THE
TO-HELL-AND-BACK
CLUB

By
Jill Hannah Anderson

pandamoon
publishing

www.pandamoonpublishing.com

Jacket design and illustrations © Pandamoon Publishing
Art Direction by Don Kramer: Pandamoon Publishing
Editing by Zara Kramer, Rachel Schoenbauer, Forest Driskel, Jessica Reino, and Jill Crosby: Pandamoon Publishing

Pandamoon Publishing and the portrayal of a panda and a moon are registered trademarks of Pandamoon Publishing.

Library of Congress Cataloging-in-Publication Data is on file at the Library of Congress, Washington, DC

Edition: 1, ver 1.02

ISBN-10: 1-945502-67-3
ISBN-13: 978-1-945502-67-5

Reviews

"In The To-Hell-And-Back Club, Jill Hannah Anderson shines light on a love that's rarely explored: the deep ties between friends. Her understanding of these extraordinary connections, and the soul twisting grief when we lose them, colors every page of this novel." — **Randy Susan Meyers, bestselling author of Accidents of Marriage, & The Widow of Wall Street**

"The To-Hell-And-Back Club is a heartwarming story about navigating tragedy and secrets with a little acceptance, a little resilience, and a whole lot of friendship. A perfect book club pick!" — **Barbara Claypole White, bestselling author of Echoes of Family, & The Perfect Son**

"Anderson's debut about a middle-aged woman surviving devastating loss, and rebuilding her life with "a little help from her friends," is at turns heartbreaking, bittersweet, funny, and darn right inspiring. Don't miss it!" — **Lesley Kagen, NYT bestselling author of The Mutual Admiraton Society, & Whistling In The Dark**

"Jill Hannah Anderson spins a bittersweet tale of loss and love, fear and forgiveness, reminding us of the brittle nature of life and its uncertainties. Tempered with brushstrokes of humor, The To Hell and Back Club illustrates the resilience of the human spirit and the healing power of friendship. You'll want to hug your girlfriends a little closer after reading this novel." — **Lori Nelson Spielman, #1 international bestselling author, The Life List, & Sweet Forgiveness**

"Set against the backdrop of Minnesota's 10,000 lakes, Anderson's debut follows the grief-stricken Peyton Brooks on her journey from despair, to hope, to wholeness in a story that reminds us of the jarring truth that life can change in an instant." — **Julie Lawson Timmer, author of Five Days Left, Untethered, & Mrs. Saint and the Defectives.**

"In The To-Hell-And-Back Club, Anderson takes on an interesting "what-if" premise: What-if your three best friends all died in the same car that you were supposed to be in? This is an interesting frame which allows her to explore a different kind of empty-nest syndrome and how you might recover from that with pathos and humor. A heartfelt read." — **Catherine McKenzie, bestselling author of Hidden, & Arranged.**

Dedication

For my husband, Don,
who never once rolled his eyes (in front of me, anyway)
and never said I was wasting my time writing a book.

And to my parents, Hal and Bunny O'Connor,
for instilling in me a love of books

THE
TO-HELL-AND-BACK
CLUB

Chapter 1

September 2010

I took a step back after knocking on my husband's bedroom door.

"What?" Jerry opened his door, golf cap in hand, at 6:20 a.m.

"When's your tee time?"

"Soon."

"Josh called. He left his spikes here. Can you take them to him?" The round trip to our son's campus would take over an hour—one I didn't have. I was meeting my friends for the day.

"Nope. Bring them yourself."

"They're waiting for me at Maggie's." I took my tenth calming breath of the morning.

"You don't need anything from that craft fair anyway."

That wasn't the point, and he knew it. The point was my fragile sanity. With both our kids recently off to college, Jerry and I were now where we'd always avoided being—alone together.

Somebody better hide our sharp knives.

"Sorry, not my problem, Perfect." My nose tingled at Jerry's shortened version of his nickname for me, *Perfect Peyton*. Nobody knew better than me just how imperfect I was. My plan to give up on our pretense of a marriage would be another imperfection of mine. Tomorrow night, when we'd both hopefully be home, I planned to bring up the word I never thought I'd utter: divorce.

Jerry and his too-strong cologne nudged past me and breezed out the door.

"Sorry? My too-wide-ass you're sorry!" My words echoed in the empty house.

I dialed my best friend Maggie's home. "You three go ahead without me, I'll drive myself. I have to run Josh's football spikes over to the campus before the team bus leaves for their game."

"Aw, Peyton, we can wait for you. It won't be the same if we don't all ride together." Maggie echoed my feelings. It was our annual day trip to the Little Falls Crafts Fair—a big event in central Minnesota every September.

"Lauren and Dana are here already. I guess the upside is that we'll have two vehicles to stuff full of our purchases." Maggie said. "How'd you end up with Josh's spikes at your house?"

"He brought his laundry over after last week's game and washed his uniform, but left his spikes here. I'm surprised Sherlock Holmes didn't ask about that. You know how Jerry feels about me coddling Josh." At least we didn't get into *that* this morning. "Anyway, by the time you're done eating at Bunny's Buns, I shouldn't be too far behind you. I'll call when I leave the campus."

My taste buds were going to miss out on the best-ever-caramel rolls my friends would be savoring. Granted, I might as well sit on one of Bunny's caramel rolls, since it would settle on my ever-expanding rear anyway, but they were worth it.

I was one cupcake away from having to buy new clothes. I settled for a tasteless granola bar and downed a small glass of orange juice.

In the bathroom, I added hairspray to my screaming-for-a-dye-job blonde hair and swiped on a smudge of taupe-colored eye shadow "guaranteed" to enhance my sienna-brown eyes. Boring face, boring life. I had to fix both—soon.

I hopped in my car and threw Josh's spikes on the passenger seat with such force I'm surprised they didn't tear the upholstery. I hit the gas and shot down our short driveway like an Indy driver in reverse, barely missing our mailbox across the road. *Ease up there, Danica.*

As I drove, I chewed on my twenty-one-year marriage. Jerry and I were gearing up for a sword-wielding standoff; I could feel it in my clenched teeth. A summer fling-with-a-surprise-pregnancy-ending tossed us into a marriage neither of us wanted. Over the years, we'd used our children as shields to avoid each other. Now our nest was empty. It was time to cut the ties.

Removing Jerry from my life would mess up our four-couple friendship with Maggie, Dana, Lauren and their husbands. It was going to suck...which is maybe why I'd put off "the talk" with Jerry in the few weeks since Josh had moved out. When you've gone twenty years without a meaningful conversation, it's difficult to know where to start.

Responsibility drove me to this marriage. Saving my sanity pushed me to end it.

Tonight, over jumbo margaritas, my friends were going to help me come up with ways to refill my life now since Karley and Josh were both in college. I would soon be living alone.

That's where my three friends came in. Working out of my home as a medical transcriptionist was like solitary confinement—no co-workers to visit with and too much time at my desk. My free nights were filled with bookkeeping for

Jerry's construction business or my part-time transcribing for a local doctor, until his retirement last year—all from my home office.

I'd filled my life with my kids' busy activity schedule over the years. Thankfully I still had Maggie, Lauren, and Dana, my social life and support. I'd need them more than ever now.

I pulled in the college parking lot where two school buses were parked. Josh stepped away from the circle of football players and approached me, sweeping me off the ground as I stepped out of my car. "Thanks, Mom. I'm super sorry." His smile reminded me why I was a softie still doing his laundry. I craved being needed. Josh needed me. Mission accomplished.

I slid back in my car and called Dana, knowing she'd be in the back seat since Maggie drove, and Lauren got motion sickness. "Are you on your way?" Dana put me on speaker phone.

"I'm leaving the campus parking lot now."

"We're leaving Bunny's now. We'll only be half an hour or so ahead of you. We picked up a caramel roll for you." They knew I loved those rolls. They knew everything about me.

In the background, Maggie shouted. "We'll meet you by the fire station. Hustle up, girl!"

And Lauren's husky voice overshadowing Maggie's. "Get your ass here! I've got your shit-list burning a hole in my purse. We've got money to spend, food to eat, and your life to figure out," she said, before good-naturedly arguing with Maggie over where I should park once I arrived.

"They're worse than my kids." Dana laughed. "Call us when you get there."

"I will. No having fun until I get there, okay?" We hung up, and I headed south on Highway 371. I shook my head and smiled, thinking of them talking all at once. We never ran out of things to say to each other. The highway was congested with other shoppers coming from every direction to assemble at the enormous Little Falls craft and food extravaganza.

As I drove the next forty miles, I passed the sun rising over shimmering lakes, reminding me of a recent canoe and camping trip we'd taken. Our girlfriend time was everything to me.

Fifteen miles from Little Falls, the traffic came to a near-standstill. "C'mon, c'mon." I drummed my fingers on the steering wheel. I was going a whopping ten miles an hour and could've balanced my checkbook, plucked my eyebrows, and filed my nails at that pace. I dug in my purse for my cell phone and called Dana. I got her voice mail. I tried Lauren next while a gazillion cars ahead of me now sat idle.

I hung up, cutting off Lauren's voice mail. The noise at the fair was probably too deafening for them to hear their phones. Sirens wailed ahead in the distance. Assuming there was an accident, at least the ambulances would be going against traffic to the Brainerd hospital.

I dialed Grace. My only sibling lived in San Antonio close to the home where we grew up. In my teens, I never thought I'd miss my annoying younger sister. Funny how things change. "Hallow?" Grace's twang always threw me back to my youth.

"Hey Grace, I'm stuck in traffic, headed to meet the girls at the craft fair." I heard my little nieces and nephew giggle at their mom's request to "Shush, please."

"What're you up to?"

"Hans has a soccer match this morning. We're up bright and early, and Mira and Gianna are boycotting eating breakfast this early. Why aren't y'all riding together?"

I replayed the scene at home for Grace.

"C'mon, P, even I could have told you Jerry wouldn't change his tee time."

"I know. I wanted to karate chop the wall in frustration." I huffed.

"Taking up karate, are you?" Grace teased.

"I might. After the fair tonight, we're stopping for dinner. They've got a shit-list for me, as Lauren calls it, with ideas on things to fill up my nights and weekends."

"When are you having the big talk with Jerry?"

"Hopefully tomorrow night. He's usually home Sunday nights. I need to get things moving."

"Other than filing for divorce, what do *you* want to do? How about getting back into swimming? And you love to cook. Maybe join a gourmet group?"

"I burned my swimsuit years ago, Grace; it was a cleansing ceremony." A gourmet group did sound fun though. I was open to most anything with my friends…well, other than the yoga-pretzel-pose group with Maggie that she'd suggested. This body wasn't Gumby.

The traffic inched forward. As Grace and I chatted, I came upon the accident scene. A one-ton utility truck was stuck in the grassy median, its back doors flung open with a trail of smashed produce scattered about. With my window rolled down, I caught the scent of comingled fruit—acidic oranges mixing with fresh-picked apples.

By now I could see the lights flashing from at least three ambulances. "Grace? I've got to go. I'll call you later." Lights pulsated from ambulances near two crushed cars. One, an SUV with a smashed in back-end; the other, a silver Chevy Impala, crunched like an accordion on the side, white paint etched on its side from

4

the one-ton utility truck. *Those poor people, there has to be massive injuries.* The police navigated us around the nightmare as paramedics scurried about.

For a second my brain flashed, *Oh! It looks like Maggie's car.* But Maggie's car was like a thousand other older model silver Impalas. Then I saw the license plate: GRG SLR.

Maggie, a chronic garage-saler, had splurged on those vanity plates. Logic told my brain no two vehicles could have identical plates. My heart screamed for the DMV to have made a mistake.

* * *

I don't remember pulling onto the shoulder and turning off my car, or the legs of my jeans getting wet as I stumbled through the tall, dewy grass in the ditch. But I do remember bulldozing my way past a cop almost twice my size to reach Maggie's car. The Jaws of Life bellowed an excruciating roar as it sliced away at the tangled nightmare.

Please be okay, please be okay. Maybe a broken leg or something, I pleaded to a god I've ignored since the unexpected death of my mom over twenty years ago.

The top of the car had been carved off, giving the rescue team easier access. Sobs wracked my body, my heart beat like a steam engine, and adrenaline fueled my instincts. I pushed my way closer and was stopped by a paramedic. "Those are my friends, I have to see them!" I screeched, my words fighting against the horrified knowledge strangling them.

She pulled at my arm. "Stay here; you don't want to see them." Her voice was firm.

She didn't know a thing about me.

"Please, let us handle things."

"Only if you promise me my friends are okay!" The look on her face was my answer. The paramedic was a little thing. I shook her off like a tiny, pesky mosquito. She followed and caught me. She was nothing if not persistent.

When she asked me contact numbers for their families, I knew…because if they could, they'd be asking Maggie, Lauren, or Dana for the information. I sobbed out a promise to answer her questions if she would let me near the car. Her fingers untangled from my sleeve.

With so many rescuers around the crushed car, I went unnoticed. They were administering CPR on Dana as they rushed her gurney toward the open back of an ambulance. She was still alive.

My stomach cramped as I approached the nightmare. The aroma from the scattered produce didn't mask the blood and coffee mixed in with something foreign. Looking back, I smelled death. Crimson and glass splattered the scene. A metallic taste filled my mouth; I'd bitten my lip.

Panic crawled like spiders up my neck as sweat slid down my body. Lauren's beautiful red-bronze hair, now plastered with blood, framed her blank stare. I yearned to reach in and gently brush her hair from her face, get a wash cloth to clean her up, and close her vacant eyes.

Instead, my hand cupped over my mouth, hoping to stifle the agony wailing from me. Maggie's dark hair covered her face, which had been pushed sideways from the impact. "Oh, Maggie, please hang on!" I babbled as the paramedic wrapped her arm around me. The powder from their airbags blanketed their bodies like snow. The slice against Maggie's motionless chest left my brain no choice but to let the truth sink in as the paramedic guided me away.

Hysterics electrified my body as I leaned against her small frame. My nose ran, and I thoughtlessly wiped it on the bottom of my shirt. Away from the chaotic nightmare, my brain could no longer ignore the horrific truth.

My heart beat at lightning speed as I broke out in a full-body sweat.

I was either going to throw up or faint. I ended up doing both.

Chapter 2

I opened my eyes under a large white pine. The same paramedic held a cool compress to my forehead. Although a flannel blanket was draped over me, my body shivered like a jackhammer. Dewy grass dampened my back. The acid in my mouth from my purging brought my nightmare front and center. I tried to push myself off the ground, and she put her arm out to support me.

"I need to see Dana, make sure she's okay." Words chattered out from my shivering jaw. She held me to her as if I were a child as my huffing sobs breathed in the scent of fabric softener from her blue jacket. This woman, Mary Beth, according to her embroidered coat, became my life support.

"They've taken her away in the ambulance. Is there someone I can call for you?"

I mumbled Jerry's cell number as I pinched the bridge of my nose. She dialed it; no answer. "Anyone else?" Who would I normally call in a crisis? The people who'd been in Maggie's car. Jerry was golfing with Lauren and Maggie's husbands. All three would know soon. I had no empathy for Maggie's husband, but my heart broke for her son who had no idea he'd just lost his mother.

"Nobody else," I whispered. I thought of my own children if I'd have been in the car. I couldn't imagine my grown kids without me. An ambulance pulled away, its siren screaming, "Get out of our way!" to the cars backed up on the highway.

Mary Beth sat in the grass next to me. Big Cop appeared in front of us. "Can I ask you a few questions? We need contact information for their next of kin. Any cell numbers you have would help."

I fumbled my cell phone out of my shirt pocket and handed it to Mary Beth. "Lauren's husband, Dylan, is on there, and Dana's husband, Bob." My mouth moved as if it were shot with Novocain.

Mary Beth read their numbers off to Big Cop after he scribbled down the numbers I'd recited. I didn't have Maggie's worthless husband's number. He'd hear anyway, through Dylan. The cop jogged away with his information and was replaced by a highway patrol officer. "Does Dana attend a church?"

I didn't have to think. "Our Savior's Lutheran Church in Pine Lakes." Dana was the only one of my friend's faithful in her church attendance. Would that merit save her?

Around us, patrol officers asked questions of several eyewitnesses.

"The driver swerved to avoid deer running across the highway."

"The driver cut into the lane of the produce truck."

Shock kept me from yelling to defend Maggie. I scrunched my eyes closed, the heels of my hands held against them to fight off reality making its way to my brain as I rocked back and forth to comfort myself.

"Stay here, I'll be right back." Mary Beth's voice was as gentle as her touch as she tucked the soft blanket around me. She left for a few minutes. Or a few hours. I'd lost all sense of reality. She reappeared. "I've gotten permission to drive you home in your car."

"Can you please take me to the hospital?" My chest and throat burned as if I'd run ten miles.

She nodded. After the ambulances pulled away, and the cops directed traffic, Mary Beth guided me into my car as she explained that the other paramedics would meet us at the hospital. During the half-hour drive, adrenaline pumped so hard through me I felt my skin would split open. I fidgeted like a two-year-old and cried like an infant. My brain scrambled images, as if I'd taken a handful of hallucinogens. It was the worst "trip" in my mind.

She reached over and gave me a not-so-gentle shake. "Listen, Peyton, you've *got* to pull yourself together." We neared the hospital, and Mary Beth led me in some deep-breathing techniques. "Dana's family is going to be there soon, if they aren't already. Spare them the details of the accident. Just be there for them…and Dana."

"Do you think she'll make it?" I held my breath for the right answer.

She took a minute. "I don't know. They'll do everything they can for her."

I willed Dana to hang on. At the ICU, I dropped my body into a chair in the empty lounge while Mary Beth spoke with two doctors in the hallway. Minutes later, she came to tell me Bob was already there, speaking with a surgeon. I hugged Mary Beth as she turned to leave, hanging on as if she were a buoy, and this ocean of sorrow would drown me if I let go.

* * *

After pacing the halls, my shaky legs were ready to collapse. I sat back down, closed my eyes, and allowed my mind to drift back to a movie theatre when Maggie, Dana, Lauren, and I went to see *Ghost*. We all fell in love with Patrick Swayze, each of us picturing ourselves molding clay with him. It was one of our first outings together, and our shared love of Patrick helped cement a good footing to build our friendship on for the next two decades.

Like a movie camera, my memory replayed various scenes. There was Lauren, tossing her long auburn hair back, hiccupping from her tears after purging confessions of her troubled past like a bad flu. Growing up on the streets with her mom, always on the move, could have done some permanent damage to a young Lauren. We were in Lauren's living room comforting her, and laughing at her hiccups as she belted out, "We Are Family" by the Pointer Sisters, in her perfect-pitch voice—interrupted by hiccups as we danced—hoping to stomp out her grief.

And Maggie, a grade school principal, lived on a shoestring budget since her husband sucked the life and money out of her. Maggie with her garage-sale purchases of goofy clothes, everything from plaid golf pants to a fox-fur hat. Things she'd wear when we'd go out, to get a laugh, to bring some joy into her life, and ours.

Then there was Dana, super-mother-of-four, who could've used bladder-repair surgery. We'd get to giggling and she'd frantically hunt for the closest bathroom. We were all at Target one day, and Dana didn't make it in time. Mortified, she hid out in the restroom. Lauren bought a box of Depends, brought them back to the restroom, and we all put one on before prancing out of there like queens. It was always "all for one" with the four of us.

I opened my eyes. It would never be that way again.

With each passing hour, the waiting room filled. Bob and their children, Dana's family from Wisconsin, workers from their business, and Jerry and I—all waiting for Dana to come out of surgery. Not yet noon, it seemed like a month since I'd dropped off Josh's spikes.

I took a walk to stretch my legs and get a drink of water at the fountain, and I met Bob, who was coming back from speaking with a cop. "It was deer crossing the road, that's why Maggie swerved into the other lane." His voice cracked.

I reached out for his arm. "Maggie did what we'd all do. I know they tell us not to swerve, but you and I both know it's a natural reaction." A reaction that caused a massive crash and roll-over.

Bob's sigh sounded like it pulled from every cell in his body. "I know, I know." His hands rubbed over his face as he closed his eyes. "God damned deer." His shoulders shook.

His chin quivered as his voice trembled. "I keep thinking I must be having a nightmare."

"I know. Me too." I folded my arms, holding in my pain as my red eyes met Bob's puffy ones. I remembered Mary Beth's advice as Bob and I continued down the hall toward the pristine waiting room. I needed to be there for Dana's family— I could grieve when I got home.

Dana and Bob's oldest daughter, fourteen-year-old Eva, had four-year-old Channy on her lap. Their son, Nash, sat numbly on a chair next to Dana's mom, who snuggled seven-year-old Finley. The dynamics of this family would forever be changed.

Even if Dana pulled through, Eva would be thrown into adulthood by way of responsibility.

Shortly after three o'clock, they wheeled Dana out of surgery and summoned her family to her room. I stared out the windows. Soon the sun would set. I begged fate to allow me to turn the clock back to when the sun rose this morning. *This was your fault, Peyton. If you wouldn't have delayed them at Maggie's, if you'd have told Josh no, the timing wouldn't have been off, and you and your friends would be laughing and enjoying the day together at the craft fair.*

If, if, if. Jerry's blue eyes caught my glance, likely reading my self-inflicted guilt. He knew what those women meant to me—everything.

Bob found me in the hall. "Do you want to come see Dana? It might help you."

"Thanks for thinking of me. Yes, I'd like to see her." I followed him into Dana's room. Dana's elf-like face was now puffy and bruised. Tubes were everywhere. Dana's mom rubbed one of Dana's legs through the thin sheet as Eva held Dana's hand. "Go ahead and talk," Bob encouraged, starting me out. Short, compact, Bob, who had the inner strength of Goliath, held a one-sided conversation with Dana, as if they were in their kitchen having coffee, and continued until I could find my voice.

Eva passed Dana's hand to me. How could it feel so soft? "We all need you. You're a fighter, Dana. You can do this!" My other hand muffled my pain, shoving it back down my throat. Dana couldn't die. I needed her…almost as much as her four children sitting in the room needed her.

I let them have their privacy and rejoined everyone else in the waiting room. I went to the window and watched a woman kneeling in dark soil, meticulously weeding colorful mums in the hospital courtyard. My mind went back to years ago when we four women did two separate digs, burying our dreams and secrets in time capsules out in the woods…leaving a little of ourselves behind.

We weren't to dig any up unless that person died. And here I sat…two dead, one barely hanging on. We figured they'd remain buried another fifty years. That was our plan. Now it was my nightmare.

Shortly before midnight, while I mindlessly reread our local newspaper, Dana's brother, George, trudged into the waiting room. His face, haggard and pale, precluded his devastating words. "I'm sorry. Dana didn't make it." His voice was monotone. His bloodshot eyes scanned our thinned-out group as his hands tapped his baseball cap against his leg in a nervous beat.

I jumped up and went to him. "Nooooooo!" I wailed, clinging to George like a lost puppy. Dana was my "sister" too, just like Maggie and Lauren. So what if we weren't from the same gene pool? Our bond couldn't have been stronger.

Jerry patted George's shoulder. It was the first time that day I'd seen Jerry with tears in his eyes. Dana was our last hope.

I looked around. Everyone was crying—and I wanted to scream. Scream how life wasn't fair! I watched Bob walk into the room, his arms around his sobbing children. His poor children who'd just lost their mother. I remembered my similar horror, even though I'd been twenty when my mom died.

I stepped forward. "Oh, Bob, I don't know what to say." I whispered against his neck.

"It's okay. I know." Dana couldn't have asked for a better husband, father to their children, and business partner. Embracing, we rocked back and forth, and I experienced a comfort I couldn't get from Jerry. Yet, I also knew this day hadn't been easy on Jerry; our circle of eight was now down to five. I was the lone woman left. My support system was gone.

What else was there to do but go home? Jerry and I rode the elevator down in silence. The long walk across the near-empty parking lot illuminated by streetlights was like walking to the electric chair.

"Are you going to be able to drive?"

My body could barely walk, much less concentrate on driving. "Let's leave my car here, and I'll ride home with you." I blew my nose for the hundredth time that day.

When Jerry and I entered his truck, my arms clenched my stomach. I'd likely be sick again if it weren't for the fact I hadn't eaten since before the crash. Leaning against his pickup seat, breathing in the new leather smell, I closed my eyes.

"You going to be okay?" There was actual concern in his voice.

"I won't throw up in your new truck. I've got nothing left inside me." Not in my stomach or my heart. Our ride home was quiet, as usual. Over the years, it had been a standard for us. We'd get together with our friends and chat up a storm. Like two strangers with the same set of friends.

We pulled into our driveway where Karley and Josh's cars were parked. Jerry must have told them about the accident. I walked down the hall and nudged open Josh's bedroom door. His lanky body was sprawled on the bed he'd recently vacated, legs hanging over the end. I opened Karley's door next. Although she hadn't lived here since leaving for college three years ago, it was still "her" room. I've slept in there since Karley moved out. We blame Jerry's snoring. We're not fooling anybody. I stood in the hallway between their open doors, wishing I could move the clock back to years ago, when each night I would check on them before I went to bed. Back when they needed me.

"Mom?" Karley sat upright in her bed. The hallway light must have wakened her. "Oh mom, are you okay? Did Dana make it?" Karley struggled to detangle her long, lithe self from the covers. Her sleepy body found its way, meeting me with a warm hug. I swallowed my tears as she pulled away, reading the answer in my eyes. I didn't have to say the awful words.

"I can't believe it!" A sob escaped her. "I thought Dad was playing a cruel joke when he called." We clung to each other, Karley's frame a few inches taller than mine. Her golden curls were tucked behind her ears, revealing the tiny extra piece of skin on her right earlobe that gave me a small pang. I inhaled her tangerine scented shampoo and drew strength from my daughter who understood my pain.

She pulled back, studying me with the same brown eyes as mine. "You know the first thing I thought? 'Thank God, Josh is such a mush-brain.' You would've been in the car with them!"

We laughed through our tears, a foreign emotion in the last twenty-four hours. Josh has been called many things; charming, athletic, but, within our family, mush-brain is an apt description for him.

Jerry walked by, poked his head in, and mumbled he was going to bed. His weathered face was drawn from exhaustion. It had been the longest day of my life. Well, it tied with the day my mom died and I was due to deliver Karley. 1,400 miles away. I didn't want to think about it now. I wasn't equipped to handle my current grief, why dredge up more?

I hugged Karley. "I need to get to bed before I drop. Thanks for coming home, honey." Thank goodness for daughters. My mind flashed to Dana's eldest daughter.

I stopped in the bathroom to wash up, noticing I'd cried away any makeup I'd bothered to put on that morning. My nose was as rough as sandpaper, my eyes swollen like clamshells. I shuffled into Jerry's bedroom after grabbing my pajamas from Karley's room. I hadn't had to share a bed with Jerry since Karley had been home Memorial Day weekend. Lying next to him, his steady breathing, his scent on the blankets…was like crawling into a stranger's bed. I craved to be held, but not by Jerry. He'd fallen asleep, enveloped in his own pain of loss. We should have been able to comfort each other. We should have been able to be there for each other. We should have done a lot of things.

I wished my children were home under different circumstances. I needed them, needed to cook for them and their friends, clean up after them, chauffeur them to school events—be a part of their lives again. I'd made them and my friends my whole world—the people who completed me. Now my children had their lives at college, and my friends were gone. And I had nobody.

Chapter 3

The day after the accident Karley headed back to her apartment by the University of Minnesota, where she'd just started her senior year, and Josh drove to his apartment near the Staples Central Lakes College campus, where he was a freshman. I had the house to myself and called Grace. In the twenty-four hours since I'd talked to her, my life had changed forever.

"Hallow?" Hearing her voice, I wished I could blink and be in San Antonio with her.

"Hi, Grace, are you busy?" I tried to keep the *please don't be busy* out of my voice.

"Hey, P! Nope, just cleaning up the kitchen. The kids are outside playing, and Garret is studying for his CPA exam."

"I need to tell you something…" The sandpaper coating my throat prevented me.

"What's wrong? You okay?"

Sharp pins pierced the inside of my nose. "Oh my God, Grace, it's awful!"

"What is? Something happened to Karley or Josh? *Please* tell me they're okay!"

"Th—th—they're fine, the kids are fine." I took a deep breath. "It's my friends…"

"It's okay, P, take your time. I'm here for you. I've got all the time in the world."

A long silence followed as I fought to push my words around the elephant lodged in my throat. "Remember when I told you yesterday I came upon an accident? Oh my God, Grace, it was *Maggie's* car. Maggie was driving! She sideswiped a produce van, and they—they—they…" I couldn't say the words. If I said them, allowed them to mix with oxygen, they'd come true. I couldn't let that happen.

Grace gasped into the phone. "No! Oh no, Peyton! Are they okay?"

My crumbling grief pulsated sobs into the phone, giving Grace her answer.

Grace's burst into full-blown crying sounded foreign. I'd probably heard my little sister cry two or three times in our lives. She knew what my friends meant to me. Knew how much I relied on them. Knew my plan to divorce was now the least of my sorrows.

Little by little, my pain worked its way from Minnesota, crossing states, to Grace's caring heart.

"I wish I could be there with you, but Garret would hang me by my teeth if I left him alone now with the kids. His CPA exams are next week. Between work and studying, he's walking a fine line already. And Dad is caring for Barbara since her foot surgery last week so they'd be of little help with the kids. I'm so sorry. You know you can call me, no matter what time, right?"

"I probably will, and I'm apologizing ahead of time for it." I rubbed my throbbing forehead. "Karley and Josh will be back in a few days for the funerals. That will help."

"Don't be afraid to get a prescription for sleeping pills, or antidepressants, or both. Whatever it takes to get you through this." Grace's voice was firm, as if she were the older sister.

"That would be the whole bottle of pills then…or shock treatment." Grace knew I was half-joking. "I'm trying to be strong and not lean on Jerry or the kids, although I think Jerry's eyes would pop out of his head if I looked to him for comfort."

"We can Skype; it might help. Maybe you could come here for a break after the funerals."

"I'm already taking this coming week off work for the funerals. I'll call you though, and Dad, too." If I kept talking to people, I could avoid the emptiness I was already feeling without my friends. Where were the support groups for people who lost best friends? I struggled to bury my anger at the injustice of those wonderful women being swiped away from all of us who loved them.

* * *

Four days later I sat in a church squished between Karley's sticky, bare shoulder and Jerry, sweltering in his rarely-worn suit. The mid-September day was warm and calm, not a good combination for an overcrowded church. It seemed a quarter of our town, population 4,270, was crammed in the pews. Stained glass windows were cranked open and ceiling fans worked overtime, yet I was as sticky as a wet jelly bean. I'd cried so many tears I should be as dried up as a prune.

A campfire torched my stomach, thanks to my coffee breakfast to offset the over-the-counter sleeping pill I'd taken. I had to get through this last funeral—Dana's. It was no easier than Lauren's or Maggie's. Watching little four-year-old Channy hug the tattered blanket she'd given up last year as she leaned against Bob undid me. If I closed my eyes, I envisioned the crash. Leaving them open, I had to face life without my friends. I didn't like either choice.

Some friendships happen by demographics: a neighborhood, or a school attended together. Maybe it's common ground: a running club or a quilting group. For me, my best friends and I were thrown together because our husbands played college football together and became best friends. A situation like ours might not work together well. For us, it was a perfect blend.

* * *

Each day after the accident, Jerry tiptoed around me, as if at any moment, I might emotionally combust. For years, I'd kept my feelings to myself at home—but this was overload. Jerry, an only child, was raised with his emotions buckled up, thanks to his fresh-from-Vietnam father and submissive mother. He expected the same from me.

The day after Dana's funeral, I sat in my recliner, newspaper on my lap, staring out our living room window at my favorite time of year. For four days, I'd had what I called "frying pan headaches," piercing pain above my eyes and in the back of my neck as if someone walloped me with a cast iron skillet. I had no desire to go out into the world…out in the sunshine.

I'd read my friend's obituaries over and over. They described so little about their lives; didn't mention the holes they left behind, their determination of steel, sense of humor, or endless comfort. I should have written their obituaries. *I* was the person who knew all of them best.

I didn't even hear Karley come into the room. "Mom, can we talk a minute?"

"Sure, honey, what's up?" Her army-green duffle bag was slung over her shoulder. "Are you heading back?" I couldn't remember if I should already know the answer.

Karley sat on the ottoman. "Yep, I can pick up a shift at work tonight, and have a ton of classwork to make up." She leaned close enough for me to count the few freckles on her cheeks. "I'm worried about you, worried about leaving you alone. Maybe I should take the next couple weekends off and come home."

"No, you need the money from your job. Don't worry about babysitting me." I'd have loved to have Karley by my side 24/7. I refused to put my daughter through that.

"Maybe you could reach out to your friends' families. It would help you and help them." Karley whispered, but I read her loud and clear.

"I'm afraid I need help before I'll be any good to others. I've been doing some research." I pushed myself up and led Karley into the kitchen.

I showed her numbers I'd written down on a notepad, knowing I needed to talk to somebody. One belonged to the minister at Dana's church. Dana had mentioned years ago how the minister had helped her get through some tough times. Now I wondered what they were. The other numbers were for grief counselors. "I'll call, I promise."

Karley's eyes met mine in approval. "You'll be glad you did."

I forced a smile. "See? I'm not so pigheaded I won't ask for help. I'll be fine. I promise." What a joke. I'd never be fine again. I was lost in the woods without a compass.

The house was too quiet when I walked back inside after a long hug goodbye with Karley. Josh had left earlier for his apartment, and Jerry was gone, helping his grieving friends in some way. I needed my sister. And my mom and dad. But my mom was dead, and Grace and Dad lived too far away. I'd need to stand on my own, again. I didn't know how I was going to do it.

* * *

Three weeks after the funerals, I was still pacing Karley's old bedroom floor at night, staring out the open bedroom window into blackness as empty as my heart. Way past the midnight hour, in the dark loneliness of my room, I caved and called Grace way too many nights, imagining her grabbing her cell phone and whispering to me until she secluded herself in their bathroom to avoid waking Garret.

Selfish, selfish me. Never once did Grace make me feel like I shouldn't have woken her up. Never. Yet, I couldn't keep it up. She had a busy life of her own with three young children. Finally, I called my doctor for a sleeping pill prescription, which she filled. When you hear someone's only friends have died, you can figure they're going to need help sleeping. It helped…a bit. I slept through those late haunting hours when your problems magnify in the dark, leaving you with paranoid thoughts.

I'd taken a week off for their funerals. Now back at work for two weeks, holed up in my home office performing my medical transcribing on autopilot, I was thankful I knew my job by heart after twenty years. If I'd needed to concentrate, I'd be out of a job. And my new uniform of black sweats wouldn't be allowed out in the real world.

Someone had taken my brain, put it in a blender, and hit the "pulverize" button.

Yes, I'd promised I'd call a counselor. The thought of telling a stranger how lost I was depressed me even more.

I could do this. I just needed more time.

Following the funerals, Jerry was the one person in my life who had to put up with me. This was when I should've been talking to him about a divorce, but I was smart enough to know I needed to work my way through this sinkhole of grief before I could deal with the tragedy of our divorce.

My daily routine of moving from my desk to the couch, wrapped up in a blanket I used to shield myself from the world, must have worn thin on him.

Jerry walked in after work on a cool October Wednesday—the only weeknight we had to avoid each other since I'd dropped out of bowling league. With the rest of my team gone, it'd be like slowly bleeding out. Better to cut the arm off right at the get-go instead of dredging up memories each week.

He hadn't come up with a Wednesday night activity—yet. He had his other weeknights covered: bowling, darts, or pool leagues kept Jerry away until after I crawled into bed. And weekends were filled with golfing, followed by hunting season, which took care of our having to see each other much until Thanksgiving. I hoped to have the strength to move out by then.

I was staring into space when he walked in, eyed me, and shook his head.

"What?"

"Some clean clothes would be nice."

"For who, you or me?" He was dreaming if he thought I was getting off this couch.

"Both." He left the living room, went into his bedroom to change clothes (*aha, apparently he did have some clean clothes left*), and walked back out of the house. I didn't know where he was off to and didn't care. It saved me from retreating to my room for the night.

After his pickup backed out of our driveway, I shimmied off the couch to grab a bag of chocolate-covered peanuts. I wandered into the laundry room which was indeed full of heaping piles of dirty clothes, most of them Jerry's. I conserved, wearing the same outfit over and over. Mustering some energy, I threw a load in. One down, six to go. Jerry would soon have to do his own laundry when I moved out. But dealing right now with that confrontation was like asking me to solve world hunger.

After I'd packed one load in, I put on my fall jacket and headed to the cemetery—an almost nightly routine for me. Bob and Joe had buried Maggie and Dana close by each other, and Dylan had Lauren's small urn on the corner of Dana's grave. With only one cemetery in our town, I was fortunate to have them together, making it convenient for me to pull up a lawn chair and talk to the only people who understood me, besides Grace and Karley.

Normally, the old me would be taking walks or bike rides with my friends this time of year, soaking up the changing colors, breathing in the earthy scent of damp, fallen leaves. I knew I should be doing those activities myself. Even baby steps would help...but I could barely crawl.

The "baby" weight I'd wished for years would drop from my body now obliged me. I couldn't have cared less. My throat seized while swallowing even the blandest of foods. That morning I realized I hadn't shaved my legs since before the accident. I had nowhere to go, no reason to ever shave again.

The people I cared to talk to—my children and Grace—were handled by phone—stiff-armed to keep their distance so they couldn't study me like some microorganism in a Petri dish.

* * *

Josh, who'd been MIA since the funerals, called me Wednesday night. "How about if me and some of my team drive over there on Sunday? You could make lasagna or something, Ma."

If I wasn't going to drag myself to his games—which I hadn't been to since the accident—he was willing to bring half the team to me. Normally I loved to cook and would have tripped over myself to cook and bake like crazy for them. I'd been far from normal this past month.

"I'm sorry. I have a meeting on Sunday." It was hard to lie, even through the phone.

He didn't argue, or call me out on what meeting I could have when I didn't belong to anything. I'd done a good job of painting myself into a solitary corner.

Although I couldn't bring myself to have a normal conversation with anyone but Grace, I still found myself picking up the phone to call my friends, before reality slapped me in the face. I saved their numbers on my cell phone, as if they'd someday get cell service in heaven.

Karley called the next day. "Hey, Mom, how are you?" She was checking on me, as usual. And if she'd spoken to Josh, she'd know of my lie about having a meeting.

"I'm keeping busy." I invented a list of activities, throwing in a fictitious meeting for good measure. I didn't tell her each day my whole body ached; I didn't sleep well—even with Ambien, didn't eat right, and talked to myself too much. Could you die from loneliness? Karley, who would soon have her RN license, could've answered that question. I continued to lie to protect the innocent.

My loneliness felt like a piranha. And it was eating me alive.

Chapter 4

Six weeks after their funerals, I was still lying to everyone, including Grace. If I didn't, she'd be on the next plane from San Antonio, marching into my house, and dragging me by my please-pay-attention-to-me hair back into reality. We Skyped often, and I always made sure to look presentable. Grace understood each day was an effort for me—still, it didn't stop her from trying to fix my life.

"Isn't there anyone around there you can call to do things with? What about your friend who had a daughter Karley's age?" Grace quizzed me on a Sunday night.

"Rhonda? They moved away after the girls graduated from high school."

"How about the neighbor who threw a block party one year when I was there?"

"Cathy? She moved to Tennessee with her boyfriend. Believe me, Grace, I've covered my options. I did this to myself. I thought Maggie, Lauren, and Dana were enough. They were."

My friends had been enough for me for about two decades. We'd had a pretty good run.

I'd even had a few phone conversations with my dad, a quiet man face-to-face and almost mute when you got him on the phone. Still, I know he tried to be there for me.

"Do you need anything, sunshine?"

"No, I'm okay, Dad. Just tired. I miss you and Grace."

"Aw, you know I always miss you." His voice held such tenderness. I longed for his big, beefy hugs. "Grace said she suggested you come visit us. I think it's a good idea, sunshine. You've had a tough go of it, and the warm weather here would do you good."

I chuckled at his use of my childhood nickname. "I will. I'm checking out last minute plane ticket deals." Dad would never think of me as his sunshine again if he saw me in person.

I'd called Wyatt twice since Maggie's funeral, wanting to make sure he was okay. In typical guy-teen-talk, he said little. I found some small comfort in the fact her son was busy at college in Boston, close to his aunt and uncle, instead of his self-centered father here in Minnesota.

I made sure to call Bob every few days. My heart physically hurt at what he and his children were going through without Dana. In my spineless ways, I handled everything over the phone instead of reaching out *in person*. I barely functioned in private.

You'd think Jerry would be tough to deceive, as he was one of the few who saw me *in person*. Yet the day we were supposed to finally make it to one of Josh's football games—together—I couldn't do it. A debilitating headache and iffy stomach made me rethink the hour drive.

"I'm staying home. I don't feel well." I mumbled as Jerry entered the kitchen.

"Again? Jesus, Peyton, get over it."

"Get over what?" Pain narrowed my eyes. "Six weeks and I'm supposed to just forget?"

"You know what I mean. Think of Josh instead of yourself all the time." His lip curled.

My stomach roiled. "If I remember right, *you* are the one who says I do too much for the kids. I've been to every single event in Josh's life. I think he'll cut me some slack for a few months." I cinched my bathrobe tighter, as if it was a rope around Jerry's throat.

"And aren't you the one to point a finger? Unless it's a sporting event, you've been MIA. I've been to every school play, band concert, sporting event, and class program imaginable for both of the kids. If they were in a spelling bee and stood there and picked their nose, I stayed through the whole damn event." I turned my back on Jerry's eyes bulging in surprise.

It took a second for his comeback. "And who took them golfing and fishing? Who played catch with them in the yard?" We rarely raised our voices, but Jerry and I could've both earned gold stars for shouting now.

Damn, he was right. It was why I'd stuck with him. He loved our kids. We just didn't love each other. Ignoring his rant, I shuffled down the hall to my bedroom, wishing I had the energy to run away.

A year ago I'd have had to be near-death to miss one of Josh's high school games. I'd now missed six college games. I heard the door slam and Jerry's pickup rev as I took a couple of Ibuprofen. It was October twenty-seventh; what would've been Maggie's forty-fourth birthday.

With the house to myself, I made some stomach-coating chocolate milk and buried myself in billing for Jerry's construction business. After a short early afternoon nap, remorse scolded my heart for allowing my emotions to derail me from one of Josh's games. Again.

Nothing sounded good to eat, and chocolate milk was getting a little familiar. A brilliant idea popped into my head. Pushing a stepstool to the cabinet above the fridge, I got out a half-empty bottle of Kahlua, a bottle I brought to our get-togethers—a congenial liquor, as happy to get along with vodka as it did with coffee or cream. I grabbed the vodka too.

I poured a shot, or two, of each over ice into a tall glass, added some half and half, and cracked open a Diet Coke. It had been a long time since I'd had a Colorado Bulldog. Slurping it down, I eyed my empty glass. My feet tingled already. *What the hell, celebrate Maggie's birthday as if your friends were here.* I poured another and made myself comfortable on the couch.

The numbing feeling worked its way through every cell, calming the nervous beast in me. Yawning, I drained the drink...and woke up an hour later. Startled, I jumped up from the couch, my head feeling like a maraca shaken too much. I got dressed before popping two Excedrin to settle my barn-burner headache. The sun would be setting soon, and I wanted to visit my friends.

I heated up a can of tomato soup, sipping it from my favorite mug, a present from Maggie. When we celebrated her birthday last year, Maggie commented, "It's my last birthday with Wyatt around." Her son, Wyatt, graduated last spring with Josh, and while we dreaded our empty nests, I'd been pinning my freedom from Jerry on mine.

Maggie had ten times more reason to leave Joe. And was ten times more afraid to.

I rinsed out the mug, and there were my pals Kahlua and vodka, staring me down. Before I thought twice, I filled a travel mug with ice and mixed up a nice-sized White Russian to-go.

Pulling on a thick sweater, I dug in the closet for mittens and an ear band. It was cold out—one step away from our first hard frost, and I headed out to the cemetery to sit among my friends.

There was no heat in the sun as it lowered on the horizon, but my drink warmed me from the inside. With my blanket wrapped around me, I sipped, still a little fuzzy from the two drinks before my nap. Colorful maple leaves whipped around me in vibrant circles, carrying with them the scent from the pine trees surrounding the cemetery.

It was too damn quiet, too damn depressing, and I was too damn lonely. I nestled myself between Maggie and Dana's graves. Maggie deserved recognition, even in death. Clearing my throat, I attempted a quiet, off-key happy birthday to Maggie.

"Happy birthday to you, h—h—happy birthday to you, happy birthday d—dear…" I choked on the trueness of the song. Maggie *was* dear, the dearest friend a person could have. I lay back on my blanket and looked up at the sky through my tears. I silently mouthed the rest of the song and hoped like hell Dana and Lauren took up where I left off.

My hands grasped fists of grass to keep my body from spinning. Damn, this was not like me to be drinking alone. *Hah, Peyton. You're alone all the time now!* I sat up, leaned forward, knees to chest, and rocked back and forth. "I need help," I confessed. "I'll call a counselor, really." I promised my below-ground friends the same empty words I'd offered to Karley six weeks ago.

I struggled for deep breaths, hoping to calm my heart and soul. *One day at a time*, I repeated to myself, as if I had some sort of addiction. I guess I did. Someone had taken my security blanket of friends and destroyed it. Not a bottle, not a pill, yet a "fix" for me all the same.

I sprawled out on the blanket, hugging the ground above their fresh graves, as if I could encompass them in a full body hug. My tears dampened the old seafoam-green wool blanket. With nobody around, I let out a howling moan, my grief escaping in the cool breeze over a sea of people who'd left this world. I should've been thankful to be above ground. I wasn't.

Rolling to the side, I struggled to sit up. My travel mug sat there, and I chugged the rest of my drink before throwing my blanket in the backseat. Backing up on the narrow road between rows of graves, I put it in drive and floored it, accidentally driving over a couple of graves and narrowly missing a headstone. I drove home in a daze, disgusted with myself. I'd crossed a line somewhere. Luckily, Jerry wasn't home yet to witness my lack of control.

I crawled into bed and promised myself that tomorrow, I was making the call.

* * *

I called two counselors on my lunch break the next day. Both were booked out for weeks, unless I was suicidal. *No. I miss my friends and mom, but I'm not ready to join them.*

I waited until after work to call the minister at Dana's old church, and was greeted by her answering machine. "Hello, this is Peyton Brooks and I'm leaving a message for Missus Reverend Bloom. Aw crap, not Missus…" Click. *You idiot.* I tried again with more success. I remembered Dana offering me an invitation to go to church with over the years. I never went…until Dana's funeral.

I was getting ready for bed when the minister called back the same night. Jerry was at pool league, and I was thankful he wasn't around to hear me admit I needed help. "Hello?"

"Mrs. Brooks?" A shaky voice asked.

"Yes."

"Mrs. Brooks, this is Eunice Bloom, the minister at Our Savior's Church, returning your call." An uncomfortable pause followed. How do you explain grief? My silence forced her to continue. "I remember you, honey, from Dana's funeral. When I spoke with Bob afterward, he pointed you out with your family, explaining you were the friend left behind."

"I appreciate you returning my call. I need to talk with someone, and Dana spoke highly of you, always trying to drag me to your church." I winced at my poor choice of words, as if I'd be pulled kicking and screaming through the church doors.

Eunice laughed. "Let's get together, and I promise I won't drag you through the front doors. My office is in the back, and you can slip in through the side door." I was thankful for her sense of humor and glad I hadn't made an appointment yet with a grief counselor.

"How does tomorrow look for you, Mrs. Brooks?"

"Peyton. Please call me, Peyton. I'm done with work at five. Do you ever meet people at night?" My words rushed out before I could change my mind.

"I meet people whenever I'm needed. Let's meet at my office at, say six-thirty? It would give you a chance to have dinner with your family first. Take the tan door on the south side of the church. My office is to the right."

I thanked her, not bothering to tell her I ate alone. If Eunice thought my grief was solely focused on my friends dying, I had this-is-just-the-tip-of-the-iceberg news for her.

* * *

A rounded, animated, seventy-something woman with the same bouncy gray curls and red-rimmed glasses she'd worn at Dana's funeral met me at six-thirty the following night. And when her soft hand shook mine, I experienced a momentary sense of peace.

"Welcome, Peyton." She led me in to an office with a calming scent of lilacs. She poured us Earl Grey tea, and as she handed me my teacup and patted my shoulder, hope blossomed. Maybe she'd be able to shed some light on what in the hell I was going to do without my friends.

"I'll let you lead the way, Peyton, as I can only guess why you're here."

I leaned back in the floral-print cushioned chair, drumming my fingers on my lap. Where did I begin? After the accident? Before? All the way back to my college years?

"Well, my obvious problem is getting on with my life without Dana, Maggie, and Lauren." I picked at my suddenly-interesting cuticles.

"As you mentioned, Bob told you about us four women being close friends. They were everything to me, besides my son and daughter, of course." No use pretending my marriage was anything but over. Would it get me kicked out of a church?

Eunice didn't flinch. I continued. "I'm angry at my friends, which I know is stupid. And I'm angry at myself for making my whole life my three friends and my children." The pain squeezing my heart for almost two months loosened its grip. Eunice leaned forward, eyes on me.

"I know nobody can fix it but me. Well, me, and hopefully you." I gave her a half-smile.

"Would you like to tell me a little about your past?"

I needed to explain the present first. "I'm sure you noticed I neglected to mention my husband Jerry as part of my life. My marriage isn't good. Never has been. We met the summer before my junior year of college." I took a sip of tea and wished for a shot of whiskey. I didn't even like whiskey.

"I had been dating Greg, a great guy, since my junior year in high school. We dated until the winter of my sophomore year at UT Austin. When he broke up with me, I was devastated. I met Jerry at a party the next summer, and we started dating. I was in rebound-mode." At the time, I'd tried to convince myself it was love. Surely, I'd never have slept with him otherwise. I almost believed it.

Eunice waved me on with her age-spotted hand. "Continue on, my dear."

"It was a short summer fling. Jerry, a Minnesota boy, had spent his summers with a cousin in San Antonio, doing construction work. When we parted ways, I was fine getting on with my college life and putting Jerry behind me." I studied her paisley wallpaper border.

"I discovered I was pregnant that fall. I knew the right thing to do was to call Jerry."

"And what did he say?"

"I caught him off guard." *Actually, Eunice, Jerry probably shit a brick sideways when I called to tell him I was pregnant.* How could I convey to her the careless abandonment I'd felt that summer? In the back seat of a pickup truck on a hot

26

summer night, a cooler of beer with us, "Amarillo by Morning" playing on the radio…more than a few times, the condom tucked in a wallet was forgotten.

And because of those split-second decisions, I'd found myself committed to marrying a man I never loved. And what was worse, I knew full well he didn't love me back.

"After we talked, I transferred to the University of Minnesota Duluth for my second semester, where Jerry was a senior." And froze my ever-expanding butt off.

Eunice nodded. "Very brave of you, leaving everything you knew and loved behind."

I wanted to correct her. I'd taken the coward's way out. "Things were tense between us. I thought of moving back in with my parents. I think Jerry would've been fine with it too." I'd have packed my bags and high-tailed it back home after Karley was born…if my mom had still been alive.

"What kept you from moving back?"

Only an act of God. "My mom died a few weeks before I was due with Karley." Eunice handed me Kleenex to dab my eyes. "She'd taken up running around the time I confessed I was pregnant. She'd come home from a run with an excruciating headache and sick to her stomach. Thinking she'd pushed herself too hard running, she went to lie down in their room. Dad found her an hour later, dead from a brain aneurysm." I'd always worried the stress I put on her had made things worse.

"I couldn't burden my dad with me and a baby, and I wanted our daughter to have two parents. After Karley was born, Jerry and I had a small wedding. It was the right thing to do." I knew people who'd married for far less reasons than a baby. Yet I'd asked myself a thousand times over the last twenty years if I'd done the right thing—for anyone involved.

"Jerry would've been fine without ever having children. I attributed it to his stuffed-shirt upbringing and his being an only child. His dad had come back wounded—both physically and emotionally—from Vietnam. Jerry called him 'The Dominator.' His years growing up weren't easy." I folded my arms over my chest. I'd made excuses for Jerry's lack of emotion for years. It was easier to blame his upbringing than to look at my part in our marriage.

"Yet you had another child together…" Eunice leaned back in her chair, her hands folded.

"Yes. Jerry never liked being an only child, and although I have a younger sister, when I was growing up, I felt like an only child because Grace is seven years younger than me." I shrugged. "We agreed we didn't want Karley to be an only child, if at all possible."

I always wanted children…but getting pregnant during college hadn't been part of my plan.

I remembered how shocked I'd been to find out Jerry's parents made him a deal: marry me and they'd pay his college loans. They wanted to know their grandchild. It was a tough pill for Jerry to swallow, but money had governed his life for so long that it sang loud and clear to him. His dad had been awarded a workman's comp claim a year earlier, and they had money for the first time since his dad had come home from the war.

It worked for both of us. I wanted my daughter to have both parents around. Jerry wanted to be debt free. I wasn't sure how it worked for his parents. According to Jerry, they'd been less than doting parents to their only child. Why would they be any more interested in a grandbaby?

It didn't matter. Within two years, Jerry's father had died from cancer.

"Have you and Jerry tried marriage counseling?" Eunice's question interrupted my thoughts.

"Yes. After a few sessions, our counselor mentioned he didn't see us putting enough effort into making our marriage work. He was right."

"Can I ask why you are staying married?"

I was surprised Eunice implied we shouldn't. "My plan had been to file for divorce last month. After my friends died, I've struggled to even think straight. The last thing I can concentrate on right now is fighting over a divorce." I gave her a self-deprecating smile. "I'm so good at side-stepping conflict, I could teach a dance class on it."

Eunice folded her hands over her ample lap. We talked of my happy family upbringing, my high-achieving personality prior to pregnancy, and the emptiness I felt at giving up my dreams. I didn't dare tell her how I'd romanticized Greg, made him perfect in my mind over the years. Putting Greg on a pedestal had likely kept me from trying hard enough with Jerry.

Instead, I glanced at my watch. "I'm sorry; I've been rambling for two hours!"

"I'm here to help. Let's talk about what you can do to move forward with your life. You mentioned your past love of swimming. How about taking it up again? It might help you sleep."

I looked down at my un-athletic shape. Yes, I'd lost weight, but I'd also long-ago lost the body of a strong swimmer. "I know I need to do something, but right now, putting one foot in front of the other is all the exercise I can handle. Anyway, I'm sorry for dumping on you."

She stood up and patted my hand. "I'm happy to help. Please, come see me again."

We walked outside as I zipped up my jacket, and before I had a clue what my arms were up to, I took a step toward Eunice and embraced her. I was long overdue for some human touch.

Chapter 5

Halloween was Saturday. Normally, I dressed up with my friends and worked the children's Fall Festival event at the school. Not this year. This year Jerry was who knows where, and I shut all the lights off in our house, grabbed my bag of chocolate covered peanuts, and holed up in my bedroom, looking through all the photos I'd accumulated over the years of my fun times with my friends.

I was back in Eunice's office the following Tuesday night. "Do I pay you for meeting with me? I don't feel right taking up your time. But I'd rather talk with you than a grief counselor."

"As long as you feel I can be of help, I'm here for you." Eunice assured me.

I had no problem uncorking more of my story of my unfulfilling marriage, empty nest, solitary job, and lonely life. I hung it all out, the dirtiest laundry I could ever expose.

"Loneliness is everywhere. And it's getting worse with e-mail, Faceplate or Facebook, and tweaking or twitting, or whatever they call those things," Eunice exclaimed. "And the texting, for heaven's sake why don't they pick up the phone and simply speak to the person?"

I chuckled at her feistiness. She was right though; it isolated us from real, human contact.

"Sometimes I feel like I'm crazy. One day I'll be okay, laughing on the phone with Grace over something one of her children said, convinced my friends are away on a vacation without me. The next day, I can barely drag myself out of bed, crying if I even look at my too-silent cell phone."

I sounded like a nut job, even to me.

"Pain and grief from loss has no time limit. What you described is normal." Eunice leaned toward me. "I know mothers who have functioned the first month after losing a child, and then suddenly fall apart. There is no rhyme or reason to how it will play out."

She reached for my hand. "There are many places where you could connect with people. Asking for help is the bravest thing you can do. Suffering in silence is self-destructive."

"It was easy making friends when I was young; I was surrounded by girls in our neighborhood, school, and sports. Now at forty-two, where will I ever find like-minded women? I feel like I did years ago when I moved here and didn't know anyone besides Jerry."

Eunice nodded. "I'm sure you will, dear. You made an unselfish decision years ago which changed your life forever. And you got through it." Her warm hands enveloped mine.

I swallowed my desire to correct her. I'd made the *wrong* decision, and needed to rectify it via divorce. "I named Karley after my mom, Karen Lynn, and taking care of Karley as a baby helped lessen the pain of losing my mom. I don't seem to have the fight in me this time."

"You're depressed. It's natural. Maybe you could see a doctor for an antidepressant?"

I wanted to shout *no!* Yes, I was depressed, but I'd get over it. "I'm petrified I'll get addicted to them." Confessions rolled off my tongue. "Sometimes I feel like an actress…pretending to live." My glassy eyes sought out her kind face. "I can't be the only one who feels like she's been sucker-punched every other day."

Eunice studied me. "There is a group of women from the area who I think could help you. Women who've gone through some difficult times in their lives. 'Like-minded' as you say. I can connect you with someone who could tell you more about the club if you're interested."

"What's the group about?" I didn't want to join a clap-your-hands-shout-for-joy club.

"It is technically called Crossroads Club." Eunice cleared her throat. "But most of the women call it the To-Hell-And-Back Club."

I raised an eyebrow. "What an interesting name."

"I founded it back in the early 70s after a great many women came to me for counseling. It was such a tumultuous time—the ending of the Vietnam War, the repercussions of the psychedelic sixties… So many changes going on in the world. These women needed other women to talk to who could relate." Eunice's voice softened in reflection. "Many had husbands coming back from the war changed men. Some had husbands who never made it home."

I imagined that generation of women—women my mom's age. I could understand how Eunice's club would've helped them. I wasn't sure my glass-half-empty attitude would improve by hanging out with other Debbie Downers. "I know

I need to meet other people, but it's hard to step out of my comfort zone. And I'm afraid I'd only bring them down."

"Chicken."

I burst out laughing. "Okay. I promise I'll think about it. I'm planning a trip to visit my sister in Texas soon, so I'll decide after I get back. Are they women only from our town?" With less than five thousand in Pine Lakes, I didn't imagine there would be too many members.

"Heavens no, dear! The Club pulls from several area towns. It has no guidelines. If you need it, it is there. There is no building, they can't shackle you." She winked. "It is run strictly by volunteering members and is non-profit. You can leave the club at any time."

"I'm happy to hear there's no dungeon." I grinned. "And I promise to follow up with you when I get back from my trip...that is, if you don't mind me meeting with you again. Please let me know what I can do to pay you."

Eunice tapped her index finger to her lips for a few seconds. "Hmmm, I could use another person to help clean the church. It's easy to work into your schedule. And I'd love to see you help the family Dana left behind. Bob and his children would appreciate your help."

I'd always liked Bob. Helping him was something I should have been doing already. Cleaning her church sounded better than sitting in my house, which had become a box of quicksand.

Before I left, Eunice gave me a list of cleaning instructions and a key to her church.

I'd been checking online every week for an apartment. There were two one bedroom apartments available in a low-income building. I drove over to meet the manager after I left Eunice's office. Dirty, dingy, and loud should've been their advertisement slogan. No way would I live there. I'd have to stick it out with Jerry until I could find something else.

When I got home, I dug out old clothes for cleaning. All my jeans were baggy. I'd gotten rid of the "baby fat" I'd been carrying around for eighteen years. I pulled out our scale. Down fifteen pounds since I'd stepped on it about a year ago. Shopping for clothes now would be fun. Lauren would've jumped for joy if I called her to help me shop for something other than jeans and sweatshirts. I missed her sassy, tell-it-like-it-is personality. I eyed our phone hanging on the wall. Did they have landlines to Heaven? It would make dying so much easier on the living.

I missed their advice, the side-splitting laughter, and talking about everything from facial hair to favorite books. On my dresser was a photo of us four friends on a beautiful fall evening, sitting in a grassy field where we'd buried time capsules years ago.

I might never find the inner strength to dig up our secrets, although likely nothing they'd written would surprise me. I knew everything about them.

Now I was alone and struggling, the worst pick for lone survivor. Dana had four children who needed her, a husband who adored her, and a hectic business. She'd have made it through.

Lauren was our street-smart girlfriend—she'd seen it all—no surprise for how she was raised with no father and a barely-there mother. If Lauren had been the last one standing, with no family other than Dylan, she'd have persevered. Not me, I'd forgotten how.

Next to me, Maggie would have had the hardest time. She wanted, and needed, to get the hell out of her marriage—yet Joe held her in a vice of mind-games and subtle threats—and although we encouraged her, along with her parents, Maggie mentioned she'd wait and see how my divorce worked out for me. At least Maggie had her busy, social job as school principal.

I had nothing of the sort. No kids at home, no adoring husband to spend time with, and no booming career. I thought of how close I came to being in the car with them, and my phone call to Maggie. I should have said, "Yes, wait for me." Or if we'd have talked a minute longer, maybe those deer would have already crossed the highway. I could suffocate in my guilt.

* * *

Over the next few days I made lasagna, chicken fettucine alfredo, monster cookies, and hot fudge pudding cake...all for Bob and his children. I'd forgotten how happy spending time in the kitchen made me. Bringing the food over to Bob's house gave me a reason to get out at night, and catching up with the children was long overdue on my part.

While we all visited in their kitchen, Eva casually mentioned an upcoming holiday dance—her first in high school. "Do you have a dress yet?" I watched her eyes, similar to Dana's, meet Bob's.

His lips pressed together as he shook his head. "No, she doesn't. I forgot. We need to go shopping." I read the sadness and knew it would be a bittersweet event for him.

"I'd love to take you shopping, Eva. If that's okay with you." I said to Bob.

He let out a sigh. "Actually, that would be great. I appreciate it." It would relieve one of a hundred things in his too-busy life and give me an opportunity to spend more time with Eva. We set a date for me to pick her up Sunday morning after they got back from church.

I spent Saturday price-checking last minute plane tickets to San Antonio. When I found a steal for a five-day trip, I checked with Grace to make sure it fit her schedule before booking it. I'd be home a few days before Thanksgiving so I wouldn't miss seeing Josh and Karley when they came home.

Jerry had been deer hunting all day and stopped in to clean up before leaving for pool league. I hated to bring up my trip to Texas, yet even though we rarely spoke or spent a minute together, I was fairly sure he'd notice me being gone for five days.

I might as well have pounded spikes under my fingernails. "Nope. We can't afford it. You know last summer was slow for my business. I'm going into the winter without much work scheduled."

"Too late. I found a good deal and have already booked my flight." I was going to Texas. It wasn't a question. As usual, he'd assumed he had the final say. Not this time.

He stormed out and got in his new truck we'd somehow managed to have money for.

* * *

An hour into our shopping on Sunday, Eva and I found a shimmery emerald green dress, which matched her eyes. Mission accomplished, we headed to the Food Court. As we shared a heaping plate of nachos at a nearby restaurant, I asked her, "How are things going at home?"

"They're okay. It's been tough for Finley and Channy. They don't get it that mom is gone for good." She blinked back tears as she talked about her youngest siblings. "Nash and I babysit a lot for dad when he works the pizza parlor at The Pines at night. We've missed a bunch of our high school events." She gazed down at her last few nachos, before jerking her head up, eyes wide. "I don't mean to complain!"

"You aren't complaining." I thought about The Pines, the seven-day-a-week pizza and bowling business Bob and Dana owned for years. "I'd like to help. I'll see if I can take some shifts." It made sense, for both Bob and me. It would help fill my nights—especially once I moved out.

"I bet dad would like that. Shelly, the manager, works most nights, but dad still helps out a lot."

For two months, I'd been self-centered in my pain, neglecting my friend's families who were hurting too. I had no sympathy for Joe, Maggie's husband. But Lauren's sweet husband, Dylan? That man worshiped the ground Lauren danced on. I'd called him a few weeks earlier, offering copies of some of the photos of

Lauren I'd accumulated. That's when Dylan told me of his plan to move back to Montana where his mom and brother's family lived as soon as his house sold. Lauren's urn would go with him, but he was leaving a small vial here at the cemetery.

Eva and I visited that very cemetery on our way home from shopping, dusting a thin layer of snow off their gravestones. Neither of us bothered to muffle our sobs as we huddled together in the chilly November day.

* * *

The following Wednesday, I'd just stepped out of the shower when the phone rang.

"Hello, dear. How are you doing?" It was Eunice. At 7:10 a.m.

"I'm okay. Is something wrong?" Thankfully, my rudeness was ignored.

"Do you have a minute before you log in for work?"

I stuck the phone on speaker so I could shimmy into my clothes. "Yes, go ahead."

Eunice cleared her throat. "I wonder if you could clean this Saturday morning as we have a church event afterwards. If you could finish by ten or so, I'd appreciate it."

I'd been cleaning Wednesday nights, to get me out of the house on the one night Jerry might be home. I thought of my empty upcoming weekend. "Sure. Or how about Friday night?"

"That won't work. We have a function Friday night. Saturday morning would be best."

I ran a comb through my too-long hair. "Okay. Any special cleaning you want done?"

Eunice sighed into the phone. "No, nothing special. Thanks so much, dear."

* * *

Saturday morning I was at the church before 7:00 a.m. In two hours, I'd finished all but the vacuuming. As I pushed the vacuum along, my mind drifted on how to fill my blank-slate Saturday. Suddenly, someone walked in front of me, and I stumbled backward in automatic flight.

My heart was still going a mile a minute when a woman pushed back the furry hood of her down jacket and faced me. I turned off the vacuum cleaner I was going to use as a weapon.

"Oh, I am sorry! I should've thought about you not hearing me come in."
She looked familiar, her olive skin rosy from the freezing temperatures outside.

I held a hand to my heart which was working its way back down from my
throat. "For a second there I thought the church was haunted!"

She let out a belly laugh as her almond-shaped eyes studied me. "You look
familiar. Forgive me if I should know you from church." She held out her petite
hand to shake mine. "I'm Mary Beth Connelly. I take care of the flowers here." As
we shook hands, I knew—she was the paramedic from the accident.

Shock choked my words. "I'm Peyton Brooks. You're a paramedic, right?
You were at the scene of an accident last September, on Highway 371. My three
girlfriends died in that accident." A brief flashback of the nightmare generated my
tears. I grabbed a dust rag to use as a Kleenex.

Bad move. I inhaled Endust, began sneezing, and surprised myself by
busting out laughing.

Mary Beth fished in her coat pocket and pulled out tissues. She plucked a
dust bunny from my cheek. "Oh yes, now I remember you!"

She led me to a wooden pew and we sat down. "You were one of Dana's
best friends. With the privacy statutes of my job, I couldn't tell you at the accident
how I knew Dana from church. I've thought of you a lot, how you must have been
feeling these past months."

"I'm so glad I ran into you here, I can finally thank you in person. I don't
know how I'd have made it through without you." I dried my eyes.

Mary Beth patted my hand. "I was happy to be there for you. I remember
seeing your husband in the waiting room with you later on, and was thankful you
had him there for comfort."

Why were people always assuming Jerry was of any help to me? We were
no more help to each other than someone who couldn't swim trying to save a
drowning victim.

Mary Beth and I talked for almost an hour. "I should let you get back to work."

"That's okay. I'm glad to have someone to visit with. I talk to myself way
too much."

"I don't suppose Eunice has mentioned her women's club, has she?"

"Yes, she has, but I picture a bunch of down-in-the-mouth old ladies sitting
around crocheting while they complain about their bunions."

Mary Beth grinned. "I don't know how to crochet. And I don't have
bunions. Yet."

"You're in the club?" Mary Beth seemed so "together."

"I joined years ago but just attend big events now. Most members have been through some awful times. The club is nicknamed The To-Hell-And-Back Club, or Hell Club for short. Some, like me, needed to get through a difficult period. Others barely made it through real nightmares. It's a great way to meet new friends who'll understand what you've been through."

Mary Beth took out her cell phone. "What's your phone number? I'll check and see what the next event is and give you a call. I'll go with you, if you'd like. If you decide to join, I'd be happy to be your mentor. Each new member gets assigned a mentor to help them the first year."

"I'd appreciate it." I recited my number as Mary Beth punched it into her cell phone. "You think I'll fit in okay in the club?"

She laughed. "We don't have a whole lot of requirements. You need us? We're there."

I stood. "I better finish up. Eunice said I needed to be done by ten for the program."

"What program?" Mary Beth's brow furrowed.

"I don't know. She asked if I could clean this morning before some church function."

"Hmmm. I'm pretty involved here, and I've no idea what she's talking about."

"So you're not here to do the flowers for some pre-Thanksgiving program or anything?"

"No. Eunice knows I'm here every Saturday morning to switch out the flowers."

I thought Eunice was the conniver. I was wrong. When Grace called me that night and asked if I'd met Mary Beth again, I shouldn't have been surprised. "So it was you? You little manipulator."

"I felt the need to nudge you along so I looked up Eunice. When she mentioned the paramedic who helped you was a member of the Hell-Hath-No-Fury Club, we figured out a way for you to meet her again." Of course. Grace was like a cobra, striking from a distance.

I laughed at her description. "It's called the To-Hell-And-Back Club, you dork."

"So did you join?"

"Not yet." I paused, "but I will."

"Good. See you next week, Sis." Grace blew a kiss into the phone.

And I counted the hours until I could see her and my dad again.

Chapter 6

During my flight to San Antonio a week before Thanksgiving, I had a conversation with my spineless self. *Learn to stand up to Jerry, you sissy-pants, or he's going to chew you up as a snack in divorce court.*

A day after I arrived at Grace's, we sat in her backyard amidst a swing set, sandbox, and flowering shrubs which would never make it through a Minnesota winter. The patio table's striped umbrella provided us shade. I pushed my chair back enough to bask in the rays. It would be another four months before I'd feel anything close to this back home.

"So, you're meeting up with your high school friends Saturday night, including Hot Greg?"

There was the double-stepped beat of my heart again at the mere mention of his name, as if I were back in college. I forced out a chuckle. "You don't even remember what he looked like." *I* barely remembered. I'd boxed away any photo I'd had of Greg and hadn't looked at them for two decades.

"You're right. But I remember your drool pools from when you dated. I thought it was pathetic, wasting all that time on a boy you swore was better looking than any movie star." Grace winked.

"Maybe he's developed a paunch, gone bald, and hasn't brushed his teeth in ten years." I didn't believe for a minute Greg would be anything but perfect.

Grace lifted her blonde hair and bunched it in a hair clip. "I'm glad you reached out to Donna. I see her around town once in a while, and she always asks about you."

"Donna and I email a lot. I can't wait to see her and everyone else in person again. I'm thankful she was able to get a group together on such short notice." I fanned my face.

"Let's go inside. I'm hungry." Grace picked up her iced tea glass and led the way.

We threw together a taco salad and made a couple of margaritas. It was noon, after all. As we ate lunch, I told Grace about a decent three-bedroom apartment I found located a few miles from my home, available April first. "I don't know how this is going to work if I have to live with Jerry until then. The stress level will send me to an early grave."

"You need your old Texas feistiness."

"I know." I hugged her shoulder. "I'm hoping we don't fight about every little thing. Unclenching Jerry's hand from our finances will be a struggle."

"I wish mom was here to instill some of her positive wisdom," said Grace.

Mom was a women's libber who liked people who marched to their own drum. We had a dog named Morrison when I was growing up; named after Jim Morrison from The Doors, who mom always said had been "hotter than steam." And there were the names she gave her daughters; me, after the racy book, *Peyton Place,* and Grace, after its author, Grace Metalious.

"You've turned into Dad over the years," Grace observed. "You've become too complacent. If you wanted to buy a green car, but the salesman told you to buy a blue one, you'd say 'okay.' Me, I'd say, 'I'll go where I can buy a green car, like I want.'"

"Gee, thanks for the compliment." In my head, I was already sympathizing with whatever car salesman ended up dealing with Grace.

"It's not your fault, P. You had an edge and misplaced it once you married Jerry." She embraced me in a long hug. "I have faith you'll get it back." As I closed my eyes, I could pretend it was our mom—minus the scent of Noxzema—back to guide me. I still blamed myself in a twisted way for Mom's death. She'd taken up running after I laid the burden of my unplanned pregnancy on her. The doctor assured us running didn't cause her aneurysm. He didn't know the whole story.

"The thing is, the few times I haven't done the right thing, I've paid for it. Like using Jerry as a landing pad after Greg broke up with me. Look where it got me."

Even Grace had a hard time arguing with that. "So...do you have your ducks in a row yet?"

I stirred my half-empty margarita glass. "I think so. I'll sit down with Jerry after the holidays. It shouldn't be a shock. You know how we've barely tolerated each other over the years. I'm hoping to keep busy with The Pines and the Hell Club until I can move out."

Grace's tan hand covered mine. "You said your friends had been going to suggest some fun things for you to join. You still need to make an effort, P, even without them. It sounds like the Hell Club has plenty of activities."

"They do, according to Mary Beth. She promised I'll find women there who I can relate to."

I needed to make new friends. Yet I was afraid of losing them again.

* * *

Over the next few days, we visited the zoo, Riverwalk, and local parks. One night we all went over to have dinner at Dad and Barbara's. Afterwards, as we caught up over a couple bottles of wine, it felt wonderful to be away from the tenseness and loneliness at home.

"See how much happier you'd be if you moved back to Texas?"

"No kidding, Grace." I rolled my eyes. "I'm sure I wouldn't miss Karley or Josh at all."

Grace held up her hand. "Okay. You might have a point there."

When Grace mentioned I'd come to Texas with a whopping two pairs of shorts in my suitcase Barbara gasped as if Grace had announced I'd been mixing plaids and stripes.

"We need to go shopping." Barbara was animated.

"You're right. P's lost a lot of weight, and none of her clothes from last summer fit her." Grace eyed me up. "What'd you bring to wear to your mini class reunion? I cringe to think about it." She talked like I'd show up in pajamas.

"And your hair could use a little update." Grace reached over and picked at my hair, her nose scrunched up as if she might find lice.

"You're in a time-warp, sis." Grace called her stylist, who squeezed me in two days later—the day of our mini-class reunion. My hair was cut in stylish, shoulder-length layers, with buttermilk-colored highlights and some caramel lowlights. It took five years off my face, which gave my self-confidence an overdue boost. After all, I'd be seeing Greg again.

I'd missed all my class reunions in the past, some on purpose, most due to lack of funds. As excited as I was to meet the group for dinner and drinks, I was also nervous. "You're going to break Greg's heart when he sees what he missed." She squeezed my shoulder as we headed down the stairs. I couldn't admit, even to Grace, that it would be *my* heart broken again when I saw him.

Driving Grace's Toyota along 410, memories from high school stirred like a bottle of pop shaken up. I missed Greg and all my friends I'd walked away from here in Texas. Greg had deserted me for the priesthood. I'd deserted my past.

Donna and I greeted each other with a hug, talking at the same time, trying to cram as much as we could into our too-short time together. Within fifteen minutes, everybody had arrived, including Greg. Damn, he'd gotten better-looking with age. This wasn't going to be easy.

He walked toward me looking like a guy out of GQ—tall, trim, his curly black hair now cut short—and his ocean-blue eyes as bright as I remembered. His charming, lopsided smile revealed two slightly crooked eyeteeth. And like an erupting volcano, I was afraid I was going to vomit.

Greg's arms were outstretched, and we embraced in a long hug, my eyes shut to suppress my tears; I swallowed hard to keep the nausea down. As much as I didn't want to let go of this man, I needed to escape to gather my wits and tie down my emotions. A trip to the bathroom was in order.

"Women must line up to go to your church!" I tried for flippant versus grief-struck as I stepped away. Greg threw his head back in a deep laugh.

"Your admiration is so twisted." Greg's ignorance of his many virtues was one of a thousand things I'd loved about him. He'd made me happy for our three-plus years together. We were greeted by others, and I took the opportunity to make my exit to the ladies' room. I wrestled my pain and regret and stuffed them deep down to my ankles. They weren't invited tonight. I'd deal with them tomorrow.

Greg and I sat next to each other during dinner but had little chance to catch up with so many conversations going on around us. After dinner, many had to leave, and after a break in conversation, Greg turned to me. "Would you like to go out on the deck for a few minutes?"

Donna flashed me a concerned look. I'd have liked to ease her mind by saying he couldn't break my heart anymore. It would have been a lie.

One table was occupied, and Greg led me to the opposite corner where we leaned against the wood railing. We both were quiet for a moment, watching the beautiful sunset. I had so many questions to ask about his last twenty years. None made their way past my tongue.

He took a swig of his beer, braced an elbow on the railing, and turned to me. My whole body ached with the desire to turn the clock back a quarter century.

"Listen, Peyton, I was glad to hear you were going to be here tonight. I've waited two decades to explain some things to you."

I couldn't meet his eyes, instead finding his shoes interesting. Greg's hand lifted my chin. "It occurred to me after your mom passed away that you probably never knew about my visit."

"What visit?"

"Before your mom died, did she tell you I stopped at your house over Christmas vacation during our junior year of college? I had struggled to not contact you that fall, thinking it was for the best. By Christmas, I couldn't take it anymore. I had to see you." His eyes met mine. I held my breath.

"I called a couple of times before Christmas, and your mom said you weren't home, so I stopped by a few days after Christmas. That's when she told me you'd moved to Minnesota the day after Christmas to be with your boyfriend. I was devastated." He shook his head. "Then, when I heard you couldn't come home for your mom's funeral because you were due any day to have a baby, I was shocked." *I bet he was!*

"I second-guessed my decision for a long time. After hearing of your pregnancy and move to Minnesota, I told myself it reinforced I'd made the right decision in joining the priesthood." He studied me as if I might cough up a confession like a hair ball. Yes, I had a doozy of a bomb, and yes, he was a priest. But it was one confession I could never tell.

"She probably never mentioned your phone calls or visit because what was the point? It would've made things worse for both of us."

When we'd broken up, my mom was a witness to my losing-Greg tailspin. She was wise enough to know I'd settled with Jerry, in hopes of proving to myself I was loveable. And I'd always wondered what else mom knew about that summer.

"When you couldn't come home for your mother's funeral, I'd wanted to contact you. My parents said it was best if I left you alone." Greg's voice was quiet. My mind was not.

For the millionth time, I asked myself if I'd made the right decision. Jerry had been a poor replacement for Greg; I'd known it from the start.

He took me in his arms. His shoulders felt too comfortable, his jawline…just the way I remembered it from all those times we'd slow-danced. He likely meant to comfort me. All I felt was cheated. In my dreams as a teenager, I never pictured my life without my mom, or living so far away from my dad, sister, and high school friends. Greg wouldn't have shunned me for the priesthood, and in my craziest imagination, I never pictured marrying a man I didn't love.

On my way back to Grace's, I had the moon roof open and blasted old country songs a decibel louder than my not-on-key voice. When they played "What Might Have Been" by Little Texas, I tried to let the regret of the words blow off me in the breeze.

Tears formed as I flew down 410, playing "if" with my life. Knowing what I'd missed made it even worse. And knowing I'd made a grave mistake sliced me like a guillotine.

* * *

I didn't sleep most of the night, my soul feeling like a peeled grape—skinned and raw. The lack of sleep and a freshly-opened scab caused a major funk in my mood. Grace mentioned as much on our drive to the airport the following afternoon.

"What's wrong, Debbie Downer? Too much booze last night?" She studied me as she pulled up in the drop-off lane at the airport.

"Of course not. I was driving. I had maybe two drinks all night." I came up with a quick, and honest, excuse. "I'm not ready to go home and address Jerry and our marriage. I feel like a different person in Texas—my old self." And after this trip, I'd never be the same.

I hoisted my suitcase out of her trunk and set it on the sidewalk. "I'm thinking of stopping on the way home from the airport to pick up a backbone." I was in need of a new one.

"Well there's a brilliant idea, Ms. Invertebrate."

"Ah Grace, I'm going to miss your sassiness." I put my arm around her.

"It's just a phone call away." She smiled and hugged me back. It was hard to let go.

Chapter 7

I managed to ignore the signs of stress until the day before Thanksgiving, when I caved and went to the Minute Clinic. I'd been fighting a bug since my sleepless night at Grace's.

For once I was glad Karley and Josh couldn't make it home for Thanksgiving—they both picked up shifts at work. Prescribed antibiotics and plenty of rest, I spent Thanksgiving in bed.

Even with no appetite and little energy, I was determined to see Eva in her holiday dress at Bob's that Saturday night. When I left for Bob's, Jerry left for snowmobiling. I took an extra dose of antibiotics before I left and thought of how little time Jerry spent with Bob now.

Eva and her friend posed for us in his living room. "You both look beautiful." I hugged her before they left for the dance via her friend's father. If sheer will could bring a person back to life, Dana would have miraculously appeared to embrace her eldest daughter.

After they left, Bob got his young daughters, Finley and Channy, ready for bed. Nash was at a hockey game. By 7:30, the house was quiet.

"Want a beer?" Bob opened the fridge. I hesitated with my empty stomach churning. Relaxing with Bob overruled my judgment. He opened our Michelob bottles and relaxed back in the chair across from me at the kitchen table.

"I can't thank you enough, Peyton. Not only for the food over the past couple of weeks, but more importantly, for taking Eva shopping." Bob's usual smile faded and his light-brown eyes showed exhaustion. "She deserved a break. I'm leaning on Eva and Nash too much." He pushed back his receding, longer-than-usual hair. Normally it was military-short.

"I'd like to help out at The Pines." I droned on with my sales pitch of my business skills.

"Gee, thanks. I could use an extra hand." He relaxed in his chair. "You sure you want to?"

"Yes. I knew it was going to be tough when Josh moved out. I'm going crazy staring into space, and working at The Pines would help me too."

Bob rubbed his face. "Okay, we'll figure out a schedule." He looked deep in thought.

"What is it?"

He paused. "You know what I miss? Dana's smell. The gardenia-scented lotion she'd use. I keep the bottle on my bedside table now, and take a whiff before bed. I swear it helps me sleep." He studied my reaction. "You must think I'm crazy."

"You're anything but crazy." I said, smiling. "It's funny, when Eva and I were shopping in the mall and spotted Bath & Body Works, we walked straight to their Gardenia Glow section to smell Dana's signature scent. You aren't alone in finding comfort there."

I made my own confession. "I miss our bowling 'Go Team' cheer we'd do after each strike." We sat in silence, lost in our memories. "I also miss Thursday lunches," I blurted. Bob raised an eyebrow. "Lauren used to come eat lunch with me on Thursdays before heading out to bartend."

I continued. "I also miss Dana's funny stories about the kids as she'd laugh about their antics. And I miss Maggie always being there to listen and give sound advice. Every day I miss something about each one of them. For you, I can't imagine the void Dana has left," I said.

Bob cleared his throat. "I think about the last time we made love. And of all the nights we'd put it off because we were both exhausted, thinking 'there's always tomorrow.' I wish I'd have known there wouldn't be another tomorrow." His voice was husky. My heart twisted in pain for his loss.

He studied his empty beer bottle. "Want another beer?"

I could already feel the effects of my first one, thanks to my minimal food intake the past few days. I ignored my queasy stomach. "Sure. Thanks." We moved to the living room where we each plopped in a cushy recliner. For the next few hours—and a couple more beers—Bob and I rehashed funny stories about our friends, kids, and activities we'd shared over the years. I stifled a yawn.

"I need to get going." I announced before getting up from the recliner. Lightheadedness hit me, and I stumbled. I remembered I'd double-dosed on my strong antibiotic.

Bob was instantly by my side to help. "You sure you're okay?" He touched my cheek, which burned like a lit torch. "Hey, it looks like you're breaking out in a sweat. I think you should sit back down."

As good of friends as we were, I couldn't bring myself to tell Bob how awful I felt. If I stayed another minute, I'd be sick. I needed fresh air, and maybe some toast. And my bed.

Bob walked me to the car, after I'd scooped up a handful of snow from his sidewalk and doused my neck and cheeks. "I don't think you should drive." His voice was firm.

"I'm fine. I had three beers in over three hours, and I didn't even finish the last one."

"That's not what I mean, Peyton. You're shaky and pale. Do you want me to call Jerry?"

"No, please don't. I'll call you tomorrow. I'll be okay. I just need some rest."

Bob looked back toward his house, likely judging whether he could leave four and seven-year-old children home alone for the ten minutes it would take to drive me home. "Don't even think about it, Bob." I squeezed his arm before getting in my car. I needed to get home. Fast.

I drove with my car windows down, my teeth chattering, my legs shaking, and my heart clawing to get out of my chest. It was a few miles to home, or a twelve mile drive the opposite way to the hospital. I fought with my decision as bile rose in my throat. Common sense told me I was okay. My amped up body wasn't listening to common sense.

A mile from Bob's, I decided on Urgent Care. Drenched in sweat, my hand covering my mouth, I drove through the cold, dark, empty roads. Suddenly, a car came around the corner too fast into my lane. I over-corrected as they continued on, and my car skidded off to the side, the back of my car hitting a tree. I leaped out of the car, my headlights shining on the empty road.

Falling to my knees, I collapsed in the pristine snow, two feet from my dented back left bumper. Thankfully, the damage appeared minimal. I doused my face and neck with snow as my knees froze before forcing my shivering body from the ground.

Ten minutes later I stood, looking like hell, at the after-hours desk. The receptionist tapped away on her keyboard as she asked me information. Then she got to my emergency contacts. "I show Jerry Brooks as your primary contact and Maggie Coleman as your secondary." It was a sucker-punch I didn't see coming. Was this how life would be? "Ma'am?"

"Um, yes to Jerry. You can take Maggie off. She's passed away." Jerry would soon be off too.

"I'm so sorry! I'll take her off right away." Her fingers flew across the keyboards, instantly deleting Maggie from my history, from my life. "Anyone else you want to put instead?"

I couldn't think of a single soul besides my poor children. It was unfair to rely on them, yet who else did I have? Even though Josh was almost an hour away and Karley two hours, I rattled off their cell numbers while leaning on the counter to keep from collapsing.

Over the next hour, they ran tests, hooked me up to IV fluids, and took blood—which in itself could send me into panic mode. An extremely young-looking doctor walked in. "Your blood pressure is high, Mrs. Brooks, and your blood glucose is low. And, you barely skid under the .08 blood alcohol level." He raised one eyebrow for effect. "But you're going to be okay."

"Are you sure?" Even though my symptoms had waned, I didn't trust them to not sneak back. My mom had neglected to go to the ER when she should have, and died because of it.

"Yes, I'm sure." He studied my chart. "I see you're on antibiotics for a stomach bug? Drinking alcohol with antibiotics is never a good idea, especially on an empty stomach. And you were dehydrated." Dr. Doogie Howser slid glasses on his nose as he wheeled his chair close to me. "Are you under a lot of stress? Feeling depressed? Not taking care of yourself?"

"Yes, yes, and yes." *Don't judge me, Doc. That's my job.*

"Okay, let's start with the drinking. Alcohol is a depressant..."

I held up my hand and cut him off. "I don't have a problem with alcohol. I had a few beers over a period of several hours with the one real friend I have left right now. I don't *normally* drink, and I don't *normally* need antibiotics. And *normally*, before these past few months, I had no problem eating."

"Let's address those eating habits."

"They could be better. I'm working on it. I'm under a lot of stress, and I'm getting help."

"If you're meeting with a counselor, that's great. Have you tried yoga? Meditation?"

"Do I look like I do yoga?" I tamped my embarrassment with a half-hearted joke.

He was kind enough not to answer. "Listen, you need to find a way to relieve your stress, some sort of relaxation techniques. Stress won't cause ulcers, but it isn't helping your health." His demeanor was kind. "Cut down on the caffeine and Ibuprofen, or you're going to end up with an ulcer. If you don't start taking care of yourself and work on reducing your stress, Mrs. Brooks, you'll be paying us a visit that will last more than a few hours." He got his point across.

I promised I'd take better care. What else was I going to do? The doctor stood and handed me some pamphlets. "These have helpful information on ways to de-stress your life. I'd like to see you back in here in two weeks for more blood work. We need to get your blood pressure and low blood glucose under control. And keep seeing your counselor."

His kindness made him now appear more mature. "Everyone needs help at times. Everyone."

I walked out of Urgent Care clutching my become-a-happy-healthy-person papers, my body pumped full of water, crackers, and fruit. It was close to midnight when I pulled in my driveway and sighed in relief. Jerry was still out. I couldn't have faced him.

Adding to the stress of losing my friends was the underlying need to talk to Jerry about a divorce. Thinking of it over the years was easier than taking that first step. Communication had always been Jerry's and my number one downfall. Bringing up a divorce was going to be no easier than any other difficult discussion we'd side-stepped over the years.

* * *

Rare early-December sunshine streamed through my bedroom windows. It was almost nine, later than I'd slept in months. My first Hell Club event was that afternoon at the Brainerd Curling Club.

Mary Beth picked me up shortly after lunch. As I slid into the passenger side, she eyed me up. "You feeling better?" She had called me earlier in the week.

"Yes, thanks to sleeping for two days straight." I smiled at her as she drove.

"I'm glad you visited with Bob last week. You need to get out and enjoy yourself more often." Mary Beth grinned. "Which, I guess, is why we're here."

She pulled in the almost-full Brainerd Curling Club parking lot, and my stomach danced in anticipation. I'd never heard of the sport of curling until the Winter Olympics a few years ago when a team from Minnesota had medaled in the event.

Inside the large steel building a commons area held a small kitchen and bar. Plexiglass sectioned off the area from the ice arena below. Mary Beth led me to the plexiglass. "There are four sheets of ice, so we will have four games going on at the same time."

She pointed out the women sliding along the ice. "They're practicing their slide. See how they use their broom off to the side as support? It looks harder than it is. You can learn the very basics the first day." We made our way to the locker room, and Mary Beth introduced me to several women.

"Everyone seems so...normal." I whispered to her as we sat down to change out of our street shoes and put on clean tennis shoes for the ice.

"What did you think? They'd have horns or something?" She nudged me, teasing. "Some might have gone through hell, but most managed to keep their sense of humor with them on the trip."

We stood up. "C'mon, we have to sign a waiver before we can go on the ice." She led the way to a small table with a "Welcome to another fun event, sponsored by the To-Hell-And-Back Club!" sign propped in the middle.

"Let's also get you signed up so when you walk out on the ice, you're a true club member."

A woman, who could have passed for a stockier version of Halle Berry in a stylish cropped hairstyle, stuck out her hand to shake mine. "Welcome! I'm Charlee." Charlee's skin was the color of polished oak, and her welcoming smile put me at ease.

"Hi, I'm Peyton." Mary Beth had warned me ahead of time, nobody introduced themselves with their last names. You started in the club on a first name only basis.

"Peyton's ready to sign up to be a club member." Mary Beth offered after we signed our waivers for the Curling Club. She'd informed me ahead of time that the club had no building or meeting room of their own. It was a non-profit club where members paid for whatever event they signed up to attend. Each member was encouraged to have a mentor. Mary Beth was mine.

"Awesome. It's a simple form, with a few boring legal regulations." Charlee shuffled sheets of paper in front of me. "This one says you won't sue the club for any injuries at any events, which, by the way, we don't have a dime to our name anyway." She chuckled. "This form is our super-huge list of rules as a club member. You'll need to sign with your blood." Her brown eyes sparkled with mischief.

I read the list of rules...all three of them.

#1 Don't ask, only offer. Meaning, a fellow club member will let you know eventually why she joined the club. However, if you're comfortable, you may offer why _you_ joined. See rule #2.

#2 Wait a year. Give us time to know you for "you," not your past.

#3 We're here to help bring you up, don't join the club just to drag us down. We'll offer a shoulder for you to cry on, as long as you shoulder your own responsibility to move forward.

That was it. "We don't tell people why we joined?" I thought that was part of the "cleansing."

"That's what your sponsor, or mentor, is for. Trust me; we humans have a tendency to pre-judge people." Charlee's eyes met mine. "Like what if I told you I'd had a boob job?"

Next to me, Mary Beth giggled like a school girl. "Are you kidding?" I asked before thinking. I wanted to kick myself for my sudden rudeness.

"No, *clearly* she hasn't." Mary Beth answered me, elbowing Charlee good-naturedly. "Charlee's point is, if it was the first thing you found out about Charlee, you might pre-judge her and think she was self-centered, superficial, or a stripper, or a rich mistress, or a…" Charlee slapped her hand over Mary Beth's grinning mouth.

"And really, I might have low self-esteem, or have been emotionally abused, or I'm a breast cancer survivor." Charlee's arched eyebrow went up an inch as she put her hand on her hip. "So, we keep our wondering to ourselves." Charlee winked.

I turned to Mary Beth. "I'm glad you clarified that for me about Charlee. Now I don't have to wonder every time I stare at her chest." I smiled as I signed my name on each membership form.

Charlee slapped the table, busting out laughing. Mary Beth shook her head at us as if we were two misbehaved children she had no hope of controlling. "That's why we have that 'Judgement Box' by the door. You'll find it at each event. It's visibly empty, but emotionally full. If we leave our judgement at the door, we're less likely to be shocked by someone's actions or words." Mary Beth explained before guiding me toward the curling arena.

The coolness inside, along with the endorphin release from laughing, strengthened my frail body and spirit. I felt like a million bucks already. Or at least a thousand.

We were split into teams of four and handed our equipment: a "slider" which was made of Teflon and slid over one of our tennis shoes to help us slide when throwing the rock, and a broom to help sweep the curling rocks to the "house."

Charlee went over the instructions, and we newbies had time to practice before starting our games. My teammates, Molly—tall and young—and Lily—petite and quiet—were new members, and poor Charlee, a seasoned club member, was stuck with us.

Before we began, Charlee lined us all up and led us through stretches, telling us we needed to "stretch and warm up our muscles" first or we'd be sore tomorrow. Someone in the group called out, "Do Kegel exercises count?"

"Only in your bedroom," Tia, a woman on our opposing team, teased back.

On my first time up to throw my curling rock, I crouched down in the hack, which reminded me of the starting blocks for sprinters, and concentrated on everything I'd learned. My foot pushed my body forward out of the hack. I slid out on my left foot while guiding the rock…and fell over onto my back like a turtle, legs in the air. "Are you okay, Peyton?" Charlee's eyes grew wide.

My gut-busting laughter answered her concern.

"We need helmets!" Molly joked. Your feet could go out from under you in a second while sweeping or throwing—and ours did—plenty.

A shapely salt-and-pepper haired woman bent down in the hack, ready to throw her rock as we waited behind her. "Hey, Charlee, does this position make my butt look big?" She asked as her rear pointed upward before she pushed off to throw her rock.

"Nope. From the back I thought you were Nicole Kidman," Charlee joked.

When it was Molly's turn to throw, she remarked, "You are all gonna be sorry I had chili for lunch," before she crouched down in front of us in the hack. After everyone's eyes widened in surprise, our laughter bounced off the enormous ceiling and echoed over the vast sheets of ice.

Over the next couple of hours, our arms burned from sweeping curling stones into the "house." Music played on the speaker system, and when "Daydream Believer" by The Monkees came on, every woman from twenty to sixty belted out the lyrics.

"I've done more sweeping today than I have for years," Lily said, as we all shook hands after our game.

Tia fanned her face. "I'm having a hot flash and need to lie on the ice for a minute."

"It'll look like the outline of a crime scene victim when you're done." Mary Beth joked.

As I shook Tia's hand, she said, "Welcome to the Hell Club." There were burn scars on her hand. I shook it gently, already wondering what her "story" was. I ached from head to toe after my body and soul were brought back to life, something I thought would never happen again. And it fed me a slice of hope that this group of once-broken women might just be what the doctor ordered for me.

Chapter 8

While others decorated their homes for Christmas and spent hectic hours shopping, I spent my free time cooking for Bob's family, chauffeuring his kids, and working at The Pines.

And coming to terms with my conscience. I'd get through the holidays one baby step at a time until I could address what Jerry and I had been putting off for years.

The Hell Club had a volunteer event for Toys for Tots the week before Christmas. Molly picked me up, along with Tia and Charlee—all women I'd met at the curling event. Mary Beth couldn't make it. "I know Tia and Charlee, and neither is a mass-murderer as far as I know. You'll be fine, Peyton."

On our drive over, Charlee, Molly, and Tia all talked a mile a minute—and did their best to yank me out of my shell again. For three hours, a dozen of us packed up toys at the Brainerd National Guard Armory, according to the lists for each family's needs. A couple of the women commented they'd been on the receiving end in years past and were happy to pay it forward.

"Where do you chicks want to go eat after we're done?" Molly rubbed her flat stomach.

We were going out for dinner before driving through the Sertoma Winter Wonderland holiday display at the Northland Arboretum. "How about Prairie Bay Restaurant? I love their pasta," said Tia.

"Fine with me," Molly and Charlee chimed in. I didn't care where we ate. Having other women to go out for dinner with again meant one less lonely meal for me.

A few of the other women joined us, and over dinner, I digested a short version of how Tia came to join the club. "Burns on over forty percent of my body, thanks to a house fire started by my drug-influenced teenage son." Tia nonchalantly rolled up one of her sleeves to show me the continuing of scars and skin grafts that I'd seen on her hands.

"How awful! Did your son make it out okay?" I couldn't believe she could relay such a horrific event in a matter-of-fact voice. Time must heal almost everything.

"He did. That was eight years ago, and after treatment for his addiction, and both of us getting the help we needed, he cleaned up his act. He's now a junior in college." Tia beamed.

A hundred questions raced through my mind. I asked none of them. I knew the rules.

The noise inside the car was at level orange while we drove through the colorful Sertoma Winter Wonderland, its scenes enhanced by hoar frost covering the branches shimmering in the moonlight. The three of them chattering at the same time reminded me of my old friends, and I grinned. Charlee entertained us with a detailed story of her recent mammogram.

"They asked if I was okay to stand for a period of time at the torture machine. I assured them I was fine…until they squeezed my lungs in with my rib cage in the god-awful machine!" She chuckled. "A man had to have invented that torture chamber. Why don't guys have their nuts squeezed in one of those to determine any cancer? They get off with a simple blood test for a prostate cancer check."

"Seems a little unfair to me," Molly agreed. "I don't have enough va-voom for them to squeeze, I'm afraid when it's time for me, they'll break my ribs in that machine." She then launched in to a story about the difficulties of buying a training bra with lace for herself.

It was after nine when Molly pulled into my driveway. I wasn't surprised to see our house dark, meaning Jerry was still out snowmobiling. "Thanks so much, I had a great time." I clutched my stomach, still laughing from all their stories as I got out of the car.

"We'll see you soon, huh?" Molly asked.

"You bet!" I didn't know what the next Hell Club event was, but I was going.

* * *

Karley and Josh arrived the morning of Christmas Eve, making the long Christmas weekend bearable. Our Christmases had always been small. Jerry's dad, who'd suffered the effects of Agent Orange in Vietnam, along with a lot of mental anguish, succumbed to cancer two years after we married. His dad's "mental absence" in Jerry's childhood was likely the driving force for him sticking it out in our marriage…to be there for his own kids. Eventually his mother remarried and moved to California, leaving Jerry and me to spend holidays with our children, unless Grace's clan showed up.

Before Karley and Josh packed up to head back to their apartments, I boxed up enough leftovers for them to add five pounds to their tall frames. "Thanks for the grub. Me and the guys never get around to cooking much." Josh mumbled as he tied his size thirteen tennis shoes. Guilt stabbed at me.

"I'm sorry; I never even thought you might want me to bring food over once in a while."

Josh gave me a blank look through his too-long hair. "Huh?"

Clearly, he wasn't dropping a hint for me to cook for him. "I'm saying when I go to Brainerd, you're half an hour away; I could be stopping by with food for you."

"He's not a baby, for God's sake." Jerry's voice boomed behind me.

"I know," My jaw clenched. According to Jerry, his parents never coddled him. Therefore, boys weren't supposed to be loved too much.

"Anywayyy…" Josh stood up and tried to put an end to a possible verbal spat. "I better get going here, and Ma, I'd love it if you stopped by sometime, food or no food."

I gave him a smile for reinforcing it was okay if I mothered him. Wasn't it my job?

Karley hugged her brother extra hard when he left, likely because he'd managed to block a war of words between Jerry and me. After Karley left, I drove to chat with my dead friends.

* * *

Typically, Jerry and I would have gotten together with Maggie, Lauren, Dana, and their husbands for New Year's Eve, but there was nothing typical about my life now. Instead, Jerry welcomed in the New Year with Joe. Alone in the house on New Year's Eve, I wandered into the kitchen and grabbed a fresh bag of chocolate-covered peanuts, a staple in my diet now. Our kitchen, once permeated with the aroma of baked goods and hotdishes, whose walls used to vibrate with our children's laughter and that of their hungry friends, now echoed loneliness.

Bob had invited me over to play games with his family. I should've gone. I waited until nine before calling him. "Kids still up?" I was already in my pajamas and thinking of going to bed myself.

"Oh yes. I've found that if I let Finley and Channy eat two bowls of ice cream topped with sprinkles and chocolate chips, their inner Energizer Bunny can probably make it to midnight."

"They'll outlast me. I'm thinking of crawling into bed soon with a good book."

"They'll probably outlast me too," Bob chuckled. "I only have to make it until eleven. Nash will be home from his friend's house by then. Eva is babysitting, and I don't expect her until well after midnight." He paused. "I wish you'd have come over, Peyton."

"Me too."

"And before I forget to mention it again, you are off duty for cooking and baking. Between you and the ladies from church, I can barely close our freezer door. We've got this."

"You sure?" I needed someone to need me, or at least my cooking.

"Yes. The kids are a big help in the kitchen. I'm not letting you off chauffeuring duties though."

"I wouldn't dream of giving that up." I needed Dana's family far more than they needed me.

* * *

My relief at starting the new year—what I hoped would be better a year—faded when I logged-in to work the first Monday in January. All medical transcriptionists working for the hospital were notified via email to dial in for a conference call at 10:00 a.m.

The gossip mill had been churning for weeks, via personal emails from other medical transcriptionists, of possible changes within the hospital. By ten-thirty, I'd been informed my job of twenty years would be outsourced by April or May, thanks to the bad economy—and downsizing—terms used often the past few years.

We "seniors" in the field were given the choice to take a voluntary layoff which would come with a decent severance pay and unemployment. And that within a few years the remaining jobs would be outsourced anyway. My formerly-a-dream goal of finishing college now burned bright.

It was bad timing for me, one more wrench thrown into my life. This was going to be a big gouge in our divorce finances. I picked up the phone and called Grace when I was done with work.

"Do you think you could find a part-time job while you finish college?" Grace asked.

"If there were a professional worrier job, I'd qualify, but I don't see ads for one." Grace chuckled at my job idea. "I'll keep working at The Pines, and I'll have severance pay. I called a Minnesota college on my lunch break to check into online classes. The college requirements have changed so much; I'll have more than a year now full-time. This just reinforces how important my accounting degree is."

"Good for you, P. I'm glad you're grabbing this opportunity," Grace cheered me on.

"I'll drop the bomb about my job loss first to Jerry, before I address filing for divorce. I'm bracing myself for the blowup." I assumed Jerry would be home Wednesday night. We saw each other so seldom; we had avoidance down to a science.

"Don't let him bully you, P."

"I won't. I feel like such a failure, even though the job loss isn't my fault. Heck, I feel like a failure with my marriage too. Like a big "F" will be written on my marriage report card. We should have tried harder over the years." I mumbled the last words, more to myself. I felt like I had tried. Looking back, I had to wonder if I'd ever put my heart into making it work.

"So you haven't been trying all these years? The old Peyton tried hard at everything. Remember her? Captain of the swim team? Salutatorian of her high school class? Remember her?"

"Gee thanks for dredging up my old accomplishments; they remind me of how much my life has slid downhill." It was easy to be a high achiever when I was growing up. My life was perfect. Once the rug was pulled out from under me, I stumbled and fell.

"My point is I've never seen you not try, P. I'm glad you're feeling strong enough again to address your marriage. This is your life. Start living it."

* * *

Jerry was a no-show after work Wednesday night, so I chose the following Sunday before I worked the late shift at The Pines. Though we rarely talked, I had a pretty good idea of Jerry's schedule. The Minnesota Vikings were playing Sunday afternoon, which meant he'd be watching the game at Joe's house. I made roasted chicken, potatoes, and popovers, one of Jerry's favorite meals.

He walked in the door near suppertime. "I figured you'd be working." Apparently, Jerry paid more attention to my work schedule at The Pines than I thought.

I had switched shifts so I could talk to him. "Not until five-thirty. Um, I made dinner."

"We had snacks at Joe's, I'm not hungry." I watched him escape toward the hallway.

I pulled out the backbone I'd purchased and installed it. "We need to talk." I used my matter-of-fact voice, and Jerry slowly turned around. I gestured to the kitchen table, and pulled out a chair for myself, feigning control. He chose to stand there, arms crossed. I had just sat down when the timer went off on the stove. It jolted me in my chair, and I jumped up to check the popovers.

Perfectly done; the one thing in my life even close to perfect.

Jerry watched in silence; although I caught him inhale the aroma. I studied his face, a rare occurrence for me, and noticed the lines of bitterness around his mouth.

I performed a mini Lamaze breathing technique before speaking. "My job is going to be outsourced in the next few months. Most of us have been given the option of a severance package and unemployment. I'm taking it." My hands were clenched under the table.

"You're crazy!" He'd never laid a hand on me in anger, yet his voice put me on edge.

"The medical transcription work is being outsourced. They're offering those of us who've been there the longest to be the first ones out. I'm going back to college to finish my accounting degree."

"That's poor planning on your part, choosing to lose your job. Do I need to remind you we need your income? You know the building industry's been shit for three years."

"I won't be done until April or May and I'll have severance pay for a while plus unemployment. If you're so concerned about money you shouldn't have bought your new pickup last summer. You might want to get a second job in the winter when construction is slow. I did it for years, doing Dr. Braun's transcribing at night, along with doing your business books these last twenty years. That's three jobs for me." *Where was my video camera so I could record myself for Grace?*

Jerry's eyes widened and his face pulled back as if I took a swing at him. I couldn't remember the last time I stood up to him. He stood with his hands on his hips, ready to reprimand me. "I'm sick of this!" His words shot out of his mouth like cannon balls aimed at me.

I understood what he meant. I felt the same.

"So am I, Jerry. Let's be honest. We need to divorce." I kept my voice under control, refusing to allow it to convey my guilt, sadness, and anger. "I've been looking at apartments."

"Forget it. I'll move in with Joe. It'll be cheaper." He crossed his arms again. "I'm more than ready to move out." He threw his shoulders back and his chest puffed up as if he were proud of that fact.

I blinked rapidly, as if he'd thrown a bucket of water at me. He'd probably been thinking of this as long as I had. I was glad I hadn't put a deposit down on an apartment yet. I slammed the oven door, the aroma of the popovers stirred with the motion.

"I haven't been any happier here than you, Jerry. I stuck it out for the kids."

"Well they're both grown up now and gone. I'll be glad to leave." His purple Vikings jersey had a salsa stain down the front and I wanted to laugh. What was wrong with me that I noticed it while we discussed the disintegration of our twenty-two-year marriage?

He paced between our kitchen table and the living room. The room wasn't big enough for our misery. Our bitter words hung over our heads, ready to slide down the pale-yellow walls in a runny blur, covering up everything we hadn't said over the years. Jerry grabbed a sunken popover and descended silently to the basement.

I slid our dinner out of the oven and let my warm tears plop on the cold burners. The stove clock read "4:32." I had to get ready for work at The Pines. *Why are you crying? This is what you wanted.* I'd have liked to call in sick, but staying home with Jerry, confined to my bedroom, would be worse. I walked like a zombie in to my bedroom and got ready for work. Nobody would know my toxic marriage had finally been sliced open to bleed out a painful death.

And our children…we were hurting them just to make ourselves happy. Another heap of guilt.

After putting on the best play-acting of my life at The Pines, one deserving of an Oscar nomination in my book, I slept little. The next morning, I watched Jerry silently walk past my office, making a few trips to his truck with packed boxes. Not one word passed between us. Pride strangled me. My right eye twitched, as if it were sending out Morse code for help. When I heard the door to the garage shut for his final trip, I took my lunch break and called Grace.

"I don't need to wait for the apartment anymore." I dumped the latest in my life on her.

"Well, it's all out in the open now. Yes, you are sad your marriage is over. Nobody is happy about a marriage breakup. Give yourself a gold star for your effort over the years. You didn't fail—you tried. Now get rid of your guilt and move forward." If only she knew the whole story.

"I have so much to figure out, and I feel overwhelmed again." What an understatement.

"You can do it, P. Nothing is stopping you now."

Nothing, and nobody. It was just me, myself, and I…again.

Jerry stopped in the next day. I was done with work for the day, and darkness had settled in outside my windows. I stayed at my desk with a cup of hot cocoa and attempted to concentrate on our personal finances. It was a good time to address our bills.

He walked by my office, ignoring my existence. I cut him off in the hallway when he came out of his bedroom. "We need to talk about finances." My voice was cool as a cucumber even as my nerves burned like jalapenos.

Jerry stopped, holding two overflowing boxes. "You'll be responsible for the house payment and anything related to this place. You're the one staying here." He shook his head as if it should've been obvious to me. He nudged by me. I pulled on his sleeve to stop him.

"Excuse me? I'm only staying here because *you* are moving out. One of us might as well live here until we can sell the house, which will be a while in this market. I can't pay for all the household expenses on my own."

"You know I don't have money coming in this time of year, and business has been even slower with the economy. I'll pay my truck payment. That's it." He turned with his full boxes and shit-full-attitude, and walked toward the kitchen.

I stuck to him like a wood tick. "Do you really want to let it go into foreclosure with only nine years left on our mortgage?" My words stopped him. "We're *both* responsible for this place." His lips compressed like a zipper.

"And what about the kids? Have you said anything to them?" I was ashamed I'd put our finances ahead of our children—adults or not, they were still our kids.

His shoulders slumped, as guilt replace his arrogance. "No. Did you want me to call them?"

I had always taken care of everything with our kids. It didn't feel right having him step into the role. "I'll tell them." My anger deflated. "I hate doing this to them."

"They're not children anymore. They'll be okay."

"They'll always be our children, Jerry. We are going to force them to go to two houses for the holidays, split their time with us, and try to dance a tightrope between us the rest of their lives." One of the biggest reasons I'd put off bringing up divorce over the years.

He had the decency to hang his head. A minute later, he walked out and loaded his truck.

And I poured myself a glass of wine.

Chapter 9

Within the week, Jerry had moved out of the house—and away from our marriage—a marriage we'd both left, emotionally, years ago. He still stopped to drop off invoices for me to pay for his construction business, and on the following Friday afternoon, as he placed bills on the corner of my desk, I decided it was time to address some questions. "Jerry?"

"Yeah?" He stepped back, as if I might bite. The thought crossed my mind.

"I wanted to let you know I'm going to file for divorce." I forced myself to look at him.

He took another step away. "Fine by me." He performed his Mr. Clean stance.

"We need to figure out our money. I've paid February's mortgage already, and I can see you've got a decent balance right now in the business."

"Maybe, but I'll need money to pay for some things at Joe's. I'm going to give him a few hundred a month until I figure out where I'll live." Jerry had backed up to my office doorway, and I watched his weathered fingers drum on the open door.

"We're both going to need the equity from this house so we can afford something on our own. We should meet with a realtor and figure out what our house is worth. I can't afford to live here, and I don't need all this room." I wanted three bedrooms wherever I ended up. I wanted room for my children to feel welcome, but this was too much for me alone.

"I'll talk with a few of the realtors around here, have them come in and give us an appraisal." Jerry offered, knowing most of the realtors thanks to his construction business.

He pushed himself away from the door and tapped the invoices against his leg as he walked out. I didn't know if I dared deposit any of his paycheck I'd be cutting for him next week to help pay for our expenses. And although I didn't want to stay living in our house, it was going to be hard to leave it. I needed to talk with Karley and Josh...soon.

* * *

The next morning, I showered, dressed, and brewed a half pot of coffee. As I sat by the living room window, I watched the sun rise, sparkling on the snow-covered lawns of our neighborhood. A neighborhood I'd be moving from someday soon. I finished my coffee, laced with pumpkin-spiced creamer, shrugged into my parka, found my winter ear band and warm mittens, and stepped in my Sorel boots. I needed some fresh air to clear my head.

I walked around our always-quiet neighborhood where the basic one-story homes initially filled with young families like ours years ago. Almost all those families moved out as their families and income grew. We stayed. Now the homes were occupied by retired couples. My boots crunched on the layer of packed snow on the street as I squelched the feeling I was stumbling again. Why was it always me worrying about money? Why was it always me worrying about our kids? I needed an emotional personal trainer to teach me how to stop worrying about everything.

My pace was as fast as I could walk in my heavy winter wear, and the walk helped relieve some of the tightness in my chest.

Thirty minutes later I was back home, shoveling the few inches of snow that fell overnight. A new dusting and the warmth of the sun was a good combination for the Hell Club event for the day...cross-country skiing. It was exactly what I needed to expel some stress.

We all met at the Brainerd Arboretum where the trails were groomed. In the afternoon sunshine, two dozen of us skied in temperatures hovering at forty. We skied through sticky snow, which meant more than one snowball fight broke out, thanks to Molly-the-Instigator. There was a good-sized hill on the trail, and Charlee was one of the first in line. Picking up too much speed, she ended up doing a mid-air-spread-eagle jump, landing on her butt, and sliding backwards the rest of the way, her hood filling with snow. Her loud guffaw and clumsy acrobats brought Lily to her knees in a fit of laughter. Their amusement was contagious, and we were all soon rolling in laughter at the bottom of the hill.

I was whistling as I parked my car in the garage while the sun set. My mood had elevated from zero to one-hundred in the space of an afternoon. They could sell the uplifting endorphins you got from hanging with the Hell Club women for a high price.

Although we'd all brought a few snacks, after all that exercise, I was famished when I got home. After I cleaned up, I drove to the nearby grocery store. I'd been out of milk since Jerry left and had nothing at home even resembling a fruit or vegetable.

I stood in the checkout lane, proud of my healthy purchases: milk, bananas, a bag of baby carrots, and a loaf of whole grain bread. Oh yes, and a bag of chocolate-covered peanuts.

"Hello, Peyton, how're you doing?" Georgia, the sixty-something woman who I swear they built the small store around, gave me a sympathetic look.

"I'm okay, better than I look, I'm afraid." My hair was still wet from my shower and I'd washed off my makeup.

She laid her cold hand over mine while looking me in the eye. "Oh? Because I sure was surprised to hear Jerry moved out on you, so I'm glad to see you standing in front of me right now. I was concerned for your well-being, you know, after all you've gone through."

Were you? Was she truly sorry or was she itching to find out a new juicy tidbit from me? I was too polite to ask. And I sure as hell was not going to say another word. I swiped my credit card, bagged my groceries, and walked out the sliding doors with my head held high.

So the word was out. Our town's population was less than five thousand, and I probably knew about a hundred. Yet somehow, my vanilla-flavored-life was spicy enough to be added to the local gossip feed. Super.

After I devoured a grilled cheese sandwich and a banana, I called Grace, and we connected through Skype. "Personally, I don't give a flying leap about what people say about me in town, but it was hard not to set her straight about me being a woman scorned."

Grace relaxed back in her chair and took a sip of her wine. I loved Skype; it was as close to my sister being across the table from me as I could get on a weekly basis. "P, remember, you live in a small town. As soon as the locals get dirt on someone else, you'll be old news."

"I hope so. I refuse to hole up in this house just because of a few loose tongues." I picked up my glass of wine. "Cheers." I grinned at my life-saver-sis as we clicked our wine glasses together via our computer screens.

You work with what you've got.

* * *

When I woke the next morning, my plan was to call Mary Beth, who hadn't been able to make the cross-country skiing event. Before I even made coffee, Dylan called. "Sorry to call so early, I wanted to catch you before you went anywhere."

"That's fine, I was up." The sound of his gravelly voice made me smile. I was going to miss him once he moved back to Montana. Yes, I rarely saw him now, but knowing he was in the same town still gave me comfort. Once he moved, another piece of my past would be gone.

"Can I stop by for a few minutes? I've got something for you from Lauren that I found."

Curiosity sat me up straight in my kitchen chair. "Sure, that'd be good."

Dylan said he'd be over in half an hour. I hopped in the shower.

Thirty minutes later he knocked on my front door, and I greeted him with a hug. "It's good to see you again." I reached up and touched his long sideburns, out of style, but never on Dylan—a chiseled, Marlboro-looking man who totally rocked his long sideburns. "I'm going to miss these," I'd named his sideburns Ernie and Bert years ago.

He grinned, betraying the haunted look still in his eyes. "They're gonna miss you too. Hell, I'm gonna miss you, have missed you these last few months." He bent down and tugged off his cowboy boots before following me into my kitchen.

"Coffee?" I reached in the cupboard for another mug and poured him a cup.

"Sure. Thanks." Dylan pulled out a chair next to where my half-empty coffee cup sat. He shrugged out of his parka and set a crumpled envelope from his pocket on the table.

An envelope from Lauren? I couldn't imagine what he'd have found. Until I brought his coffee cup to the table, along with the pot to refill mine, and saw *Shit List* written on the front of the envelope, in Lauren's loopy handwriting. Oh my God.

I gingerly sat down, as if my chair might break. I forgot about filling my mug. "Wow."

Dylan watched me, taking in my recognition of the envelope. "So you know about this?"

It was a list to help me start a new life, and instead, my life was destroyed that day. A list I'd forgotten about. "Yes. It's the list Lauren was going to give me the day of their accident." My eyes were glued to the envelope, like a small child yearning for a piece of cake but not daring to reach out and help themselves.

"I'm sorry, but I read it. I didn't know what it was at first." He grinned. "I was afraid it was for me when I read 'shit-list,' thinking Lauren had made up a honey-do list for me."

Our eyes met. "You just found this?" Where had it been for four months?

His lips compressed. "I'm gonna be honest with ya, Peyton. After I got Lauren's purse back, I went through it a week or so after the accident. When I opened the envelope and realized it was for you, I didn't think I should give it to ya."

I'd have asked him why, but I had a feeling I'd know in a minute. "Can I open it?"

He slid it toward me. "Normally I'd leave ya alone to read it, but if it's okay with you, I'd like to stay, and explain something when you're done reading."

"Yes, please stay." I unfolded the single sheet of paper from the envelope as if the paper would disintegrate, and saw Lauren's writing with haphazard comments all over the page:

Peyton's Shit List to fill her life back up again to replace her college babies ~

First off, this is about YOU sweet-cheeks. Once Jerry is out of your life, it can't be what he wants, or what your kids want you to do, not even what WE want you to do, although we sure as hell will give our opinions. You know me. I'll tell you if I think your head is up your ass. 😊

So, first off, we're here for you when you stand up to Jerry. We'll be here when you feel the guilt of splitting up your family. We'll help you find happiness again. We promise.

Here's Maggie's two cents. She says she'd join a cooking class with you, or a gourmet group, or whatever you want to do. "Cooking and baking makes Peyton happy, this way she can get out of her house and meet others who enjoy the same thing." Awww, ain't she sweet?

Dana thinks you should get your ass back in the water. Well, you know her, she said 'rear,' but whatever. Swimming to be exact. And says you could volunteer at the YMCA to help teach little kids how to swim and shit like that, and it would make you feel all warm and fuzzy inside by doing something for others, esp. kids, plus you'd feel better getting back to your swimming. Dana's so damn smart, isn't she?!

Okay, for me, I'm up for doing just about anything out in the real world with you. I'll go hang-gliding, rock climbing, parasailing, scuba-diving, whatever you want to do. But if you're asking me what I think would be fun (but remember, this is all about YOU) I'm up for taking a dance class. Maybe salsa dancing, or some kinda similar shit. Don't you think it'd be fun? 😊

I'll do whatever you want. Let's get some fun back into your life, maybe swear more, worry less, chill out, and color outside the lines, girl. And don't expect perfection. Only fun!

I read it twice—hearing Lauren's boisterous, upbeat voice—as if she were sitting next to me talking like our old Thursday lunches together. I didn't even realize I was crying, until Dylan got up to find a Kleenex for me.

Walking back to the table with a paper towel, he asked, "You okay?"

I dabbed at my eyes and laughed. "You know what? Reading Lauren's list is like a weight off my chest. It makes me feel like she's right here knocking some sense into me." My mouth quivered as I patted the empty chair next to me where Lauren used to sit for our Thursday lunches.

"I know what ya mean. Things like that I've found around our home make me feel like she's back with me. They make me sad she's gone, but happy I have those memories of her."

"I can't tell you what a wonderful gift this is. I might frame it; it means so much to me."

He sat back in his chair, nodding at the paper. "I couldn't give it to you while you were still with Jer. Lauren had told me you planned on talkin' to him 'bout a divorce. I didn't want to have Lauren's words influencing you at all. Now that he's at Joes, it doesn't matter."

"This was perfect timing. I'm sure our split was no surprise to you, and Lauren's list is a reassuring gift to me." I refilled our coffee, and we sat for an hour reminiscing and talking about the future. I felt as energized as if I'd received a blood transfusion by the time Dylan left.

I called Mary Beth after he left. "Do you have time to meet somewhere for coffee this morning?" I sensed a budding friendship with her, and I was overdue to reach out on my own.

"I'm heading to church, but I can meet you at The Hungry Loon Café at ten-thirty."

I felt a twinge of guilt for not attending Eunice's church on a Sunday morning after leaning on her for help. But not guilty enough to attend. "Sounds good. I'll see you there."

Over coffee and blueberry muffins at The Hungry Loon, I learned Mary Beth was divorced, no children, and besides her job as a paramedic, was in charge of Meals on Wheels through the church.

"Wow, you're one busy lady." Mary Beth served others. I was a self-centered slug.

"Not so much. I don't have a family to care for, so for me, it's a good balance."

"Was it hard on you, your divorce? How did you get through it?" Any advice would help.

Mary Beth folded her hands. "It was long ago, now I think I look back on it with a better perspective. I'd been friends with Kurt for years; he was one of my best friends."

"I don't get it, why did you divorce, if you don't mind my asking?"

"He's gay." She shrugged. "If I'd have listened to my inner voice before we got married, I'd have known. Kurt was miserable. Then he started a relationship with a man."

"What did you do?"

"Nothing. I know a lot of people think 'well, an affair is an affair' and he still cheated on me, but I couldn't look at it that way. Yes, he'd been lying to me, but he was done lying to himself." Mary Beth refilled our coffee from a tan carafe.

"I was angry at first, feeling like I'd wasted six years. Eventually, with the help of the Hell Club, I got past it. Now I spoil my brother's children and am happy with my life." She folded her hands on the Formica table. "Between my marriage, and my initial struggles seeing accident victims on the job, I *needed* the Hell Club. They've been there for me ever since."

After her confession, I gave Mary Beth a brief outline of my life. I also told her about Lauren's shit-list and how it reinforced I was heading in the right direction.

I studied my too-short fingernails. "The thing is, I've never lived alone, so it's been an adjustment. I went right from home, to college with a roommate, to living with Jerry." My eyes met hers. "There's 'alone,' like those rare occasions I had the house to myself when the kids were growing up. I enjoyed it then. The *'alone'* time now…where I know nobody is going to walk through the door at night, or the next day—nobody but me sleeping in the house—feels hollow. I'm having a hard time adjusting to this new kind of alone."

I'd even dragged out my old alarm clock so I could set the music to fall asleep to. Even though it ran an hour, there were nights I had to reset it for another hour, my mind unable to relax at night.

"You aren't alone anymore. You've got us crazy Hell Club women now." She grinned.

"Thank goodness. I'm afraid I'm going to need you all in the months to come." My life had been turned upside down more than once. I had a feeling it wasn't done doing somersaults.

Chapter 10

Night class through our local community college had already started by the time I got to the campus at the end of January. But I left campus with a bounce in my step. I'd signed up full-time for the summer session—some online and some on campus—all through the college I'd checked with a few weeks earlier. For the first time in over twenty years, I'd taken an important step to change my future.

Over the weekend, I called Josh. I mentioned I took Wednesday off from work and wanted to take him out to lunch. He didn't have class until two on Wednesdays. It was time to tell our kids face-to-face their dad had moved out two weeks ago.

As I parked on the street outside his apartment, I realized I hadn't called to remind him. My mind had been too busy concentrating on the gazillion things I had to think about: the sale of our home, filing for divorce, juggling our finances, making sure we budgeted enough to help our children through college, going back to school… If Josh wasn't in his apartment, I'd call his cell.

I climbed the dirty, narrow steps to the third-floor apartment Josh shared with three college friends. A blend of distinct scents permeated the air outside their apartment door as I knocked once, twice. A loud crash was followed by a string of swear words before I heard footsteps and the door unlock.

"Oh…hi, ma."

"High is right." I was no expert on drugs, but I was no dummy either. Masked by stale beer, smelly socks, and leftover pizza, I could detect the underbelly scent I remembered long ago from my high school and college days—similar to burnt grass clippings and a certain wood I'd smell in campfires. My son's eyes resembled blanched tomatoes.

The door in front of me was blocked by Josh, now slumped against the door frame. Clad in a t-shirt full of holes, and bagged out nylon running pants, I barely recognized my respectable high-school star athlete son who smelled like something a cat would barf up.

Closing his eyes, he groaned, his voice raspy. "What are you doing here?"

"Gee, I missed you too." I counted to seven, it was close enough. "Remember our lunch date?" My fingers clenched the Tupperware I was holding. One filled with chocolate chip cookies, the other, lasagna. Both for my party-boy son.

"I guess when I was making these I didn't know I'd be feeding your munchies frenzy."

"It looks worse than it is, or was." He took the containers I offered, and opened the door to set them on a small kitchen table. It was overloaded with empty beer cans, stale food, and a wadded-up towel I'm guessing was used to clean up something I didn't want to know about.

"I'd invite you in, but you probably don't want to come in here. Can you give me five minutes and I'll meet you in the car?"

I had five minutes. Hell, I had five hours if I needed it to talk some sense into my child who was still close to perfect in my eyes.

I sat in the car and waited…playing over and over in my head what the right way was to handle things. Seven minutes later he hopped in, showered and wearing clean clothes.

"Subway?" It was one of his favorite places to eat.

"Sure." He hung his head and apologized for the tenth time. I let him.

And over lunch we had what I hoped was a level-headed conversation about drugs and alcohol. I was sure he hadn't touched either in high school; he was too into his sports. Yes, he drank some over the summer at graduation parties…I wasn't clueless. But pot?

"Mom, it's not so bad. It's safer than alcohol."

"Which you also ingested."

He rolled his eyes. "You've admitted you and dad drank all the time when you first met. I'm sure you weren't a saint." *No shit, Sherlock. How do you think I got pregnant?*

"I wasn't a saint, I won't pretend I was. And you're an adult; you'll do what you want. But you know pot is illegal. So is underage drinking. Do you really want to go to jail for it?"

He didn't answer my question. "Um, you aren't going to tell dad, are you?"

Since he didn't answer my question, I felt no need to answer his. Mostly because I didn't know the answer myself. I went back to discipline-mode. "You need to stop this, right now. Pot leads to other, more dangerous drugs." He wisely kept his mouth shut. The upside to this discovery was finding my son wasn't perfect *before* I told him Jerry moved out. He'd be less likely to blame his parents for screwing up his life today.

Still, Josh was surprised when I mentioned our split. "You're kidding, right? I called Dad the other day about a problem with my brakes, and he never said anything."

"Unfortunately no, I'm not kidding. And I'm sorry I didn't tell you or Karley sooner." I reached for his hand, and Josh squeezed mine. Although he still looked like hell, I eased my guilt by blaming it all on his partying the night before. "I thought maybe Joe told Wyatt, and you knew already. Don't you and Wyatt text each other every five minutes?"

"No, he hasn't said anything to me. But he doesn't talk with his dad much." He expelled a long breath. "Hey, Mom, I'm sorry. I wish I'd have been there for you."

I reached out to touch his flannel shirt. "Thanks. Please don't be angry at your dad or me, this wasn't a rash decision. We've been struggling for years and I'm guessing you kids noticed." Josh ran a long-fingered hand through his still-wet hair and looked away to avoid meeting my eyes. It was as close to an admission as I'd get. Our children were no dummies.

An hour later, as I drove to the Twin Cities to visit Karley, disappointment ate at my conscience. I replayed my response to his drinking and smoking pot. Did I say the right things? Should I tell Jerry? How could I not tell Jerry? I groaned at the thought of telling Jerry.

* * *

I stopped at a mall and bought some non-mom-jeans and tops that weren't baggy, finally dressing in the current decade's style. I'd called Karley a few days ago to make sure she'd be free for dinner and worried about how she'd take my news as I drove to her apartment in Uptown. She was a younger version of me—she could worry about worrying. Karley inherited my type-A personality and was a taller replica of me at her age. An *almost* replica…other than a few key things I ignored.

We walked the two blocks from her apartment to Stix, a small sports bar with great burgers and fries. While eating, we talked about her nursing classes, getting her Master's degree, and my earlier shopping trip. "You got new clothes, Mom? Wow."

"I know, it's the new me." I smiled at her and took a deep breath. "Actually, there are several things changing in my life. One of them being my marriage." Karley stopped all movement, with a french fry halfway to her mouth. I'd waited until I thought we were done eating.

"What?" She put her fry back on her plate.

I'd quit eating, this was hard enough without making myself sick. I reached for her hand, and she clutched mine back. "Your dad moved to Joe's recently, and we plan to file for divorce. I'm sorry, Karley, but as I'm sure you noticed over the years, it's been a long time coming."

I didn't know what else to say, didn't want to get into details and didn't want the blame-game in my speech. Karley said nothing, so I filled the void. "Honey, I know nobody wants to see their parents split up. But your dad and I can't seem to be happy together."

The tears in Karley's dark eyes pooled, and I fished for a tissue from my purse.

"I'm not surprised, Mom." She wiped her eyes. "I've seen how you are together. You light up when Josh and I are around and deflate when we leave. I knew it'd be bad after Josh left for college. After your friends died, I'm sure it's been even worse for you."

She leaned forward. "I agree—you and Dad will be happier on your own, and I think this will free you to start a new life."

My Karley, ever the adult, and smart enough to see I needed to start over.

"You were telling the truth about joining the Hell Club though, right?"

"Yes. And it's been great for me. I've met a lot of nice women in the club."

She stood and came around to my side of the booth and enveloped me in a citrus-scented hug. As I inhaled her perfume, I closed my eyes with a sigh of relief.

"Then I can deal with it, and so can Josh." She mumbled into my neck.

Ah, Josh...no need to tell Karley that Josh had problems of his own to deal with.

By the time we walked back to her apartment complex, the anvil of guilt I'd been carrying on my back since Jerry moved out had been lifted. I'd been responsible for caring for my children for half of my life. It was time to care for myself. Time to be responsible for my own happiness.

On my drive home, I called Grace. I needed to bounce my discovery of Josh's recreational pastime off someone, and I thought how this was another time I needed my friends. "I'm sorry to dump on you again," I said as soon as she answered.

"For what? Remember I told you months ago to call me any time."

"I know, but I feel bad because I used to be able to spread my problems over three friends, and now you're stuck with all of it."

"Bring it on, I can take it."

"How will you react if Hans starts smoking pot? Are you going to be the cool or crazy mother?"

"Are you kidding? It will totally be sweet little Gianna who is my wild-child." Grace laughed. "Actually, you just never know with kids. Quiet, responsible

Mira could surprise me and become my party-girl. No matter who it is, I hope I'll be somewhere in the middle of those two extremes, P."

After we hung up, I took a long, slow breath. For the first time, since the day I found out I was pregnant with Karley, I felt I was regaining control of my life, which was crazy, given the uncertainty in my future. Yet telling Josh and Karley my infected marriage needed to be gutted cleansed my soul. I may not have done things right in our marriage, but neither had Jerry.

Chapter 11

Eunice called me Thursday morning before work. "I've signed you up to help at the soup kitchen with our group from church, two Sundays each month. Will that work?" Her sweet voice made me smile. She knew I'd never say no to her. I owed her so much.

My first stint was scheduled for Sunday. I woke early that morning, and after a shower, breakfast, and a short walk, I slipped into a pair of new jeans, feeling confident. I was to report there by 11:00 a.m. I drove to the soup kitchen in the nearby town of Brainerd, walked in the door, and could already smell the chicken cooking in the big roasters. I headed back to the kitchen as two women were busy preparing the meal. It was obvious they started food prep long before eleven.

I marched into the harvest-gold colored kitchen. "Hello!" My voice was salesman-loud.

"Hello!" The women responded before introducing themselves.

"We're thankful to Eunice for sending you over." The one named Jane, who looked close to my age, beamed at me as if I were Mother Teresa. A tall, elderly woman with a bouquet of silver curls introduced herself as Maude.

"What can I help with?" I asked. Maude started me out by having me make the coffee and filling the beverage cart. The whole meal ran like a well-oiled machine, and by two o'clock, we'd fed over a hundred people.

When it was time for cleanup, I stood at the sink cleaning out the industrial-sized coffee maker. "Is it always just you two?" I asked. It seemed like a lot of work for a few people.

"We get random help, like you. Someone always steps in—thanks to Eunice." Maude explained. "Also, my granddaughter, Mallory, has been helping the past year or so, but not much these last couple months since she's pregnant and still has morning sickness."

Once everything was cleaned up, Jane and I walked out together. The day was losing what little warmth it held as the sun lowered on the horizon. "So, you'll be back?" Jane asked.

I leaned in to start my car and warm it up. "Sure. I can't believe how fast the time went, and how many people you serve here." I was humbled by how grateful everyone was for a meal I could have any night of the week in my own comfortable home.

"Are you here every week?" The church was scheduled for certain days each month.

Jane smiled. "No, we're scheduled two Sundays a month. Each group who volunteers here has their own schedule. It works out well."

I was happy I'd met Jane—someone my age and a mother of four sons—and someone outside the Hell Club. By the time I pulled into my garage, the sun had set. I never was a night person, especially in winter. I didn't miss the long nights of the kid's high school activities, yet I now knew it had helped keep me busy and sane in my marriage.

The attorney I wanted to represent me was on a medical leave of absence. I made an appointment with her for mid-March, which gave me six weeks to get my information together. Jerry and I had yet to settle on a listing price for our home. Getting the ball rolling was proving to be a herculean task. I itched to kick that ball to the moon.

* * *

Mary Beth called me the following night. "The Hell Club is having their annual Valentine's dinner and a movie event on Saturday night. If you're interested in going, I'll go with you."

She didn't have to sell me on any Hell Club activity now. "Sure. What movie is it?" I wouldn't have cared if it was about a bunch of monkeys picking bugs off each other.

"The theatre in Pequot Lakes is playing the remake of *True Grit* from a couple months ago, and afterwards we'll eat at the A-Pine Restaurant. They make the best pies," Mary Beth said.

Thirty women showed up for the Saturday event. "Each event can vary from a handful of women to close to a hundred. Once women have been in the club for a while, they usually form their own small group with women who've joined around the same time." Mary Beth explained.

More faces looked familiar, and I knew a handful by name—Lily, Charlee, Tia, and Molly, among others. After the movie, Mary Beth and I sat with them at a round table in the A-Pine Restaurant. We were also joined by another woman in a wheelchair.

"Nice to meet you, I'm Yvette. I joined the club a few years ago." She leaned forward from her wheelchair to shake my hand before finding a spot at our large table. I looked around at the seven other women at our table, guessing there was a good twenty-year age span between the oldest and youngest. I knew a little about a few of them—Molly had inherited a store from a woman she'd never met, which brought her to a nearby town where she'd known not a soul. Lily was quieter, but mentioned her husband had died and she was in the process of rebuilding her life with her children. Tia had told me of the burns from her house fire, and I imagined Yvette, whose right leg was amputated, had a similar story as to why she joined the club.

Over the past couple of months, we'd all shared a bit about our story, sans the gritty details. They knew of my friends dying in a car accident, and my plan to file for divorce. It was the sub-layers we newbies would wait on for at least a year.

* * *

Karley came home Saturday morning. I'd offered to watch Bob's younger children for the afternoon so he could get away for a few hours to go snowmobiling with some friends, and Karley was coming with me to Bob's. It seemed long ago since I'd been stopping by with food or running the kids to practices, and I missed his children.

The afternoon was warm and sunny, a perfect, sticky, snow-making combination. After lunch, Karley and I, along with Bob's younger children, Finley, and Channy, made an enormous, super cool snow fort. I decided Minnesota winters weren't so bad after all.

On our drive back home, Karley and I discussed Jerry living at Joe's. "Your dad won't want to stay at Joe's forever. We're meeting with a realtor in the next couple weeks to put the house on the market. I don't imagine it will sell for a while, but we need to get the process started."

"I'm okay with you and Dad selling the house. A lot of my friends' parents have downsized their homes. I'm just glad to see you happy again, Mom. For years, you let Dad call all the shots. You never stood up for yourself."

Oh Karley, if you only understood how guilt can root a person. "I found my backbone again. It makes it easier to stand on my own." I covered my remorse with wit.

"You know we weren't blind to how you guys acted with each other. I've been around enough happily married people, couples who touch in passing, who complement each other, who share a joke." Karley shrugged. "I didn't see that with you and Dad. When I got to high school, going to my friends' houses, I began to notice some great marriages, and," She leaned in, "some not so great ones, ones that would make you guys look like the parents on *Modern Family*." Karley's smile was wicked.

"Quirky?"

"No. Happy."

Back at home, we went for a walk through the nearby woods. A flock of swans flew above us, their majestic wings whooshing. The earthy scent from surrounding balsam evergreens hung in the air, and I was glad to share this day with Karley. She left after our walk to meet Jerry somewhere for dinner before heading back to the Twin Cities. So this was how things would be. My family fractured…but not completely broken.

On Sunday, I showed up for my second round at the soup kitchen. I worked with the same women, along with Mallory, Maude's pregnant granddaughter, and felt much more at ease.

After we closed up, Jane, Maude, Mallory, and I went out for late afternoon coffee and muffins. Although Maude was old enough to be our mother, she had as much energy as Mallory and a great sense of humor. They were full of questions since they all lived in the Brainerd area and had heard of the accident months ago. I talked briefly of what led me to Eunice.

"It will get better." Jane sounded confident. "I'm glad to hear you joined Eunice's club—it should help to get you out of the house and meet new people."

"It has. It was hard for me to leave my comfort zone after having the same three friends for years" I shrugged. "But breaking out of that shell has been well worth it."

* * *

I hadn't been much of a snow bunny in my years of Minnesota winters. Yes, I had warm Sorel boots, but when I found out the next Hell Club event was snow-tubing at a local hill, I marched out and bought my first pair of snow pants since my kids were young.

The turnout was the biggest I'd seen yet at an event. A van pulled up in the parking lot, and I watched Yvette hoist herself into her chair and wheel down the van ramp. I'd ridden to Prime Time Snow Tubing with Mary Beth, Molly, and Charlee. We walked over to greet her.

"This is going to be so fun!" Yvette was grinning ear-to-ear. I understood her excitement; this was an event where she'd be on equal footing (so-to-speak) with everyone else. A tow rope would pull us up the snowy hills as we sat on our large inner tubes. Very little walking was needed, and the rest of us would be there to help Yvette along the way.

After we all purchased our tickets, everyone headed outside and grabbed a fat inner tube. One by one, we lined up at the tow rope, pushing, laughing, and throwing snowballs.

"Let's all wait at the top so we can ride down together!" Molly shouted.

An hour into our fun, I was heading up the hill again, and ahead of me was Abby, a woman in her mid-twenties home from fighting in Afghanistan, where she'd donated her left arm to the war. But she hadn't lost her determination. Abby was full of sass and spunk and clung to the fast-moving tow rope just fine with her one arm...until it was time for her to get off at the top of the hill. She had no second arm to push herself up off the tube, out of the way of the woman behind her, and in her hurry, got the giggles, and created a small tube-landslide.

One of the guys working the hills leapt to rescue Abby and the trail of runaway tubes, tiny icicles hanging from his goatee bounced as he ran. I'd managed to catch mine but fell onto my back near the top of the hill and lay there staring up into a cobalt blue sky, feeling the cold snow on the back of my head and the warmth of the sun on my face

Molly plopped down next to me. "Isn't this great? What a beautiful day."

"Yep, and I never thought I'd be snow-tubing in my forties, but this is so fun!"

Charlee snuck up behind me, grabbed the rope for my tube, and took off running as she jumped on hers. "Hang on!" she shouted, as we sped alongside each other down the hill.

Four hours of non-stop tubing was going to leave a mark on our bodies. "Ugh, the back of my arms ache," said Lily as we sat at a large table inside the warming house. We nursed our steaming hot chocolate.

"I know what you mean," Tia agreed. "I was sure the tow rope was going to yank my arms out of their sockets."

"Oh no, look!" Abby held up her stump and grinned. It hadn't slowed her down much on the hills. Same with Yvette. I didn't expect to find inspiration in this club, but it was all around me.

"My stomach muscles got a good workout from all the laughing," Charlee said before passing out plates around our table for the two platters of nachos Molly set in the center.

"I think we'll feel it for days," I referred to the physical effects from tubing. The energy derived from a day with the club made me feel I could conquer the world. Or at least Jerry.

Chapter 12

On the night of March eighth, what would have been Dana's fortieth birthday, a night I should have been out with my friends celebrating, I tossed and turned in bed, unable to sleep. I'd moved back to our old bedroom so Karley could have her old room when she came to visit. It was time to make it *my* bedroom, no matter how long I stayed in the house.

The next morning, I stripped the bed and made a trip to the laundromat to wash away any trace of Jerry in the blankets and comforter. I cleaned everything from the ceiling fan to the hardwood trim around the carpet. I stopped at the hardware store and picked up boxes to pack up his remaining clothes still hanging in the closet.

My hair was pulled back in a short ponytail as I stood, hands on hips, surveying the room. It screamed "paint me." It had become lifeless over the years, much like the love life inside it.

Target and Home Depot were my new best friends on Sunday afternoon. I bought moss green paint and material for new curtains to replace our dark shades. Fueled by a sense of renewal, I set to work. Maybe it would help sell the place.

The radio blasted on Sunday afternoon while I applied the paint tape around my bedroom windows and baseboard. "Eleanor Rigby" by the Beatles came on. Popular before my time, still, I knew the song, and for the first time ever, the words sunk in. Poor Eleanor. Living in a dream and waiting for someone to show up at her door. Oh, how true…where do all the lonely people belong? Thanks to the Hell Club, I was no longer Eleanor.

* * *

I'd talked with Jerry very little since he'd moved out, and those conversations focused on his business and taxes, until I mentioned my mid-March first meeting with my attorney. "We need to get together and go over the three appraisals so we can get this house listed."

While I was on the phone, I opened the door to the garage. We had so much to go through. Who was going to get what? I dreaded the work and the probable arguing. "How close were the appraisals?" I asked him. He'd asked three realtors to each give us their estimate of a listing price for our home. Four years earlier it would've listed for more. We were divorcing in a down economy. But really, was there ever a good time to divorce?

"We also need to sit down sometime and talk about all of our stuff," I added.

"Yep. There are a couple things I needed to talk to you about anyway."

I looked at the calendar hanging by the garage door. "My appointment is next Monday with my attorney. I need a dollar figure on the house for her to work with."

"I'll stop over Wednesday night with their appraisals," he said, before hanging up.

Three days later, I paced my kitchen after work, waiting for Jerry's arrival.

He showed up grubby, fresh off a muddy construction site. He tossed the printouts on our kitchen table. "They're all within ten grand of each other. I think we should go with Jack, he's the best realtor around."

I took my time reviewing their estimates. "I don't suppose they have any idea when the housing economy will turn around?" Their recommendation of our listing price was over fifty thousand less than what the market value was just a few years earlier.

Jerry's fingers drummed on the table. "Well shit, Perfect, that's anybody's guess as to when the economy's going to turn around. I need my cut of the equity. I'm waiting to build."

"I'd like to move, Jerry. I'm not going to pay this mortgage alone every month."

He stood up, grabbed the real estate papers, and pushed his chair in. "I'll see what I can come up with next month."

"Next month? If you want me to keep doing your books, I'm going to start charging you. I'm done doing them for free. Pay up, and I'll apply it toward the mortgage each month." I considered my offer generous, something Jerry never had been.

Jerry looked out the window, likely contemplating my offer. I asked about the other reason he stopped by. "You said there was something else you needed to talk to me about."

His arms folded over his chest. "Here's the deal. Joe and I agreed it was time for me to get my own place. They've opened new apartments outside of town, near Brainerd. I've looked at them and put a deposit down. I'm moving in April first. I need to save some of my income for that."

You could've heard a mouse fart in the next room while we calculated our next moves.

"Things will be tight until this place sells." I stated the obvious. It was a prelude to when we'd divorce. We'd both be living on a shoestring. Another reason I needed to complete my degree. We'd never lived extravagantly; I'd been raised to worry over each dollar. Jerry didn't go too overboard in spending thanks to the rough upbringing he had...unless the purchase had a motor in it.

After he left, I contemplated the many emotions wrestling in my head at the thought of our divorce. It was like watching a terminally ill patient breathe his last, painful breath. You hate that the end has come, but in the same instant, you are thankful for the agony to be over.

On a Monday in March, I was ushered in to my attorney's pristine office in Brainerd. Ann Ryerson looked more like someone who'd lead a church choir, with her horn-rimmed glasses, crisp white blouse, navy suit, and sensible pumps.

"Welcome, Mrs. Brooks. I'm sorry to meet you under these circumstances."

"Thank you. I'm probably jumping in before I'm ready, but I wanted to find out what I should be doing to proceed with a divorce." I could afford a one hour speed-session to help steer me in the right direction. Her two-thousand-dollar retainer fee up front was going to take some doing on my part.

I ran through our assets and expenses, our children now over the age of eighteen, and my upcoming job loss, college, and Jerry's recession-hit construction business.

"If you can get your house sold, it would help give us better ground work on splitting your assets. The more you and Jerry can agree on yourselves, the less you'll each pay in attorney fees."

My short time with her was money well spent. I feared our house wouldn't sell until the economy turned around. But I was no longer stuck in limbo.

* * *

A few days later, Shelly and I sat on the porch at The Pines on one of the first warm nights of spring as the scent of freshly-bloomed lilacs filled the air. It was no surprise business was slow; bowling leagues were over, and everyone had waited too long for these nice nights to spend them indoors. It had been a helluva emotional fall and winter.

We watched a small group of women biking on the trail which weaved through town about a block from us. I nodded toward them. "There's a sure sign of spring." I watched them with envious eyes. "I miss biking with Dana, Maggie, and Lauren."

She shook her head when she read the hopeful look on my face. "Oh, not this fat little body. You aren't getting me on a bike." As we watched the women round the corner, Shelly said, "but, there's nothing saying you can't be joining those women. You should check into it."

"Check into what?"

"Those women bike from Lakes Gym. It's about a five-mile bike ride from here. I've seen them go by previous summers. I hear they meet at the gym and bike down the trails."

"Really?" Lakes Gym was nestled among several of our small towns, but I'd never thought of joining. Had no interest before.

"They've got a nice big pool there I take my grandkids to once in a while."

"Listen to you, the wealth of health information." Shelly did her best to help Grace and Eunice expand my horizons. And there was another nudge to get me back into swimming.

We headed back inside as the phone rang. While Shelly took an order for pizza, I thought about swimming again. Feeling buoyant and free. Feeling like the young me.

The following day, I drove by Lakes Gym. Three times. The thought of exercising with a bunch of buff strangers opened up a whole box full of insecurities for me.

After having children, I had let myself go, plain and simple. Now I'd lost the weight I'd wanted to, but it didn't mean my body was a sculpted muscle mass. I had body issues to tackle.

I ran it by Jane one night at the soup kitchen, mentioning how I'd never got any muscle back after my children were born. "I know what you mean, after having my boys, I really struggled. You should do it, Peyton. You'd love it, at least I do."

"You go there?" I asked, as we arranged cupcakes on a tray.

"Don't act so floored. Can't you tell?" Jane wiggled her average-sized butt in jest.

I blushed. "That came out wrong. I assumed I wouldn't know anyone who went there. I pictured body-building women with tanned skin."

Jane feigned hurt. "And your point is?" We laughed as I confessed my concern of looking like a hick at the gym. Jane explained I'd fit right in with the majority. "That's why people go there, silly, to get in shape. For most of us, it's a good routine to get in. They have yoga classes, water aerobics, spinning classes, and regular aerobics. And you'd love the pool."

"You're right about the pool. I'm just not sure about wearing a swimsuit in public. It was one thing at my sister's in Texas. Lakes Gym is another."

"Did you get a new swimsuit after you lost weight? You might be pleasantly surprised when you go swimsuit shopping."

I rolled my eyes. "Do you know a single woman over eighteen who is happy to shop for a swimsuit? And yes, I bought a new one." After gathering more information, I promised to visit the gym with Jane the following week. It was better than continuing to drive by.

My heart quickened the following Thursday as we entered the swimming pool area. Swimming had been my drug of choice in high school and college. Once I moved to the "Land of 10,000 Lakes" I had plenty of lakes to swim in, but only a few months of good swimming weather. It became my excuse as I got older. I found myself sitting on the beach watching my children swim. Sitting at work, sitting in the car driving to the kids' events, sitting at their events, sitting at my desk at night doing Jerry's books. I'd been sitting away the last twenty years of my life.

No wonder this pool was calling my name.

I joined the following week and attended my first spinning class with Jane. In the locker room, Jane introduced me to a few women, including Michelle Montgomery, one of the women I'd watched bike down the trail a couple of weeks earlier. I asked her about their bike nights.

"We bike on our own, whenever the weather looks decent. We meet in the parking lot here with our bikes at six o'clock. If the weather's nice and you're free, you should join us." Michelle reached up and pulled out the ponytail holder from her shoulder-length blonde hair.

I thought about the times Maggie, Lauren, Dana, and I would go for a bike ride and do our "synchronized biking," laughing as we'd stick our legs out to the side in unison, ride one-handed as we'd cruise down the bike trail, pine cones from the trees lining the path crunching under our tires.

I could see myself eventually conning some of these women into doing the same crazy actions. Even if Jane didn't join us, I accepted there were some things I'd have to do alone.

* * *

I helped organize a Hell Club bowling and pizza night at The Pines before their busy summer season for pizza and beer. I'd managed to avoid bowling since the week before Maggie, Lauren, and Dana died. It felt strange to be back—this time with three women I was beginning to think of as friends. My teammates were Molly, Lily, and Charlee, the women I was getting to know best at the Hell Club, other than Mary Beth.

As I laced up my bowling shoes, Lily plopped down next to me.

"Can you help me choose a ball? I've never bowled before."

"You're kidding. I thought everybody bowled at some point in their life."

"With three children, I didn't have much free time, and my main sport since I was young has been running," Lily said.

We walked over to the rows of balls. Lily was maybe one hundred ten pounds. I chose a ten-pound ball for her to try, and we went over the basics.

Charlee hadn't bowled much either. "Hey, I've lived in the sticks for years, with four kids and no money. Bowling is a rich man's sport." She winked.

"Guess it's you and me," said Molly as we sat down to keep score. The time flew by, and it didn't feel strange at all to be playing with three new women.

"Son-of-a-bitch!" rolled off Molly's tongue with little effort, and we'd laugh at her high expectations of a strike every frame. I'd come to think of her as a younger Lauren.

We were losing big-time. I didn't care. It was great to see Lily get up there, knock more than a few pins down, and do her "victory dance" with a huge smile. There was a lot about Lily I didn't know, but I did know one thing—I hadn't seen her smile much before today.

"So you work here?" Charlee asked after our three games were over.

"Part-time. My day job as a medical transcriptionist will be done by May, then I'm going back to finish my degree in accounting."

"I did the same thing—went back to college in my thirties. Same with Lily. It's never too late." Charlee reassured me.

"You amaze me, Charlee. I don't know how you've done all you have with four children to raise on your own." Charlee's husband-at-the-time had gone to Alaska to visit a brother and forgot to ever come home again. He left Charlee and their children out in the country in a rugged home with no running water, no money, and no car or phone.

"Usually it's the fight-or-flight situation we're put into where we either pull ourselves out of the shit-hole, or sink into it. For me, when one of my children almost died, and I had to run to a neighbor's home almost a mile away to get help, I had to do something. Going to college to get my nursing degree was my 'something.' It gave me money and security, which gave my children safety, and a better future." She smiled at Molly, Lily, and me, the newcomers. "Isn't that why we all joined the Hell Club? We've all been through 'something tough,' and came out the other side stronger women."

She was right. We were all in the club because we'd *survived* a personal hardship, came through it, and were starting fresh. It wasn't too late to start over, finish your degree, start working out again, or make new friends.

* * *

It was painful to watch the REMAX realtor pound a "For Sale" sign in our front lawn the week before Easter. A neighbor with young grandchildren had a blow-up Easter bunny in their yard. I now had a "For Sale" sign decorating mine. A yard Jerry had mowed a thousand times, one I'd planted flowers in, one Karley did cart-wheels in, and Josh played catch in. A yard which would hopefully soon be taken over by another family with better luck staying together.

The April air was filled with promise: buds on the lilac bushes, tulips sprouting from flowerbeds, and birds chirping in the trees. The seasons changed, no matter what. Just like life.

On the last Friday in April, I put in my final day as a medical transcriptionist. There were no coworkers to high-five, no going away party. The twenty or so of us who all worked from our homes and were taking the buyout could have gotten together, but we'd never formed that sort of relationship. We were spread out all over the county.

Even though I'd grown tired of my too-solitary job, it had been a good and stable income. For some reason, I felt like a failure even though I'd chosen the buyout, chosen to go back to college, chosen to improve my life. My failed marriage didn't help my confidence. Nobody pushed the guilt on me—I heaped it on myself.

I gave myself a pep-talk. *Stop feeling like a failure. Your parents always wanted what was best for you, maybe this is it.* It was true. They wouldn't want me to be alone. *If you're lonely, get a dog.*

As soon as the thought entered my mind, it made sense. I talked to myself way too much. A dog was a comfort I needed. I might not know where I'd be living in a year, but wherever I ended up, the dog was going with me.

I celebrated my last day of work by going out to dinner with Mary Beth, Charlee, Molly, and Jane. "I'm going to the animal shelter next week to find a dog." I announced over our glasses of wine.

"Wow, you sure know how to celebrate job freedom." Molly teased.

"Hey, how about a nice little kitty instead? I think our cat is pregnant," Charlee said.

"Does she have a belly on her?"

"Not yet. But she has been gone a lot and comes back with a rather contented look on her face. The other day she slinked home with a smile and lit up a cigarette." Charlee giggled.

We all laughed at her description. "You'll be the first to know if I don't find a dog."

* * *

The first week in May was the first time I'd been unemployed since I'd turned sixteen. It was strange to wake up without a set schedule. It was temporary. I still had my part-time job at The Pines so technically I wasn't unemployed. To celebrate, I made a trip to the animal shelter and picked up the cutest little mutt. To hell with Jerry, who'd never wanted a dog. It was a step toward my independence.

The small, brown, cuddly, male mutt didn't roll his eyes when I voiced an opinion or thought, he liked the same music and TV shows as I did, and he didn't snore when he slept at the foot of my bed. They estimated him to be around seven, which, in dog years made him past his too-playful stage. I stared into his big black eyes and tried to determine his heritage... Shih Tzu and a larger breed? He was big enough to hop on my bed, but not too big to hog all the room.

Because he gave me the opposite feeling I got from Jerry, total acceptance and unconditional love, I named him Reggie. Reg, the opposite of Jer. Phonetically anyway. I could relate to him. Both of us not sure where we belonged, yet ready to make a new life for ourselves.

Chapter 13

I might not have liked the solitude of my job over the past twenty years, but it was such a constant in my life that I now felt like I'd lost a limb. Like when Josh moved out. And when my friends died. Even when Jerry moved out. Phantom pains came to mind.

After spending most of my day boxing up items from our basement, making a "Jerry" pile, one for me, and a pile marked "both," I was ready for a break. I packed my water bottle and cell phone and hit the bike trail late in the afternoon. Early May sunshine caressed my shoulders over the miles as the breeze carried sounds of a baseball game from the nearby high school. Since I had no schedule, I stopped in at The Pines when I noticed Bob's van outside.

"Hey there, Peyton. You don't get enough of this place?" Bob welcomed me in a hug.

"I was out biking and thought I'd stop to say hello." I smiled into his shoulder.

"I'm glad you did. I'm not too busy right now if you have time to visit." He led me to a table in a corner close to the bar. The few other customers sat at a table close to the bowling alley, leaving us in privacy. Bob usually worked during the day, and most of my shifts were at night. I missed him.

He'd poured us each a 1919 root beer, and we talked about his children, the business, his in-laws coming to visit, Karley graduating soon from college, my job loss, and Jerry moving out.

Bob looked down at his glass, his finger tracing the moisture. "When Jerry told me he moved out, I didn't know if I should be happy or sad for you."

"Are you kidding?"

"I know. Dana probably shouldn't have told me about your plan to file for divorce, but she did. It's been obvious how unhappy you've both been for years. I think Jerry stuck around for the kids, and the money. I didn't think he'd leave in this poor construction economy."

I chuckled. "I guess after all these years, you know Jerry well. Yes, my plan was to file after Josh moved out, I just hadn't worked up the nerve to do it. And then when Dana, Lauren, and Maggie died, my world, and plans, fell apart."

I leaned in and nudged Bob's shoulder. "I imagine your plans for your future have changed even more." I sure wasn't going to complain to a man who lost a wife he loved.

"I'm lucky," Bob said. "I had a happy marriage, and although I miss Dana like crazy and hate that she's missing out on experiencing everything in our children's lives, I look at it as 'better to have loved and lost than not loved at all.'"

My mind wandered to years of watching them together, thinking of what a great couple they made. "You and Dana put a real effort into your marriage—something Jerry and I never did. Instead, I put my effort into raising our kids. So, as much as I'd like to say shame on Jerry, I have to also say shame on me."

"Things were rough for Dana and me the first few years; I won't pretend it was always smooth sailing. But it was worth the rough spots."

"The good thing about never having a real relationship with Jerry is I never relied on him for anything. But the quiet of the house is driving me nuts. I'll be glad to get out and start college full-time next month."

We talked about my divorce-in-limbo situation. Jerry was in his busy season—as busy as his construction work was in this economy—and said it was pointless to meet with his attorney until we got an offer on the house. I agreed, to a certain extent, but I also thought we should drop the price of the house. I couldn't afford to keep it up.

"Once the season picks up after Memorial weekend, I can give you more hours here if you'd like," Bob said as he walked with me outside. It was time to get back on my bike. I was meeting some of the women from Lakes Gym at six o'clock to bike.

"I might take you up on the offer, depending on how much time this old brain needs for studying." We hugged before I hopped on my bike. I didn't know what I'd do without Bob in my life.

Later at night, before I turned off the lamp by my bed, I turned and faced what used to be Jerry's side. Being honest with myself, I admitted—it wasn't always bad with Jerry; we had some good times too. Unfortunately, those times never outweighed the bad.

I thought of the nights years ago when the kids were babies, when we'd have to sometimes let them cry themselves to sleep. We'd lie in bed with the same lamp on I had now, making shadow animals on the bedroom wall. We'd laugh at each other's made-up animals, and it was simple entertainment for us. I also let my mind wander even further back to the so-not-me casual sex I'd been more than willing to have with Jerry. Before him, it had only been Greg.

Being with Greg had been making love. My months with Jerry were make-me-feel-wanted-sex. My fault, not Jerry's. I never felt hate toward Jerry. Anger, yes, and indifference, which was worse. Each year became lined with more bitterness.

Yet, there had been some fun times. In honor of them, I made a few shadow animals on the wall.

* * *

I spent a week in mid-May de-cluttering our house like a small tornado. Now was the time since I'd start classes the first week in June. With housing sales in our area down, and so many foreclosures on the market, I didn't expect a quick sale unless Jerry agreed to drop the price.

The following week, sunshine and time on my hands inspired me to dig up the time capsules my friends and I had buried. When I'd thought of them over the winter, I wasn't sure I'd ever be ready. Nothing said I had to open them, but at least I'd have them if I moved out of town.

Loading a shovel, work gloves, a thermos of water, and some food in my car, I drove the few miles to the field where we'd buried them. Nestled in county land, we knew the place would remain untouched since a small river ran near the cluster of white pine trees we'd selected as the burial site. County land couldn't be sold if it had a body of water on it. The last stretch of road was dirt, pocked with various sized hoof prints left by deer. It was a haven for them, and I hoped to leave it as undisturbed as possible.

Coming over a gentle hill in the field, I spotted the grouping of white pines. Tall grass waved in the breeze. I stood for a moment in the quiet, eyes closed, the sun soothing my body, like a warm hand guiding me toward the time capsules.

My mind took me back to those happy times when we snuck out here at night, flashlights and time capsules in hand. Lauren's husky voice swearing a blue streak when she'd tripped over a large rock still rang fresh in my mind, sounding so sultry and real I opened my eyes and looked around. I was alone, of course. It was my overactive imagination, and wishful thinking.

Grass grew over our so-called graves, but I had a good idea of where they were. It had been seven years since our last dig, and the forest had re-grown as if we'd never disturbed it.

My two separate time capsules were easy enough to find; all I had to do was lay down, feet at the base of the pine tree closest to the river, with my head facing the river. Mark the spot where the tip of my head ended and start digging. And uncover the last link to my friends.

I hoped my friends would, theoretically, be by my side, reading along with me when I decided to open them. Dana laughing so hard she'd pee her pants, Lauren, slapping her knee in hysterics, her throaty ha-has echoing into the quiet air, and Maggie's smile, wistful. The years with Joe had taken such a toll on her happiness. I hoped she got that back in Heaven.

I spent a half hour digging to retrieve my time capsules. Why had we buried them so deep? I set my cooler and jug of water under a shady tree, already sponging my neck to cool off. I remembered the way we marked our digs, each three feet apart, hence the need for a yardstick. I dug them all up, taking a break between shoveling. What a joke, as if we'd have been able to dig these up in our eighties!

After uncovering all eight capsules, I wiped my grimy hands on my shirt and finished off the last of my water. I sat barefoot under the tree in the shade and mowed my way through the lunch I'd packed; cheese sandwich, a few cookies, and an apple. I'd worked up a good appetite and was thankful my arm muscles were up to par from swimming, or I'd have never made it past digging the first hole.

It took three trips to the car to load everything up. I drove home and showered and then lined up the time capsules along my dresser—all eight of them stared at me as if they dared me to open them. Our first dig had been on a whim, the second dig was more in earnest; we felt the need to leave our dreams and regrets behind. I tried not to think of my own.

Lying in bed that night, I thought of our many late-night conversations over the years, our sleep-overs with kids in tow as we shared laughs and a few tears. And secrets would unfold layer by layer. Now the burden of my secret weighed on my heart. One I'd never be able to share.

I tossed and turned, my aching arms and shoulders kept me awake. The next morning, I poured myself an extra cup of coffee and stood in the morning sun, studying my dormant vegetable garden. Last summer I'd contemplated letting our small garden go. It was a lot of work, but I enjoyed it and the therapy it provided— even more important than the healthy harvest it produced. Many times, those prickly cucumbers were yanked off the vine in frustration over something Jerry did. And the lettuce, which was supposed to be gently cut, would sometimes get yanked out by the roots. It kept me from pulling my own hair out in aggravation.

It was likely I'd be living in our home at least through the summer, thanks to very few people looking at our home. I decided to plant a small vegetable garden again and offered to help Bob and the kids bring Dana's old garden back to life. Nash and Eva accompanied me to our local Ace Hardware to help pick out seeds. We agreed to stick with things they'd actually like to eat.

The Hell Club was also doing a harvest garden at the community center, with proceeds going to the Women's Shelter in central Minnesota. A few of us from the club shopped for seeds Thursday morning, and I smiled when I saw Lily was one of the women in our garden group.

"I'm surprised the whole Hell Club isn't here," Lily remarked as we chose our seeds.

"Why?"

"Because I think gardening is one of the best therapies around."

"I'm pretty sure gardening kept me out of prison." I joked and thought I saw Lily wince. I silently scolded myself, remembering things I said in jest may hit too close to home to these women I still knew very little about.

I spent the Friday before Memorial weekend on my hands and knees helping Bob's children plant their garden, showing Finley and Channy how to dig holes deep enough for tomato plants. I tackled my own garden late that afternoon. Reggie and I struggled to get out of bed early the next morning. Excitement helped fuel my steps. I had a college graduation to attend.

Chapter 14

Karley's graduation from the University of Minnesota took place on the Saturday morning of Memorial Day weekend. Jerry had driven down for the graduation and then drove back to Pine Lakes, leaving Karley and me free by mid-afternoon. We headed for Como Park, walking around the zoo first, enjoying the antics of the animals before walking to Como Lake.

"Ben offered to make us dinner tonight." Karley mentioned as I took in the beauty of the sun glistening around the Pavilion, the white swans gliding along the edge of Como Lake while Reggie led me along. I nodded, my brain not processing her words. Until Ben's name was mentioned again.

I stopped walking. "Who? You're going to move in with a guy?"

"Mom, I told you. Weren't you listening to anything I was saying?"

I threw my hands up. "Okay, I was daydreaming. I was thinking what a pretty area this is." I didn't get into the thoughts following it—I could move to the area. Heck, I could move anywhere I wanted once we sold the house. I was no longer rooted to our home or a job. I could go anywhere...do anything... Except I'd miss the women from the Hell Club if I moved.

Right now, I had more important things to think about. My daughter had a new boyfriend, apparently. And one serious enough Karley was ready to let live with her. Yikes. Karley was sensible; she thought things through. At least she always had before now.

"Did you hear anything I said about Ben?"

My thoughts did a quick rewind. "I heard you mention you've known each other a few years. He's one of the friends you hang around with, and you didn't want to say anything to me before because of all the things I've been going through." I smiled, hoping I'd redeemed myself.

"Yes, and I want you to meet Ben. Josh likes him. They get along great."

I yanked Reggie's leash to keep him from chasing a squirrel. "Josh has met him already?"

"Don't be upset, you know Josh has come down a few times to visit, so he's met most of my friends. I've talked about Ben plenty to you over the years, but since we were just friends, he probably didn't stick out in your mind."

"He will now." I turned and grinned at Karley.

"Anyway, he's working today but asked if he could meet you later tonight and offered to make us a late dinner at my apartment. It would be a good time for you to get to know each other."

"If he wants to cook for us, I like him already." I hugged Karley before standing back and taking her face in my hands. "I want you to be happy, Karley. That's all I care about."

Karley grinned. "I am, Mom, very much."

Ben won me over and Reggie as well. After we ate the flavorful spaghetti dinner Ben made, the three of us sat out on her small apartment deck while Reggie snoozed on Ben's lap.

I observed their interactions, noticed Ben look at Karley with interest when she spoke, watched how relaxed Karley was around him. Being friends first helped.

As I drove home on Sunday, I thought of how they had a better foundation for their relationship than Jerry and I ever built. And they showed respect and appreciation for each other, things which had been missing between Jerry and me.

On Monday, I woke early to attend the Memorial Day service at Pine Lakes cemetery. I'd done it for years, although I hadn't known anyone buried there before now. I always went for my mom—buried too far away from me—and gleaned some comfort in walking among the headstones, hoping someone who didn't know my mother was doing the same for her in San Antonio. This year I had three more reasons to go.

When the service was over, I cried for the first time in months, missing Maggie, Dana, and Lauren with a rawness glazed over since I'd joined the Hell Club. Three hours later, I met Lily at the Community Center so we could start on the club's community garden. I wouldn't begin classes until the following Monday, but Lily had to work the rest of the week.

Petite Lily reminded me physically of how Dana looked before she had her children, but personality-wise, Dana was much more reserved. I still knew little of her past. She was there already when I pulled up, hair tied back in a short ponytail and wearing cute short overalls, which would've made me look like I was trying to relive my youth.

Lily's rare smile greeted me. "I'm glad the rain is holding off so we can get these planted." We both looked up into the cloudy, gray sky.

"Yes, and if it rains later, I hope it doesn't pulverize these seeds and plants." I unloaded the pallet of cherry tomato plants from my car trunk. We had plenty to do and were happy to be working with raised pallet beds.

"Have you always had a garden?" I asked.

"I helped my mom when I was growing up and had my own for years when my children were young. It's been a while now because I've lived in an apartment for a few years. It feels good to help with this garden."

I took small nails and strips of magazine paper to wind around the stem of the plants to keep the cutworms at bay. "I know what you mean. I planted a garden for years out of necessity when we were newly married and broke. I kept at it because I enjoy the peace and calm." My eyes met hers. "And like you said before, it's a great place to take out life's frustrations."

I told her about helping Bob with his family garden. "Oh, is he your boyfriend?"

"Nope, but we've been friends for years. He's the husband of one of my friends who was killed in the crash. Speaking of boyfriends, have you dated at all since your husband passed away?" I imagined Lily would attract the attention of a lot of men.

She was at the pallet next to me, busy planting green beans. "No, not yet." She kept her eyes down, intent on her rhythm of planting. There was an uncomfortable silence between us for a few minutes as we kept digging, planting, and watering. I shouldn't have asked.

Suddenly, Lily stopped. "Peyton?"

I had finished my last row. We were done for the day. "Yes?"

"I know I can tell my story whenever I want, and it's not like I'm keeping a secret from anyone, but I feel like I'll be walking naked in public once I do."

"I understand, Lily." I took off my garden gloves. "I wouldn't have been able to say that honestly a year ago, but I'm learning we all make mistakes, life throws us so much we can't control, and all we can do is move forward."

Lily dabbed at her eyes. "I feel the same way. So much of what's happened to me over the past decade was beyond my control. I guess now I finally feel like I've regained some control, and I want to hold on to it before having it possibly ripped to shreds again."

As we packed up the remaining plants and seeds the other Hell Club members would plant later in the week, I was glad I'd had this time alone with Lily, glad to be part of our club, and thankful for other new friends like Jane. I was becoming comfortable picking up the phone to call Jane, Mary Beth, and a few of the Hell Club women. They, along with Eunice, my strong supporter, and Grace, had all played a part in getting me back with the living. I felt like a woman who had won an Oscar. "I'd like to thank the following people, for without them, I wouldn't be standing here today…" The statement wasn't too far from the truth.

* * *

At 3:12 a.m., the shrilling ring of my cell phone on the end table jolted me from a deep sleep. I switched on my lamp and grabbed my phone before they hung up.

"Hello?" My heart thundered loud in my eardrums.

"Mrs. Brooks?"

"Yes?"

"Um, this is Zach, Josh's friend. Can you come over here?" His words stumbled out while my foggy brain fought to remember who Zach was. Oh yes, one of Josh's roommates.

"Where is 'here'? And what happened, Zach?"

"We're at my parent's house." He rattled off an address, and I asked him to repeat it as my shaking hand located a pen and paper on my dresser.

"But what happened? Is Josh okay?" Clearly not, or he'd have been calling me instead.

"Josh was in a motorcycle accident. He's here with us, but he's pretty banged up. We thought you better come here."

My heart fell to my toes while my mind played hopscotch. Josh didn't even own a motorcycle.

"Why aren't you taking him to the hospital? I'm fifty minutes away. Maybe I should meet you at Essentia Health Hospital in Brainerd."

It sounded like Zach put his hand over the phone, and I heard him talking to someone else. "We don't think it's a good idea, Mrs. Brooks. Please, can you drive over here? We don't think anything is broken, but we want you to see him so you can decide what to do."

By the time we hung up, I'd gotten dressed and was in my car. My legs were jittery and my teeth chattering—adrenaline rushing through me with the fear of the unknown.

"*Shit, shit, shit!*" I drummed on the steering wheel as I made my way through our dark, deserted town. Should I call Jerry? *No, wait until you know what happened.* It was after 4:00 a.m. when I arrived at Zach's parent's house. Three young men hovered in the living room where my battered and bloodied son was stretched out on a couch with a sheet on it, an ice pack on his forehead.

"Josh?" I bent down next to him and reeled from the smell of alcohol still permeating through his pores. No wonder his friends didn't want to take him to the hospital! I got no response from Josh, other than a small groan. I turned and eyed his friends.

"Will someone please tell me what in the hell happened?" I held Josh's large hand while checking his pulse. It was there, slow and steady.

Zach looked at the other young men. I didn't recognize either of them. "We were partying at our apartment, and Josh kept bugging me to take my bike for a spin. I said no, but he found my key and went anyway." All three squirmed in discomfort.

"When we realized he was missing, along with my bike, we went looking for him. He missed a curve a mile away from here, and we found him and the bike alongside the road. We took him here, it was closer than our apartment, and I knew my parents were out of town for the weekend."

"We'd have taken him in, Mrs. Brooks, but we're afraid they'd arrest him."

"I can smell the booze. It's obvious he's had way too much to drink. Anything else?" I met Zach's eyes, I didn't want any lies. I also didn't want to think about me drinking and driving to the cemetery last October. I could have killed someone on my short drive home. Most accidents happened close to home. Josh's had been only a handful of miles from his apartment.

"Maybe something else. There were a few drugs brought to the party. We didn't know those guys, Mrs. Brooks, so we don't know what they had, or what Josh took. We thought we better call you. I used Josh's phone and thought you'd be the one to call instead of his dad."

His dad. I'd forgotten all about Jerry after initially wondering if I should call him. Now I was glad I didn't. I didn't need to hear his ranting and raving while trying to make a clear decision, which I was having a hard time doing.

They had cleaned Josh up a bit, his scrapes on his face and hands were clean. Thank goodness he'd had a jacket and jeans on. But who knew what he looked like underneath? Zach helped me remove Josh's clothing. After taking it all in, I made a decision.

I walked in to their small kitchen for privacy and dialed Mary Beth's number, knowing she'd be up soon anyway for her work shift. After explaining what little I could find about Josh's injuries, Mary Beth instructed me in her calm voice. "Apply ice packs to his chest, but don't wrap him in anything; his ribs need to keep moving so he can breathe or cough normal. Is he alert yet?"

"Barely. He did a lot of moaning and groaning while Zach and I removed his clothing and cleaned his wounds. Alert enough to say he doesn't want to go to the hospital. He's banged up real good, but it's mostly his shoulder and ribs I'm worried about."

"If his accident was around 3:00 a.m., and he was drinking right up until then, his alcohol level will be high for hours. Yes, he might have some broken ribs, but you have to decide what you want to do. What risks you want your son to take, *and* what responsibility." Before we hung up, I promised to keep Mary Beth updated.

"You know they'll arrest me if I go in, Mom." Josh mumbled into his chest after I hung up. He was alert enough to hear my conversation. His eyes stayed closed, but his face held a look of shame. I would've killed him myself if I weren't so thankful he'd been smart enough to put Zach's helmet on. It likely saved his life.

In the end, Josh waited until the next afternoon to see our regular physician, waited until the drugs and alcohol left his system. The doctor could do little for Josh's few cracked ribs and extremely bruised shoulder. Josh was lucky as far as his accident was concerned. We had yet to tell Jerry.

* * *

Jerry busted out his whoop-ass-rant when he realized two days had gone by before he was told. And in-between that time, I remembered I'd never said anything to Jerry about my discovery of Josh's drinking and smoking pot when I stopped at his apartment last winter. I actually felt bad. Jerry was his father, no matter where he lived. He deserved to know what was going on with his son.

Jerry stopped by on his way to a construction site. Reggie made a beeline for my bedroom as soon as Jerry walked in. Reggie had good dog instincts.

It took Jerry about a minute to accuse me. I hopped on the defense. "What did you want me to do? Call you in the middle of the night? Or call after I realized he was drunk? At what point did you want to know, Jerry?" I was seething.

If I'd have called him, he'd have been ticked at his middle-of-the-night wake-up call, or even more ticked at finding out his son had been trashed before "borrowing" a bike. "What condition is Zach's bike in?" Jerry enunciated through clenched teeth. Josh was in my living room with us—I'd brought him home with me for a few days. His school was over for the summer.

"It's totaled."

"I bet he loves you for that." Jerry rubbed his hand across the stubble on his jaw.

Josh shrugged, wincing in pain. "He didn't have insurance on it. I owe him three grand."

I suppressed my heavy sigh. This was news to me.

98

Jerry stood. "It sounds like you'll need to get two jobs this summer." He studied his son. "I've got to get back to work and finish up for the night." Jerry walked himself to the door.

"I have to go soon too, Josh. My first class is in less than an hour." Josh hung his head. Regret hung between us. Had I gone wrong somewhere as a mother? I hadn't handled my discovery last winter about Josh's drinking and smoking pot right. I probably should have dragged his sorry ass to the hospital the other night and let him suffer the consequences.

Those consequences would've been huge. I thought of my drive to and from the cemetery last October on Maggie's birthday. Who was I to point a finger? If I'd have been pulled over, I'd have failed the sobriety test. I couldn't think about my own stupid decision right now. I needed to get to my first college class in over twenty-two years.

Chapter 15

Between recharging my brain for college and the Nurse Nancy role I found myself playing to Josh, I was emotionally drained. Watching for possible pneumonia, applying ice packs, and making sure he wasn't having a drop to drink while balancing his pain meds… All new stress I didn't need.

Arguing with Jerry was getting old. "You should've let them take Josh to the hospital, and if they threw him in the slammer, maybe he'd learn." He'd called and caught me off guard.

"Well, I didn't. It's not like you never partied before you were of legal drinking age."

"I never touched drugs, Perfect."

One point for Jerry.

"Yes, I called and talked to Zach. And you covering for Josh kept him from understanding he was a damn lucky guy to crawl out of the accident in as good of shape as he did. Next time he might not be so lucky."

My heart seized at the thought of Josh ever being so stupid again. After hanging up with Jerry, I hoped he was wrong. I didn't want to think about whether I'd made the right call or not. At 4:00 a.m., I'd done what I thought was right.

The majority of the next couple weeks were spent with my nose in accounting books. What little free time I had was spent caring for my garden, Bob's, and the club's. And worrying about Josh—who had moved back to his apartment, away from his helicopter-mother.

It was after my Monday night class, two weeks after his accident, when Josh called, back safe at his apartment. "I'm sorry for putting you through all of this, and I hate to dump more on you, but I think I need your help."

Was he thinking he had a drug or alcohol problem? I was hoping he was just an unlucky, bad-decision-making, typical teenager. "Josh, you know I'll help you in any way I can."

"Um, Mom, I need money. I owe Zach a little over three grand for his bike, and I don't have it."

I'd been getting ready for bed. I sunk down on my bed, clutching the phone. Of course, Zach would want to replace his bike so he could enjoy it for the rest of our never-long-enough summer. "Oh Josh, I'm living on a tight budget myself. With your dad at his own place, and me living on my severance pay and paying for college, I'm strapped." I rubbed the back of my neck.

"I can't work the construction job for Zach's uncle because of my shoulder and ribs. I got a job as a cook at the café down the road, but it doesn't pay like the construction work did."

"I'll see what I can do." After we hung up, I laid in bed while my brain scrambled for answers. Sleep played hooky, and my mind spun like a hamster on its wheel.

The upside to not sleeping is you lie there thinking of everything imaginable. And what I remembered was the ten grand Jerry and I had stashed, little by little over the years, in our bank safe deposit box for emergencies. With Jerry's seasonal work, having emergency cash stashed was a comfort…one we'd managed to avoid dipping into for years.

Until today. I didn't have class until one. I was at the bank when it opened at nine. When I signed in for the box, I was surprised to see Jerry's signature above mine from a month earlier. I hadn't been in our deposit box for over a year. Jerry used it more than I did, keeping vehicle titles, paperwork for his construction equipment, etc., for safe keeping.

After the bank clerk left me alone in the room, I sat at the table, opened the large box and dug through the various papers, emptier than I remembered it. *Where the hell was our cash?*

Panic set me on fire from head to toe. My heart danced a fast-paced-polka as my hands dug like a gopher through the handful of papers again. Our two vehicle titles, four-wheeler title, the abstract for our house, a few random papers, some old coins…and that was it. Not a single hundred-dollar bill. I doubled over and sobbed angry tears.

That self-centered son-of-a-bitch! I'm going to kill him! Anger vibrated me, adrenaline bouncing inside like a percolator. I couldn't leave the room, couldn't make myself go out until I had myself somewhat composed.

Once I climbed down from the freak-out-ledge, I hurried out of the bank, my hand clenched around my cell phone, wishing it was Jerry's neck. I waited until I slid behind my steering wheel so the outside world wouldn't hear me come unglued with my not-soon-enough-to-be-ex-husband.

"Where are you working?" I dug my short fingernails into my palm, deflecting my anger. If Jerry had any inkling, I'd never find him. My tires screamed out of the bank parking lot.

"We're over on Gull Lake. Why?"

"I'm coming over. What's the address?"

"Jesus, I'm busy. What do you want?"

"I need to talk to you about something with Josh." It wasn't a lie. I'd planned to loan Josh some of that money Jerry took—and possibly spent. *Please tell me you didn't spend it all!*

"Shit. Just a sec." I heard him move from the construction noise. "I'll call you after I'm done with work tonight."

I'd driven out of the parking lot and pulled over to the side of the road. I didn't want to be a road rage driver. "This can't wait."

"We'll it's gonna have to. I'm busy." Click.

It was a good thing I wasn't driving; I'd have rammed another driver in my frenzy. I shut off the car again, got out, and stamped around on the side of the road. Anyone passing by might think a snake had slithered up my pant leg. Instead, I'd been married to a snake.

After my blood pressure cooled to below-heart-attack level, I drove home. I ran in my office and fired up my computer. Silly me; Jerry said he was working on Gull Lake. I pulled up my billing spreadsheet of current construction sites, and there it was. One job on Gull Lake was a cabana they'd finished last week. The other was a remodel on a cabin: 87935 Eagle Nest Way.

It wasn't yet ten. I had class at one. I could make it there, have a bloody-knuckle, knock down drag out fight with Jerry, and drive home well before I had to get to class.

Twenty minutes later, I was stomping down a cushy, well-manicured lawn toward the lake, where construction noise reverberated in the humid June air. Jerry was nowhere to be seen, but as soon as Pete, one of his workers, spotted me, he pointed to the garage.

Lucky for Jerry, he was alone reviewing floor plans, which were spread out on a picnic table. I got right to the point. "What did you do with our cash from the bank safe?" My voice was as level as I could keep it, but Jerry must have felt the venom as he spun around to face me.

My eyes spit fire while my hands itched to strangle him. My brain fought the desire.

He didn't answer right away. His brain was likely carefully choosing his words. "I needed it for the deposit on my apartment and first month's rent. Joe and

I went to Canada last month for a fishing trip, and I put some towards a retainer for my attorney."

I wanted to puke listening to my arrogant husband rattle off his expenses—paid for with *our* money. "You've hired an attorney?" Funny how that one thing stuck out for me.

"Yes, and you told me you did."

"I did, but I've only paid her for my one meeting with her. I can't afford the retainer, and you said you didn't have time to file until fall. I find it hard to believe you needed *all* the money. You didn't have any saved for your apartment after living with Joe for three months?"

"What did you think I lived on over the winter? You know I don't bring much money in during those months and you sure as hell weren't forking over any of your paycheck." His cell phone rang. He wisely chose to ignore it. "What did you need the money for anyway?"

"First of all, I wasn't forking over any of my paycheck because I was paying *our* flippin' mortgage!" Surely smoke was billowing out my ears. "I was going to lend some of our savings to Josh. He needs to pay for the motorcycle." I was certain neighbors a block away could hear me. I didn't care. I didn't know these yuppie people. But I also didn't want to give Jerry the satisfaction of me having a heart attack right there on the plush grass. I took a deep breath.

"Josh can't work for Zach's uncle because of his injuries and asked if I'd help him out. I forgot about our emergency cash until last night. Apparently, you didn't."

"Josh is going to have to figure out his own cash-flow problem. Stop bailing him out."

My fingers tingled at the desire to slap him. "I was doing it more for Zach since he's the one without his bike—thanks to our son." The ache in my jaw told me to stop grinding my teeth.

Jerry took off his cap and wiped his grimy forehead. He didn't argue.

We volleyed sarcastic, snide remarks back and forth a few more minutes before I nailed him again about the money. "If you're using our money for your attorney, I'm entitled to half, so I can pay my attorney's retainer." I held my breath, and then reminded myself I was asking for my own damn money and to stop being such a chicken.

"It'll be a month before I have enough to pay you. Can we talk about this later? I'll figure out a way to get Josh some money. He needs to pay Zach." Jerry's voice lowered a decibel.

"The sooner the better—for both Josh—and me." I didn't want to let him off easy, but as I marched back to my car, I breathed a sigh of relief that we'd be able to help Josh's friend.

I had over an hour at home before I needed to leave for class. Reggie and I went for a walk, and I took my cell phone with me, needing to release some of my frustrated energy. While I walked, I vented to Grace. They were coming for a visit in July, and I couldn't wait. For now, she was sympathetic—and in the middle of a t-ball game. I let her go.

Next, I dialed Charlee. Mary Beth was working, so she was off my ranting list. Charlee had an ex-husband and four teenagers. After listening to me huff and puff out my story, I let Charlee talk. "I get where you're coming from, Peyton, but I'm going to play Devil's advocate here. It will help keep you from murdering your husband.

"Hang on a second," Charlee said. I heard a creaky door shut. "Sorry about that. I was in our garden with the kids."

I hadn't been to Charlee's house yet, but knew she lived out in the country and had a garden about the size of my house. "Okay, from what you've told me about your past, you already knew he puts himself first, so Jerry thinking he's entitled to all the cash shouldn't surprise you. And even you've said before how he generates very little income in the winter."

I stopped on my walk and sat on a huge boulder on the edge of the woods by our house. "You're right, why am I surprised?" Reggie found a shady spot and plopped down.

"I'm not saying what he did is right. He should have talked to you about it first. I'm surprised he went to Canada though if he didn't have any money."

"I asked him the same thing. He pointed out I'd gone to San Antonio in December." I was exhausted and it wasn't even noon. And I had class to get through yet.

"The big thing for you two is to figure out how you're going to handle helping Josh out with his finances." I agreed with Charlee. Josh was far more important than money.

"Sometimes saying no to our kids is the best move—and the hardest too," Charlee said. "And, at least it sounds like Jerry will get you your money next month for your attorney."

"Thank goodness. I feel like this divorce is never going to get rolling."

"Come out with us tonight, Peyton. Remember the Hell Club is going out for dinner and dancing at Harpo's in Merrifield?"

"I have class until six." I didn't bother adding I was on a tight budget. I deserved to go out.

"So? We aren't meeting until seven, and it sounds like you could use a night out."

I was weighed down with studying, worrying about Josh, and now money issues. But, Charlee was right. I needed to cut loose.

After an hour at Harpo's Saloon with my friends that night, I forgot I even had children.

We shared pizzas, pitchers of beer, and funny stories. There was a table of men nearby, and a few of them broke into our conversation, asking women to dance in the small space by the juke box. I was visiting with Mary Beth when someone tapped my shoulder. I turned around. A good-looking man with dark, shortly cropped hair, tanned face, and a trim body was asking me to dance.

Hearing the familiar beat of "Pretty Woman" starting, I'd have normally been tongue-tied but for the positive reinforcement also known as beer. I followed him to the dance area.

My hands rested lightly on his shoulder and hand as he twirled me around the postage stamp-sized dance floor. I felt the heat of him through his Rolling Stones t-shirt. When the song was over, he introduced himself.

"My name is Todd, and I'm a regular member at Lakes Gym. I've seen you there recently."

"Oh yes. I joined in April."

"I noticed. You're friends with Jane, right?"

I was flattered he'd noticed me. No man had noticed me for years—including Jerry.

"I'd like to take you out sometime. No wedding ring, so I assume you're available?"

I looked down at my left hand as if I were surprised my simple band was no longer there. I'd taken it off after Jerry moved out. "I'm still married, we're separated right now."

"So, will you go out with me?"

My palms were sweating. I hadn't been asked out since college—a different lifetime. My heart did a dance of the butterflies, but I didn't know this guy from Adam, and he was way too good-looking. His eyebrows were better groomed than mine. What was he asking *me* out for? "I don't think so. I'm not ready to date yet. But thanks for asking."

He feigned hurt, clutching his chest, and I laughed at the flattery. "But, if it changes, I'll let you know." The words breezed out of me as if I was asked out every day. If I hadn't had a couple beers, I would have needed to sit down from the shock.

Todd promised to keep checking with me. I excused myself so I could get back to my friends; one of them being Mary Beth. "Watch out for him, he preys on women at the gym."

"How do you know? You don't even go to the gym." I laughed at her concern.

"No, but I used to, and I know other women from there who've talked about him."

"I told him I'm not dating yet so you don't need to worry, Mother. I won't sneak out of the house to meet him." I hugged Mary Beth, thankful someone was looking out for me again.

I called Josh the following night. "I'm sorry, but you're going to have to find a second job. Your dad will get you some money soon, but it sure won't be three grand." I wanted to add "since he took all our cash, I've got no reserve funds to help you out." I bit my lip instead.

"I'm having a hard time finding a job I can do which pays decent and doesn't require me to use my body much. I already talked to Dad. He said this is a good reminder for me to be responsible." His voice was somewhere between taking responsibility and a whine.

I couldn't argue there. "My concern, Josh, is your partying, not to mention taking who knows what drugs from total strangers! And then you hop on that motorcycle and not only take your own life in your hands, but others as well." He didn't respond. "Do *you* think you have a problem? If you need help, we'll come up with the money somehow." I wanted someone to convince me this wasn't unusual college-party-live-life-to-the-fullest behavior. As I made the promise to him, I worried about the cost. Why did everything revolve around money?

"I think I've got a handle on it. It was a super-stupid thing I did. Dad's right—this has been a good wake-up call for me."

"That's exactly what I hope it is, Josh, a good wake-up call. Next time you might not be so lucky." I closed my eyes, thinking of how easily I'd slid behind that wheel on my drive to the cemetery last October. I should've known better. I hoped there would never be a "next time" for Josh, or me. And I reminded Josh how much I loved him before we hung up.

* * *

The next Hell Club event was a big one—their annual picnic on the last Saturday in June. I was surprised to see Michelle from Lakes Gym in the crowd. I shouldn't have been. When we were at the gym one day, Jane had mentioned Michelle's ex-husband had physically abused her and stalked her. He was finally put away when he came into the bank she works at with a loaded gun, aiming to "set her straight."

I went and put my arm around her shoulder. "I'm happy to see you here!"

"I joined during the court proceedings before my ex-husband was convicted. These women propped me up and helped me move on," Michelle explained as she gestured to Mary Beth, who was visiting with a family. "I saw you with Mary Beth. We joined about the same time."

As Michelle and I walked around, she introduced me to other women who were there with their families. In the distance, I spotted a tall redhead from behind with wild curls and long legs. I knew it couldn't be Lauren, but my heart didn't listen. I ran ahead of Michelle to catch a glimpse of the woman—who looked nothing like Lauren. It felt like a child seeing their dad in a Santa suit.

My letdown was soon replaced by anticipation as the games began. They had tug of war, three legged races (which Mary Beth and I tanked), paddle boat races, and swimming events—my baby. With three months of near-daily swimming, I'd found my calling again.

After winning the Women's Freestyle 40-50 age bracket, I was thrown in with the winners of the other age groups. A twenty-two-year-old kicked my butt. I didn't care. I was still beaming later when I was teamed with two teenage boys for the paddleboat races. I wasn't sure what ached more, the muscles in my calves as we pedaled like steam engines or my stomach muscles seizing up from all our laughing. The day was a great reminder of what it felt like to be a carefree teen: damn good.

Chapter 16

I'd spent so many 4th of July's with Maggie, Dana, and Lauren that the holiday would never be the same for me without them. We four couples would go to the park with our children for the concession stands, games, and fireworks. My old friends were on my mind so much, like a constant scratching on a wound, reopening a scab over and over.

They would understand what I was going through with Jerry and Josh. But they weren't here.

I turned to them anyway. I rode my bike to the cemetery. On my way home, I made a decision—I was ready to open the time capsules.

I poured myself an iced tea and carried Maggie's two time capsules out to our patio. With her being my closest friend out of the three, I was certain I wouldn't read anything too unsettling. We'd all chosen fictitious names, and I remembered our second ones were all buried in large mason jars. I opened the other jar first.

Maggie had chosen the name Ethel, her grandma's name. And there, in her familiar sharp, small printing (in crayon) was her list.

June 2001

NOT-SO-SECRET-WISH—I hate my life right now
FANTASY DREAM—to have wild sex with Matthew McConaughey in front of my husband
MY LEAST FAVORITE FOOD IS—onions
I WANT TO BUY—a little red corvette
FANTASY JOB WOULD BE—interior designer

I tried to remember our lives ten years ago. I found her dream to have sex in front of Joe a little disturbing, but hey, it was her fantasy. And it likely stemmed from knowing Joe cheated on her for most of the years they were married.

Enclosed was a Boy Scout program, which listed Wyatt receiving awards and another piece of paper folded and refolded many times as if it had been a worry-stone for Maggie. It read "Hang in there for your son, love, Mom." Maggie's parents were what kept her going, along with us. I thought about how long Maggie *did* hang in there.

There were times I was concerned for her health. She'd get so thin, I was certain I could crack her like a wishbone. She always promised me she was okay. Now I wondered.

I opened her second time capsule; my fingers went first to her "treasures." One sheet was a copy of her acceptance letter to the grade school where she was principal, accepting said position. Her name and date were blacked out.

She had also enclosed a junior-high football program from Wyatt's recent game. The other item in there was a rubber, thankfully still in its wrapper, with a small post-it note attached saying "found in hubby's wallet." Since we all knew Maggie had her tubes tied a few years after Wyatt was born, it was another sign of the sad state of their marriage.

October 2004

I WANT TO—get a divorce when my son graduates
WISH-IT-COULDA-BEEN-DIFFERENT—I'd have married my H.S. boyfriend D.Z.
DEEP DARK SECRET—I hate my husband
HOPE FOR THE FUTURE—Start a new life
MY BIG REGRET IS—attempting suicide when my child was young. My husband is sooo not worth me ending my life. Someday I'll find the courage to be on my own. If you are reading this, I hope you understand and forgive me. You have helped keep me going.

Hooooly shit. Maggie? If there were going to be any secrets, I hadn't suspected they'd come from her! We all knew each other so well—or so I'd thought. Maggie and I had been friends from the time our sons were born. Why did she never confide this to me, even years later? And why hadn't I, her best friend, ever notice her deep depression? A searing pain of regret stabbed me. I'd failed her.

Yes, I had my own secret, but it wasn't life-threatening, like Maggie's. When Wyatt was young, he idolized Joe. Always traveling, Joe was rarely home to discipline, he was the "fun parent," which he played up. By the time Wyatt was a teen, he'd seen the "real" Joe. I'd forgotten how hard everything was for Maggie back then. Too hard for her to deal with? Too hard to confess to her friends?

I set Maggie's paper down, wishing I'd have gone to watch the fireworks with the Hell Club. Instead I had nightmares, like walking in on Maggie in a pool of blood, or turning to say something to her in the car and finding her with a knife in her chest. Horrible, twisted dreams.

The next day I was back out at the cemetery for a one-on-one with Maggie. I knelt in the cool grass next to her grave, my hand touching her headstone. "Why couldn't you tell me, Maggie? Did you think I wouldn't understand? I knew you shouldered too much! I'm sorry I didn't pay more attention and insist you get help." A single hot tear slid down my cheek. "I would've helped you, Maggie." I whispered. Sorrow dripped through my hand to her headstone.

In the back of my mind, I wondered how many times she did try to tell me…and I'd ignored the signals, not wanting to dig below to her pain and confront it. I'd avoided my own issues. Why did I think I would I have had the strength to deal with hers?

I biked home, threw my gardening things in the car and drove to the club's community garden. Lily, Tia, and I had a date to weed the garden before the heat of the day, and I needed to unload my feelings about Maggie. They'd understand.

The club's garden was growing like crazy. Six of us had our own small plots to care for, and by the looks of things, we'd be raising a good crop to sell for the area women's shelter.

I stepped out of my car, and my flip-flop seemed to sink into the steaming blacktop of the Community Center parking lot. I unloaded my garden tools as Lily and Tia pulled up in Tia's ancient Escort. "Isn't this a scorcher?" I asked as we unloaded gardening tools from Tia's trunk.

"Yes, and I can't wait to get back inside my air-conditioned apartment. I can't believe I'm saying that after being stuck inside so much in the winter." Lily groaned as we got to work. An hour later, we were done and sat in the shade, drinking water from the thermos I'd brought.

"Can I ask you both something?" With the tidbits of information I had on Tia and Lily, I hoped they'd be able to help me sort my feelings out about Maggie.

"Sure, what's up?" Tia took a big swig of water.

"I've told you about my friends who died." I fiddled with my paper cup. "I recently found out some disturbing news about one of them from years ago, and I need help making sense of it. I'm upset she didn't feel she could confide in me, and even more troubled that I, as her friend, didn't see the signs and try to help her." I filled them in on what Maggie wrote.

Lily took my hand in her petite one, and gave it a gentle squeeze. "When people are in extreme pain, many times it's too hard for them to reach out for help. It's easier to box it up and keep it hidden inside you. If we admit to others we need help, it's like Pandora's Box—you can never fold the pain back inside again. Someone else knows your 'secrets,' and they can no longer be ignored." Her mouth was set, her eyes downcast.

I understood better than Lily knew. It's amazing what your mind can block and bury for years if you want to badly enough. I planned to never open my own Pandora's Box.

"I'm sorry, Lily. I've probably dredged up bad memories for you."

"It's okay. I want you to remember this Peyton: your friend not reaching out to you for help is no reflection on what kind of friend you were to her. It's a reflection of how much she loved you and didn't want to drag you into her misery."

Tia nodded, her spiky, dark hair sticking out in disarray. "Lily's right. The fire at our home was a culmination of a whole heap of problems I'd been too damned depressed about to bother asking for help." She picked at a hole in her shorts. "Before my son got into drugs, before he accidentally torched our home, I was a mess. I'd lost my job, had no support from my ex, and crawled down a deep depression hole I couldn't seem to hoist myself back out of."

Her eyes focused on me. "I needed help long before my son did. And look what happened to us because I couldn't seem to find the words which now are easy to say. *I need help.*' That's it." She linked her freckled arm through mine. "But it's damn hard to say when you've got a semi pushing you down the tunnel. And I'm guessing that's how your friend felt."

Their words were like bees in my brain hoping to pollinate some understanding. "Thank you both. You've been a big help. I never would have looked at it that way." I put an arm around each of them, and we embraced in a long, sticky hug before standing to pack our things up so we could get out of the heat.

* * *

Grace and her family were coming to visit. I'd scheduled time off from The Pines and got my class assignments ahead of time so I could complete them before they arrived.

They flew in Saturday morning, and we walked to a nearby park where the kids could play while we visited. On Sunday, one of our warmest summer days so far, we headed to our local beach to cool off.

Later that night, after Grace and Garret's kids had unwound enough to be tucked into bed, the three of us sat on my patio, enjoying the last of the daylight. Dad and Barbara were driving up and would be joining us tomorrow.

"Why don't you two go out for a while? Don't you want to show Grace all the wild haunts you hang out at when you pretend you're twenty?" Garret kicked back in his lawn chair with a beer as he winked at me.

Grace sprang up from her chair. "Hey, great idea! Where do you want to go?" Her green eyes lit up with excitement. The decision was made for me.

We chose Zorbaz, a local pizza/beer place on Gull Lake. It had a nice, laid-back atmosphere, and we were in time for a beautiful sunset. Their windows were all open, screens allowing the call of the loons from the calm lake to filter inside.

Grace ordered us each a tall glass of Blue Moon beer. By our second round, we'd finished a mound of nachos as I filled her in on some of the women from the club. "Charlee has been good for me with my 'Jerry issues,' and Lily and Tia were a big help after I read Maggie's time capsule secret." I'd already filled Grace in on what I'd uncovered.

While I was yapping away, Grace's eyes suddenly bulged. She sucked in so much air she resembled a blowfish. Reaching over the scarred table, she grabbed my arm. "Ow! Watch it; you're clawing me like a tomcat."

"Shhhhhh," Grace said before turning her head to look out the window at near-darkness. "Look out the window, P." She released her vice grip on my arm.

"What? Is there something going on out there?"

Barely opening her mouth, like she was some kind of spy, Grace muttered between her clenched jaw. "No, dummy, I don't want you turning around and staring."

"At what?"

"It's Jerry. Behind your right shoulder. Don't look! Keep looking out the window."

Did I need to tell her how foolish we looked peering out into darkness? There was a quarter moon out, which made it hard to see anything. Jerry was here, so what? Although I did get the queasy feeling you get when faced with an unwelcome surprise. "And? It's a small town."

"Not just Jerry, you idiot, he's with a woman."

I tried to not be offended by Grace calling me both an idiot and a dummy. I was intrigued and curious. Okay, envious too. Jerry was getting on with his life.

"What does she look like?"

Grace's eyeballs rotated in their sockets as she was able to peer around without turning her head. It was impressive. "She's got long, wavy blonde hair. Kind of pale skin for summertime, and a white knit top hugging her chest like you wouldn't believe. She's skinny and looks pretty young. Do you think you know her?"

My mind was tallying up what Grace had relayed. Why couldn't Grace have told me she was heavyset, pimply, greasy-haired with a slight moustache?

"Listen to your description, Grace. I know this is Hicksville compared to San Antonio, but your generic description could fit half the tourists around here."

"Well, I don't know what else to say about her," Grace defended herself.

After a few more seconds of peering into darkness like a fool, I took it upon myself to ever-so-slightly turn my head. Once Grace gave me the okay, of course.

Jerry and this woman were deep in conversation, facing each other and leaning over the table. I got a good side view of both of them. There was no question it was my husband.

My throat went dry, so I downed the rest of my beer. And something resembling insecurity crept inside me. I don't know why—I had no reason to feel that way. Jerry dating someone had no reflection on me as a person. I repeated the mantra a few times.

"C'mon, Grace, let's get out of here." I pushed back my wooden chair, ready to make a break out the side door.

"Are you sure? We shouldn't let Jerry ruin our fun, P." Grace was apologetic. "You have every right to be here, and if we have to go, can we at least walk by their table so I can pretend I noticed him for the first time, and make him introduce her to us?"

"You know I'm not a good enough actress to smile while Jerry introduces me to Squeezebox."

"Fine, you stay here. I'm going to the bathroom via the scenic way past their table. I can play dumb real good, you know that." Grace winked. As much as my common sense told me to get up and leave, it would be too obvious. I wanted to see how this played out. I slipped over to Grace's side of the table so I could have a clear view of the event.

I couldn't hear what they were saying, but Grace's animated surprise of seeing Jerry there could've won her an Academy Award. After a couple minutes of conversation with plastic smiles on both sides, Grace pointed over at me for Jerry.

When I met his uncomfortable look, I flashed him my own fake smile and gave a little wave. As if seeing him out with another woman was no big deal. I swear Grace was going to pull up a seat and visit all night with them, as if she and Jerry's date had become best friends. Grace had always been outgoing. She could talk to a wall.

After Grace made her gratuitous trip to the restroom, she came back to our booth, smiling like the whole world was one big ray of sunshine.

"Okay, now can we leave?"

"If we leave now, he's going to know it's because of him." Grace was right. "Besides, don't you want to hear what I said?" I let her relay her speech." It went something like 'Oh my gosh, is it you, Jerry?' He gave me an 'I know you from somewhere' look. I said 'Jerry, it's me, Grace! I'm here visiting Peyton.' I used my high-pitched, friendly-surprise voice. That's when I pointed you out. When he didn't introduce me to his friend, who, if it makes you feel better, up close has a pointy chin and her front teeth are a little crooked, I stuck out my hand and said, 'Hi, I'm Grace Patrick, from Texas. What's your name?'" Grace exhaled after her long-winded dialogue.

"What did she say?"

"She put her hand out to shake mine and introduced herself as Melody something-or-other, and said it was nice to meet me, and didn't I have such pretty eyes. I kind of expected some bubble-brained blonde, but she was pretty nice."

Great—Jerry's new girlfriend was pretty *and* nice. "Jerry and I discussed the house, bills, and when we'd file for divorce. We forgot to talk about dating."

Grace reached over and put her hand on mine. "I guess you got your answer." She squeezed my hand. "It's another step in getting on with your life. You've done so well, P. When you feel up to dating, the men will be lined up."

"I don't know if I'll ever be ready, and you need to get your eyes checked if you think men are going to line up." Yes, I was dressing in clothes from the current decade, and had more muscle and a pretty new hairstyle. Still, I was now in my early forties and not one of those women who spent a lot of time on themselves. I said as much out loud.

We headed outside across the parking lot barely illuminated by the sliver moon. "Those are high-maintenance women—trophies. The man you'll be happy with will be looking for a woman with a heart as big as the moon, a sense of humor, a brain, and natural beauty. Someone like you, P." Grace hugged me hard. I struggled to convince myself she knew what she was talking about.

Dad and Barbara arrived before noon the next day. Grace and Garret had taken their kids to the park, and Barbara was taking a nap. "I need to stretch my legs," Dad said. "How about taking a walk with me?"

"I'd love to." I put on my tennis shoes, and we headed for the path through the woods, where we'd escape the afternoon heat.

I'd recently confided to him how I felt I let him down by not succeeding at my marriage. If Mom would've still been alive, I was sure she'd have wanted me to keep working at it.

As we walked, Dad cleared his throat three times before bringing that conversation up. "My dear little sunshine; always the worrier, always trying to be such a good girl." He chuckled, and the guilt seizing my chest lessened. Maybe he wasn't so disappointed after all. "You should take a cue from Grace. She's never had any problems being someone who did what she felt was right for her." He was right. Grace would have no qualms saying she gave something her best, it didn't work out, and she was moving on. Not me. Guilt to the end.

He slapped his big, beefy hand against his leg as we took a seat on an enormous boulder. I sensed more hesitation on his part in the weight of his unsaid words. "I have something to tell you, something your mom wanted to speak with you about years ago, before she died." He paused and gently took my hand in his. "She wanted to do it in person, when she'd have flown to Minnesota to help after Karley was born. Of course, it never happened."

My chest constricted. Dad was dredging up mom's two-decade-old speech?

"Your mom didn't want you to marry Jerry just because of the baby. She thought you'd regret it afterward, but knew you were trying to do the right thing. She wanted to explain how we all make mistakes; getting married wouldn't change the fact you were having a baby. She hoped you would change your mind, and move back home."

I sensed there was more, and dad was having a heck of a time spitting it out. "You know your mother was what they used to call a flower child...peace activist, that sort of thing...?"

Where was he going with this?

"Wellllll, we never told you girls that your mom had been married before we met."

"What?" I inhaled so deeply I swallowed my gum.

"It feels good finally telling you. I don't like keeping secrets, and I'm sure your mom would've figured I'd tell you before you married Jerry. She mentioned she'd tried bringing this up with you a few weeks before she died, suggesting you move home instead of feeling like you had to marry Jerry."

His steady voice was quiet. "She hoped you might consider it. Of course, once she died, I had a tough time getting through the days, working, caring for Grace, and taking care of the house. I should've been encouraging you to move back to Texas. It would have been good for all of us." He shook his head. "I'm so sorry

I dropped the ball. Then you married Jerry, and afterwards, I thought, what was the point of bringing up your mom's past?"

My stomach couldn't have hurt more than if my dad had sucker-punched me. The anger burning and growing like wildfire inside me was humiliating. How could I be upset with my dad? I was a big girl when I'd made the decision to move to Minnesota.

Finding out that if my mom hadn't died, she'd have rescued me in time, reassuring me we all made mistakes…was one of many just-missed-life-changes for me.

"You okay? I'm so sorry to drop this on you now, sunshine. I wanted to reinforce how most people have some big thing in their life they regret. You aren't alone."

I pinched my nose, hoping to stop the tears. All these years with Jerry, I tried to do the right thing—at least for the kids. I'd always been told to do the right thing, feeling guilt for my "mistake." And here my mom had made her own first marriage mistake. I stood and paced. *Don't think about it, Peyton, it's all in the past. Only look forward. Look forward, dammit!*

I couldn't. "Why didn't she say something *before* I moved to Minnesota? All you both kept saying is how disappointed you were in my actions—how it was going to affect me the rest of my life. Well guess what? It could've affected me a lot less if I'd have known it was okay to make a mistake and not suffer for it the rest of my life!" Regret hung on each angry word.

"Okay, calm down, sunshine." Dad's hands were in front of his face, as if I'd claw him. He scratched his head, likely struggling to remember how he felt twenty-two years ago. "We were disappointed, but it was because you had to drop out of swimming, and you'd been missing so many classes from your morning sickness. You're the one who insisted on moving to be with Jerry so your baby could have a father." He shrugged. "I couldn't argue with that. I wouldn't have handled it well if you and Grace hadn't grown up living with me." Dad dabbed at his eyes.

And I deflated. Of course, how would he understand my regret at not moving home with Karley anyway, and raising her on my own? I was angry, at my own self. And what difference would it have made? I'd wanted to marry Greg, my one true love, and instead he'd chosen to marry the church. My future had been decided by him too.

"I'm sorry," I plopped back down next to him, wrapping my arm through his. "You're right." I nestled in his shoulder and sighed. "Why are you telling me this now?"

"Because you need to hear everyone makes mistakes. It doesn't have to be anyone's 'fault.' Sometimes things just can't be worked out. You gave it over twenty years of trying, and you needed to hear your Mom made a decision she regretted. Nobody's perfect, honey, not even my little sunshine."

"Does Grace know?"

He laughed his big, hearty laugh. "No, you go ahead and tell her."

Later, while Grace and I were alone in my kitchen cleaning up after supper, I brought up our mom's first marriage. It was less than satisfying on my part, because she didn't give me the "Oh my God!" response I was hoping for.

"I kind of sort of knew there was some hidden secret like that for years."

"Did not."

"Did too."

"You did not, Grace, you're just trying to get one up on me."

"I did so, P. It was years ago, after you'd gone off to college, we were having supper. I had to do a paper for school on drug use, and was quizzing them on the psychedelic sixties, and 'free love,' when I asked Mom point-blank if she ever did anything wild. She was in the middle of taking a drink of milk and choked on my question so much that milk came out of her nose. That's when I knew I hit on something. Of course Mom wouldn't admit to anything. So there."

I slapped her with the dish towel. I missed her already.

She'd be leaving too soon—the story of my life.

Chapter 17

It was hard to go back to my empty home once I drove Grace's family to the airport on Saturday. Dad and Barbara had left the day before, and I missed them all already.

There was no reason to be inside on such a beautiful July day. Homework and housecleaning could wait. I spent an hour weeding my garden I'd neglected for over a week, and then called Bob to see if their garden needed some TLC.

"Sure, feel free to come over whenever you want," said Bob. "In fact, I was getting ready to take the younger kids to the beach. Want to join us? We can help later in the garden."

I was hot, dirty, and sweaty and had planned a swim later anyway. "That sounds perfect."

"I'll pick you up in half an hour." After we hung up, I jumped in the shower to wash off the grime from gardening.

I packed a small cooler with snacks and drinks before Bob arrived. I crawled into his van, was greeted with a blast of energy from rambunctious children, and received a smile from Bob.

We drove the few blocks to the beach, unloaded our gear, and in about two seconds, the kids had made a beeline for the water. Bob and I found a treasured shaded area and set up our beach chairs. We kept our eyes on the kids, who knew they had to stay behind the first row of buoys, while we visited. Bob rested his arms on his knees, his whole body relaxed.

"So, it looks like things are going okay this summer…?" I hadn't talked to him much since school let out for his kids.

He shrugged. "I've got a handle on things for the most part. Eva and Nash have been a huge help. The first couple weeks of summer vacation were tough, getting our schedules figured out. Dana's parents come over from Wisconsin once or twice a month to visit, which gives me a break. It's a win-win for everyone." His smile was boyish, and in his baseball cap, he appeared almost youthful. He looked too young to be a father of four. Or a widower.

After a bit, we made our way into the water, swimming with his children for the next couple hours. When it was time to pack things up, Bob asked, "After we're done weeding the garden, would you like to stay for supper? I'll grill some burgers."

"Sure." I was as comfortable around Bob as I'd been with Dana. And I'd known him almost as long as I'd known Jerry but enjoyed his company far more.

The evening temperature dropped about ten degrees by the time we finished with supper and working in the garden. Finley and Channy were inside the house watching a movie, and I planned on walking home. It was only a few miles and it wouldn't be dark for another hour.

"Why don't you stay? We can have a beer out on the deck. I'll drive you home later."

"Just *a* beer for me though." I smiled. I'd told Bob that afternoon about Josh's drinking. And I'd admitted I shouldn't have driven home from his house that night after drinking.

We sat outside, listening to the frogs in a nearby pond compete with the movie the kids were watching in the family room downstairs. I mentioned my run-in with Jerry and his girlfriend. Bob was surprised to hear of her. "I guess I'm so busy, I don't see the guys anymore."

"How about Dylan? Have you heard from him lately? The last time I talked to him, it sounded like he had a possible buyer for their house."

"Yep. He closes in a few weeks. He's already made a trip out to Montana with some of his things and put an offer in on a house there." Bob took a swig of beer.

"I drove by his and Lauren's house last month and was sad to see the 'For Sale' sign in their yard. I have so many good memories of being there with the girls." Lauren and Dylan's house was on a lake. We'd spent a lot of time there during the summers.

"Speaking of houses for sale, are you getting any bites on your house?"

I shook my head. "I wish. Being on a lake has helped Dylan, but our home is just one of many ramblers out there. I think we're going to have to drop the price soon."

"Do I dare ask how classes are going? It's got to be a shock to your system."

"Oh, it was." I laughed. "It's getting better, though; my brain has dusted off the cobwebs, and I'm enjoying learning again and taxing my brain. My old job had become so boring."

He tilted his head and studied me, the sliver of moonlight dancing on his tanned neck.

My face flushed like I'd swallowed a fireball. I wasn't sure if it was a good feeling or not, but I was sure of one thing; Bob's caramel-brown eyes were studying me.

My senses heightened. The crickets and frogs—too loud, and I could feel Bob's body heat even though it was several inches away. He reached over and touched my cheek before his fingers caressed the back of my neck, guiding my face toward his. He leaned in, kissing my lips with the tenderness of a whisper. My brain wondered if I was imagining it or not.

Pulling back a few inches, Bob looked into my eyes but didn't take his hand off my neck. Checking for shock and finding none, he continued. His mouth explored mine, and I responded, although the whole time my brain screamed *"what the hell are you doing?"* I couldn't believe I was kissing my friend's husband. It didn't feel right, yet I didn't know how to stop.

A day's growth of stubble on his face tickled my cheek, and the foreign feeling pushed reason back into my brain. I pulled away. "Holy shit." I swallowed. And burst out in giggles.

Bob eyebrows rose as he pulled away. "What?"

It was a waste of time trying to stifle my laughter. "I'm sorry!" I gave him an impish look. "I think I now know how it would feel to kiss a brother." My grin matched his as Bob slapped his knee and threw his head back in laughter.

"You're right. Something was a little off. I figured I lost my mojo." Bob elbowed me in jest. "We gave it the old college try though, didn't we?"

I leaned into him and we hugged. "Good thing we didn't ruin our friendship, right?" Bob looked at me, serious for a moment. "You deserve happiness, Peyton, and I hope you find a man who appreciates you…more than just a brother would." He winked.

We sat in silence a few minutes, and I replayed what had happened. Bob was a good friend, someone I could be myself around. Comfortable enough to feel no need to bolt after our kiss. "Good thing we stopped." I smiled and nudged him. "I wouldn't want to ruin you for any of the women I hope you'll date someday."

He grinned, the uncomfortable moment passed, and everything re-balanced between us. As nice as the kiss had been, my heart wasn't racing, my palms weren't sweating, and no sparks were flying. Damn, why couldn't I fall in love with Bob? He was perfect.

Switching subjects, Bob asked about the time capsules. "Have you decided to dig them up?" He picked a sure way for me to forget about our kiss by bringing up my dead friends.

"I dug them up in May and have had them sitting on my dresser. I worked up the nerve to open a couple and chose Maggie's, thinking there wasn't a thing I didn't know about her and would find no surprises." I took a sip of my beer, as if it could wash down the knot of emotion forming in my throat. I'd been wondering who I could ever ask about Maggie's confession.

"By the look on your face, I'm guessing you uncovered something you didn't expect."

"Yes, and I'm glad you brought it up because it's been haunting me, and I didn't know who to talk to about it. I sure wasn't going to ask Joe." Bob knew there was no love lost between Joe and me. Although Lily and Tia had helped me understand why Maggie hadn't confided in me, I hoped Bob would be able to shed some light on what I might've missed.

"One of the things we wrote was our deepest secret." My nose tingled as visions of her possible attempts flashed through my head again. "Maggie's was an attempted suicide."

Bob grabbed my hand. "You're joking, right?"

His reaction told me he hadn't known either. "I know. Crazy, right? I was shocked. It said something about 'when my son was young,' so it was years ago, but still…we were friends, and I'm kicking myself for not being there for her."

Bob's face wrinkled in thought. "Do you think Joe even knew? He traveled so much…"

"I doubt it. I'm sure he was what drove her to it. He's cheated on her from day one, spent every dime she ever made, and was never there for Maggie or Wyatt. I'm guessing she felt like she was at the end of her rope." We held hands, and Bob's touch was comforting. "It's the unknown eating at my brain. Why she did it, how she did it, and how I could have helped her."

"Don't beat yourself up, Peyton. You can't change the past. Are you going to open the other time capsules?"

"Not anytime soon." I laughed around my words and the emotional ball strangling me. We sat a moment longer in silence, lost in our own thoughts.

As he drove me home, we talked about the upcoming one year anniversary of the accident. "Only fifty-six more days," I said. When I looked at all that had happened since, it seemed like a different lifetime. In a way, I guess it was.

* * *

I took Eunice out to eat the following Tuesday. It was such a scorcher out I'd have loved to wear just my bra and underwear. I tossed on a sundress so I wouldn't be arrested.

Today's luncheon, other than catching up on each other's lives, was to discuss a new "option" for me. I'd made the mistake of telling Eunice I had more free time going to school full-time than I thought I would. God forbid I start wandering around without a purpose.

"I've got to make sure I leave myself open with enough time to do my homework. Don't forget this brain takes a while to digest things now." I stabbed at my chicken salad.

Eunice wrapped her hands around her teacup as she smiled at me. "I've found a couple of women who are willing to take over the church cleaning so I'm taking you off cleaning duty and putting you on something else."

"Something else…?" Eunice could be clever; before I knew it, she would talk me into leading a Zumba class or something.

"This has to do with a club member. Normally we don't ask new members to help others until you've been in the club a year, but I've met with a few of the senior members and they can't think of another woman who might be able to help Josie the way you could."

If you had strength in an area where another club member could use help, a match might be made if both parties agreed. "I'd love to help." As I said the words to Eunice, I wondered what possible gift I had that would help someone else.

"Josie joined a few years ago and has an extreme fear of even stepping into a lake or pool, even though she's lived in Minnesota all of her life. I thought with your old lifeguard experience and your rebirth into swimming, you might be able to help her get comfortable a bit before the lakes turn cold."

"Sure! Let me know what you'd like me to do, and I'll make sure to fit her in my schedule." I'd never thought of my swimming as a gift before, but was confident I could help this woman, and couldn't wait to pay it forward.

I called Josie as soon as I got home. "We can take this at whatever pace you're comfortable with, Josie, you'll make the call." Eunice told me Josie was in her late twenties, and I didn't remember meeting her at any events.

"I'm ready to start whenever you want. I work the three-to-eleven shift at the hospital most days, so if you ever have time in the mornings, they'd work best for me." Josie said.

"Mornings work for me too." I checked my whiteboard filled with my activities. "The only morning I can't meet is Wednesdays. Would nine o'clock at Round Lake beach work?"

"Yes. So, do you want to start tomorrow?" Josie sounded nervous. From what Eunice had told me, we'd be taking baby steps.

"Sounds good. We'll work our way up, and once we get past our knees, we can worry about swimsuits." I hoped my words would comfort her, knowing I wasn't going to drag her in past her comfort zone—whatever it may be.

I met Josie at the beach the next morning. We sat on the cool sand as she told her story. "When I was six, I was at a beach similar to this, with some friends and my older brother and his friends. Trevor was fifteen and a good swimmer. He was out on a floating raft with a couple of friends, diving off." Her voice grew soft, and I could tell this was difficult for her to talk about, even twenty-some years later.

She stared out at the calm lake in front of us, and I waited for her to continue as the scent of drying seaweed permeated the humid air.

"I'd been watching Trevor, jealous that I couldn't swim out so I could jump off the raft. His two friends swam toward shore and headed toward the concession stand. Trevor was the last one left. I watched him go to dive, slip, and hit his head on the corner of the diving raft...and not come back up after he fell into the water."

Hearing of her frantic search for the lifeguard who was further down the beach and busy scolding kids throwing rocks, then running to get Trevor's friends at the concession stand, before seeing them all diving for Trevor and the lifeguard swimming to shore with Trevor's limp body—I pictured it all—a scared, younger sister unable to help her brother. She never set foot in a lake or pool afterwards. I was eager to help her conquer her fear.

We took it easy. The first week we never made it past our knees, instead we stood in the shallow water getting to know each other and sharing our stories of what brought us to the club. As haunting as her experience at six was, Josie had endured other life changes which had pushed her into the arms of club members. Maybe I couldn't help her in other areas, but this? This I could do. To get Josie comfortable in the lake was as important to me as it was to her. And helping Josie reminded me we were all in this together.

I talked to Lakes Gym about teaching swimming lessons when I found out their previous teacher had moved away. They offered me a part-time swim instructor position. I'd start in September and would transition Josie to the pool then. It had taken me months to get my swim-groove back after years of dormancy; I expected Josie's traumatic hurdle to take much longer.

* * *

Jerry had a habit of dropping off invoices and bills once or twice during the week. He still had a key to the house—as long as he paid part of the house expenses—our agreement.

On a hot night in early August, I was in the middle of making salsa with some of the tomatoes, onions and peppers from my garden. I was sweaty and as hot as a jalapeno. And, I wasn't expecting Jerry to show up. He knocked twice before opening the door from the garage. As he stepped in the kitchen, I was busy wiping my face with a paper towel. He looked exhausted, grimy, and thin, so I didn't feel too bad about my appearance.

He tossed some invoices to pay on the kitchen table, and I offered him a beer. He took it without any thanks and leaned against the counter. "I loaned Josh three grand a few weeks ago, when I got paid from the big job over on Last Turn Trail. So, until he pays us back, I figure we each get thirty-five-hundred of the remaining seven grand. I should have yours next week."

I was so surprised, I had to sit down. "You gave Josh all three thousand?" I'd kept my nose out of Josh's business, telling myself he'd have to figure things out on his own.

"Not gave, only loaned. I told him when I build a house next year, or whenever we sell this place, I'll be expecting him to help me out. He'll be good and healed by then."

I should've known there was an ulterior motive for Jerry's sudden generosity. Still, I was thankful Josh was able to pay Zach back. I was worried I'd let him off too easy. Since Jerry didn't bring it up, I didn't. I was overdue to call Josh anyway. It had been a few weeks, and I needed to say what had been gnawing at my conscious over the past couple months.

I turned my mind back to our finances and upcoming divorce. I'd be able to pay my attorney retainer soon, and I wanted to schedule an appointment with her. "We either have to sit down ourselves and decide on our finances, or we'll end up paying attorneys to do it."

"I told my attorney I'd meet with him in September. I'm too busy right now."

"So, what do you want to do?" I wanted to know what my next move should be.

"I sure as hell don't want to pay an attorney more than I need to. You're the one who takes care of the bills and accounts. Can't you write up some stuff?"

My eyebrows rose in surprise. "You want *me* to split up our assets?" I was all for it, but I didn't think Jerry would trust me.

"Well, to me, it's easy. We sell the house, split the profit, split our savings, and go our separate ways." He drained his beer and set the bottle in the sink.

"There's more to it, Jerry. Our vehicles aren't the same value; your truck is six years newer than my car. You have a ton of money invested in your business equipment which was purchased with our joint money. And I have my 401k through work. Also, I think we need to lower the price on this house or it won't sell."

Jerry had been leaning against the counter, and pushed himself away and toward the door. He wrinkled his nose as if the kitchen now smelled of pig shit instead of salsa. "I don't know, Perfect, figure it out. I'm busy and tired. I'm going home."

As usual, I was left trying to figure out what the hell I should do next.

Chapter 18

After Jerry had promised I'd have the money any day to pay my attorney retainer, I took it as a sign to get on with my life. Todd, the man from Lakes Gym who I'd met when I was out with the Hell Club six weeks earlier, had been asking me out whenever I saw him at Lakes Gym. A few days after Jerry was at the house, I ran into Todd after my spinning class. When he asked me out, I said yes. Nausea bubbled in my throat. I forced it back down.

"Really?" His groomed eyebrows rose as he smiled a toothpaste-ad smile.

"Yes." The expression on Jane's face was grim as she strode toward the locker room. She had echoed Mary Beth's opinion the night I met Todd. Images of Jerry out on his date while I watched them with Grace—feeling like a pre-teen not permitted to date—fueled my resolve.

"How about catching dinner and a band at the Wooden Wheel this Saturday night?"

I hadn't been to the Wooden Wheel for years, but I'd heard they hosted great bands.

We agreed on a time, I gave him my address, and left for the locker room, feeling like I'd rather have a root canal done than go on a date.

I should have taken the root canal. I was pacing my living room when Todd arrived.

An hour later, after my stomach settled, we sat at the Wooden Wheel eating thick, juicy burgers. Over a couple of beers, I learned far more about Todd than I cared to know. "I graduated with honors from Penn State, had twenty great job offers fresh out of college. I chose to settle here, where I grew up."

Lucky us, I wanted to add. He never gave me a chance.

"Do you like to golf? I can golf a twenty-nine at the Whitefish Golf Club, thirty-one at Maddens. I could teach you a few tips."

I should've stopped him right there and informed him my soon-to-be-ex already had me turned off of golf. No worry for me—Todd continued to tell me how wonderful he was in other sports as well. I nodded off and on, like a mute bobble-head doll.

Finally, a band took their place on the small stage, and cranked out music from the 80s and 90s—my kind of music. The dance floor filled, and although only a blind woman wouldn't notice Todd's good looks, his hand felt like a tarantula crawling down my lower back as he guided me on to the dance floor. I reached down and pulled it off before his hand found its way to my rear. Was dancing with him going to be any more pleasant than listening to him drone on about himself?

I decided no. After one slow dance, it was time to make excuses. I had a headache, and a fake early morning meeting. Could he take me home?

Todd made no effort to hide his annoyance, and guilt tugged at my brain until we arrived at my house. Before I could bolt from the car, he'd put it in park and reached over to plant a forceful kiss on my lips, giving me the fingernail-on-a-chalkboard chills down my spine.

I pushed away, doubt I thanked him for dinner, sprinted to my door, and struggled not to yell, "And you wonder why you don't have women falling all over you?" In the safety of my home, I locked the door behind me. As he peeled out of my driveway, it reminded me of when I did the same thing a year ago on that fateful day.

Getting ready for bed, I scrubbed my face—and lips—extra well. Dating was awful. I'd never ventured past Greg, until I met Jerry on an alcohol-fueled night. A sober date twenty-plus years later…what had I expected? I hadn't hit middle-age full stride yet but realized dating wasn't any easier now.

The next morning I was scheduled to work the soup kitchen at 10:00 a.m. I called Josh first.

"Hullo?" It was nine o'clock, and he didn't sound too groggy.

"Hi, honey, I have to leave for the soup kitchen in about a half hour, but I need to talk to you about something I hoped we could talk about in person." I'd tried to meet with him off and on. Between my hectic schedule, and Josh's busy life, it hadn't happened.

"I've been busy between cooking at the café and caddying at the Gull Lake Golf Course."

I was aware he'd gotten a second job, something his healing ribs and shoulder could handle. "Did you have a late night?"

"I worked at the golf course all yesterday for a tournament, then they had a dinner last night. Great tips though." Josh sounded tired. I hoped it was tired and not hungover.

"Your dad told me he lent you the money from our savings so you could pay back your friend for his motorcycle." I paused, wanting to choose the right words.

"Yeah. I really appreciate it."

"Well, I'm afraid I haven't done a good job of driving home how I felt about you getting on your friend's motorcycle all buzzed up. I want you to think about if you'd have hit a car, or a pedestrian…innocent people."

Josh sighed so hard, I thought it would rustle the hair by my ear. "Mommm…"

"Don't whine, Josh. I know you didn't mean to hurt anyone, you weren't thinking clearly. But, you could have. A car with a family, an adult crossing the street, walking home from the late shift…a car with three girlfriends who would leave their families, and their friend, behind. It could've been anyone." I chewed at my lips, knowing I was scolding myself too.

"I know." His voice was quiet. During a long pause, he cleared his throat. I wanted to fill the void, tell him it would all be okay, but I couldn't smooth it over for him.

"Um, it won't happen again, okay?"

My children had always been so perfect in my eyes, my one great success. I didn't want him going down the wrong path. "I hope that's a promise, Josh. I don't want you hurt, and I certainly don't want anyone else hurt." We talked a few more minutes, and I sat holding the phone long after we hung up. I needed to get together with Josh soon, in person.

It was an effort to put our conversation aside as I drove to the soup kitchen. Twenty minutes later, I was helping Maude do some good elbow-grease cleaning in the soup kitchen before we started cooking for the day.

"What's up, buttercup?" Maude's granddaughter, Mallory, walked in the kitchen from the dining area, swinging a pail with rags as she greeted me in her singsong voice.

"Hey, Mallory, you're looking good." Mallory was due with her first child in November, and was now over her longer-than-normal morning sickness.

"Thanks. This past month has been much better. I'm enjoying the pregnancy now, but I'm excited to see what the baby looks like."

Mallory had long, thick, light brown hair, was tall like her grandma and thin with a small baby bump. "I bet it'll look like a string bean," I teased.

Mallory laughed. "My husband and I are both five foot ten, but he's stockier, so you never know. It can come out like a circle, and I won't care. I'll love it up no matter what!"

Her enthusiasm overflowed. And it reminded me how much I loved my children.

No matter what.

* * *

Jerry dropped off a check for two grand two weeks after he'd promised me the money, which was quicker than I thought I'd see it. I called my attorney's office to let Ann's secretary know I'd be mailing a check for my retainer. I mentioned that Jerry wasn't meeting with his attorney until September. Ann's secretary scheduled me for a mid-September date. *Finally,* the divorce ball was rolling. A year after I'd thought it would.

The last Saturday in August was a Hell Club mini golf event. We met at Pirate's Cove, and divided into teams. My team consisted of Michelle, Lily, and me, and we found ourselves competing with Molly, Mary Beth, and Charlee, who were golfing one hole ahead of us.

"Got a hole in one here!" Molly shouted back to us as she did a happy dance with a pirate made out of metal.

"It doesn't count if you kick it in," Michelle teased.

A couple of holes later, I was ready to putt when Charlee came around and snuck up behind me, throwing a rubber snake at my feet. "Yaaarrgh!" My feet came up under my butt, and I swear I was suspended in air for a minute. When I heard Charlee snickering behind me, I chased her around the nearby clubhouse, while we both giggled like little school girls.

"Don't make me laugh, I'll wet my pants!" Charlee begged as she crossed her legs.

"You started it." She danced around with her legs crossed. I burst out laughing. And crying.

Charlee warily walked back to me, her eyes searching mine. "What's wrong?"

"I don't know. I guess I'm happy to hear you were going to wet your pants."

Charlee's dark eyes bugged out. "Well, I'm glad one of us is happy about that."

I impulsively reached out and squeezed her hard. "You reminded me of my old friend, Dana. Thanks for that."

A look of understanding crossed Charlee's face. She knew enough about my old friends to "get it." To lighten the mood, I said, "You owe me a chocolate malt though for scaring me." We walked back to resume our game, after Charlee made a quick stop at the bathroom. By the time all sixteen of us were done mini golfing, along with Charlee owing me a malt, Molly owed Lily a foot rub, and Michelle owed Mary Beth a weekend of doggie-sitting.

I took my ice cream payment right away as we invaded The Chocolate Ox where they served more flavors of ice cream than I could count. Crickets chirped in a nearby pond. I hated to see summer end. The air was already cooling off at night, a sure sign of fall approaching.

I was so glad to have new friends to enjoy the seasons with again.

* * *

After Labor Day weekend, I started teaching swimming lessons at Lakes Gym. Wednesday mornings I taught water aerobics to a sweet group of elderly women, followed by a class of energetic toddlers. Saturday mornings were three children's classes: tadpoles, walleyes, and sharks. And most mornings, whether I was giving swim lessons or swimming on my own at the pool, I met with Josie. She had made amazing progress. I hoped by the end of the year she'd be comfortable enough to put her head under water. For the most part, her anxiety attacks in the water were gone. I was so proud of her.

With my full class schedule, swim lessons, working at The Pines, and everything else I was accumulating, the beginning of September was so busy I nearly forgot it was approaching the one year anniversary of the crash. *Nearly*. Each day something reminded me of my old friends. I'd spot a pair of high-heeled fancy sandals, knowing Lauren would have loved them, or I'd hear a child's comment reminding me of one of Dana's kids. Maybe it was hearing about an abused woman, thinking Maggie was now free of Joe's emotional torture.

On Saturday morning, at the God-awful crack of dawn, I sat cross-legged on my living room floor, with tears rolling down onto my Hard Rock Café t-shirt. I had the sense ahead of time to grab a box of tissues. Reggie eyed me from the other end of the living room. I hadn't had an emotional breakdown in front of him before. Well, he was going to have to adjust. "Life isn't all daisies you know." I huffed to Reggie between sobs.

A drum in my head had been incessantly playing the death march for the past week. *A year ago, everything changed.* It pounded out "remember, remember, remember." As if I could ever forget. Tomorrow was the one year anniversary date of their deaths. We should have been heading to the Little Falls Craft Fair today.

I threw on jeans and a sweatshirt, laced up my tennis shoes, grabbed my cell phone, and took Reggie for a brisk walk. I needed to exercise away the horrific memories.

Karley called my cell phone while I was on my walk. "How're you doing?"

Leave it to my daughter to remember the anniversary of my friends' deaths. "I'm okay now, honey. I had a bit of a meltdown earlier, which poor Reggie had to witness." We chuckled, making jokes about how a male dog might be ill-prepared to handle an emotional female. I longed to reach out and hug my daughter. Yes, she was only two hours away, but since she had to work today, it was two hours too far. After we visited, I reminded her how much I loved her.

You just never knew if it would be the last time you'd be able to tell someone that.

After we hung up, I called Bob. "How are you and the kids doing today?" I didn't have to say, "on the first anniversary of Dana's death." We'd been talking about it for weeks.

"We've got Nash's football game today in Grand Rapids, so we are all going to watch him play. How about you? Do you have anything going on today?"

"I'm leaving soon to teach swimming, and then I'm meeting some of the women from the Hell Club for lunch. I might even open another set of time capsules later on."

"Hmmm. I hope it goes better than it did with Maggie's. Whose will you open next?"

"Probably Lauren's. Save Dana's and mine for later." I slowed my pace with Reggie and noticed some of the anxiety from earlier had faded, thanks to the best stress-relievers for me—exercise and an old friend.

As Bob and I said our goodbyes, I turned and headed for home. I had some rambunctious children to teach at the pool.

Eight club women met for lunch at Prairie Bay, where we shared four scrumptious appetizers before walking a few miles on the Paul Bunyan Trail. I came home and mowed my lawn, hung laundry out on my clothesline, and trimmed the shrubs—anything I could think of to be outside on a beautiful September day. After a light dinner, I cracked open a Coors Light, grabbed Lauren's two time capsules, and headed out to my backyard patio table. Setting them on the table, I took a deep breath.

Twisting off the rusty top of the Miracle Whip jar from our first dig, I braced myself for another trip down memory lane. Lauren's large, flowing writing reminded me of her shit-list, which was now framed and hanging in my bedroom. Inside were two mementos; one a concert ticket stub from one of the few Garth Brooks concerts she'd attended, the other a bar napkin from a Sturgis motorcycle rally. It was one of the many fun trips she took with Dylan each year, and something I'd always envied; having a husband you'd actually want to do things with.

I unrolled her paper, seeing "June 2, 2001" written boldly at the top.

MARTHA'S 2001 INFO—
NOT-SO-SECRET-WISH—my hubby & I could have a baby to love of our own
FANTASY DREAM—record a duet with Garth Brooks
MY LEAST FAV. FOOD IS—anything that doesn't go with beer
I WANT TO BUY—my own Harley
FANTASY JOB—duh, professional singer

I laughed at her remark about beer. It made her sound like a drunk, which she wasn't; she was always so careful not to relive her youth. And I was happy to know she'd achieved her goal of her own Harley. There was no surprise reading of her desire for a child—we all knew how bad Lauren and Dylan wanted one. And Lauren had been blessed with an amazing voice, one she used in the lounge where she bartended.

Inside Lauren's second capsule was a piece of tan Berber carpet I recognized from their living room remodeling. The other item was a faded photo of Lauren with the band ZZ Top from a concert she'd gone to with Dylan. Lauren was a tall, stunning woman who could be very persuasive. I hadn't been surprised to hear how she'd managed to get them invited backstage. Although Lauren and I had completely different upbringings, we did share one thing; we were the only two from our group without a college degree. "I'm going back for both of us, Lauren," I said to the photo I held in my hand.

"OCTOBER 8, 2004" was written in crayon, cursive penmanship.
I WANT TO—celebrate my 50th anniversary in Hawaii
WISH-IT-COULDA-BEEN-DIFFERENT—my childhood, DUH
DEEP DARK SECRET—had an abortion at 15 which was botched so bad I'm sure it's affected my chances of ever having a normal pregnancy. Yes, my friends, I'm sorry I never told you this but was always afraid you'd judge me, which I know is stupid shit 'cuz you know about my crappy past. Hopefully I'll get the courage to tell you all someday before we bite the big one.
HOPE FOR THE FUTURE—Another try for a baby. I know. I don't deserve one.
BIGGEST REGRET—I'm too old to try out for American Idol!

Oh, God! I held the paper still for quite a while. An abortion? How many times over the years had I voiced my negative opinion in front of Lauren about women having abortions? Had she flinched right in front of me, and I didn't notice? Why didn't Lauren ever say anything to us? It saddened me to think our friendships didn't encompass everything, didn't dig as deep as I'd thought. Hurt, I questioned if I should've never opened any time capsules. Yet really, who was I to talk about holding back secrets?

I remembered how over the years we all felt so bad for Lauren and Dylan, never able to conceive. In 2003, when Lauren and Dylan finally got pregnant, our group was as excited as they were. And each time Dana had found out she was pregnant she'd struggled to tell Lauren.

Reading of Lauren's abortion at age fifteen, I forced myself to remember her horrid stories of her upbringing. Never knowing who her dad was, living in cars and on the street with her mom…reminded me we can't have it all. Yes, Lauren had a great marriage, but she also carried the knowledge of a past she couldn't change. Getting pregnant at age thirty-seven was amazing for Lauren, and we all rode their tide of joy until her miscarriage at nine weeks.

I wasn't sure she and Dylan were going to recover, but they did. As Lauren said, "It's been just the two of us all along, and we know how to survive together, we've had lots of practice." It had to have been added torture for Lauren, always wondering if her abortion had affected her ability to conceive. What a weight for her to carry.

I re-read her dream of them celebrating their fiftieth anniversary. They hadn't even made it to their twenty-fifth. Neither had I.

Chapter 19

I met with my attorney on September nineteenth, four days after Jerry had met with his. During that hour, Ann and I went over my options, changes, what I needed most for my future as a single woman, and what Jerry and I should work out between us.

"From what I can see, there should be no reason to go to court." She informed me since Jerry filed first, his attorney would prepare a stipulation for termination of marriage once we hashed out the details. I had no control over whatever would happen next.

"Have you had any bites on your house yet?"

"No. I know it would help get our finances finalized. Jerry and I need to talk about lowering the price so we can unload it."

Ann brought up Jerry's construction business, and the "blue sky" built up over the years. "If he's going to get half of your retirement, you should get half of his business equity. There's not an exact dollar figure tied to 'blue sky.' It is something you two should discuss."

Dividing up half of my life was tough to see dissected in black and white. And it sounded like I had more finance matters to bring up with Jerry.

* * *

Mallory was back to helping again at the soup kitchen, glowing with her blossoming pregnancy and full of energy. So, it was a surprise the following Sunday to hear her say toward the end of our serving the meal how she suddenly wasn't feeling well.

Maude was showing me how to run the enormous dishwasher when Mallory piped up. "I'm going to call Dad and have him come pick me up."

Jane's fourteen-year-old son had helped us serve. "Why didn't you drive yourself?" He shot Mallory a curious look. I'm sure to a young teen, driving any chance you got seemed logical.

"Dad was going to be running errands anyway, so I asked if he could drop me off on his way."

"Do you want to take her home, Maude? We can finish cleaning up." I offered.

Mallory, who had been wilting like a flower, came back to life. "No! I'm sure Dad has nothing going on. You stay here, Grandma." Mallory grabbed her phone and dialed. "Dad won't mind."

Five minutes later, I was mopping the floor and didn't hear the side door open. I never looked up until Mallory tapped me on the shoulder. "I'd like you to meet my dad, Daniel Monroe. Dad, this is Peyton. She's been working here with our group since this spring."

I wiped off my wet hands on my jeans and shook his hand. Nice firm grip and even nicer smile. One dimple in his right cheek made him look about thirty. Mallory clearly got her smile and height from him, and his square jaw was similar to Maude's. "You have a wonderful daughter and mother." I smiled at Mallory, who appeared antsy. I assumed she wanted to leave since she wasn't feeling well.

"I guess she's okay. I mean what can you do when they push their way back home, and pregnant besides?" He teased, as he reached around Mallory and gave her a big squeeze.

Her husband wasn't coming home from Afghanistan for the birth, instead saving his time to get out in a few months. Her dad would be the one in the delivery room as her coach. I thought that was sweet, especially since Mallory had told me two weeks earlier how she lost her mom when she was a few years old. "C'mon, Mal, let's get you home and tuck you into bed."

As they left, Mallory looked back at us and dragged her feet...not appearing sick at all. The rest of us finished wiping tables, vacuumed, and locked up. As I drove home, I thought about Daniel Monroe. His boyish smile kept popping into my head, along with his dark blond, wavy hair which framed his tanned, rugged face. And he looked familiar for some reason. I shrugged it off as him reminding me of someone. For all I knew, he was remarried. Mallory hadn't mentioned a step-mom, but I hadn't been listening for one before now.

* * *

The first Saturday in October was sunny, warm, and beautiful, with the leaves changing to their red, bronze, and pumpkin colors as a number of us from the Hell Club drove to The Farm on St. Mathias—a farm outside of Brainerd with miles of dirt roads for their hay wagons and an enormous corn maze right in the center. Forty of us signed up, enough for three hay wagons.

I rode to The Farm with Mary Beth, Michelle, and Molly, and with the crisp, fall weather, the place was busy. We walked in the pathway between enormous cornstalks, hearing kids screaming in delight through the maze. Molly snuck up ahead of us, and when Michelle and I walked by, she reached out and grabbed Michelle's waist from behind. I'm sure Molly meant to surprise Michelle. Instead, Michelle's blue eyes bugged out and her mouth twisted in horror before she swung around, knocked Molly down and ran away. I caught three seconds of surprise on Molly's face, and three seconds of terror on Michelle's.

"I'm sorry!" Molly recovered first, and rubbed her arm as she ran to Michelle. "I'm so, so sorry!" She hugged Michelle from behind as Michelle stood with her hands over her face.

I jogged over to them. "Are you okay?"

Michelle nodded. "I'm the one who is sorry, and embarrassed," she said into her hands. "I guess all these years later, my ex-husband still has an effect on me."

"I picked the wrong one to scare!" Molly turned to me. "Would you have slugged me?"

"I might have, for good measure." I tried to lighten the mood.

The three of us continued on through the maze. "The thing is," Michelle said, "this is one of my favorite things about the Hell Club." She leaned her head on Molly's bony shoulder. "Yes, you didn't have an ex who abused you, but you get it. We all have our issues from the past."

"I love that nobody judges each other," she said as her chin quivered.

"So, I shouldn't ask if you think this corn maze would be fun at night?" Molly joked.

Michelle laughed. "Definitely not with you."

We finished the corn maze and lined up for the hayride. As I sat in the sea of women, the air heavy with the scent of freshly cut hay, I studied each woman. No matter the pain behind why we'd all joined, I'd never witnessed so many hugs, tears, and laughter—the best prescription. Even tears helped wash the pain away.

* * *

When I arrived in the soup kitchen the following Sunday, I was stunned to see Mallory's father in the serving area setting up tables…with an apron on. I shot Maude a questioning look.

"Mallory is due November second, so she decided to take off these next few weeks, to minimize the time on her feet." Maude said as she whipped an enormous batch of potatoes in preparation for another large turnout.

I was organizing the veggie tray when Jane walked in. "Sorry I'm late; I had to drop two of my boys off at basketball practice." She grabbed an apron. "I see Daniel's truck. Did Mallory con him into working for her after all?"

"Apparently. I told her it would do her good to keep busy, not sit at home with her legs up. She's not retaining any more water in those skinny legs than I am." Maude shook her head.

Daniel peered into the kitchen. "You talking about my conniving daughter who seems to think I'm her puppet?" He smiled at the three of us as he went to the sink and washed his hands.

"What's up with Ms. Mallory all of the sudden? Normally she's got enough energy for ten people." Maude held two sheets of biscuits and motioned for someone to open the oven door.

"Maybe because she's eight months pregnant?" My sympathy was with Mallory.

"I accused her of trying to tie up my rare free day, but she got all wide-eyed. Guess you ladies are stuck with me until she has the baby, and for a while after that."

Jane reached over and pinched Daniel's smooth cheek. "And aren't we lucky women to have you?" I'd noticed a few differences since the day I met him. He'd shaved, and his wavy hair had been cut a little shorter. Either way…he was one ruggedly handsome man.

When I showed up at the soup kitchen again two weeks later, Daniel was back working with us. If I happened to take extra care at straightening my hair and perfecting my makeup, I convinced myself it was because I had the time to primp. I pulled on a soft gray sweater, stepped into my favorite jeans, and left for the soup kitchen. When I walked in, Maude piped up. "Look at you, all gussied up. Going somewhere afterwards?"

I wanted to shush her; I hoped Daniel would think I looked like this every day. Well, almost every day. "Sure she is; we're going shopping after we're done here," Jane said.

It was true. Jane and I were going to Target—and I'm pretty sure Jane knew I hadn't primped for that. "Peyton, would you mind helping Daniel set up tables and chairs?" Jane asked.

He was already in the dining room, sleeves rolled up to reveal some impressive forearms. "Hey, Peyton, how's it going?" He smiled, looking my way.

"Just fine. I came to offer you my muscles." I flexed my swimming muscles.

"Wow! Remind me not to wrestle with you." He winked.

I went to the other end of the table he was carrying. We unlocked the legs of the table before we turned it over—as I vividly imagined wrestling with Daniel.

"So, you're going to be in the delivery room with Mallory?"

"Well, her mom's gone, her husband's in Afghanistan, and I didn't want her to be alone."

"Do you have any other children?" I wanted to add "as in step-children?"

"Nope, just my bossy prima donna daughter who invaded my house." He winked.

"You mean the prima donna who invaded your heart?" I teased as we unfolded a table.

He laughed. "Yes, that too."

We finished setting up and received our serving assignments. While we filled plates, I stood next to Daniel. He looked every person in the eye, greeted them, and smiled...treating them as if he were serving them in a five-star restaurant. Even though common sense told me a guy like him was either remarried or dating some amazing woman, it didn't stop my mind from playing "let's pretend."

* * *

On Halloween, the Hell Club volunteered to work at a haunted house in the nearby town of Nisswa. The chicken in me was leery of signing up, but Molly convinced me it'd be fun. I opted for working the front line, taking people's money and stamping their hands. Molly jumped at the chance to dress up like Freddy Krueger and scare the bejesus out of everyone.

And both Yvette and Abby were making the most of their disabilities in a scene where they had a "possessed" chainsaw which supposedly cut off Yvette's leg and Abby's arm. Molly took great joy in slopping fake blood all over them. I thought they were all a bit twisted, but I loved their spunk and sense of humor.

Charlee, Molly, and I went out for a drink after the haunted house closed for the night. "A customer of mine rented one of those tree house places up at Spirit Mountain in Duluth for this coming weekend," said Molly. They can't use it, and have already paid the deposit on it, and asked if I knew anyone who could use it. I thought it'd be fun to get a group of us together and go for the weekend."

I was scheduled Friday night at The Pines, but with four days' notice, I figured I'd find someone to cover for me. "I think I'm free. I've seen photos of those places, and it sounds fun."

"Hmmm, as much as I'd love to go, my kids aren't old enough to leave alone for a weekend. Not without me coming home to total disaster anyway," Charlee said.

"Shoot. I wish you could get away." I felt sorry for her. Four kids, no husband.

"Believe me, I do too."

Molly drummed her fingers on the table. "I'll put the word out to a few of the other women. It sleeps up to six people and reservations are for Friday and Saturday nights."

"I'll let you know if I find enough women to go," said Molly as we finished our drinks.

The following Friday, I dropped off Reggie at Jane's house, promising to bring him back a special treat. Mary Beth, Michelle, Yvette, Molly, Lily, and I headed to Duluth, happy the weekend was going to be mild. Early November in Minnesota could be cold and snowy.

The tree houses were located on a ski hill, and although it was too early for skiing, they had a zip line and alpine coaster—both of which I watched Molly eye up as we parked. We unloaded our bags and walked the short distance to the top of Spirit Mountain.

"Who's game to do the zip line?" Molly asked. We all said we'd give it a try.

"How about the alpine coaster?" She raised an eyebrow, knowing that was a scarier ride.

"I think I'll pass," Lily said.

"Me too." Michelle and I chimed in.

"C'mon, you sissies," Yvette egged us on. "If I can do it, you can!"

"Yes, what have you got to lose?" Michelle joked.

"My other leg," Yvette said with a straight face before busting out in a chortle.

Every time I heard Yvette laugh, it inspired me. I knew enough about her story, how she'd lost her leg in a car accident, and her two young sons as well. It was inspiring how she could drag herself out of bed and face each new day without her children.

Molly badgered Lily and Michelle so much that by Friday night, we'd all done the zip line and the alpine coaster. Flying down the zip line, my hair tucked inside a helmet, the hilltop air blasting at my face as the ground blurred below me was the most invigorating feeling I'd had in years.

We sat next to the fireplace Friday night and had a couple drinks and a lot of laughs. It reminded me of going off to Girl Scout camp when I was a kid, minus the alcohol and poker playing, of course.

"Stop cheating, Michelle!" Molly teased after Michelle won three hands in a row.

"Stop looking at my cards, you rubber neck," Lily deadpanned to Yvette.

"Geez, these new club members are sore losers." Michelle said to Yvette and Mary Beth.

"Don't I know it. We've let a bunch of pansies into the club." Mary Beth shook her head as if we'd brought shame to the club.

So, I reached over and poured a good dose of peppermint schnapps into her virgin hot chocolate. "Chill out, Mary Beth," I teased as we all giggled and passed the bottle of schnapps around to liven up the rest of our hot chocolates.

Saturday was spent along the lake walk. When the wind picked up and the temperature dropped, we quickly stocked up on chocolate treats at Rocky Mountain Chocolate Factory before driving back to the Mountain Villas. The temperature forced us to tuck ourselves in for the night, and we watched chick flicks late into the evening.

I never heard Yvette's cell phone ring at six the next morning. It wasn't until we were sitting around in our pj's, drinking coffee and eating blueberry muffins that she told us.

"I got a call this morning from Charlee about a fellow club member." She paused and I could see Mary Beth and Michelle already knew what Yvette would tell us "newbies."

"This member hasn't been to any events recently, I doubt you've met her. She joined eight years ago, after an abusive relationship with her ex-boyfriend. It sounds like she's been seeing him again, and he beat her so bad last night she was airlifted to Minneapolis." Once you'd been in the club for a year, if you wanted, your name went on a "care list" for club members who might need help. Via phone calls and emails, members were kept updated on where help was needed.

"She has no family, so we'll take shifts to sit with her," said Michelle. By the time we left Sunday, Michelle, Mary Beth, and Yvette were on the shift schedule at North Memorial.

"As you know, the club isn't all laughs. Many members carry some potentially explosive baggage, and when it blows up, we need to be there for them," Mary Beth explained.

"It's also what I like best about the club," Molly said. "Knowing you women have our backs."

Chapter 20

My butt was dragging by the time I got home from our girls-weekend-away trip to Duluth on Sunday afternoon. When I got a call from Maude that evening saying Mallory had delivered her baby girl earlier in the day, it put a sparkle in my step again.

Up early on Monday, my car plowed through heavy snow on our side roads as I headed out shopping for baby outfits and a plastic baby tub—the one thing Mallory mentioned she needed. I stopped by the hospital afterwards, since Maude had said Mallory and baby would get out of the hospital by Monday night.

I knocked before swinging the partially closed door open a bit. I heard murmured voices, so I figured Mallory wasn't sleeping. I told my heart to behave itself as I laid eyes on Mallory's dad, rocking and talking to his granddaughter in his masculine arms. The infant looked long, even in Daniel's tall frame. Mallory was sleeping.

"Oh, I'm sorry," I whispered, feeling like I had intruded on a private moment.

"No, it's okay. C'mon in and meet my little granddaughter, Maren."

I put down my gifts on a nearby chair and stepped closer to Daniel. Close enough to smell the outdoors on him, close enough to notice a few gray hairs in the various shades of blond, close enough to feel the warmth of his body, and close enough to notice his palm was larger than Maren's face.

Maren was wrapped like a burrito in a soft pink baby blanket, eyes wide open, while her pale pink lips made sucking motions. Daniel's pinky tenderly brushed against her cheek.

"She is beautiful, and isn't it amazing how you can pick out their parents features on them right away? Maren has Mallory's almond-shaped eyes, doesn't she?" Daniel asked. I wanted to mention I'd noticed his eyes were the same. I didn't.

Those were the very same eyes I'd been avoiding for fear he'd see in mine an interest I was trying to ignore.

And I squelched the distant memories pushing to the surface of when I had my own children. The way I'd studied every inch of them, noticing every detail…and imperfection. When I'd noticed the tiny extra piece of skin on Karley's earlobe, I'd told myself it was nothing. It was easy to do, I was still grieving the sudden death of my mom, focusing on caring for Karley was enough, without questioning if her earlobe was "normal" or not. Few people mentioned it, including Jerry.

Daniel gazed fondly at his granddaughter. I was certain he'd notice anything unique about her.

"Of course I think she's perfect, like I thought Mallory was—until she became a teen anyway." We laughed, knowing many parents felt that way.

"Has Mallory been asleep awhile?"

"Yes, in fact she was stirring before you came in, and I thought she'd wake up. She was a trooper, and I'm so thankful it all went well."

"Were you able to be in during the delivery?"

He grimaced. "Yes, and now I understand what they mean when men say they can't stand to watch their wife in so much pain. I wasn't with Mallory's mom when she was giving birth, and even though I went through birthing classes with Mallory, I don't think anything can prepare you for seeing someone you love in so much pain." Daniel kissed Maren's tiny hand.

"And there she was; a true miracle. I don't know how you women do it."

"We get through it because we know the end result is worth it." I reached over to touch the soft-as-whipped cream patch of blonde hair on Maren's head.

"Sit down, stay a bit, I'm sure Mallory will wake up soon."

I pulled up a chair. "I can't wait to have grandchildren."

"How many kids do you have? How old are they?"

"Karley is twenty-two and has a serious boyfriend. Josh is nineteen and flies by the seat of his pants. I'm hoping he doesn't settle down anytime soon."

"Would you like to hold her?" Daniel held out his granddaughter for me as if he were handing me the Hope Diamond.

I took Maren, who was now sleeping in a purr-like state, while he told me of the sporting goods store he'd owned for years, selling everything from water skiing equipment to hunting supplies. Although it was a busy deer-hunting weekend, he had plenty of help covering for him. He told me of Maude coming to take over for him during labor so he could run back to his shop to fix a problem with the scale his customers used to weigh their deer.

"She was all wound up when I got back. 'Daniel, did you change your clothes? Did you take a shower again?' Reprimanding me for going back to the shop where I might have touched a dead deer carcass, sure I was going to bring some flesh-eating germ into the hospital room."

I chuckled. I could envision Maude chewing out Daniel as if he were some irresponsible teen.

"I reassured her I had indeed changed my shirt, washed up, and wasn't going to infect 'HER great-granddaughter' as she refers to Maren. As if I would endanger *my* granddaughter."

After returning Maren to the hottest looking grandpa around, I thought about how wonderful it would feel to be a grandma someday. We visited for a while until Maren woke and started to fuss, which woke up Mallory, proudly grinning with a smile as wide as Texas.

Mallory went in to great detail about her delivery with amazing energy.

"I'm so happy all went well. Your daughter is perfect." I squeezed Mallory's hand. "I should get going now. I need to study. I hope you drop by the soup kitchen with Maren though, when you feel up to it." I leaned down and hugged Mallory in her hospital bed and placed a kiss on Maren's forehead.

Daniel walked me out to the elevator. "I guess I'll be filling in a while at the soup kitchen until Mallory is willing to let me watch Maren while she volunteers again."

I hoped Mallory took a couple months off. All I could think of as I rode the elevator to the main floor was if he was remarried, wouldn't his wife have been there? Or maybe she was at work. Hell, why didn't I just ask Mallory before if she had a step-mom, or ask Maude if her son was married? I knew why; I didn't want to admit I was attracted to him. The attraction I'd hoped to feel with Bob, and hadn't mustered with Todd—I had no difficulty feeling it with Daniel.

* * *

I'd signed up to serve the community Thanksgiving meal at Eunice's church hall since I was going to be alone Thanksgiving Day. The kids were going to Jerry's for mid-day dinner and coming to my house later on for snacks. Josh had mumbled the information to me after a recent football game. Digging his cleats into the grass, the same cleats that changed my life last year, he kept his head down as if I were going to be angry with him for deserting me on a holiday.

To be honest, I was more hurt than anything else, which was stupid and unreasonable. At times, I could be stupid and unreasonable. So, volunteering to serve Thanksgiving dinner to those who would be otherwise alone seemed like a good way for me to spend the day. Knowing Mary Beth would be there to help made it easier to swallow. She had no children—part time or otherwise—and never complained about it.

As I dressed for the community dinner, I thought of Karley bringing Ben and wondered if she let Jerry know ahead of time. I was wishing I could have been at Jerry's place when they walked in the door. Now, for Josh to bring someone to dinner? That was another story, but one quickly abandoned. One more mouth meant less food for Josh.

On my way to the church, I picked up Mary Beth. She waited with her usual smile.

"Honestly, Mary Beth, you know what you need?" I commented as she stomped off the snow from her boots before sliding into my front seat.

"What?" Mary Beth said, facing the back seat as she unloaded two pans of pumpkin bars, setting them next to the two pumpkin pies I'd baked. "I wasn't aware I needed anything."

"You need a husband and kids so you aren't always so happy." I pulled out of her driveway, windshield wipers fighting off our first major snow of the season. We both laughed, knowing I didn't mean the part about children. We arrived at the church hall where a dozen or so volunteers were already scurrying along like ants. Eunice handed us both aprons and led us to the potato peeling production line.

Men showed up to set up tables and chairs, carve turkey and help with dishes and serving. A long line was formed by noon when the doors opened, and as surprised as I was by it, I was even more amazed to see Mallory with her dad in line. Daniel was carrying an infant car seat with a tiny, sleeping Maren inside.

I don't know what I expected, more like a soup kitchen type of line of people who couldn't afford a decent meal. What I observed was a kaleidoscope of locals; elderly couples, single parents, the down and out, and the upper-middle class.

Sandwiched between Mary Beth and a quiet young man, I asked about the crowd this dinner drew. "It's a free will offering, stressing to come and enjoy a good holiday meal with others. We want people to come together as a community, no matter the size of their wallet. And we always end up making a nice profit. People are generous." Mary Beth explained as we carted large trays of bars over to the end of the buffet line.

In a few minutes, we'd be serving the public, and in there somewhere was Daniel, a man I had thought about too many times lately. A man who made me wish I had a mirror to check and see if the steam from boiling potatoes had flattened my hair and smeared my makeup. *He's here for a meal, Peyton, not to eye you up as his next meal, no matter how much you wish he was!*

I panicked. They were coming toward us, and I was sure I'd slung a glob of mashed potatoes in my hair or something. "Mary Beth?"

"Hmm?" She continued scooping potatoes from the roaster onto plates.

"Do I look okay?" I sounded like a self-centered teen.

"What?" Mary Beth missed a step in her process.

"I mean, do I have food in my hair or mascara running down my cheek?"

Her eyebrow shot up before she served the next person. "Yes, you look fine. Nervous, but fine."

Counting ahead, I had less than a minute before they'd be in front of me. I licked my lips, fluffed up the back of my hair with my forearm above my gloved hand, and braced myself.

I would never make it in a stage production. My "Hey there, Mallory!" sounded as surprised as a dollar scratch-off winner.

"Hey, Peyton. We thought we'd come here today since Grandma's out of town for the weekend. She's visiting her sister, and Dad didn't want to cook for just us two." Mallory's glowing face looked so serene. She stepped ahead, and it was hard for me to drag my eyes to the next person…her dad. Daniel's arm was swinging the infant seat back and forth by its handle, as if it were a small Easter basket. And his left hand had no ring on it, not that it meant anything. Jerry had never worn his wedding ring because of his construction job. Mallory said just the two of them. Unless she had a step-mom who never ate, I was sure there wasn't one.

Daniel's arm was partially covered by a form-fitting tan sweater with the sleeves pushed up, displaying his golden-haired arms. I had yet to bring my eyes up to his face, and my hand had apparently quit working so Mary Beth reached over and scooped some potatoes on his plate. I also realized he hadn't stepped forward in line yet.

Leaning down, his face was level with mine. "Hello, Peyton, nice to see you again. Mallory said you'd be working here today." Pause. Engaging smile. Waiting for my answer.

"Um, yep." *Wow, genius, way to reel him in with your clever words.*

"Ahem," the gentlemen behind Daniel cleared his throat; we were stopping the line. My large spoon was still perched halfway above the roaster oven, and I thought of how Daniel's eyes were the color of chocolate Dove bars. Both yummy.

He continued on with his charming smile, on to the lucky women who would be serving him green beans, forging ahead with his happy daughter and sleeping granddaughter, and I would continue on serving people mashed potatoes I now realized were the same color as my blouse. Why didn't I wear red? Red was my color, not bland-potato-white, in November.

A half hour later, the line slowed a bit. "Can you go around with coffee and see who wants a refill?" Eunice shoved a couple carafes in my hands.

Good old Eunice, tossing me out into the crowd. As I made my way to Daniel and Mallory's table, I spotted Daniel drinking coffee. "Would you like a refill?"

He took a quick sip to finish off his coffee and pushed the cup toward where I stood. "Sure, thanks. This is a great meal, Peyton. So much better than me going through the hassle of making a big meal. I've never been here before."

Daniel seemed comfortable in a kitchen, I'd seen him first-hand slice, dice, and sauté his way around the soup kitchen. "It's my first year here too." I told him, in no hurry to leave their table. Lucky for me, Mallory was in her twenty-question mode.

"Are your son and daughter coming to your house tonight?"

"Yes, they'll be there for snacks later on."

"So, it's just the three of you. They should have come here—we could've met them." I was smart enough to know Mallory was up to something.

"They're at their dad's right now. My daughter's boyfriend is with them, so there will be four of us tonight."

"Dad said he's enjoyed working at the soup kitchen with you."

I looked at Daniel who rolled his eyes upwards and drummed his fingers over his full mouth. "You aren't too old for me to spank, are you?" He mumbled to Mallory.

When an elderly gentleman waved his empty coffee cup at me, I had to move on, missing out on Mallory's answer.

Two hours later, Mary Beth and I stepped out into the snowy late afternoon. I gave a heavy sigh as I slid behind the wheel. She waited about half a second after I turned the car key. "Okay, who is he?" Her dark eyes searched my face. I turned to look out my rear-view mirror before pulling the car onto snow-packed roads.

"You mean the gal and her dad who was holding her baby? That's Mallory; she works at the soup kitchen, and her dad, Daniel, has been filling in the past month. Her daughter is two weeks old, and her husband is serving overseas, so she's been staying with her dad." I pulled out onto Highway 371, the slush sliding my car around. These were some of the worst driving conditions in Minnesota, where temperatures hovered around freezing and created black ice or slushy roads which could make you easily lose control. I slowed my speed.

"I've heard you mention Mallory. I guess I never heard you say her dad was such a sexy looking guy. Unmarried, I assume?"

"Mary Beth, you said a man was sexy. I was starting to think you forgot there was an opposite sex." I winked at her.

She reached over and tapped my arm. "Don't change the subject, girl. And yes, I know there's an opposite sex, and choose to keep them as friends, co-workers, or dogs."

I turned on to Mary Beth's road. "You've heard me talk about Maude too—Daniel is Maude's son. I think Mallory's mom died when she was quite young, so he's been her main parent. I haven't heard anything about a new wife. No wedding ring, so I guess, you know…"

Thank goodness Mary Beth didn't expect an explanation. I had no answer as to why I was eyeing up another man while I was still technically married. Emotionally, I hadn't been married for years, if ever.

After dropping her off, I drove home, made a grilled artichoke dip, wild rice soup, and cut the extra pumpkin pies I'd baked last night. Anything to pass the time while I waited for Josh, Karley, and Ben to show up.

When the three of them walked through the front door, stomping the sticky snow off their boots—I sensed something was off. Nobody would look me in the eye. "What's wrong? Did something happen?" I didn't add, "at your dad's."

Josh bent down to untie his bootlace, thus avoiding my answer and eyes, while Karley cast a sideways glance at Ben, as if she hoped he'd answer for them.

"We're fine, Mom, just tired." Karley took a deep breath. "It smells good in here, and we ate around one, so we're hungry for whatever you've whipped up." Her forced smile read "please, let's change the subject," so I went along, reminding myself my children were adults and would have to let me know if they needed me to step in.

It wasn't until Josh was well into his second piece of pie, before he accidentally spilled the beans. "Your pumpkin pie is soooo much better than Angela's. Her crust was mushy and no spices in the pumpkin." He continued to plow his way through the last of his pie, head down near his plate in case, God forbid, he'd miss a crumb. And was ignorant of what he'd said.

"Who's Angela?" *Oh, why did I ask?* Karley's lips came together in a stern look for her brother, and I guessed she was trying to kick his long legs under the table. She must have succeeded. Josh shot up, alert.

"Oh, she's a lady I know."

"A lady who made you a pumpkin pie?"

"Yep."

"Why?"

"Uh, because she knows how much I like to eat."

"How nice of her." Josh squirmed while I quizzed him. Ben's eyes volleyed back and forth, taking in Josh's and my banter. His expression reminded me of a poker face with moving eyes. It was all too much for practical, level-headed Karley.

"For crying out loud, Josh! How stupid do you think Mom is?"

I held up my hand. "Don't answer that."

We all laughed and the tension collapsed. "Your sister is right, Josh. I've pretty much figured Angela must have been at your dad's place, which, unless he is now inviting the homeless in for meals, I'm guessing she's your dad's girlfriend?"

Three sets of shoulders lowered in relief, thankful to not have to carry on the pretense anymore. "Yeah, I guess she is. Actually, Mom, she was nice." Josh shrugged his shoulders, while informing me my not-yet-divorced husband was dating someone serious enough to have her at a family gathering.

"I thought they broke up? The woman I saw him with last summer…"

"They did, this is someone new. I think they met when Dad did some remodeling on her house a while ago, although they kind of acted like they've known each other a long time. Which, by the way, Dad said he should have enough inside projects to keep him busy most of this winter." Karley was becoming a professional on guiding the subject elsewhere. After years of living in a tension-filled house, she knew how to diffuse a bomb.

I let it slide; my children didn't need me playing twenty questions with them about their dad's love life. Jerry's business profit was still my concern until we got this house sold. I made a mental note to go through the billing from the past few months to find a certain Angela I might have billed for Jerry's business. Some things I struggled to let slide.

Chapter 21

I was browsing through the sale ads in the Sunday paper when Jerry called me.

"It's about time. I was starting to think you didn't live there anymore."

"Hello to you, too. I didn't know you had been trying to get ahold of me." I guess it should have been obvious by the number of times his cell number showed up on mine. He never left a message, which I pointed out.

"We need to talk, Peyton."

"Gee, I thought only women said that."

He ignored my wit. "I'm sure by now the kids have told you about meeting Angela at Thanksgiving. I want to get our divorce finalized. I've submitted my construction equipment values to my attorney, and he said he'd contact your attorney."

After what my attorney told me at our meeting, I wasn't sure it was going to be as easy of a split as Jerry envisioned.

"Have there been any bites on the house?" He asked.

"No, a few showings, but this time of year, the realtor told me not to expect much."

"I want to build this spring," Jerry stated.

"He said house sales are picking up a little, but the economy is still slow. He's strongly suggested to me that we drop the price ten grand or so. If we don't do it by January, when people start looking again, they might not bother to look at our house."

"Yep, I guess if that's going to get us our money out of the house, I'll do it."

For the next fifteen minutes Jerry and I hashed out things with housing expenses and the kids, as far as continuing them on insurance and splitting holidays. We were married by paperwork only. Within the next few months, we would be divorced the same way.

* * *

In early December, I made a trip to the sporting goods store, Gander Mountain. Josh had asked for warm socks for Christmas. Elbow deep in a sea of moisture-wicking, thermal, and wool socks, I was ready to find a store clerk for some assistance when I sensed someone watching me.

"Hello, Peyton. Need some help picking out socks?" Daniel appeared at my side.

Dear Fate, where is the nearest mirror? I'd been studying all day and hadn't bothered with makeup. Had I even combed my hair? Thank goodness I'd at least changed out of my sweatpants and into jeans. "Hi, Daniel. Yes, my son wants socks for ice fishing that will be warm and dry. I'm on information overload here." My cheeks warmed up like hotcakes.

"I'd say go with the SmartWool socks. They're expensive, but worth it. I don't carry them in my shop because of the price, but they're great."

I had retreated thirty years to the mute thirteen-year-old I'd have been if the star high school football player talked to me. My brain wasn't registering what Daniel was even saying. Something about socks. Who cared about socks? Oh yes, I did. Well, at least my son did.

"I forgot you have a sports shop." I couldn't even remember the name of his shop, couldn't think of anything but his charming smile...and my sweaty palms. Great. I didn't feel this way at the soup kitchen. I had the other women to buffer me there. Here, it was Daniel, me, and a sea of socks. He rifled through the bins and found a few different styles for me to choose from.

When he asked me about Josh and what sports he liked, and if he hunted too, or enjoyed summer fishing, my nervousness melted. Ask me about my children and I could talk all day. And we did for the better part of an hour. When Gander Mountain employees began switching off sections of lights, we knew it was time to go. I had my Christmas socks for Josh, and Daniel made his way to a fleece baby blanket he'd eyed the week before for Maren.

After we checked out and parted ways in the parking lot, I played our conversation over in my mind. Talking with Daniel felt as comfortable as visiting with Bob. And, unlike Bob, I was positive if Daniel kissed me, my whole body would self-combust.

* * *

In mid-December, I joined a couple dozen other women from the Hell Club on a trek to the Twin Cities. We'd booked hotel rooms in downtown Minneapolis and were eager to watch the glittering, colorful Holidazzle Parade.

After checking into our hotel, we loaded onto a metro holiday-blinged-out bus headed for Nicollet Avenue, dressed in our warmest attire.

Lined up in a crowd of thousands, we'd arrived in time to nab a curbside view of the holiday parade. A group of us made a trip to Bob's Java Hut for a hot chocolate run before the parade started, maneuvering our way through the energized crowd with Molly and Mary Beth leading the way.

"I sure miss the cities sometimes," Molly said as she opened the door to "the best hot chocolate place around" according to her.

"You lived around here?" Molly had mentioned before that she moved from the Twin Cities when she inherited her store.

"Yep, born and raised about ten miles from here." She took off her mittens and blew on her long fingers before giving our order.

"Do you get back here to visit much?"

"I visit my best friend. My dad lives in New Mexico now, so I've got no family here."

"We need to get the new club members together so we can hear each other's story. It's hard to believe it's been almost a year since I joined," I said. "I told Lily I'd wait until she was ready, since we joined about the same time."

"Me too." Molly agreed. "My story isn't that exciting, but I don't want to pressure Lily. I want her to be comfortable telling us and not feel like she has to. Charlee mentioned maybe next summer a group of us new members and our 'mentors' could rent a pontoon or something."

"That's a good idea. We did it years ago when Charlee, Michelle, and I joined." Mary Beth remarked as we grabbed our cardboard holders containing four hot chocolates each and made our way through the festive crowd back to the rest of the club women. I thought about the domino effect in the club—one woman in need seeking help, in turn helping another woman in need... It was better than any pyramid scheme I'd ever heard of. This one actually worked.

After a night of little sleep but lots of laughter, we made the two-hour drive home with Michelle at the wheel. Mary Beth was in front, and Molly and I sat in the back. Traffic crawled on the slippery, black-ice roads. A pickup in the middle lane of 494 swerved in and out of traffic, traveling too fast for the road conditions. "Crazy driver," Mary Beth mumbled. In her profession, I'm sure she'd seen plenty of accidents caused by reckless drivers pushing the limit.

As we came over a hill, the traffic sat at a standstill. Two vehicles were in the median, one overturned. Two others were blocking traffic in two lanes, smashed and turned sideways. And one of those vehicles in the ditch was the pickup we'd watched snake through the traffic.

It took a while for traffic to maneuver around the accident scene, going from three lanes down to one. Police and ambulances appeared, coming from the other direction to help the many people who were injured—some lying on the ground, covered with coats and blankets. And in those minutes, I broke out in a sweat, my neck and face clammy as the scene spun around me.

"I don't feel well." I tried to keep my voice calm. I rolled down my window, even though it was below freezing outside, and unzipped the hoodie I was wearing.

Mary Beth's medical training kicked in. "Can you pull off at the next exit, Michelle? Peyton, honey, put your head between your legs."

Molly reached over and helped me unbuckle my seat belt since my hands were shaking. "It's okay. You're going to be okay." Molly, normally energized, spoke softly in a soothing voice.

My legs were shaking as I whipped off my hoodie, feeling hot and cold at the same time. Within minutes, Michelle took the next exit and pulled into a parking lot. Before she'd brought the car to a complete stop, Mary Beth had her door open and had run back to open mine.

"Okay, nice and slow breaths, Peyton, we're here for you. It's okay." She crouched down next to me. "Do you want to lie down in the back seat for a few minutes?"

Molly hopped out her side of the car and helped Mary Beth lay me down. Michelle grabbed a bottle of water from the cooler. "Here, take a drink."

I did and then lay down as Molly and Mary Beth covered me in their jackets. "I'm so embarrassed. I don't know what's wrong with me." My teeth chattered as I spoke.

Mary Beth was now by my head, tenderly rubbing it. "I think you're having an anxiety attack. Keep doing the slow breaths with me. We're here for you, Peyton. You'll be okay."

I closed my eyes and concentrated on breathing along with Mary Beth. Of course I was having an anxiety attack. The minute I saw the accident, my brain sent me into panic-mode. In my mind, I was back at my friends' accident, reliving it all over again…feeling so helpless. And again, Mary Beth was at my side, along with two other friends who understood. I didn't feel embarrassed, didn't have to explain. After a few minutes, my heart slowed its frantic pace.

When they dropped me off at my home two hours later, I got in my car, went to pick up Reggie from Bob's home, and then made a stop at the cemetery. Seeing the accident was a too-raw reminder of what my friends must have experienced in those seconds before they died. I needed to be with them again, in the only way I could.

* * *

Mallory came back to the soup kitchen the week before Christmas, with Maren in tow. Maude was out of town again, and Daniel was working at his shop. "Don't worry; she'll sleep most of the time." Mallory promised Jane and me as we prepared the meal.

"We don't mind at all, Mallory, it's nice to have a baby around," Jane reassured her.

Maren slept through until the last meals were served. Mallory snuck back to the kitchen and fed her. When I brought the empty roaster back to the kitchen I heard Mallory on the phone asking her dad if he could bring her a diaper for Maren.

"I thought your dad was working at his store today." I said.

"He is, but it's next to our house, and I know he's not working alone today."

Still, I felt bad for Daniel. "We can clean up here, Mallory, you don't have to stay."

"Don't worry, Peyton. Mallory had this all worked out ahead of time, didn't you?" Jane chuckled at my concern.

Mallory chose to ignore Jane. The fastidious Mallory I'd come to know wouldn't have forgotten to pack diapers, and wouldn't be so demanding.

I loaded the dishwasher while Jane rinsed the dishes before handing them to me. "Can't you smell a meddler? Mallory knows her dad will do anything for her, knows he won't mind dropping something off knowing you're here." Mallory was suddenly fussing over a content Maren. If her diaper was full, she didn't seem to mind. "Isn't that right, dear?" Jane asked her.

Mallory's face flushed as she turned to me. "Well Jiminy Cricket! I had to fake sleeping at the hospital so you two could visit, and all you guys did was talk about boring stuff. So, I dragged Dad to the Thanksgiving meal at church, and you were too busy to visit."

Just then, Daniel showed up with the all-important diapers. We all stared at him as if he'd grown an extra arm. Had he honestly been willing to stop here for a diaper—and to see me?

"Hey, Peyton. I was going to tell you the other night, if you need more help picking out things for your son, I'd be glad to help you." Daniel cleared his throat.

"Thanks. I think I have everything I was going to get for Josh. If I need help with anything else, I'll call your shop." As if I'd have the guts to do that.

"Yep, well, I guess I better get back to the shop." He stood there, and I had stopped making any pretense of working, so Jane stepped in and finished loading the dishwasher. "It was good seeing you again." Ten heartbeats later, Daniel tipped his head, turned, and walked out the door. A minute later my brain registered to get back to work. There was nothing in my will to wipe him from my mind.

* * *

Karley called me every other day the week before Christmas. "What's up? I love hearing from you, Karley, but c'mon, you're normally so busy with school and things, I'm the one trying to connect with you every week."

"I'm trying to finalize my plans between seeing you, Dad, and Ben."

"Isn't Ben coming up with you?" I asked, as I rolled out sugar cookie dough on a quiet afternoon. Karley explained he had to work, then went back to hammering out my schedule, as if it were now more important in her life than Ben. That should've been my second clue.

Two days before Christmas, Grace called me, asking what I was doing. "I'm getting ready to leave for a quick trip to the grocery store. Can I call you back?"

"What're you doing later on this afternoon?" She knew I had two weeks off school.

"I have the weekend off from The Pines, so I'm doing Christmas baking. What's up?"

"Well, if you aren't busy about four o'clock, could you swing by the Brainerd Airport to pick up me and my family?"

"Are you kidding me? You're flying to Minnesota?" I shouted into the phone.

"We're already in Minneapolis. We've got a layover here. Our estimated touchdown in your area is 4:10. Are you sure it's okay? I'm sorry to surprise you like this, but it's what I wanted it to be. Karley assured me you had the room, didn't have anything pressing in your schedule, yada, yada, yada..." Grace's hurried words were interrupted with her telling Hans to quit kissing Mira.

"Ah, so that explains Karley drilling me like a staff sergeant over my plans this week." Now it all made sense. After assuring Grace I'd be at the airport before four, I left for the store, mentally adding items to my grocery list as I thought of quick things to make for their visit.

Back home an hour later with more groceries than I'd bought since their visit last summer, I took out a couple of chickens, threw together a wild rice chicken bake to have ready for dinner, whipped together two pie crusts, and made chocolate cream pies, knowing Grace's children would love them. Okay, it was one of my favorites too, and now I had a good excuse to make it. I was going to have a full house for the holidays; it was the best Christmas present ever.

The Brainerd Airport was almost empty. I paced the small area as I waited for them to make their way through check in. "Auntie P, Auntie P!" Mira ran to greet me with a fierce hug while Gianna, cookie in hand, clung to my leg. And it was so good to see Grace in person again.

I stifled a laugh when Hans remarked how he couldn't wait to see Josh so they could play together. To him, their twelve-year age difference didn't seem to matter. How sad our children hadn't grown up together, both in ages and in geography.

The car ride back home was deafening and packed, yet I couldn't stop smiling. We weren't home for more than a half hour when Josh showed up unexpectedly. "Am I too late for supper?" he bellowed after stomping the snow off his boots.

I peered in the kitchen, waving him into the living room. "You'll never guess who's here!" I could feel my eyes shining with happiness.

"Um, let's see," he stalled as he lifted me up in a vice-like hug. "Could it be Aunt Grace and Uncle Garret and those rotten kids they keep at their house?" His smile was broad.

I pushed away from his chest. "You knew? You, Josh, were able to keep this a secret?"

"What? I'm not seven anymore, you know." He waved his rolled up sleeping bag in front of me; he was prepared to sleep on the floor. Whew.

I laughed, and kissed his stubbly cheek. "I know. The problem is poor Hans seems to forget you aren't, and he's counting on you playing games with him."

"Don't worry, we'll find stuff to do. I brought my old baseball card collection since Grace said he loves sports and playing cards. And I figure I'll show him how to play poker." He winked before I gave his shoulder a good punch.

If I had known Josh was showing up too, I'd have made three pies. Karley arrived early enough the next day to celebrate Christmas day with us. I glowed like an LED Christmas bulb. As far as my "family" went, the only people missing were my dad and step-mom. After our meal, we gave them a call and passed the phone around. It was as good as it could get for me, which was pretty darn amazing.

When Josh left, I walked him out to the car and slid in the passenger seat as he started the car to warm it up. "How's it going? I know the holidays are a hard time for people to not drink." No matter how hard I tried, I couldn't turn down my worry-meter.

He turned in his seat to face me. "I know you worry about me. Things are going well. I go to parties and behave myself. I'm fine." He rubbed his hands together to warm them up.

"I'm so proud of you. I knew you could quit." I reached over and hugged him hard.

Josh leaned in, and I held on tight. Life could be a struggle—no matter what your age.

The morning before Grace and her family were scheduled to fly back to Texas, Garret announced, "I'm taking the kids out for lunch and to a matinee. Give you two some alone time."

After a lazy, play-with-new-toys morning, four sloppy kisses from Gianna, and vice-like hugs from Mira and Hans, we watched them pull out of the driveway in my car.

Two seconds later, Grace blurted out, "You got some wine around here?"

"Geez, Grace, it's not even noon." I rolled my eyes. "Yes, did you want a glass already?"

"Yes, I do, and so do you. You might want to find yourself a nice extra-large wine glass."

I reached into the bottom shelf of my fridge door and took out a bottle of unopened Pinot Grigio. "This okay?" I waved the bottle in front of her face, which, upon close inspection, looked a little pinched. "Hey, are you all right?"

She grabbed the wine from me, rummaged through my utensil drawer for an opener, and sank into a kitchen chair. "I'll be fine in about ten minutes. You? I'm not so sure."

My senses were on high alert, as if someone were going to come at me with a hatchet. *This is your sister, not some mass-murderer who let himself into your house.*

I opened the cabinet to grab two wine glasses, probably not big enough according to Grace, before cautiously sitting across the table from her. "Okay, what's up?"

She didn't answer me, too busy uncorking the bottle like a pro and pouring a glassful for each of us, before gulping her wine down…not-so-much like a pro. When she set her empty glass back on the table and folded her hands in front of it, tears were sparkling in her eyes.

My suit of armor melted in fear. "Grace, you're making me nervous. What the hell is going on? We're drinking wine at 11:30 in the morning for god's sake."

Her eyes brimmed with pain as they bore into my soul. "I met Greg."

I performed a record-breaking intake of air. "Oh?"

"Is there something you want to tell me? Because my suspicions have been running like she-devils in my head since I met him." Grace leaned forward and clutched my hand. "Oh, P, am I right? And if I am, why didn't you tell me? I'd have understood!" Her face was pinched as if she'd start crying. Grace doesn't do crying.

Adrenaline begged me to jump out of my chair, grab her words out of the air, and shove them back in her mouth. If only I could bury my shame with them.

Chapter 22

Clutching the stem of my wine glass so hard I was afraid it would break, I drained the glass—a much better way to reduce tension. Grace refilled my glass, along with hers.

"I didn't know for sure until we met again on my trip to Texas last year." My head hung as I stared at my wine glass, as if I were confessing to it. "I hadn't seen Greg since that summer before he went in the seminary. When she was young, it was easy to bury any possibility Karley was his. I was married to Jerry. Greg was married to the priesthood."

I looked at Grace. "Where did you see him?"

"I was at a Thanksgiving program for the kids, and your friend Donna was there, watching her little nephew. We were visiting, she said how happy she was to see you last year...and then this good-looking dude came up to say hello to her."

Without realizing it, I'd downed my second glass of wine in the time it took Grace to say those few sentences. My overactive-mind imagined the scene, every detail right down to Grace's jaw no doubt dropping onto the polished school auditorium floor.

As the wine burned like incense in my throat, a calming wave took over my body. "What was it, his smile?" It had to be. That's what sealed it for me.

Grace squeezed my hand. "Yes, that unique grin with his slightly crooked eye teeth—and his goofy earlobe—both an exact replica of Karley's. I couldn't help but gawk, which, by the way, I'd have done anyway since he's so damn gorgeous. When Donna introduced him, and I realized he was your old boyfriend, it didn't take long for my brain to connect the dots." She shook her head. "I must have swooned. Donna grabbed ahold of me, asking if I was okay." Grace whispered, "She doesn't know, does she?"

I pushed my chair back, jumped up, and paced. "*Nobody knows*, including Greg!" Once his name passed my lips, I burst into tears, muffling them with my fists. "Oh Grace, I had no idea, I really didn't. Maybe it was my brain's way of dealing with my pregnancy. Honestly, I assumed it was Jerry's. If I'd have even allowed myself to think it could be Greg's, I'd have never moved to Minnesota, never have married Jerry." My words went unfinished between blubbering sobs as Grace came around the table and took me in her arms. Grief over my grave mistake coated me.

"It's okay, it's okay." Her soft sweater against my cheek and her hand rubbing my back were almost as calming as her Texas twang. I could imagine it was my mother talking, telling me from heaven that it was just a horrible mistake. So many things I'd done in those few months were mistakes, and it could've happened to anyone. I wondered for the hundredth time if my mom sensed what had happened, if it was why she asked me many times if I wouldn't just be better off staying in Texas.

As my sobs wound down, Grace asked, "Are you going to tell me what happened?"

I nodded. I swore it would be Karley I told first, if I ever told anyone, and Jerry second. "I need to get some Kleenex first." I grabbed the whole box from the bathroom while Grace refilled my glass.

Planted back in my kitchen chair, this time with Grace sitting next to me, holding my hand, I poured out my heart. "You knew Greg and I had broken up my sophomore year in college. Since you were only twelve, I was pretty sure you'd never remember what he looked like. I dove head first into a nobody-will-ever-love-me-again tailspin that spring and summer. Then I met Jerry at a pool party." I dabbed at my eyes. "It didn't take long for Jerry's and my relationship to get physical, something I normally wouldn't have done if I wasn't looking for reassurance I was loveable."

Although Grace knew it already, I wanted to remind her of what fueled me to act the way I did. "Then Greg came home that summer for a week. He'd been working out of town. We ran into each other at the grocery store, and although I was dating Jerry, Greg and I met for dinner that night. That's when he told me he was joining the seminary after college. I was shocked beyond words." I focused on Grace through my tears as she rubbed my back.

"My feelings for Greg were as strong as ever. We met each other for the next two nights until he went back to work. I think we both felt 'this is it, our last chance to be together.' When he left, I'm ashamed to say I went right back to sleeping with Jerry, as if it would help wipe Greg from my mind."

It had, in a sense, because when I found out I was pregnant ten weeks later, I never even thought it could be Greg's child.

"If his smile wouldn't have jolted my brain, the tiny extra lobe on the bottom of his ear would have done it," said Grace. "When Karley was born, didn't you think of that?"

I nodded. "Yes, but with mom being an only child and me having never met her parents, I told myself it probably came from her side of the family. Plus, I went to college with a girl who had a similar earlobe. I figured it wasn't that unusual."

"You never suspected anything over the years?" Grace eyed me over her wine glass.

"When Karley's eye teeth came in, my brain tried to alert me. She was about eleven, and her smile became more and more familiar. That, and the similar bump on her earlobe, should have knocked me over. But when the answer to your suspicion creates a whole new tragedy, it is easy to stifle."

A sob shuddered out of me. "Still, the possibility nagged at me enough that I couldn't wait to get braces on Karley's teeth, to mask what I couldn't change. That was around the time Jerry fell off the roof and was out of work for a year. Any thought of us splitting would've been financial disaster. It took us four years to recoup his construction company's lost income." I cringed inside, realizing how many decisions in life were based on money.

Grace leaned in and hugged me hard. "Oh, P, I can't imagine how hard it was for you!"

Mopping my eyes, I sat back. "It was easier to just do what was best for everyone—stay married to Jerry and squash any other options. There was no point in remembering how careless I'd been the summer I'd gotten pregnant with Karley. After Greg and I broke up the previous winter, I'd gone off the pill." I sighed. "It was a tough time for me emotionally, and then when Mom died, I couldn't even think about Karley's dad being anyone but Jerry. I couldn't think straight anyway. Plus, she had blonde hair like Jerry and me, not dark at all like Greg."

I closed my eyes. "I can still see the surprise and happiness on Jerry's face after Karley was born. When he held her, he kept repeating 'Wow, wow.' For someone who didn't want to be a father, didn't want to be with me…seeing that instant love on his face? It was enough for me."

"Are you ever going to tell Karley or Jerry? Or Greg?"

"I don't know. It's something I've struggled with ever since I saw Greg last year. I'll probably never tell Greg, why muddy that water? It won't change the fact that Jerry is Karley's dad, plain and simple. He's the one who raised her, the one who loves her. And she loves him. Yes, he drives me crazy, and I think he's been a self-centered husband, but he's her dad, whether it was his sperm or not."

We sat back in our chairs, our emotions squeezed out and hung to dry. After a minute, I asked, "What would you do if you were in my place?"

Grace drummed her fingers on her lips. "I'd wait. You'll know if and when the time is right." Her voice was quiet as we sat there engulfed in a pool of "what if's."

As sad as I was to drive Grace and her family to the airport the following day, I was also exhausted from a whirlwind week I hadn't expected. Not to mention the extreme emotional drain from my confession to Grace. I barely made it until seven before falling into bed that night, with Greg front and center in my mind. Again.

* * *

The next day was New Year's Eve, and I spent most of the day cleaning. At five, I got ready for Jane's. She and her husband threw a huge party every New Year's Eve, and Jane insisted I go and meet new people. I arrived at Jane's crowded party solo, something you couldn't have paid me to do a year earlier, or five years earlier, for that matter. My friends had been my safety net for years.

Michelle was there, and we spent the first hour mingling as she introduced me around. Michelle had spent all thirty-seven years of her life in the area, and being a loan officer at a bank in Brainerd, knew most of the townspeople. Jane's home was enormous, with a grand staircase leading up to a great-room consisting of pool tables to the side, a long mahogany wet bar, couches, an enormous stone fireplace, ceiling-tall windows overlooking a pond, and even waiters carrying around trays of appetizers and drinks. There had to be a hundred people or more.

As the night went on, I paced my wine intake while meeting people whose names I'd only heard in passing before. Then Michelle introduced me to a man who'd been facing the other way in the corner of the room, with a petite woman painted to his side. He was talking to another man who was making steady eye contact with Michelle.

"Hello, Isaac." Michelle's smile was warm for the man who'd been watching her.

"Hey, Michelle." He cut his conversation short with the couple whose backs were to us.

Realizing the interruption, the couple turned our way, and I fumbled my wine glass. Daniel! How could I not have recognized his build and hair from behind? Probably because I'd been at the party a couple hours and hadn't seen him. And would've never expected to find him here, much less with a leech hanging from his side. *Jane, Jane, Jane, why didn't you warn me?*

"Hello, Daniel." Michelle offered him a smile before her eyes focused again on Isaac. "Isaac, Daniel, I'd like you to meet my friend, Peyton." Her eyes took in the woman clinging to Daniel. From her reaction, I guessed she was one person Michelle didn't know.

Heat rose up my neck and covered my face. Daniel's expression stretched as if he were lying on a nail bed as he shook off the parasite hanging from his arm. The rest of them were clueless. He reached out and took my hand. "Nice to see you again, Peyton." Michelle's eyebrows rose in question. "Peyton and I work at the soup kitchen together once in a while," Daniel explained.

I didn't realize he was still holding my hand, and apparently, neither did Daniel. It wasn't until the dark-haired woman took her claw and pulled Daniel's hand back down to put it in hers without saying a word that the whole situation became even more uncomfortable.

Isaac rocked back and forth on his feet, a tight smile on his face as he exchanged a knowing look with Michelle. I interpreted it to mean, "can you believe Daniel is with this protective parasite?' I had no problem thinking nasty thoughts about this woman I didn't know.

"Ah, Michelle and Peyton, I'd like you to meet my friend, Deb Jamison." Daniel was trying to be genial, but in typical man-style, he said the wrong thing. Even *I* knew when you were dating a woman it was never a good thing to introduce her as your friend. The look Deb cast at Daniel could have burned metal. But he wasn't looking at her.

If I didn't know better, I would have guessed he was giving me a "Please, I can explain" look, which was crazy thinking on my part. He hadn't indicated any real interest in me. So far it only seemed to be Mallory pushing him my way. I was making up my own fantasies, or had more to drink than I thought.

Which would explain what happened an hour later.

After our uncomfortable scenario, I chose to down another glass of wine, which is never a good thing for me, a lightweight when it comes to drinking. Michelle and Isaac spent some time talking, while I entered a group conversation of women talking about their empty nests—a topic I could relate to. I was engrossed enough in the conversation to not notice Daniel, until he tapped me on the shoulder.

He leaned down to whisper in my ear. "Sorry to interrupt. Can I talk to you a minute?"

I don't even think I answered him. I excused myself from the women and followed him. He seemed to be searching the room, as if he were counting each person in there. He guided me into the hallway and down to a quiet, dark office.

"I've only got a minute, but I wanted to explain." His words rushed out in a loud whisper. "Deb is in the bathroom, and I know as soon as she gets out, she'll be circling like a vulture looking for me."

I laughed. What a perfect description of her. With my back up against the wall, Daniel had braced his arm above me, cutting me off from reality. And he was looking at me like he wanted to kiss me. I could all but taste the kiss.

His words rushed out. "Maybe you don't care, but I wanted to explain she is *not* my girlfriend. This is our first and last date. A friend of mine fixed us up, and I'll throttle him for it tomorrow. I didn't want you thinking I was dating someone, because I'm not. And I know you're still married because I asked Mallory, and she told me you're getting divorced, but it hasn't happened yet, and well, I wish I was here alone tonight so I could spend more time getting to know you." He took a breath and looked toward the door to see if anyone was coming.

"Man, this is ridiculous, I feel like a teenager worrying about being caught by his parents. I'm so angry I brought Deb here, and am probably overstepping my boundaries since you haven't said a word, and maybe don't care if I'm dating ten women." He'd boxed me in with his arms and now stepped away. He ran his hands through his hair. I was itching to do the same with my hands.

I should have, since what I did next was far worse. I took a step toward Daniel, never taking my eyes off him, and reached up to kiss him. *Just a quick peck on the lips,* my mind told my mouth. *Nothing more than a friendly early New Year's Eve kiss for a nice guy.*

My independent, long-ignored mouth wasn't listening to my brain. And, I swore I could hear Maggie whisper in my ear, *"Don't wait any longer to live your life!"* The green light went on for me. My initial contact with his mouth was brief. Brief enough for me to pull my head back from his, and see the surprise on his face in the shadows from the hallway light.

Honest to Pete, I can't even say it was the wine. I could blame it on hormones and the lack of sex for what seemed like a decade on my part. I liked this man, and remembering my friends, I made a judgment call I was going to live for the moment.

I pulled Daniel's collar toward me, stepped back toward the wall, and kissed him again, as if at any moment he would leave this Earth. We were twenty years younger in my mind, carefree, childless, and horny as hell. I'd morphed into some sex kitten, which was a joke since I sure didn't look like one. It didn't matter. The way he responded to me made me *feel* sexy. It was as if he'd been holding back, and I'd given him a free pass. He pressed me to the wall, kissing me with such intensity I expected the room to catch on fire. My hands cupped his face, experiencing each crease around his chocolate-brown eyes, the cleft in his chin, a day's growth of stubble, and the width of his neck below his soft shirt, as if I were reading his face in Braille.

What I really wanted to do was drag him over to the mahogany desk, swipe off its contents, and pull him on top of me. Someone had located my packed-away sex drive and hand delivered it to me tied up in a pretty bow. I was raring to make use of it.

Lucky for me, I was one glass short of that rash decision. I settled for sinking both hands into his thick, wavy hair, cementing his face with mine. If I only got one chance, I was going to make damn sure it was memorable—for me, anyway. Eventually my brain kicked my head, reminding me more than a few minutes had passed. A certain someone was likely circling the wagons for Daniel.

"As much as I hate to say this, you probably have someone looking for you out there."

He pulled his face back, as if I threw a glass of cold water on it. "Aw, hell! I forgot all about her." Daniel shook his head. "You must think I'm a real piece of work. Taking one woman here and then cornering you like Don Juan." He stepped back.

"I'm not, you know. I can't believe I kissed you like that. I'm so sorry. Well, I'm not sorry I kissed you; I'm sorry I'm stuck with Deb, and I don't want you to think badly of me." Daniel crammed his hands into his jean pockets and hung his head. "You can ask my mom or Mallory; I'm a nice guy." He looked like a little child waiting to be reprimanded.

I stepped to the side, a safe distance from him—for his sake—smoothed back my hair, and straightened my blouse, smiling. "Oh yes, I'll make sure and ask your mom if this is typical behavior for you." We both laughed, releasing the pent-up tension between us.

"You don't owe me an apology, Daniel. I kissed you first. And I want to tell you I've never acted like this, at least not since my teen years. I'd like to blame the wine, but you don't see me going around kissing other men, so I'm thinking that's not it. Anyway, let's both agree it was a New Year's Eve kiss, and leave it at that."

I didn't wait for him to answer. I picked up my half-full glass of wine from the desk, gave him what I hoped was a carefree smile, and walked down the hall to the closest bathroom, where I closed the door and leaned against it. *What in the hell had I just done?*

Chapter 23

Watching Tom Hanks' movies on New Year's Day afternoon, I remembered I'd done the same thing nearly a year ago right after Jerry had moved out. *You've Got Mail* played, and I watched Tom and Meg Ryan crossing paths over and over. Had I, at some point in my life, crossed paths with the man I should have married? Someone other than Greg, of course. Maybe I passed this man on a street, or sat next to him in a restaurant?

Even while thinking of all these possibilities, Daniel Monroe's face was blinking like a neon light in my mind. Had our paths crossed over the years? I kept thinking back to my actions the night before. I'd forgotten what it was like to feel such an attraction. Was I forcing myself to feel that way? I didn't think so, but it had been so many years since my heart hijacked my common sense, I second-guessed myself. Yet, if I was forcing myself, I'd have made it work with plastic-model Todd. Better yet, I'd have made sure things worked out with Bob—that would've been perfect. It was something else, like the to-my-toes feeling, this-could-be-right sensation I'd had with Greg years ago.

Hoping to divert my mind from Daniel, I decided the new year was a good day to open Dana's time capsules. It was time to cleanse myself from the old, and I felt strong enough to weather any possible secrets enclosed in her capsules. I couldn't imagine anything too exciting. She was too busy with her children, husband, and business to do anything too crazy.

I took her two capsules off my dresser and left mine sitting next to two hardcover books of Maggie's I'd borrowed last year. I guess they were my books now, Joe wouldn't want them.

After my dinner of an egg sandwich and a salad, I opened Dana's time capsule from 2001. Her first jar held a pregnancy test, which I'm assuming had shown positive at one time. I chuckled, trying to think of which child it would have been.

HILDA'S TREASURES ~ "JUNE 2, 2001" was printed at the top.
MY NOT-SO-SECRET-WISH—time to myself! I don't see it happening anytime soon with baby #3 on the way!
FANTASY DREAM—see above! ☺ *Or a long motorcycle trip with Colin Farrell*
MY LEAST FAVORITE FOOD—pizza in any shape or style, I'm SICK of it!
I WANT TO BUY—some new boobies that don't sag!!!
MY FANTASY JOB—be a CSI chick ☺

It was all so Dana-like, all the exclamation points and happy faces, ever the optimist.

I cracked open Dana's 2004 jar containing a handful of small items; Barbie shoes, a baseball card, marbles, and a pacifier. She had to have owned stock in those things. The other item was a copy of her quote from Edina Plastic Surgery on a boob job. I unfolded her paper.

HILDA, ROUND TWO -
I WANT TO—travel to Australia for a second (okay, first) honeymoon
WISH-IT-COULDA-BEEN DIFF.—my sister wasn't dying of cancer
DEEP DARK SECRET—when I kept having miscarriages I hated my body betraying me, and sort of blamed my hubby too, until we met with Dr. Phneu, ☺
HOPE FOR THE FUTURE—all my kids and my husband stay healthy. Boring, I know.
MY BIGGEST REGRET—Damn, I never wanted to address this, so I'm thankful I'm dead if any of you read this. Years ago, in a drunken stupor I had sex ONCE with one of my best friend's husbands, and I am SOOOO sorry and hate what I did. Regret doesn't begin to cover it.

The paper fell from my hands as if it had sent volts of electricity through my body. My brain couldn't grasp the words as I reread the last few sentences a dozen times, sure I'd missed a "ha ha, joke's on you" line in faded print. It wasn't there. Never in a million years would I have guessed this. Lauren's? In a sense, it wasn't a total surprise, knowing the painful stories of her upbringing. Even Maggie's. As shocking as her confession had been, once I had time to reflect, her years with Joe were so miserable. But this? Dana was more wholesome than apple pie.

An elephant crushed my heart. My nose hairs tingled as I closed my I-want-to-unread-that eyes. We all had said many times how we were like sisters—the women we would turn to for anything. How could she do this to Maggie? Yes, we all knew what a slime-ass Joe was, so it was no surprise Joe would have hit up Dana for sex. The big surprise was Dana giving in, drunk or not. I rarely saw Joe now, which was a good thing for him. I was positive I'd kick the shit out of his groin if I ever laid eyes on that scum-slime again.

I was well-aware it took two. I was distraught Dana could have done that to Bob and Maggie, and was sure it had to be many years ago before they became such close friends, especially since Dana seldom drank once she had children. It still didn't forgive her. She was married. I told myself there was more to the story than Dana could write, and it was all best left buried. Something I was already wishing I'd have done with her time capsule.

I was surprised to read the effect her miscarrying had on their marriage in the beginning and wondered if her cheating took place around those tough times in their marriage. After the doctor diagnosed Dana with an incompetent cervix, fixed with a surgical procedure, she had no problem carrying her babies full term.

Before those days, we all got together occasionally. For the most part, I was so busy with my own young children. Dana and Bob were trying to have kids and also get The Pines up and running. And I don't remember Dana ever bringing up those tough early years.

I shut my eyes to block out the headache forming. Emotional exhaustion took over. This was more than I could wrap my head around…my best friends had kept huge secrets for years, just as I was doing, making me wonder if we ever really know the people we love.

I called Grace before I went to bed, knowing I'd never sleep if I didn't share this weighty discovery with her. "That's disgusting!" Grace drawled. "You know how Joe gave me the willies the few times I met him. I can't believe he'd stoop so low as to fool around with his friend's wife."

"Joe has always screwed anything not bolted down," I reminded Grace.

For Dana's part, it was inconceivable to imagine her with Joe. And before I fell asleep, I thought of Bob. I sure wasn't going to give him Dana's time capsules as we'd talked about months ago. I kept going back to Dana's words. *Drunken sex.* For a number of years, Dana was pregnant or nursing and had precious little time between to drink. So, she'd carried this huge burden for years in private agony. She had to have told Bob, or she'd have never written it down for us, would she?

* * *

I called Lily the next evening. "Can I meet you sometime for coffee or something? Anything? I need to talk to someone, and I think you'd understand best."

"Sure thing, Peyton. How about dinner tomorrow night?"

We set a time and place, and I collected my thoughts. I couldn't confide in Mary Beth—she knew Dana. Lily had been so helpful in explaining why Maggie had kept her secret. I hoped she could help me again.

After our large bowls of wild rice soup, we nursed a couple of beers while enjoying the endless popcorn at Last Turn Saloon in downtown Brainerd. I'd peppered our meal with my relaying of Dana's confession in a nameless manner; Lily and I sipped our coffee as she dissected it all.

"I think you need to ask yourself what is bothering you the most. Number one, it's not the guy she cheated with since it sounds like you don't care for him at all. Number two, his wife, your best friend, already knew he was a major cheater, so I'm guessing that discovery isn't what's upsetting you." Lily took a sip of her decaf.

"I think it's a combination of things: You thought your friend was perfect, like you thought your other friends were, and it's a letdown to find out she did this one major wrong thing. Also, I'm sure you feel awful for her husband, who you said is a good friend to you. I think the fact this was another friend keeping a huge secret is what's weighing you down."

My brain ingested Lily's words. She was right; it was a combination of things eating away at me. I was upset all three of my friends had done things I'd have been shocked to hear about when they were alive, which is probably why I didn't. My secret was not the result of something I did on purpose. Everything they had done was a conscious decision.

"We're all capable of doing awful things; you know that from the Hell Club. You have to get past this, Peyton."

"I know. My sister has pointed out I struggle with forgiveness, for myself and everyone else." I leaned forward. "Thanks, as usual, for listening. I owe you one. More than one."

"Remember this when we tell our stories, okay, Peyton?" Lily shrugged into her coat.

"Lily, you're so sweet, I can't imagine you ever doing anything bad."

Her eyes were sad. "You thought the same thing about your friends."

I flinched at Lily's honest words as we left the restaurant.

* * *

I avoided the cemetery for over a week, until I could bring myself to "face" Dana. Stupid? Yes. I still had a long way to go in forgiveness. I needed to remember all the good in Dana—the friend I loved for so many reasons. When I climbed over my too-high expectations and made my way back to visit my friends, I apologized for my absence. I couldn't judge them any more than I could judge the women in the Hell Club, or myself. My job was to "care for the place setting in front of me," as my mom used to tell me. The weight of carrying a grudge hurt only me.

My holiday break from class was spent cleaning and boxing up the items neither Jerry nor I wanted for Goodwill and studying ahead on my classes. My class instructors wanted us to start focusing on graduation requirements and job searches. There were a number of internships out there, and the new clinic opening soon in Brainerd was looking for help in their accounting department. I thought of the difference now. I knew so many more people, new connections with job information. It never would have happened if I had continued to hole myself up in my house.

I also talked to Bob over the phone a couple times and was glad we weren't face-to-face, worried I'd give Dana's confession away. Eva needed a dress for their upcoming Sno-Daze dance, and I volunteered to take her shopping.

When I picked up Eva on Saturday morning, she was unusually quiet. My heart sank as I drove, figuring, "Here it is; she's too grown up to spend time with me." I didn't take it personally; she was older than Karley had been when she insisted I just drop her off at the mall.

So, I brought it up. "I suppose it would be a lot more fun for you if your dad let you shop with your girlfriends." I wanted her to know I wasn't upset. She watched the slush from our tires cast off into the graying snow piled alongside the road and pulled on her bangs as she looked out the window, a nervous habit of hers I'd noticed over the past year.

"No, that's not it. I'm glad you're taking me." Her voice was flat. I didn't need to be a therapist to figure out something was eating away at her.

I was going to have to pry it out of her. "So, what is it, Eva? Is it something you can't tell me? Something you need to talk to your dad about?"

"No!" she said, wide-eyed. Which told me it had something to do with her dad. I thought of what changed in their household the past couple months. Bob had recently begun dating a woman named Liz. Her husband had passed away, she had young children of her own, and the one time I met her, I thought she was nice. Bob had told me he'd talked to his children about dating Liz ahead of time. It sounded like she was rethinking her "That's fine, Dad" response.

"Is it Liz?" My voice was soft, understanding.

"I guess," she mumbled.

"Have you talked to your dad about this? You know he'd be honest with you. I was sure your dad said he sat down with all you kids."

"Yeah, he has. He asked us kids last month if we'd mind if he took her to The Pines Christmas Party, saying she was just a friend. She seemed nice enough, and Dad explained she's lonely too." She paused, picking away at a snag on her jeans. "He talks to her most nights now on the phone, laughing and being all goofy like a little kid. He's acting so immature!" As she burst into tears, I veered off to the side of the road.

"How about we shop in Brainerd instead?" Eva nodded as I fumbled around in my glove compartment for tissues.

"Good. Before we shop, let's go to Starbucks and get ourselves a chocolatey, whipped cream something or other. We can find a table in the corner and have us a good talk before we shop, okay?" I reached over and smoothed her hair away from her damp face.

She nodded again as her jaw quivered. A few minutes later, we arrived at Starbucks.

We sipped our spruced-up, double mocha cappuccinos and dissected her feelings. "I can understand your feelings about your dad dating. Honestly. I was in your shoes years ago. Granted, I was older and married, but I get where you're coming from. You probably think your dad must not have loved your mom very much if he can date someone else."

Her eyes searched my face as if I might be lying. "Here's the thing. It took my own dad finally explaining it to me. He had dated a number of women, most of them only a few times, as if he was trying on different outfits, determined to find one that fit perfect. Like the favorite outfit he'd had for years. My sister and I took it as a betrayal to our mom."

"He told us he wasn't dating other women because he didn't love our mom or miss her, but precisely because he did love and miss her." I watched her shred a napkin. "So, knowing your parents like I do, I am quite certain your dad is dating Liz for the very same reason."

She hashed over my words. "So, Dad is dating Liz because he misses Mom?" Her voice was high-pitched and she scrunched her nose.

"Yes," I answered. "I know it probably doesn't make sense to you, it didn't to me at first when my dad explained. Now I live alone, and I understand. Loneliness can eat away at you until you think you'll go crazy. Sure, your dad has you kids, but you all have your friends and your own interests, and when you go to bed at night, your dad is there, all alone. Shouldering the parental decisions alone and wondering if he's making the right choices, wishing your mom was there to offer her own wisdom."

"He cries sometimes at night." Her words were quiet.

"Still?" I had hoped being with Liz would lessen Bob's grieving and loneliness.

She shook her head, her brunette ponytail, swinging back and forth. "It's been a while now, probably a few months. At first, I was sad hearing him cry too, knowing he missed Mom like we did. When I didn't hear him cry, I realized I wasn't crying much anymore either. I guess I expected him to be okay, you know, not looking at other women."

"Maybe you think your dad doesn't need anyone but you kids right now, but you all won't be living there forever. Take it from me. It took a lot of bad things to happen to me to force me to put myself first, so I would be a happier person for others. Your dad needs to take care of himself, and deserves to have a life."

I reminded myself I deserved it too.

After my shopping trip with Eva, I thought about Jerry dating and maybe getting married again. What if she had children already, and he focused on them more than ours? What if she tried to "mother" my kids, or my future grandkids? The thought made my stomach queasy.

Never mind if I married again, the same thing could happen to Jerry. I excused it by telling myself he hadn't been as much a part of their lives as I had, so Jerry wouldn't care about another guy in their lives. Yes, it was skewed. It was the way my mind worked.

Chapter 24

I had to go back to class the next day, and my cupboards were bare. It was time for some serious big grocery store shopping, something more than the standards I'd been relying on for too long.

I drove to Cub Foods in Brainerd, walking down each aisle to scout for new ideas. My easy choices needed some adjusting. I took my time pushing my metal cart down each aisle, looking for healthy alternatives to my existing comfort foods.

When I hit the coffee and hot chocolate aisle, my eyes settled on the jars of Ovaltine. Dana had grown up drinking Ovaltine and had passed the virtues of vitamins in their chocolate milk down to her children. When I was at their house and Ovaltine was served as her kids' snack, she'd make me a glass. It was such a different taste from the Nestle Quik I was used to, I never changed over. With the orange and brown plastic container in hand, my mind wandered back to those good times with Dana and her kids, all with their chocolate mustaches and smiles.

I stared at the list of ingredients, not seeing them at all.

"Must be some interesting ingredients in there."

I jumped back and dropped the Ovaltine into my cart. Good thing the jar was plastic.

"I'm sorry; I didn't mean to scare you," Daniel said. "I didn't realize you were traveling on a different planet."

I watched him fight with a smile.

"Where were you?"

"Daydreaming, although I'm sure you've figured that out by now." My heart was skipping rope. And my brain reminded me in front of me stood the man I'd been thinking of way too often, the man I hadn't seen since New Year's Eve. And here I was, in scruffy jeans, a down jacket adding thirty pounds, and my hair pulled back like I was going to get a facial.

Rule number one, I scolded myself, if you ever hope to enter the dating market again, you can't go around town looking like you rolled out of bed. Or you can bet your meager life savings you'll run into Daniel, George Clooney, or Bradley Cooper. Even if the last two live states away.

We chatted for a few minutes about Mallory and Maren. "So, do you have time for a cup of coffee somewhere?" Daniel asked. "Or a drink or something?"

"Well it can't be a drink because we both know what happens when I'm drinking." *For Pete's sake! Could somebody please go to aisle twelve and buy some duct tape for my mouth?* This is when I needed my girlfriends, so they could slap their hands over my motor-mouth.

Daniel's eyebrows rose. "Well, I wasn't going to bring it up, but since you mentioned it, maybe we should stick to coffee. I don't want to risk you taking advantage of me again."

I was horrified, and I'm guessing my face showed it, because he chuckled and reached for my jaw to close my mouth. "Relax, I was kidding. Although, I've thought of our kiss every day since New Year's Eve. Let's drop this uncomfortable subject, or I know you will refuse to join me for coffee."

I wanted to deny it was me that night. He saved me from lying. "Please, Peyton, let's just go visit. I've thought of calling you, but I figured you'd be embarrassed and hang up on me. I think that great coffee shop, Mixed Company, is still open. Should we go there?"

I looked at him. Why did he look sexy when his hair wasn't combed? Why didn't men need makeup? And why could a flannel shirt and faded jeans look like he was meant to model them? How could he look so yummy just going to the grocery store? I reflected on how I likely looked and wondered how I could improve my looks between here and Mixed Company, just a few miles away.

In the car, I scanned my image in the rearview mirror while the car heated up. Nothing in the teeth—check, lipstick on—check, headband yanked out and hair fluffed up with comb—check, mascara smears under the eyes wiped away—check, mint in mouth—check.

We nursed our decaf coffees, so engrossed in exchanging bits and pieces of our lives—my going back to college, his raising Mallory without a mother, the stresses of his self-employment, my searching for a new job when school was over—we didn't notice the employees cleaning up, and every table empty but ours. Tucked in a private corner, we were oblivious to the now quiet coffee shop until the barista kindly came to tell us they were closing for the night.

Was this going to be a habit for us, staying in shops until they closed? We walked outside, talking in the sub-zero temps. "I better get home, let my dog out, and get my frozen groceries put away." Regret etched my words.

"Yes, I'm sorry I've kept you out here in the cold." Daniel turned serious after telling me a funny story about Mallory trying to suck cooked spaghetti noodles up her nose as a teen. "I'm not going to push you, but I'd like to meet again and visit, if that's okay." He picked up my gloved hand and held it between his bare hands.

"My divorce will be final soon, so I'm okay with dating." It had dragged on long enough. I wasn't passing this guy up.

As soon as the words were out, I cringed. "Oh boy, you said you wanted to get to know me better and I mention dating!" *You need to start carrying duct tape, Peyton, or keep your lips zipped.* I kicked snow with my old tennis shoe, concentrating on my foot so I didn't have to meet his eyes.

When I looked up, he was grinning. "Yes, that's exactly what I meant. We don't even have to call it a date. Can we meet once in a while to visit?"

"I'd like that." Daniel had mentioned he'd had no problem conning my phone number from Mallory, so right after he promised to give me a call soon, he leaned down, planted a whisper of a kiss on my cheek, and I inhaled the cold air coming off his whiskered face.

Driving home on tires so frozen they bounced me around, I congratulated myself for venturing out on such a cold night. I'd already run into Daniel shopping twice. Karma.

* * *

My attorney called at the end of January to let me know Jerry had turned in his spreadsheet on his company equipment to his attorney. Finally, another move forward. My relief was brief. "Jerry's figures look out of date to me. I can send you a copy, since you've done his books and taxes for years. You can compare it to what you've been booking for his equipment inventory and assets."

She scanned and e-mailed me the spreadsheet while we were on the phone. "Thanks. I'll look it over and get back to you soon."

It didn't take long for me to see the discrepancies Jerry had worked into his business' "worth." Even though I could have scanned or emailed my concerns back, I decided this was worth a face-to-face. I hopped in my car with my copies of the most recent records of Jerry's construction equipment and drove to Ann's office.

"How much do you want to push here, Peyton? I'll do what you want, but if you can sit down in a civilized manner and discuss the $50,000 discrepancy with Jerry, it'll save you paying me to step in."

I could only hope for civilized. "I'll call him. Thanks for bringing this to my attention." My half of the price discrepancy would make a big dent in my assets. I was not about to roll over and play dead.

I figured there was no time like the present to call Jerry.

"We need to discuss a few things about your business' net worth."

"We're in the middle of putting up a beam." I could hear his workers in the background.

"So, what do you want to do?" I was referring to our divorce discrepancies, not the beam. I had my own ideas of where he could put the beam.

"I'm not budging on my business figures."

"I'm not an idiot, Jerry. I know the history of your business and the assets. You might want to rethink the spreadsheet figures you gave your attorney."

"Don't threaten me." Jerry used his you're-being-ridiculous voice.

"It's not a threat. I have the facts." I wasn't backing down. Not anymore. Click.

Grrrrr. Fine, I could wait. At some point, we'd have to sit down together and be adults. Apparently not today.

* * *

My old San Antonio heartthrob, George Strait, was coming to the Twin Cities, and I put the event idea out to other club members. He was a piece of my past, back to the days when he'd play at Gruene Hall in New Braunfels, and my friends and I would drive the forty miles to go see him.

A few days before the event, I spoke with Mary Beth. April, a club member and close friend of Josie's, had been admitted for a heroin overdose. Mary Beth had asked me in December, when I'd been a member for a year, if I was ready to be added to the club's "care list."

I was happy to be included, knowing at any time any one of us could be on the care list. Needless to say, Josie wouldn't be going to the concert with us now. In my swimming time spent with Josie, she talked often about how proud she was of April's ability to kick her heroin habit from years ago. April had a young daughter, and I guessed that's where we'd be stepping in to help.

I checked my email an hour later, and there it was. April's mom would be caring for her three-year-old granddaughter, working full-time herself while her husband was recovering from cancer. She'd be looking for volunteers to take April's daughter to and from daycare and help with meals. This was my first "care" opportunity, a way to give back to the Hell Club.

I was already thinking of what I could make for their meals. An opportunity to help a child? Sign me up.

* * *

We had enough club members sign up for the George Strait concert that we were able to rent a bus. I fought to control my like-a-teenager excitement as we made the two-hour drive.

"I don't even like country music," Abby confessed in the seat behind me.

"Blasphemy! How can you say that on the way to a George Strait concert?" I joked.

"Cuz I looked him up online and for an old dude, he's pretty cute." Abby winked. "Plus, you've built him up so much; I expect gold to come out of his mouth when he sings."

I sat next to Yvette, her wheelchair tucked in the back of the bus, and we spoke about music on the way to the concert. And her car accident—which I still knew little about.

"The night of my accident, my husband and I were supposed to go out to a local pub where a band we loved was playing for the night and have dinner for our eighth anniversary." Yvette stated as her hazel eyes studied mine. "I had my two young sons in the back seat. It was pouring rain. My husband, Andy, and I were so excited to have a friend take our kids for the night, we wouldn't have cared if it was a blizzard out."

I forgot to breathe, my body tensing up for an ending I already knew. "Andy was running late from work, I offered to drop the boys off, and he'd be cleaned up and ready to go when I got back home. My friend lived six miles from our home." I reached for her hand. Yvette might appear calm, but reliving her accident couldn't be easy.

"A man in an old pickup had faulty brakes and didn't stop fast enough at a stoplight, driving right into the back of my car—where my boys were." I squeezed her hand.

Yvette dabbed at her eyes. "Both of my sons died instantly. I was in intensive care for three weeks, and my poor husband was barely hanging on emotionally." She paused. "I'm telling you this for a reason, Peyton. I've heard you talk of your struggles, and of the secrets you've discovered about those you love.

I'm here to tell you I'd have killed myself after the accident, if my husband wouldn't have stepped in. He still loved me and didn't blame me for the accident. The problem was, I couldn't love myself or forgive myself. It took years."

From the beginning, I knew there were worse things than losing your friends. Losing children was the worst. I hugged Yvette to me, breathing in the cinnamon gum she'd been chewing, feeling the softness of her knit top. "How did you get through it?" I asked into her wavy hair.

"I sunk to the deepest depression you can. And it wasn't until Andy gave me an ultimatum. Start living, or he was leaving. That was two years after the accident."

"Whenever I tell my story to a new club member, I see a bit of the old me in them. The part of me holding on to the past, the guilt, perceived wrongs they couldn't right...and I hope that in telling my story, I'll inspire people to stop dredging shit up and instead, clean it up."

We talked for the next hour, and I moved Yvette to the top of my ever-growing list of amazing women I'd met through the Hell Club.

Once inside the Xcel Energy Center, all sixty-two of us—members from area towns who'd joined the Hell Club over the past decade or so—settled in our pretty-darn-good seats. I was like an animated wind-up doll amped up on an energy drink as I chatted with every woman around me. For the next few hours I became one with the stage...feeling and remembering when George played his early hits, the ones popular when I lived in Texas, the ones coating my memory banks with sugar.

I'd always been a music junkie. How had I never dated a musician?

On our late-night bus ride home, we belted out some of George's hits. Some, like Abby, butchering the words to songs she hadn't heard before tonight. Our energy made up for our word errors. And when Yvette started singing "Amarillo by Morning" next to me, I took a minute before chiming in. Enough time to swallow the ball of painful memories lodged in my throat.

* * *

I was busy cleaning up tables near closing time at The Pines when Bob asked if we could talk a minute. "I want to thank you again for spending time with Eva. I've seen a real improvement in her attitude toward Liz and me, thanks to your talk with Eva."

"So, she told you? Well, I'm glad I could help." I continued clearing off the tables. "Sometimes I think kids assume parents are invincible and can get through anything, that nothing affects us much."

"Well, I'm bringing this up for a reason, and I'm telling you right now, please feel free to say no to me. You've done so much already, and I know you've got a busy schedule."

"And…?"

"I'd like to take Liz out to dinner for Valentine's Day next week. There is a dance at school Eva wants to go to, and Nash has a basketball game that night. My back-up babysitters are all going to the dance too. Would you be willing to come over about five and watch Finley and Channy for a few hours?" Bob's smile was charming.

"I'd love to."

He helped me carry the dirty dishes back to the kitchen, and I thought of our chemistry. Too bad ours was only the friendship kind—there was nothing to dislike about Bob.

On Valentine's Day, Daniel and I met at The Barn, the best homemade pie place in the Brainerd Lakes area. I sat across from him at a small red-checkered tablecloth table in the quaint cafe and was certain I was heading down Smitten Street. I'd have met Daniel at McDonald's. I didn't care what we ate or where.

He ordered banana cream pie. I went with the French silk. He wore a navy-blue Henley shirt with his sleeves pushed up. I wore a besotted smile.

"You're in an exceptionally good mood today." He said, as he poured creamer in his coffee.

"How can I not be? The sun is shining—a rarity in February—and I get to eat yummy dessert with you." I may have had candy hearts floating out of my eyes.

He grinned. "Well then, how do you feel about going ice fishing with me sometime soon? I've got a portable fish house we can take out if the weather is bad. Next week looks cold again. Maybe the following week? I'd like to get out before the lakes get slushy."

"Sounds great! I haven't ice fished in years. Can we go on a Wednesday or Friday? I don't have class those days." *I'd sit in an outhouse with you if that's what it took to spend time with you.*

"Just about any weekday works for me. I'll keep an eye on the weather and see if we can get out there by early March." His dark eyes studied my face, and I wondered if I had whipped cream on it. But it was my lips he was focusing on. He grinned, pushed back his chair, leaned forward, and kissed me briefly. It was long enough to ignite an electric charge from my hair down to my toenails.

I struggled to focus on our conversation, which veered from fishing, to his sporting goods rental business, to my upcoming college graduation. And I didn't want our afternoon to end.

But I had a date with Bob's children.

Chapter 25

I was greeted at Bob's by a pigtailed Channy, who I swore grew six inches in the past few months.

"Hullow, Peyton. Can we play cards?" Energetic Finley, wearing a pink tutu and purple sparkle shirt, tugged at my shirt. Bob and I laughed at her greeting.

"Of course we can." Finley pulled on one of my hands, with Channy on the other, leading me toward their kitchen table. Spaghetti and garlic toast permeated the air.

"Dinner's ready whenever you all want to eat." Bob waved toward the stove.

We talked a few minutes before he left for his date with Liz. I thought back to the brief kiss between Bob and me last summer. If we'd have both felt a spark, it could've been me who Eva and Nash were trying to keep out of their lives. Funny, how things could go one way, or another. You just never knew what the future held.

It wasn't until later when we were all in the bathroom upstairs, brushing their teeth and getting ready for bed, that something made me do a double-take. There was an old cross-stitch saying framed on the bathroom wall. Although I'd been in Dana's home thousands of times over the years, they had a main bathroom off the living room we usually used. This one was off the master bedroom, which the two younger children apparently shared with their dad.

The cross-stitch was framed in thick, dark wood. *To my Valentine, 2-14-02: You have given me so much, more than a FAMILY, I treasure what I've shared with you ~*

Forgiveness ~ Adventure ~ Mozzarella ~ Independence ~ Laughter ~ Yearning

I read and re-read Dana's message to Bob. *Forgiveness?* Did Bob know? Probably. They had too good of a marriage for Dana to keep it from him all these years. Everything she stitched rang true in what I'd experienced watching their marriage: solid, giving, both appreciative and respectful. There were so many adjectives I could have added to describe what they had. And I wondered—would I ever have a relationship like theirs? A relationship where you were best friends?

One sprinkled with humor and teamwork? Would it be possible with Daniel? And did I have it in me to contribute to that sort of a relationship? I definitely hadn't with Jerry. What made me think I could get it right with someone else?

* * *

Daniel and I scheduled our fishing date for March fourth. "If it's okay, I'll pick you up at seven. Fishing is better in the morning. I'll bring my portable ice shelter in case the wind picks up, but it looks like it will be sunny and no breeze, so we shouldn't need it." I had never done much ice fishing; fishing was something I enjoyed more in the summer. When our children were young, Maggie and I would take them fishing for crappies along the banks of Eagle Lake in the spring. I missed those days.

A relaxing day on the lake with Daniel would help take my mind off another recent head-to-head with Jerry over our finances and his business assets. I wondered if our divorce would ever be final at the rate we were going. I'm sure he kept waiting for me to back down. He'd have a long wait.

The ice was getting slushy, and although still safe, Daniel and I decided to park at the lake access and drive out on the lake using his four-wheeler. We unloaded his wheeler from the back of his truck along with a sled he used for pulling his portable ice shelter and fishing equipment. It took a bit of drilling holes with his ice auger and testing the fishing to find a good spot where the perch and crappies were biting. The sun shone down on us by mid-morning while Daniel and I sat on overturned five gallon buckets, jigging our lines. With a mild, cool breeze and most of the small lake to ourselves, you could hear a dog bark a mile away.

"Is all of this fishing equipment from your store?"

"Yep. I carry fishing supplies for both winter and summer, and pretty much every sporting goods item for boating and hunting. I got out of the bait business years ago and instead added a rental section for big items like kayaks."

"It sounds like a great sports shop."

"I like it. It works for me, and it was a great place to raise Mallory, with our home nearby. From the time she was about six, she helped me out in the store. It's been a good bonding experience for us over the years. I'd like to think it helped shape her to be the outgoing woman she is today." Daniel beamed with pride.

"You have reason to be proud. She is a sweet young woman, with an enchanting personality." Jerry had interacted with our children on a one-on-one basis over the years, but by no stretch of the imagination could I see him in a day-to-day full-blown father mode.

I sighed as I watched the steam from my coffee hang in the sun rays. My blood pressure had to be at an all-time low. "This is so relaxing."

"Yep, it's when I do my best thinking. It makes up for the rest of life getting too hectic sometimes. Mallory and I got into fishing when she was little, after Jackie left."

His choice of words on the few times he mentioned Mallory's mom had me confused. I had to get this clarified. "Daniel, when you say 'left,' do you mean Jackie left you? I was under the impression from Mallory that Jackie passed away years ago."

He shook his head. "Nope, as far as I know, she's very much alive. She went out to California with a few girlfriends years ago; a trip I have to say she sorely needed. I was never home; she was. She never came back." His expression was matter-of-fact. "Jackie's leaving forced me to stop the crazy-corporate-ladder-climbing. I avoided a stress heart attack and became a better parent to Mallory."

"Mallory makes it sound like she doesn't remember Jackie at all." I was busy digesting the fact he was divorced and not a widower.

"She was three when Jackie left. Most of what she remembers is from photos I kept of Jackie with Mallory. Those first few years, I kept expecting Jackie to show up unannounced. Just like when she left, especially when Mallory's birthday or holidays rolled around. You know, like a normal mom would have?" He scratched his chin.

"I'm sorry, Daniel. For both you and Mallory. It must have been tough."

"When Mallory was around seven, Jackie contacted me. She had a new life in California and felt we were better off without her. We got a divorce via mail. It gave Mallory and me closure, which was about all I could ask for at that point."

There was so much about this man I wanted to know. "What else do you do for fun?" We'd talked about his business, our families, but little about his interests outside of sports.

"Well, I enjoy the band. I mean, sure, its work, but it's a fun kind of work. My dream job, I guess you could call it."

Huh? "What band?"

"Our band, The Bobbers. I play the guitar and sing. We've been together about a decade now and stick to playing area bars and nightclubs so we don't have to travel overnight."

A faint memory clicked in my brain. "Do you ever play at the Wooden Wheel?"

"Yep, why? Have you heard us play before? I didn't figure you made it out to bars much over the years, from what you've told me."

I now vividly remembered my one date with Todd, and how I enjoyed the band, just not dancing with him. I replayed the band up on stage, and realized it was why Daniel looked familiar when I met him a couple weeks later. No need to mention my disastrous date.

"I think I did hear you playing there last fall. It was right before I met you, and I think that's why you looked familiar to me when we met."

We went on to talk about music for a while, a love of mine even though I could barely sing the ABC's without torturing every dog in the neighborhood. When we'd caught our limit of crappies along with a few perch, we loaded up our things and reluctantly headed for home.

"Thanks! I had fun today." He was parked in my driveway while I gathered my things from the seat between us.

"I'm glad you went so we could catch twice as many fish." He teased as he reached over and chucked me lightly on the chin.

The truck was quiet while we smiled like idiots at each other. I couldn't help myself, I laughed.

"What?" Daniel's eyebrows rose.

"I can't believe you like me. I mean, have you looked at yourself in a mirror?" Michelle had known him for years. Why hadn't they dated?

He tipped his head to the side, studying me. "You're kidding, right? Do you know how many kooks are out there? Take Deb, the gal I was with at Jane's party, for instance. Most women are either too young, too old, too much of a gold-digger, too boring, you name it. Most women would never have ordered pie when we met for pie on Valentine's Day."

"They wouldn't have? At The Barn, the best-ever pie place? Was I supposed to just have coffee?"

"No, I *want* you to order pie when we go out for pie. You're a breath of fresh air."

Me? Didn't he mean neurotic, over-analyzing air? "What about Michelle? She's perfectly normal." *What is wrong with you, Peyton? You sound like you're trying to get rid of him.*

"Are you trying to fix me up with Michelle? Because, although she's nice, I'm pretty sure she's got eyes for Isaac, and I've never felt a spark with her." He held my hand. "With you, however, I do feel a spark. Maybe it's your sense of humor, or your tenacity to start a new life, your intense love for your kids, or that nice rear of yours."

"My flutter kicks in swimming are paying off?" I grinned.

"Yep, they're doing a great job." He took my hand and kissed it. "Now, back to these fish. I was thinking, maybe you could come over this Sunday, and I'd do a fish fry for us and invite my mom too. You'd be well-buffered between my daughter and mom, so I couldn't ravage you." He wiggled his eyebrows like there were evil thoughts traipsing through his mind. Maybe there were. They were front and center in my mind.

"The fish is okay for a few days?"

"Yep, I'll clean them and they'll be in ice water until we cook them. I'd have suggested Saturday but my band is playing at a fundraising event out of town. How about five on Sunday?"

"Sure. I'll bring a salad and dessert."

"I don't care if you bring anything…as long as you show up." He leaned over and kissed me with such a passion, I couldn't have recited my own name. Too soon for me, Daniel pulled back, his eyes intent on my face. He turned away, opened his door, and came around to open mine.

I don't think either of us said anything else before I walked dazed into my house. What was there to say? Thank you for turning me on? I hadn't been in the dating scene for decades, but I was fairly certain it wasn't an appropriate way to say goodbye.

* * *

Excited nervousness drummed through me as I drove to Daniel's on Sunday. This would be different dynamics than when we all worked the soup kitchen. I was Daniel's "date" in a sense, and although I figured Mallory was happy, since she's the one who had tried to get us together, I wasn't sure how Maude felt about it. I had to trust things would work out.

Daniel met me as I pulled into his long, tarred driveway shadowed by tall white pines. "My mom isn't here yet, and Mallory is napping with Maren."

He reached in to take the black forest cake I'd made. I handed it to him before turning to grab the pan holding a seven-layer salad.

Holding my hand, Daniel led the way to his one-story, log-sided rambler. We went through the entryway, which opened into a large cathedral ceiling kitchen with a small breakfast nook off to the side. Everything was trimmed in oak and spotless. Either he was a neat-freak or Mallory was.

It whispered *Country Living* magazine spread. I loved it. "Did you say you built this place?" I was impressed.

"Yep. I bought the property, got the store up and running, and Mallory and I moved from our old house I sold into an apartment while I built this. It's nice being this close to work, yet we have privacy back here."

He led the way down the hall, showing me the bedroom Mallory and Maren shared, a sleeping Mallory spooned her baby on her bed alongside an empty walnut stained crib. Next was his office, the first room I noticed with any clutter, and across the hall, his master bedroom. Looking at his king-sized bed covered in a cushy comforter decorated with deer and moose, my heart danced a little jig envisioning Daniel lying there, his hair all tussled, nothing on but his sexy smile and a sheet draped over him. My cheeks were warm, and I hoped Daniel had no idea of the visual playing in my head.

Thank goodness Maude arrived at that moment, and we heard her moving around in the kitchen. He led the way back, where I was greeted by Maude.

"Hello, Peyton. What do you think of the place?"

"It's beautiful. You have a very talented son."

"I have three very talented sons. The other two live out of state, so guess who is the golden boy?" She leaned forward and kissed Daniel's cheek.

I had witnessed before how Maude put Daniel on a pedestal. And I was a little worried she'd think Daniel being with me would tarnish him.

Mallory appeared with a still-sleepy Maren. "Hey, Peyton, thanks for helping Dad catch my favorite meal."

I planted a kiss on Maren's forehead, inhaling the fresh scent of baby lotion, before helping Maude in the kitchen. As Daniel fried the last batch of fish, we set the table.

"This fish is fantastic," Mallory exclaimed after we'd all sat down to eat.

"Must be one of the crappies I caught." Daniel winked at me.

"Daniel's so busy; I'm surprised he had time to take you fishing," Maude said.

I looked at Daniel and he raised one eyebrow. "Yes, I'm lucky it worked out."

"With his business open seven days a week, helping me with my house repairs, and now being here for Mallory…I don't know how he has time to date."

I stopped eating and looked at Maude. She'd known me for a year now. Was she insinuating Daniel shouldn't waste his time on me? As much as I'd have liked to ask her, I didn't want to ruin our meal. It couldn't be because I was getting a divorce; Daniel was divorced. And there was no way she knew about Karley's birth father. What was wrong with *me*?

Mallory tried to switch subjects. "Did I tell you how well Maren is sleeping at night?"

"Wow, how great!" I jumped on board. "It helps get you through anything if you get some rest at night."

"Of course, Daniel is busy helping Mallory when he can, so she gets a break."

I wasn't sure if Maude was trying to sell me on Daniel or tell me he was too busy for me.

"I don't help her as much as I should, Mom."

"Because you don't have the time. That's what I'm saying here, how will you ever find time to date Peyton?"

"Grandma!" Mallory admonished Maude between bites of fish.

Daniel put his fork down and folded his hands. "What's going on here? You like Peyton. You've been singing her praises to me, just like Mallory has, for the past year. Why are you trying to put a wedge between us?" His words were slow and controlled.

Maude, normally a laugh a minute, looked grim. "Because if you toss her aside after a bit like you've done with all the other women these past twenty years"—Maude's voice was firm—"and break her heart, I'm coming after you, Daniel Charles Monroe." She slapped her hand on the table and everyone's silverware jumped. Maren flailed her arms, startled in her infant seat.

I was busy staring at Maude, surprised at her outburst; I didn't notice Daniel get up from across the table. He walked around and stood behind his mom, massaging her sturdy shoulders.

"Mom, don't worry. Peyton and I have this, okay?"

Maude now busied herself with her napkin. "I don't want Peyton hurt, and I need her at the soup kitchen. If you tick her off, she might tell me to go piss off."

Mallory and Daniel laughed, and I smiled in relief. Maude wasn't trying to oust me after all, but I couldn't quiet the tiny voice in my head. What made me think I was any different than the other women Daniel apparently had worked his way through over the years?

Chapter 26

The following weekend was the St. Patrick's Day parade and celebration in Crosslake, a town about twenty minutes away. A handful of us from the Hell Club had decided to get together and make a day out of the events. The local bars would have bands playing on Saturday night, and I wished Daniel's band would have been playing at one of them instead of at a wedding dance. As it turned out, it was a good thing he wasn't around.

We unloaded our folding chairs at the curb along the parade route. There wasn't a spot of Irish blood in me, but it didn't stop me from wearing a green t-shirt and green beer stein hat. It was hot out for March in Minnesota—forty degrees warmer than normal. Instead of being hunched against the cold wind in our parkas, we were basking up the sun in our shorts and t-shirts.

After the parade, the town buzzed with other activities. We made our way to Riverside Supper Club, where a bocce ball tournament was taking place on the quickly-thawing grass. Normally ice golf was an event on the frozen Whitefish chain of lakes, but with the warm temperatures, they'd changed plans so people weren't standing in six inches of cold water above the ice.

After bocce ball, we walked to Crosslake Town Square, where they held an egg tossing contest. Mary Beth and I were partners. After missing my too-high egg toss, she was given a lime green "My Sham Rocks" t-shirt to replace her egg-smeared shirt. It was a day full of sunshine, laughter, blarney burgers, blinky buttons, and green beer.

At dusk, we stopped at the Whitefish Lodge where some of the women were spending the night. A band was playing at Moonlite Bay, a restaurant overlooking the Whitefish chain of lakes, and we cleaned up before heading there. Mary Beth and I were driving home that night, thanks to our dogs.

If I had a fairy godmother, *then* would have been a good time for her to tap me on the shoulder, wave her wand, and say, "Oh dearie, perhaps you should skip the dance and just take the next pumpkin coach home now along with your happy memories of the day." No fairy godmother appeared.

We drove three vehicles the few miles to Moonlite Bay, where a rowdy crowd had already formed. We put a couple empty tables together in the corner. Tables and chairs were pushed back for the dance floor, and lights were dimmed for dancing. The rock band tuned up, and before long, enormous speakers pulsated rock songs through our central nervous system. The dance floor filled up, and I was content to watch, unable to visit above the noise. I was engrossed in a group of young women hopping around the dance floor. Until my eyes caught sight of a familiar face in the semi-darkness.

There he was, thrusting and prancing with a young woman who appeared to have drunk her fair share of green beer. A three-alarm-voltage performed a jump-start to my brain.

I'd like to say I don't know what got into me, but honestly, I did know. I'd been building up anger and hatred for years toward the man who made my best friend's life miserable. He was still alive and having the time of his life. And she wasn't. The topping on that anger-ball was what had happened between him and Dana. As if someone shoved a firecracker up my rear, I catapulted out of my seat like a rocket across the dance floor, focused on my target—Joe—Maggie's heartless husband.

"You! You piece of shit!" *Ooh, listen to me!* Somebody had uncorked my bottle of whoop-ass, and the fetid thoughts I'd been nourishing about Joe for years spilled out.

I pushed him so hard he stumbled backward into other clueless dancers who should have been paying attention and gotten out of my way. The look of surprise on Joe's slimy, fake-tanned face energized me. His dark hair, as jet black as ever thanks, no doubt, to Mr. Grecian Formula.

"What the hell are you doing, Peyton?" I think he was surprised to see me out in public, back in the mainstream of life. I'm sure the last he'd heard, I was still neck-deep in depression.

"I know about you, I know what you did!" By this time, Michelle and Mary Beth were beside me, trying to pull me away from this man they didn't know.

"Hey, hey, hey!" Joe's hands were in front of his face in defense, seeing as how I was trying to claw his cheating eyes out. I changed my plans and kneed him in the groin. As he toppled over, his friends, none of whom I recognized, came up to drag him away from me.

"C'mon, let's go sit down." Mary Beth led me by the elbow, talking with her let's-be-reasonable voice in my ear. But I had unfinished business. I didn't know when I'd get another opportunity to go head to head with Joe, who I hadn't seen since Maggie's funeral.

"No!" I shouted above the band, who continued on. "I'm not leaving until he tells me how sorry he is for ruining my friend's life. Scratch that, ruining, two of my friend's lives."

Joe slowly pushed himself back on his feet, although I was happy to see him leaning to the right. No doubt his privates were pleading for ice. "I don't know what the hell you're talking about. Jerry's right; you *are* crazy!"

Well there was a whole different fight I could have had with him, but I wanted to focus on the mission at hand. "You know what I'm talking about; years ago, when you screwed around with Dana. Of course, she was one in a long line of many for you!"

His eyes grew wide when it registered what I was talking about, although his mind had to have been smoking to rifle through his years of cheating and remember he'd been with Dana.

Hesitating for a second, he sneered, "She was asking for it."

I don't know what I expected Joe to say, I was hoping he'd deny it, although I certainly wouldn't have believed him. But this? I couldn't stand him accusing Dana of coming on to him.

Fortified by the B52 shot I'd enjoyed earlier at the bar, I lunged forward, slapping him so hard across the face my hand stung. "You liar!" I screamed, and things went downhill from there. Our friends separated us, but Joe's cutting words stayed with me.

"Fine. It wasn't me, you bitch. Maybe you should save a slap for your husband." His lip curled with each enunciated word. He didn't have to shout. We were now away from the band and crowd.

I quit squirming. "What did you say?" My voice was low, the words tasting like grit as I spit them out. Michelle and Mary Beth still had my arms, and likely didn't believe for an instant the calmness in my voice was real. I'm sure they heard every word Joe said.

"You heard me. Go ask Jerry. I'm sure he remembers the night well."

My mouth was dry, aching for a beer or something to wash down my shock. Joe laughed, knowing he had my attention. "I still remember the night; they were both so fall-over drunk, they had to hold each other up, but hey, when there's a will, there's a way. You'd have been proud of Jerry." He described their stumbling into the pole barn together, giving me way more details than I needed.

The sneer on his face told me Joe was well aware of the effect his words were having on me.

You don't realize how crazy you can get, if all the right buttons inside you are pushed. But it can happen. And it was happening to me. Mary Beth and Michelle pulled me against my will into the restroom, where they attempted to calm me down.

My mind swirled like a tornado, spinning anger, remorse, and shock around. Mary Beth handed me a wet paper towel and I dabbed my neck. Where was Lauren when I needed her? She'd have fixed Joe so he'd never walk again.

My knees nearly buckled, all fight drained away. "I'm sorry; I can't believe I let him get to me like this." I apologized over and over.

"Think nothing of it. The only thing that kept me from letting you slap the living shit out of him was the fact you might get arrested for it." Michelle piped up, and after my surprise of hearing Michelle talk tough, a laugh bubbled out. I couldn't stop it, becoming knee-slapping hysterical at the hilarity of it all. My husband, who I'd married to give my daughter the good family life I'd had, had cheated on me long before I ever entertained the idea Karley might not be his child.

What a train wreck we were. We should've never gotten married...for so many reasons. And where had my head been when Jerry and Dana betrayed Bob and me? What else had gone on while I'd lived in my cocoon world?

Michelle, the edge now out of her voice, asked, "Do you think he was trying to get your goat? You know, maybe he was lying..."

I shook my head no. Joe had described the old pole barn of a guy who used to throw huge parties years ago, before he moved out of town. I'd come across group pictures of those parties not long ago. Joe had too many details; my gut told me he was involved somehow.

"Oh Peyton, I'm sorry," Michelle said.

"I'm sorry too, sorry that we ever got married. Jerry didn't want it any more than I did." I was ready to go curl up in my bed and ignore life. It was 9:18, and I'd ridden with Mary Beth.

I didn't even have to ask her. "I'm taking you home, Peyton." Mary Beth put her arm around both me and Michelle, encompassing us in a group hug as warm and comforting as the ones I'd imagined over the months from my friends at the cemetery.

Michelle went out to the bar ahead of us to be on the lookout; as if at any moment, Joe might have escaped his friends, waiting to pounce on me. She waved us out of the bathroom, our shoes clicking a muffled beat on the wide planked hardwood floor as we headed back to our table. As if someone blew a whistle like Christopher Plummer in *The Sound of Music*, the rest of the women stood and we filed out in marching order into the still-warm night, amidst endless hoots and hollers hanging in the night air from the many people out celebrating in the streets.

"You can all stay. Don't let me wreck your fun." I didn't want to put a damper on their party.

"Naw, we're good. We're going to go check out some of the other bars with bands." Josie said. Most of the women were in their twenties and thirties. They'd make a night of it. For me, I was glad I hadn't booked a room at the Whitefish Lodge, although at the moment, I'd have liked nothing better than to curl up in front of the enormous fireplace in their gathering room and sleep away my sorrow. My mood would have been a real fun-extinguisher.

Mary Beth and I walked to her car. Once inside, I leaned my head back and shut my eyes. I had no problem envisioning what Joe had described. Was it worth asking Jerry about now?

"Now what?" I asked myself and Mary Beth. She didn't answer. I opened my eyes.

"Mary Beth? Are you okay?" She was sitting behind the wheel, staring ahead.

Of course, Mary Beth knew Dana through church, and now heard a different side of Dana she also never expected to hear. "This must come as a bit of a shock to you too."

"I can't believe it. I can't begin to imagine your surprise."

I leaned my head back against the head rest and closed my eyes. "I have to remember, Dana and I barely knew each other when we'd go to the parties at the pole barn." And although I might convince Mary Beth it was long ago and didn't affect me, I was lying. Big time.

"Don't you think you deserve to know the truth from Jerry? Not that it will change things at this point…" Her voice trailed off.

I kept my eyes closed as they pulsated like strobe lights. "Yes. Now, whether I *want* to hear it is a different matter. You know how I said I've always been real good at ignoring the elephant in the room? It's hard to ask. And, what difference does it make now?" I could have answered that. It mattered because in my heart I wondered if Jerry ever looked at Karley and questioned whether she was really his child. Were his actions a result of that doubt?

"Thank you so much for being here for me, Mary Beth. Again."

Her smile was wistful. "You're welcome. I'm glad the club was there with you tonight." She turned toward me, her smooth hair swishing across her shoulders. "You didn't need this."

"I agree. But it's another reaffirmation that we should've never gotten married."

Twenty minutes later, Mary Beth dropped me off, hugging me tight, and reminding me to think it over before I said anything to Jerry.

I lay in bed, unable to sleep. Over the years, I'd briefly wondered if Jerry ever cheated on me since our sex life hovered somewhere just above zero most years, but I never let myself believe it might've happened. Joe was the well-known cheater. Had Dana been the only one for Jerry? I'd never heard any gossip, so it was easy to tell myself, no matter the status of our anemic marriage, Jerry was faithful. I had been, and assumed he'd done the same. Dana had regrets. I wondered if Jerry did too. As for me, I was wallowing in a tub full of my own.

Chapter 27

I stewed for a week, having a hundred vivid conversations with Jerry in my mind. What had been going through Dana's mind the countless times we women talked of Joe's cheating over the years? Did she study my face to see if I knew? Was there guilt in her eyes and I'd missed it?

And Jerry. How could he do that not only to me, but to Bob, one of his best friends from college? Yes, drinking was involved, but Jerry had always done a pretty good job of holding his own. I had a hard time believing it was his excuse.

I wanted to talk to Dana—impossible. I'd have loved to talk to Bob. Even if he knew, he wouldn't want it dredged up now. I had to ask Jerry. I had to know. And then I'd have to bury my hurt.

There was irony. I'd cheated on him with Greg, but we'd been *dating* at the time. It was a little different than cheating in a marriage.

I was positive this took place when Karley and Josh were young, right after Bob and Dana moved to Pine Lakes. Hal, who threw those parties, had a daughter Karley's age, and they moved out of town before the girls started kindergarten. Dana and I weren't friends yet. They were new to town and I was all-consumed in my two young children—and emotionally disconnected from Jerry. We were already leading separate lives.

Here's where my acceptance came in—I was partially to blame. I'd made little effort to love Jerry. Bob had a slice of blame in this too. In their early years, he'd been hell-bent on getting their business up and running, while Dana was miscarrying one baby after another.

I needed a one-on-one with Dana. It was a cold Sunday morning when I drove to the cemetery and stood in the newly-thawed grass next to her grave. "How could you do that to Bob, and to me? And how did you carry such a horrible secret for years?" I clenched my fists inside my jacket pockets, weighing my next words.

"The thing is; I forgive you. I forgive your poor judgment years ago. I've made a similar mistake and know how that split-second decision changes our lives. I choose to remember everything wonderful about you...like your genuine kindness for everyone. You've done so much for me over the years, I can never repay that. All I can do is forgive, and tell you I still love you and miss you."

A tear plopped on the grass, followed by another. And while my forgiveness calmed me, I imagined Dana in Heaven, crying in relief from the weight of her burden lifted.

When I got home, I picked up my landline and called Jerry's apartment.

It was after ten. I was hoping he'd be free so we could meet to talk. When a woman answered, I almost hung up, sure I had the wrong number.

"Is Jerry Brooks there?" *Pretty sure he's the only Jerry there, Peyton.*

"He's in the shower. Can I have him return your call?" The sweet-sounding voice asked.

"Nope, I'll call later. Thanks." I hung up, too unsure of whether I wanted to exchange names with the woman. I was guessing she was none other than soggy-crust-tasteless-pumpkin-pie Angela. I pictured this vixen with claws. But if that was the case, why go after Jerry? He couldn't even *see* rich from where he sat, especially after I got half of our mediocre dynasty.

I was elbow-deep in rolls I was making for a fundraiser at Eunice's church when he called.

"Did you call?" No hello, always on the defensive. Is this what we'd done to each other?

Did Jerry think I was calling to argue about the bottom dollar figure we'd yet to agree on for his business? This should knock him for a loop. "I'm wondering if you have some free time today. I need to talk to you about something, and I don't want to do it over the phone."

"Hmmm." I pictured him pacing in his apartment I'd yet to see. "Why?"

"I don't want to talk about it over the phone, Jerry. It won't take long. I can stop by your apartment after I work at the soup kitchen."

"Nope. We can meet somewhere else."

"What's the big deal about me stopping by your apartment? Can't your girlfriend leave?"

"You know that's not it."

Testiness outlined his words. Probably defending his girlfriend living there. "Oh, for Pete's sake, Jerry, I know what's going on. I'm not stupid." Did he think I didn't know she probably spent most, if not all, of her time there?

He sighed. "Well then, let's get this done with on the phone. If you're gonna be pissed off at me about Josh, I don't need to hear it in person. Maybe if you'd have let him fall the first time, he wouldn't be in this situation." His words were controlled, but they clawed at me like a wild lion.

I didn't know what in the hell he was talking about. "What situation?"

"Don't play games. I'm not going to apologize for Josh, and he's not making any excuses either. He'll call you when he's ready to deal with your disappointment."

I paced back and forth in my kitchen, my stomach performing impressive somersaults. "I'm serious, Jerry. I wasn't calling about anything to do with Josh. It's something else entirely, although right now it doesn't sound as important as what I think you're talking about. Did Josh get in trouble again?" I didn't want to hear the answer, but being left out of the loop was worse.

"You don't know?" Jerry's voice rose in surprise. "I figured that's what you wanted to talk about, and why you wanted to meet here. Josh got picked up for a DUI on St. Patrick's Day. He spent the night in jail and called me the next morning to bail him out. I let him think about it all the next day before I bailed him out that night. I figured you were pissed about that."

"He called *you*?" I thought back to that night. Had Josh tried calling me and I'd missed his call? While I was on my landline, I picked up my cell phone and scrolled back for any missed calls last week. Nope, nothing from Josh. When I hung up, I'd check my landline. Surely, he called me first.

"Yes, he called me. I figured you were out of town. I'm not happy with him, and he knows it, but at least he's taking responsibility for it this time. He'll stay here a few more days. His license is suspended for a month, his car insurance will go through the roof, and, of course, he's got a helluva fine to pay. Something *he'll* have to be responsible for. Don't you dare try and 'fix' things for him."

"Of course." My mind played leapfrog with questions.

"I'll tell Josh to call you call later, when he's ready for your disappointment. You should've let him fall, Perfect. We've all done stupid shit before. Maybe he'll learn from his, this time." Jerry hung up as I stood; phone in my hand. I scrolled through my calls. No call from Josh for over two weeks.

I stared out the front window at the "For Sale" sign in our yard and thought about the people who'd lived in this house for twenty years. My family. My soon-to-be ex-husband who I never connected with, my son who didn't feel he could confide in me, and my daughter, who I now had to wonder if she too felt the same way. I didn't bother stifling my sobs. Living alone had its benefits.

Tears burned my eyes as my indignation turned to thankfulness. Josh was okay, and he hadn't hurt anyone else (Jerry said it was a fender bender), yet fear crept through. How many times had I asked him if everything was okay? I thought Josh was doing so well.

And, I thought my children would always turn to me first. I'd always prided myself on being the better parent. The one my children would turn to for help. I was wrong.

My friends and family had been filtering what they'd share with me. Jerry had pegged me right. I wanted to be perfect, fueled by my hopes of rectifying my actions years ago. Nobody was perfect, especially me. And because I'd always felt Jerry was tough on Josh, I'd overcompensated and been a marshmallow, paving the way and making up for Jerry's toughness.

I blew my nose, got a drink of water, and picked up the phone again. "Jane? I'm sorry, but something's come up. Can you get by without me at the soup kitchen today?"

"Sure. Are you okay?" Steady-Jane, a woman I was pretty sure would never expect her four sons to be perfect. Then I remembered the women in the club. Nobody got through life unscathed.

"I think so. I need to meet with Josh." I'd call him later and see if I could meet him somewhere. I had to go out anyway to drop off the rolls I'd made for Eunice's church.

Weary and worn out, it wasn't yet noon when I crumbled on my couch, searching for the answer as to why I expected too much from everyone, including myself. My mom had been a carefree go-with-the-flow kind of person. But dad? Dad was a perfectionist, albeit a calm and quiet one. When you graduate top of your class and excel in your sport of choice, as I had, you expect to do everything right. And you tend to expect others to try and do what's right. I'd failed in so many ways. When I'd gotten pregnant and tried to do the right thing, I'd failed there too. I'd only made things worse.

As a mother, you only want what's best for your child. Josh getting a DUI was not in his best interest. I picked up my cell phone and called Grace.

"You need to get real," Grace said after I relayed Josh's latest actions. "You'll go through the rest of your life disappointed if you think your kids aren't going to stumble."

"I know. Nobody wants to look like a failure in the eyes of others." I recited. "It's one of the many mantras I've learned in the Hell Club." I'd also learned *look forward, not back.*

Daniel called me a few minutes later for one of our many-times-a-day two minute chats. Over the past few weeks, we'd opened up so much to each other, confessing many of our imperfections. I told him about Josh, sensing he wouldn't judge.

"He's a good kid, right?" Daniel's voice comforted me. "This is a bump in his life, and I bet he learns from it. It will be okay, Peyton. It might not seem like it now, but it will."

Daniel was level-headed and caring, becoming entwined in my heart.

After we hung up, I called Josh. "I'll pick you up outside your dad's apartment complex at one. We can visit over malts at the Dairy Queen." And I'd keep my disappointment to myself.

* * *

It was crushing to hear Josh tell me the weight of my high expectations made him feel like even more of a loser. "You're not a loser, Josh. I worry about you, and for good reason. I worry about Karley too. That never goes away, whether you live at home or not."

"But Karley's never let you down. I'd rather have Dad angry at me than you disappointed in me. People make mistakes, Ma." Pain aged his face. Oh, if he only knew how well I understood how people made mistakes. Big mistakes.

I understood where Josh was coming from. He'd been demoted from star athlete in high school to regular Joe at Staples Community College, and pressure from me hadn't helped. I'd experienced the same feeling from my parents with my surprise pregnancy and the effect it had on my college and swimming. Now I'd done it to Josh. Add it to my long list of mistakes.

I called Jerry the next day. I still wanted to talk to him about Dana so I could put it to rest.

"Josh said your talk went okay." Jerry's voice was curt.

"Yes, it did. I'm sorry to hear he'll be taking next year off of school, but I get that he needs to work to pay off his debt." A debt which would cut into our payout from the house when it sold, thanks to a business line of credit Jerry had drawn on—something we'd managed to avoid for years. "I'm glad Josh is joining Moderation Management." It was hard to grasp my son would be attending meetings to control his drinking and attraction to drugs. Yet there it was. He needed help, just as I did when I'd turned to the Hell Club.

"What the hell are you talking about?" Jerry asked.

I grinned into the phone. Aha, something Josh told me and not his dad. "He can ride his bike to the meetings, just like he'll have to do for work. They're not AA, but members take personal responsibility for their own recovery and behavior to get their drinking under control. Josh said he's only ever done any drugs when he's drinking. It will be up to him to tackle both through his meetings. He met a few guys from school who go, and they said the meetings help."

I turned my focus back to the matter at hand with Jerry. We still needed to talk.

"Can we meet sometime tomorrow to talk? I have something I need to discuss with you."

"I'm going out of town for a few days. What is it, Peyton? Can't we talk about it now?"

"Not over the phone. And I have to leave soon. Let me know when you're free." Some of us girls from the Hell Club were going to open curling at the Brainerd Curling Club in an hour.

As we hung up I was certain Jerry wouldn't call me. I tabled it for now. One less thing I had to deal with at the moment.

Chapter 28

It was the last weekend in March, and in typical Minnesota-style weather, our balmy March weather had done a one-eighty—freezing rain mixed with snow. March was not going out like a lamb. Mary Beth was hosting a birthday party at her house for Charlee.

She called me Friday afternoon. "If you can make it here, bring your pj's. We'll all have a sleepover so nobody has to drive home. And a blow-up bed, if you have one."

"You aren't canceling?" I asked, not sure about wanting to venture out of my house.

"I would have, but Charlee lives half an hour away, and has been in Brainerd anyway for an appointment." Mary Beth explained. "I told her to plan on staying here tonight. Charlee's neighbor lady will check in on her kids. I've been telling everyone to pack an overnight bag."

"I've got Reggie." It was a dinner party for Charlee. There was no way Reggie could last more than twelve hours.

"Bring him along. He can play with my dogs Minnow and Moose."

Two hours later, I loaded my car and then crept along on the icy roads out of town with Reggie in the back. When I pulled up to turn onto Highway 371, to my right was Bar Harbor Supper Club. In such bad weather I watched people precariously walk through the Supper Club parking lot.

Then I saw him.

I watched him get out of his truck, open the passenger side door, and escort a woman out. When a horn honked behind me, I realized the light had turned green. Without having to think, I turned right, taking the service road into Bar Harbor's parking lot. There was Daniel and some beautiful woman smiling at each other while they walked arm-in-arm inside the supper club.

What in the hell? I pulled in a parking space and put my car in park. I'd talked to Daniel two nights ago. What did we talk about? I couldn't remember other than I mentioned I had Charlee's party tonight and worked The Pines tomorrow night. His band was playing this weekend. Now I couldn't remember if he had said they were playing tonight or tomorrow night.

I shut the car off. I couldn't think while driving on icy roads. Daniel had dress pants on. This was no jeans night out for him. And the woman wore a dress and nice jacket. My stomach burned as if I'd drank acid, my throat like I'd swallowed a lit match. On the heels of my recent discovery of Jerry's cheating and Josh's accident, I didn't know how much more I could take.

What are you going to do? Walk in there like a crazy woman and stake your claim? A claim I didn't have. Lick my wounds and go home? Continue on to Mary Beth's and cry my heart out to my friends? I chose door number three.

I pulled out of the parking lot with my eyes glued to the door in case Daniel came to his senses and ran back to his truck alone. It didn't happen, so I plodded along to Mary Beth's.

There were a few members who'd joined before Charlee, whom I'd never met, at her party. I was kind enough to wish Charlee a happy birthday and give her a bear hug before I burst out with my self-centered news. Mary Beth had made spiked punch, and I helped myself to a large glass. "Okay, let's have it." Charlee patted the cushion next to her on the couch.

I relayed what I witnessed and wondered if the women at the party who didn't know me thought I was a paranoid kook.

"Hmm. What did Daniel tell you he was doing tonight?" Charlee asked.

"That's just it, I don't remember if his band is playing tonight or tomorrow night."

"I've known Daniel for years," said Michelle, "He's not a two-timer. He's a good guy."

I told them what Maude had said the night of the fish fry at Daniel's house.

"I'd ask him point-blank what's up," Mary Beth said. "From what you've said before, it sounds like he's been waiting for your divorce to be final before getting too serious." She leaned forward. "We all know here how important it is to stand up for ourselves. You can do it, Peyton."

She was right. I'd never know what Daniel wanted from our relationship unless I asked.

And I knew in my heart that if I expected honesty from him, I was going to have to give the same in return. Another hurdle in my future. But I refused to live like an ostrich any longer.

"I'm sorry for being a wet blanket." I finished my glass of punch. "C'mon, Charlee, open those presents and let's get this party started." Another glass of punch and I could almost forget I even had a thought-he-was-my-boyfriend.

We'd all brought appetizers, and Mary Beth had come up with some goofy games for us to play. I'd unwound enough and was in the middle of a relaxing conversation with Michelle and Mary Beth about winter vacations when Braelie, a cute blonde who looked to be a handful of years younger than me, spread old photos on the living room coffee table to show Charlee.

"Oh wow, look at Faith here in these old photos!" Charlee exclaimed to the others. "Come here, Michelle, you've got to see Faith. Remember her from when we first joined?"

Michelle and Mary Beth both excused themselves for a minute to go look at the old photos. The other women with Braelie had joined the club a few years before Michelle, Mary Beth, and Charlee. As I heard them all exclaim over this Faith who had lost over a hundred pounds after joining years ago, I went to look at the club photos from more than a decade ago.

It was as if someone grabbed a baseball bat and hit me in the kneecaps. I let out a wail in that indefinite split-second when your brain says, "There's something wrong with this picture" and the time it registers exactly *what* is wrong. I didn't have time to cover my mouth and stifle my cry—to shove it back down my throat where nobody could hear my gut-wrenching discovery.

Maggie, my old best friend, stood front and center in the photo with Braelie and four other women who I'd never seen before. My moan had caught everyone's attention.

"What's wrong?" Michelle asked as she put her hand on my shoulder.

I collapsed onto the corner of the couch. The air had been knocked from my lungs. "Was this a club event?" I gasped to Braelie, pointing to the photo.

It was hard to tell. The small group of women stood next to a Ferris wheel. Maybe Maggie had run into them and knew one of the club members. That had to be it.

"Yes. We had gone to the fair, and Faith was telling us how she loved to ride the Ferris wheel growing up but had gotten too heavy over the years. After that, she lost a hundred pounds. When Charlee, Mary Beth, and Michelle joined, they never knew the "other" Faith. Charlee and I were talking about Faith the other day so I went through my old photos and found these."

"Faith and her family moved to Germany years ago. She was a hoot." Michelle's smile at the memory faded. "I'm sorry. We're reminiscing, and you're upset about something."

Everyone's eyes were on me, the room silent. I cleared my throat. "I know one of the women in your photos. I guess it's a shock because I didn't know she was a member."

"I've lost touch with most of these women over the years." Braelie studied me as she fingered a photo. "Who do you know in here?"

I pointed to Maggie. I'd had no clue about her attempt at suicide. Why should I be surprised she'd joined this club years ago and not told me—her best friend? For all I knew, she gave them a fictitious name.

I didn't know a damn thing about the people in my life.

"Oh, Maggie!" She picked up the photo I'd pointed to, the one where Maggie was wearing a purple boat neck shirt identical to the red one I'd bought with her all those years ago.

"I haven't seen Maggie since she dropped out of the club. I think it was around 2002. She'd gotten a promotion at work, and it changed things for her. I moved to Duluth the following year and never heard anything more from Maggie."

When Braelie said "Maggie," I watched Mary Beth, Charlee, and Michelle's eyes all turn to me. They'd heard me talk about Maggie, Lauren, and Dana so much they'd have known them if they walked in the door. Clearly, they hadn't known Maggie was in the club all those years ago.

"How's Maggie doing?" Braelie leaned forward, anxious to hear about her old friend.

Mary Beth's hand patted mine as she got up from the couch and waved the others to follow her to the kitchen. I took a deep breath.

"Maggie died last year in a car accident with two of my other friends." My voice wavered like an elderly person. "They're why I joined the club. I never knew Maggie was a member years ago." My throat felt coated with cotton. And like a true friend, there was Mary Beth bringing me a glass of water, knowing what I needed before I did.

As the rest of the group subtly made their way back to the kitchen to visit, Braelie told of Maggie's joining after her first attempt at suicide. Yes, her first. The second time she swallowed a bottle of pills and a few minutes later, Wyatt woke up crying from a bad dream, and Maggie panicked. Instead of dialing 911, she dialed a club member who dialed 911. They pumped Maggie's stomach.

That was 1999. Right at the peak of her crappy marriage with Joe's emotional abuse, his unfaithfulness, and draining of the finances while Maggie taught school and cared for her young son. The women from the club had been there for her. I hadn't.

"Don't take it personally." Braelie was now holding my hand, comforting me even though we'd met only an hour ago. "It's easier to tell a stranger of your weaknesses and misery. Telling a friend or family member is hard. They watch you, judge you. Why do you think people go to counselors instead of talking to the people who know them best?"

She was right. Looking back, Maggie likely thought I had enough on my plate. Still, I should have read the signs; her edgy nervousness and extreme weight loss on an already thin body. I'd ask—and she'd make up an excuse. I'd accepted it. It had been easier than digging my heel in at the truth.

Hell, I hadn't even been able to face my own truth. I would have done no better with Maggie's.

"You know what we always told women who didn't understand the need for our club?" Braelie's smile was wistful. "If you can't relate to the club, you just haven't lived long enough. I was young when I joined, after getting raped at college." She swallowed hard. "We all get dealt crap in life, and sometimes turning to a stranger is easier than the person right next to you. Don't blame yourself. And don't blame Maggie."

"Clearly the club helped Maggie. I owe you all a debt of gratitude for helping her." I told her of Maggie's years since she became principal at the grade school, of her hope to eventually file for divorce, and her success in raising her son to be a fine young man.

Hours later, as nine of us camped out at Mary Beth's, I tossed and turned, listening to the unfamiliar sounds of the house. Emotions entwined around my heart like prickly vines. My mind regurgitated its new information as I searched for answers to too many questions. I didn't succeed.

* * *

My brain was fuzzy when I awoke. I needed to swim—the only thing that would clear my head. I side-stepped the coffee and muffins the rest of the women were enjoying in Mary Beth's kitchen, mumbling my apologies as I made a quick escape for Lakes Gym. Nobody questioned me.

Anxiety fueled me as I slipped into the Speedo swimsuit I kept in my gym locker, marched through the obligatory pre-swim shower, tossed my towel on a chair next to the pool, and dived in.

My mind replayed the past twenty years with Maggie, and where I went wrong as her best friend, as I pushed off the edge of the pool and cut through the tepid, chlorinated water. My stomach burned like it did after the accident, as if I were mourning all over again. I missed Maggie even more now than I did after she died. Regret added to my loss. I thought I'd been a great friend to her—and Lauren and Dana—but looking back, I wondered if I could have "been there" for them more.

My mom's sudden death, my living so many miles away from my family in Texas, my empty marriage…my plate was full. And because of that, my best friend had turned to others for help.

So I swam. The one thing I could do to help me think. And feel. My salty tears meshed with the chlorinated water as I systematically pumped out one lap after another, like a steam engine with no clear destination.

My body told my brain to stop. Muscles ached, nerves were raw, and my limbs were shaky. I'd overdone it to the point my blood sugar had dropped. One more lap. One more lap. Every time I pushed off the pool wall I promised myself it was my last lap. And I don't know if I'd have ever given in to rational thinking if a mother hadn't shown up with her three young children, all eager to jump in the pool I had filled with my pain.

They broke my concentration, and my body collapsed, as if someone had deflated the guilt-ridden energy that had been pushing me ahead to find the answers to questions I had dodged for years. It was now impossible to ignore the feeling I'd let Maggie down.

Add it to the long list of screw-ups in Perfect Peyton's life.

Dragging my limp body out of the pool, I wept into my towel, catching a glimpse of the mother who watched me warily as I stumbled inside the locker room.

As I showered, I watched the hot water swirl the drain, thinking how easily I could circle the drain again, let myself unravel and sink into isolation-depression. I wouldn't. I couldn't.

If my mom hadn't moved on after her first marriage, she wouldn't have married my dad, and I wouldn't be here. If Lauren hadn't gotten past the trauma of her upbringing on the streets, the horror of her abortion, she'd never have had the life she did with Dylan. If Dana and Bob hadn't been able to move past her infidelity, they'd never have had the great family they did.

If I wouldn't have married Jerry, I wouldn't have had Josh. And Karley wouldn't have had a father. They were positive effects from my mistake.

If I didn't give Daniel a chance, I'd never know what might have been.

If I didn't let Josh stand on his own two feet, instead of always picking him up, he'd never become responsible.

And if I didn't forgive myself for not being there for Maggie, and instead learn from my human error, I'd never be able to move forward.

If. A small word with so much weight. And heavy consequences.

I'd always tried to do everything right and ended up doing quite a few things wrong.

I drove home, unpacked, and walked by a photo of us four women canoeing, Maggie smiling in the sunshine. I picked up the photo and looked at her, *really looked.* And thought of a time years ago, back when Maggie was scary-skinny, and we'd taken the children to a local park. Maggie and I sat side by side on a picnic table, watching our children swing and slide.

We'd been talking of our money struggles, and lack of help from our husbands. Maggie turned away from me, staring out at the tall pines surrounding the park. "I don't know if I can keep going." Maggie's monotone voice was so quiet. Distracted by young Josh hanging upside down from the monkey bars, I asked her to repeat what she said.

"Oh, nothing."

Then her words registered. "What do you mean? Of course you keep going. You keep going for Wyatt." My fear at her words came out as aggressiveness in my own. What did I know? Joe was horrible to her, but did I understand the toll it was taking on Maggie? I wanted her to dig her heels in and stick it out like I was…even though her situation was so much worse. Some friend I was.

I'd leaned forward so I could see Maggie's face, and I witnessed a veil cover the anguish in her eyes as she said, "You're right." And I'd let it drop—taking the ostrich way out.

My matter-of-fact response had pushed Maggie into deciding there was no hope in confiding in me. I'd given the vibe I wouldn't understand. I should have wondered what she was covering up, what she was feeling. I should have wondered a lot of things.

And I should be thankful Maggie reached out to the Hell Club years ago, instead of feeling jealous she hadn't turned to me. They probably saved her life.

Chapter 29

After unpacking at home, I crawled into bed and took a mid-Saturday nap. When I woke three hours later, Daniel had left two messages on my cell while I napped away half of my day. I called him back, got his voice mail, and left a message.

My stomach roiled like a cement mixer churning too many emotions. I walked into my office. Outside the window, sleet fell, melting the slush accumulated from yesterday and graying my day even more. Grudgingly, I fired up my computer to spend some time spiffing up my resume. I was determined to put my soon-to-be college degree to good use for a brighter future.

I nibbled away at an excuse for a meal—grapes and toast—before lacing up my boots and grabbing a heavy winter coat I'd hoped to pack away by now. Walking in the fresh, cold air calmed me, enough so when Jerry called early in the evening, I didn't jump head-first into defensive mode.

"I dropped off a new spreadsheet of my business assets and liabilities with my attorney. Can we get this wrapped up now? I want to break ground in June, once our house closes."

"As long as your figures are realistic." I was sick of fighting—about everything.

"They're realistic, and final. I'm done, Perfect. I think we can both agree to just be done."

He was right. I wanted to be done, as long as his figures bridged the gaping hole of discrepancy they showed before. The last thing I wanted to do at this point was drag our divorce on one day longer than need be.

After my draining discovery about Maggie, I tabled the idea of bringing up Jerry and Dana. It was one more thing I didn't need to deal with right now, and really, what was the point?

I crawled into bed early, caved, and took a couple Tylenol PM to ensure my overloaded brain would zone out, and muttered "sissy" as I swallowed them. I woke nine hours later.

I'd just stepped out of the shower when Daniel called. "Tag, you're it."

"Good morning." Instant anxiety seized my heart. Here was another uncomfortable conversation I needed to have—one I couldn't bring up over the phone.

"Did your band play last night?" It was easier to ask than if he'd had a date Friday night.

"Yep, I got home about two. I didn't want to call you back and wake you."

I pinched the bridge of my nose and sighed enough to steam up the bathroom mirror. "If you're not busy today, I thought I'd stop over and see you. I have some errands to run anyway. Is that okay?"

"Sure. I'm not working the shop at all today. Stop by whenever."

After we hung up, I dressed in new jeans and a Kelly-green sweater, nicer clothing than what I'd normally wear going to Walgreens and the grocery store. An hour later I pulled in to Daniel's driveway, rehearsing my speech all the way. There was a black Lexus parked in front of his garage. Daniel didn't say anything about having company. I stalled before knocking.

"Come in," Daniel shouted through an open window.

As I stepped inside his kitchen, I came face-to-face with the woman I'd seen with him Friday night. The beautiful woman who'd been smiling up at Daniel as her arm linked through his. She was sitting with a cup of something in front of her, at home in his kitchen.

"Hi. Daniel will be out in a second. Come sit down." She stood up and pulled out a chair for me. "I'm Gigi, Daniel's sister-in-law."

The breath I'd been holding deflated me like a grounded hot air balloon. Sister-in-law? I thought Daniel's brothers lived out of state. Just then, Daniel walked in the living room with another man—a younger version of himself.

"Hey, Peyton. I see you met Gigi. She's the poor soul who married my brother."

The other man gave Daniel a gentle nudge before putting his hand out to shake mine. "Hi, I'm Peter, Daniel's much younger and nicer brother." He had the same grin and the same height as Daniel, and I liked him already.

I shook Peter's hand, and we all sat down at Daniel's table. "Peter and I were brainstorming on ideas for Mallory's room once she moves out," Daniel explained.

"I was brainstorming, Daniel was daydreaming." Peter teased.

My own brain was trying to play catch up while rearranging my emotions after the surprise of finding out Gigi was Daniel's sister-in-law, not his new girlfriend.

"Would you like some coffee?" Gigi asked me. "I'm having tea."

"They're expecting their first baby." Daniel informed me.

"Congratulations! When are you due?" There wasn't even a slight baby bump yet.

"I'm a little over three months along, due after Labor Day."

Conversation went on around me, and I tried to contribute, but all I could think of was how I'd jumped to conclusions about Daniel. "I should let you all visit. I wouldn't have stopped if I'd known you had company," I said.

"I'm glad you did. Their visit was a surprise; otherwise, I'd have organized something so you could meet. They have to leave soon, so please stay."

"Yep, we stopped in Mankato to tell Gigi's parents in person we're pregnant, and we wanted to tell my mom in person too." Peter beamed with pride at their exciting news. "We're leaving soon to stop by Mom's again before heading back to stay the night in Mankato. We'll drive back to Chicago tomorrow." Peter stood up and brought Gigi's cup to the sink.

They left a half hour later. As soon as the door closed, Daniel turned to me. "Alone at last." He smiled and took me in his arms. His kisses started at my neck and worked their way down.

I wrestled with my sliver of self-control, and pushed him away. "I need to talk to you."

"*Talk?* I haven't seen you in four days and you came over to talk?" Daniel winked as he took my hand and led me to his couch.

The speech I'd rehearsed last night was now ripped to shreds after meeting Gigi. Still, on the heels of discovering Jerry's infidelity and Maude's speech to Daniel about not throwing me to the wind like his previous girlfriends, it was time to find out where I stood with Daniel. I knew where he stood with me. I was falling in love with him, feeling similar to how I had years ago with Greg.

I hugged a pillow from the couch against my chest. "No interrupting now when I explain how my crazy mind works. For the past two days, I thought you had another girlfriend."

Daniel burst out laughing. "No laughing either." I tried not to giggle along with him. "I was on my way to Mary Beth's Friday night and saw you walking arm-in-arm with Gigi in to Bar Harbor's parking lot. All dressed up and smiling at each other." I watched Daniel's face reflect an "ah-ha" moment. He kept quiet.

"I was upset, sure you were dating her behind my back." I was careful choosing my next words. "I asked myself what right I had to be upset. I know I've told you how I didn't want to take our relationship to the next level until I had my divorce papers in hand, so this is my fault. I never asked what *you* wanted from our relationship, and Maude's words have been swimming in my head since she mentioned all your old girlfriends." My voice faltered.

Daniel lifted my chin. "I'm glad this has come up. I guess we've never talked about this, and I want to." There was no laughter in his eyes now.

"Peter and Gigi showed up at my shop late Friday afternoon after they'd stopped at Mom's. I had no clue they were coming to town. You'd told me you were going to Mary Beth's with your friends Friday night, so I didn't call you. By the time you saw us, we all had been at the restaurant already, waiting for a table. Except Gigi. She'd taken a nap because she's tired from her pregnancy and had called and was ready to be picked up. I offered to get her so Peter and Mom could visit longer. It was icy out so I held on to Gigi. I didn't want her falling in her high heels."

It all made sense now. Two days ago, my imagination had built a different story.

"The good thing is, it's brought to the surface us talking about what we want." Daniel had turned on the couch and was now facing me. "I know my mom planted a seed in your brain that I chewed up and spit out a lot of women over the years. In typical Maude-style, she exaggerated."

He kissed the top of my hand. "I've had one long-term relationship since Mallory's mom left over twenty years ago. I've dated women, but very few more than a handful of times. I feel different with you, Peyton. I'm comfortable with you, trust you, have fun with you, and I want you in my future." He smiled. "And I wish like hell your divorce papers would show up."

My eyes blinked back tears, unable to find the words to respond.

"I'm in this for the long haul, Peyton. Once your divorce is final, you won't be able to get rid of me." His hand gently brushed back my hair from my flushed cheek. "And, if I'm going to be part of your future, I want to get to know your past. I'd like to go with you to the cemetery. It's time to formally introduce me to Maggie, Lauren, and Dana."

The following Wednesday, Jerry and I accepted an offer on our house from a young widow friend of Mallory's. When she heard of me trying to sell my home, she told a war-widowed friend of hers, Britin, who was looking for a home, and bingo, we had a buyer.

Soon, Britin and her young children would move into our house and hopefully fill it with love and laughter. By early June I'd move closer to Brainerd for work—meaning I'd be further away from the cemetery. It was okay. I talked to my old friends every day in my head.

That Saturday, after a long bike ride on the Paul Bunyan Trail and a dinner of fish tacos at Tall Pines, Daniel and I drove out to the cemetery. We'd left our lightweight jackets in his pickup, still warm from our biking even though the sun was already contemplating setting for the evening. We stood next to their graves, and Daniel took my hands in his warm ones.

"I'll tell you a little story about each one." I took a deep breath, inhaling the earthy scent of damp leaves covering the ground. "I've told you how Maggie was our serious, smart friend." I nodded towards Maggie's granite headstone. "But she could be carefree too. One day, she went to get her hair cut and came out of there with a god-awful bowl cut. We were meeting for dinner, and when we saw her Dutch-boy haircut, we got our dinner to go." I laughed at the memory. "We stopped and picked up some wine, then went to Lauren's, where Maggie let the three of us hack on her hair until she ended up with a cute pixie cut." I smiled. "Maggie was a good sport about things. I guess being married to Joe, she learned to roll with the punches."

"And here's Dana," I said, "Bob's wife." Daniel and Bob had met a few times now. "I've told you how she was always upbeat, even if she had four kids home with a stomach bug. She was down-to-earth and innocent, too. When the four of us took a weekend trip to Lanesboro, in Amish Country, we drove around the countryside, visiting the Amish shops located on their farms. We were looking around in a small shop, and we see Dana wander through the open door and into the people's home. I watched her pick up a wall quilt from their dining room wall and examine it, looking for a price tag. She turned around to ask the people how much the quilt was and realized they were eating at the kitchen table, mouths hanging open at her wandering around their house!" I was now crying from laughing as I retold the story. He let out a guffaw, likely happy to see me so happy with my memories.

Once I got my giggles under control, I told him of Lauren. "And lastly, there's Lauren." You know how I've said Lauren was our tough survivor. She also was a charmer. Years ago, when Maggie's son, Wyatt, was confirmed in the Catholic Church, they had the Bishop there. After mass, we all got to meet the Bishop. Lauren was wearing stiletto heels. She twisted an ankle right before stepping up to meet the Bishop, and shouted, "Son-of-a-bitchin-god-damn shoes! Oh, hello, Bishop Schneider, it's nice to meet you." Daniel bent over, clutching his stomach.

"The thing is the Bishop didn't even flinch. He took Lauren's outstretched hand as she smoothed things over, saying how she loved his sermon, batted her eyes, acted like he was her best friend, and a minute later the Bishop was smitten with Lauren. She had that way about her."

"Your friends sound like a blast. No wonder you miss them."

"I know. I have some awesome memories." It was the whole better-to-have-loved-and-lost way to look at it. I'd had roughly two decades with them—a real gift.

"You know, Peyton, everything you said about your friends, I see in you." He put a hand on each of my shoulders. "You are smart, like Maggie, you bring sunshine to others, like Dana, and you're a survivor, like Lauren. Your friends would be proud of you."

"Thank you." I beamed. I was proud of my friends. They'd been great women.

As we climbed back in Daniel's truck, he said, "It's such a nice night out, do you want to come over and I'll get a bonfire going?"

"That sounds relaxing." I wasn't ready for our day to be over. I could easily spend every day around Daniel. The thought should've scared me, but it didn't. And I didn't need a bonfire to warm me. My hormones had been on fire all day, itching for a release with Daniel. What in the world was taking so long for my divorce papers?

Arriving at his home, I went in to use his bathroom and inspected myself in the mirror. Rosy cheeks, hair in total disarray after a windy day, no lipstick… I looked a mess. I figured it wouldn't matter, we'd be out in the dark, and wasn't campfire light as flattering as candlelight?

When I came back out of the bathroom, he was in the kitchen with his head stuck in the fridge. "Wanna beer?" He poked his head back out, waving two beer bottles.

"Sure."

He grabbed two bottle Koozies, a bag of pretzels, and ushered me back out the door, while I grabbed the jacket of his he'd offered me. Wearing his jacket and smelling his scent embracing me made me want to drag him back to his bedroom. Instead, I helped gather firewood stacked in rows on the edge of the woods, and soon we had a nice fire roaring. The heat thawed my chilled feet, and the beer cooled my too-warm face.

We settled in Adirondack chairs around the fire, and he told me entertaining stories from his youth, painting Maude as a softie who let her three sons get away with a lot. I wasn't surprised.

When Daniel went in to get us a couple more beers, I followed; it was time for another bathroom break for me, and I needed a glass of water.

"Hungry?" Daniel asked as I came back out of the bathroom.

"No, just thirsty." I took the glass of water he offered as he poured himself one too. The kitchen was quiet except for the gentle hum of the refrigerator. As I took a long drink of water, my eyes locked with Daniel's. His danced with blatant desire, the intensity filled the room. What were we talking about before we came inside? I couldn't remember.

Especially when Daniel took a few steps toward me, took my glass from my hand, and set it on the table. The air was all but gone from my lungs.

He slipped his arms around my lower back, my face mere inches below his. "Peyton?" His voice was husky and deep, echoing in the open room. I wasn't sure if he was asking me anything because no words followed. It was just as well, I couldn't have answered if my life depended on it. All my energy was put into keeping my legs under my body, so my wet-noodle-frame didn't collapse onto the hardwood floor.

His kiss started slow, controlled. My brain had other plans. My hands found their way around his lower back, meshing with his well-worn jacket, soft from years of washings. It was something sturdy to hold on to as my eardrums beat the tempo of my racing heart, making me literally swoon from vertigo. All the blood whooshing through my head and heart explained why there was none left to strengthen my legs.

Daniel had a firm grip on me. As his body held me up, his mouth conveyed the emotion of our day together. He pushed the metal trash can out of the way, and I was backed up against the kitchen wall. The refrigerator next to me would have averted its eyes…if it had some.

We were sixteen-year-olds stuffed with a fresh batch of raging hormones. *Where was the woman who lived in my body for years, the one who swore she didn't care if she ever had sex again?*

I'm not sure how long we thrashed like dogs in heat, not sure what might have happened next, if in the throes of it all I (or Daniel, not sure who) wouldn't have kicked over the round metal trash can, so the loud clang of it made us both jump. Surprise jolted us apart.

My heart raced, but I wasn't sure if it was from the loud bang or the fueled passion. It didn't matter; we needed a diversion, and the crash was as good as any.

"Sorry about that!" Daniel paced around his kitchen, running his hand across his face, before stooping to right the trash can.

My face could have fried bacon, my hair no doubt a rats' nest, my lips chafed and swollen…probably looking like a woman ravaged. Nix that thought— *nearly* ravaged. And I wasn't sure if I was happy it had come to an abrupt end or not. But, I was happy to be with Daniel. So happy, I busted out laughing—a wonderful release for my happiness.

"What's so funny?" Daniel asked.

"I'm happy, and this whole situation seems funny to me. Good funny, not bad."

"Oh yeah? Well I'm feeling frustrated, sexually frustrated." Daniel took a long, slow breath. "And, because I respect you, I think it's time I took you home before I start something you might regret before those damn divorce papers are in your hand." He went to the counter where the two beers stood, still unopened, and put them back in the fridge.

When he turned back to me, he took my face in his hands. "How much longer, Peyton?" He whispered before kissing me again.

I didn't give a flying leap about those papers three minutes ago. Jerry had been out of the house for sixteen months. It was long overdue to be final—for both me, and Jerry. And by the sounds of it, Daniel too. Determination fueled my decision. "I'll call my attorney Monday to see what the holdup is. She told me two weeks ago it would be any day now." I made a deal with myself. If they weren't in my hands within the next two weeks, I was moving ahead with Daniel. Jerry sure as hell hadn't waited.

Chapter 30

I invited everyone for Easter dinner, mingling my past with my present. I didn't care if we had to sit on the floor. It would be my final hurrah in the house. We were closing in five weeks.

As Mary Beth helped me with the preparation the day before, we talked about my "enlightenments" over the past few weeks—Jerry, Josh, and Maggie.

"See a pattern here?" Mary Beth joked as we put together a vegetable salad to marinade.

"I know; forgive and look forward, not back, yada yada yada…" I recited some of the preachings from the Hell Club.

"If Maggie had confided in you of her struggles and thoughts of suicide, how would you have reacted?" Mary Beth continued to dice the carrots while I chopped broccoli. "Would you have helped her, offering support for treatment and not judged her? Or would you have deemed her too crazy to be your friend?" Her dark eyebrow shot up in question.

I stopped chopping. "I'd like to think I'd have offered support. Maggie was a wonderful friend, a wonderful mom. I never once thought she was 'crazy.' I just never realized how bad things got for her. She did a good job of hiding her misery. I should've pried more. She didn't deserve that life."

Mary Beth set her knife down on the cutting board, reached out, and squeezed my arm.

"Her actions were a call for help. We all stumble at some point. I could give you women's names from our club who you could discuss the stumbling blocks of life with—drunk drivers, thieves, even a murderer or two."

I inhaled at the word "murderer," my nose filling with the tangy aroma of marinated vegetables.

"Yes, most have had bad things happen *to* them, but some have done things they aren't proud of. Nobody's perfect. The Hell Club is full of examples."

Gone was my unrealistic expectation of perfection for everyone…including myself. An imperfect club was exactly where I belonged.

* * *

Bob, Jane, and Charlee's children all played outside, the older ones hiding eggs for the younger ones to find—mostly under leaves I'd failed to rake last fall. Daniel met women from the Hell Club, and they got to meet the man I'd been talking about too much.

Karley, Ben, and Josh were home, and Karley spent a lot of time visiting with Mallory. It was the first time my children met Daniel, and within minutes, Josh, Ben, and Daniel were in a lively debate over baseball players.

By late afternoon, the only ones left were my children, Daniel, and Mallory. I walked past the kitchen, and Ben stopped me. "Can I talk to you in private for a minute?" he whispered.

My heart raced. Was something wrong with Karley? I suggested the garage, and we snuck out without anyone noticing.

"What's up?" Did I sound carefree? I doubt it. Panic was my middle name.

"Well, you know Karley and I have known each other for years, and have been dating quite a while now, and I think she's the greatest thing in the world." Silence. Was he waiting for me to disagree? I thought she was the greatest thing in the world too.

"I know she's crazy-busy in graduate school, and things are a little tight for us, but I love Karley with all my heart, and I want to spend the rest of my life with her. I'm asking for your permission to ask Karley to marry me." His eyes shone.

My heart puffed up with happiness, growing three sizes in a matter of seconds. I hugged Ben hard, my soon-to-be son-in-law, before leaning back to look him in the eye. "Of course you have my permission. I've never seen Karley happier!"

"Thank you. I'm asking Jerry when we go there tomorrow. Karley and I are planning on going to a big Cinco de Mayo celebration next weekend, and I want to ask her then." He grinned.

After Ben snuck back in the house, I took a walk around the yard as if looking for extra plastic eggs to pick up. In reality, I was relishing the peace and calm in my heart, surrounded by freshly mowed grass and sunshine. I could all but feel grandchildren in my arms in the future, a new step in the process of lives moving forward. Mine being one of them.

Two weeks later, newly-engaged Karley came home for Mother's Day to help me pack up household items. We'd worked late into Saturday night, tackling her bedroom and Josh's. I'd agreed to store what I could until they both lived in something bigger than a shoe-box-sized apartment.

I treated myself by sleeping in until nine on Sunday. The coffee was brewing when Karley made her way into the kitchen, stretching and yawning.

"Where do you want me to start?"

I reached for a second coffee cup as Karley got the creamer from the fridge. "How about the pantry downstairs? I've got plenty of empty boxes on the floor, and ones with the dividers work well for canned goods. I'm going to tackle the kitchen today." I'd already set aside a few necessities in one cupboard for me to use in the coming few weeks until I moved.

After a breakfast of pumpkin bread and fruit, we changed into our grubby clothes and got to work. I was standing on a step stool in the kitchen, unloading the cupboard above the stove, when Karley walked in about an hour later. A warning siren should have been wailing in my brain.

She stood with my senior yearbook open to a large photo of Greg and me at our Senior Prom. Her face was pale, her mouth hung open…and my heart seized.

The wine glass I'd been wrapping in newspaper slipped from my hand, shattering on the kitchen counter. "Where did you find that?" It came out as accusing. It covered up my shock.

Her mouth opened and shut, as if she were a fish gasping for air. I stumbled off the chair and took the few steps toward Karley. In the middle of the open yearbook sat the letters I'd saved from Greg, letters he wrote even after we broke up…some dated the summer Karley was conceived. And if I remembered right, at least one mentioned our steamy week together that summer. *Why didn't you throw them away twenty-two years ago? You stupid, sentimental, love-sick fool!*

"Mom?" Her eyes searched mine, glanced down at the too-large photo of Greg and me, and then back at my face again. A thousand questions pooled in her brown eyes. In that photo, Greg's lopsided grin with his crooked eye teeth, the way Karley's had been before braces, was too big to ignore. Not to mention his unique ear lobe—an exact replica of hers.

Karley was smart. Karley was observant. Karley was devastated.

I was never good at pulling together a poker face. Taken off guard, I didn't have enough time to hide the shock and secret. I wanted to snatch the letters she'd obviously read, to re-read them after twenty years and see exactly what secrets may have been revealed. I didn't dare.

Karley's body turned rigid with understanding. "Oh my God…Mom?!"

Her white-knuckled hands clutched my high school yearbook against her heaving chest.

My daughter's life was shattering in much the same way the wine glass had.

I was speechless. This was a discussion I hadn't planned for…had hoped would never surface.

"Mooommmm," her plea came out in a wail, a long moan from deep within her, laced with questions she wasn't armed to hear answered.

I enveloped her, with my musty-smelling-should've-been-burned yearbook sandwiched between us. Her back heaved in uncontrolled sobs.

"I'm so sorry," I murmured over and over in her ear, rocking her back and forth as my hand clutched her soft t-shirt like a security blanket. My paltry words wouldn't soothe her pain. How many times had I said those words over the past months? And how effective had they been?

Why hadn't I made an off-hand comment that yes, their similarities were ironic, and point out that Greg and I had broken up months before she was conceived? Instead, guilt floated to my face.

Without warning she pushed me away, stumbling back until her legs hit the kitchen table. "No! *No!*" Karley growled as her glassy eyes lost focus, searching the room as if the answer to her paternity was written on the walls.

"I can explain, honey. Please." I grabbed her hand, still clutching the green yearbook.

The dam opened on Karley's face. *"What? You can explain what?* That it's just a coincidence my crooked smile and goofy earlobe are exactly like your old high school boyfriend's? The one everyone wrote about, saying you were the 'perfect couple'? Or these love letters from him right up until you met Dad? The summer you got pregnant with me?"

I hadn't seen Karley so out of control since she was sixteen and Josh accidentally stepped on the hem of her prom dress and ripped it minutes before her date arrived. Karley was reasonable and level-headed, just as Greg was. And it was time I told her about him.

So I did. Over the next two hours. Through a box of Kleenex, four glasses of water, a couple of Advil, some chocolate-covered peanuts, a little bit of ranting, and a lot more of listening…Karley finally heard it all. She heard it, but it would take a long time for her to digest it.

Given enough time, I hoped we could heal.

"I wish I'd never have opened the box!" Karley sniffled beside me on the couch, hugging a twisted Kleenex to her nose, distrust rimmed her eyes.

"What made you look in there?" I was sure I'd packed them away in the basement bedroom.

"I went to get more empty boxes from the extra bedroom and found one marked 'old keepsakes' on the side of the box. I opened it, thinking maybe my baby book would be in there." Karley pressed the heels of her hands against her wet eyes.

Ah, her baby book. The one listing Jerry as her father. That would never change. He was, and always would be. Genetics be damned.

I wasn't surprised when Karley left shortly afterwards—calmed down enough to drive safely home. As I swept up the shards of shiny glass off our faded linoleum, I hoped Karley's sensibility would eventually kick in. Our goodbye resembled two stiff cardboard cutouts, both hearts bleeding in red against their brown chests. Karley and I had a rocky road ahead of us, and a possible meeting in her future with Greg, but we loved each other, and I felt in my heart that she'd come around. I'd leave the decision up to her about meeting Greg. I'd screwed up the past, I'd let her control her future.

Now I needed to tell Jerry.

* * *

I called him that afternoon, strong-arming my way to insistence that we meet right away. I couldn't take the chance Karley would cry on his shoulder. The buried secret had been resurrected.

I had two hours to talk about two life-changing things with my hopefully soon ex-husband since he was meeting a client later on. It might not take long to talk about them, but it would take forever to forget the topics.

Jerry's apartment building was a new, brick, four-story complex. The halls smelled of new paint and carpet. Walking down the hallway to #212, I tried to imagine living there myself, after owning my own home for two decades. For Jerry, a contractor building other people new spacious houses, now stuck going back to a small apartment at his age…it was unfair.

Just as my coming clean with him was going to be unfair. There would be no winners here. Yet I was *so* sick of all our lies, broken promises, and deceit. I stopped before his apartment door, leaned against the beige wall as I inhaled the scent of meatloaf from apartment #216, and did a few deep breathing techniques. My short fingernails dug into my palm as I knocked.

"Just a sec." Jerry's voice was muffled. I assumed Angela would be gone; I hoped Jerry was wise enough to know this talk was between the two of us. I'd been clear this was important.

With a click of the lock, Jerry opened his new place up to me. I was careful not to touch him in passing as he stepped aside. I walked straight to the card table and chairs we'd dug out of our basement when he moved out, taking a quick inventory as I sat down.

It was neat and bare, but what did I expect? I recognized all the items from our house, other than a new recliner. This looked more like a college kid's place. A college kid with OCD.

He pulled out a tan folding chair, and I took my place across from him as I shrugged out of my jacket. Placing my hands flat on the table, I cleared my throat.

How does one start a conversation with their spouse about extramarital sex while also confessing their error years ago in picking their child's biological father?

"First of all, let's not talk about Josh, and focus on why I'm here, okay?" I didn't want him wandering off on something we'd hashed over already. "I have a couple things I need to discuss with you. I hope you'll hear me out and we can talk in a civilized manner.

"I'm guessing Joe told you about running into me at Moonlite Bay on St. Patrick's Day. That's the first thing I want to talk about, not that it matters at this point, but still…" It was easier to address his mistake first. Maybe because once I mentioned Karley's paternity, our conversation would likely be over.

Jerry sat back, his arms folded across his chest. "I haven't talked to Joe in a while."

I leaned back too, as if our conversation meant nothing to me, and hid my surprise at Jerry and Joe not talking to each other every day. "You remember years ago how we women buried time capsules a couple times?" Jerry nodded, likely wondering what they had to do with him. "Well, in Dana's last time capsule, she wrote something about her worst regret was having sex with one of her best friends' husbands."

My words hit the air and a split-second later Jerry's eyes widened with his deer-in-the-headlight look. If Joe had never pointed a finger at Jerry, and I had casually mentioned my discovery in Dana's capsule to him, his reaction would've told me the truth anyway.

"Do you remember? Were there others over the years?" He had the decency to look away. There was my answer. "You know what? It makes no difference now. I don't want to know." *I'm itching to know!* "We should've never gotten married." The level tone of my voice impressed even me. Jerry had to be floored that I wasn't coming unglued. My lack of emotions resembled a Stepford Wife, thanks to my own guilt.

"I should've known. We rarely had sex." My painful admittance came out in a squeak, which betrayed my steel exterior. I lowered my voice. "After I read Dana's time capsule, I thought it was Joe. You know what a womanizer he's always been." I let my eyes wander up to Jerry's face. Had our friends considered him a "womanizer" too? No, there was no way he'd led the in-your-face-I'm-screwing-who-I-want life that Joe did.

I laid out a condensed version of my word-spat with Joe. Jerry uncrossed his arms and got up. "I'm getting a beer, do you want one?"

"I thought you were meeting a client soon." Nagging was hard to quit.

He turned from his bare fridge. "It's Carl, from the Nisswa strip mall. I'm not worried about him thinking I'm drunk off one or two beers."

"I don't suppose you have any wine in there, do you?" Hearing from my soon-to-be-ex-husband he'd cheated on me with my friend, and who knew who else, would be a good time to have a mid-day drink. And I'd need the liquid courage for my free-the-guilt speech.

"Angela has some Chardonnay in here…"

Her name rolled off Jerry's tongue. "She's another subject, since you brought her up. I assume she's who the kids met at Thanksgiving, and who answered your phone the other day?"

"Yep, and in a way, she's a part of our history." He hesitated. "Man, I want to be done with this, and I don't mean that in a bad way."

I accepted the glass of wine from him as he sat down across from me. I wanted to be done with all of it too, but sometimes we didn't get what we wanted in life. He had no idea about my next bomb that held the stench of a pig barn…one that would crush him. Thanks to me being all nostalgic and keeping my high school yearbooks, I no longer had a choice.

Jerry sat there with his ice cold MGD in front of him, his palms slowly spinning the beer. He exhaled. "Have you ever looked back and thought about how your life would have been different if you wouldn't have gotten pregnant with Karley?" He waved a calloused hand in defense.

Oh boy, have I ever!

"Don't get all wound up now. I love our kids. I know I don't show it in the way you want, but I do. But let's be honest here, if you hadn't gotten pregnant, we'd have never seen each other again." He began peeling off his beer bottle label, avoiding my eyes.

I didn't say anything; I was too busy holding my breath to see where this would lead.

"When you called and told me you were pregnant, I didn't believe it was my baby. Stupid, I know. It took a few days to admit to myself we'd had unprotected sex a handful of times, and I had spent so much time with you all summer, you wouldn't have had time to be with anyone else. But like a jerk, I kept hoping you'd say the due date was wrong." He cleared his throat. "I was scared shitless to tell my parents, thought my dad was going to cut my nuts off."

Here it comes, he knows! Oh no, he couldn't possibly know.

Jerry glanced at me. "Put yourself in my shoes. Of course, by then, you'd already mentioned you should move to Minnesota, but I didn't think you'd do it. I figured you'd go back home, have your parents help you raise the baby. God, I sound like such a creep, even to myself."

I was in no position to hop on the Jerry-bashing-train with him.

"It wasn't until I went to the doctor visit with you that January, heard the heartbeat and heard the doctor say your due date was in early May. The date coincided with when we were dating. When Karley's hair grew out curly like mine, and she was always tall for her age, like me, I felt like shit for doubting you. But I was angry my life wasn't going as I'd planned. Hell, you had to have felt the same way. After your mom died, you kept saying how we needed to do the right thing for our baby. I didn't think getting married was going to fix anything—and at the time, wasn't positive Karley was really mine. But right after Karley was born, my dad paid me a visit. Backed me up against the wall and told me in no uncertain terms I'd best marry you, and soon." Jerry shook his head at the memory.

My body tensed like a member of a bomb squad bracing for an explosion. When his parents came to visit after Karley was born, I mentioned how alone I felt, how after my mom's death I didn't know quite what to do. And how I wanted to give Karley a good, stable home.

Apparently, his dad listened to me and pressured Jerry into doing what I'd thought was the right thing at the time. I looked at Jerry; he was clueless. My chest constricted so much, I feared dying of a heart attack in his apartment. The thought of coming clean made my knees rattle. Before I could utter a confession, Jerry broke the silence.

Chapter 31

"My father threatened me that if I didn't marry you, he'd make me join the service. 'The Dominator' waved the unrest in the Persian Gulf in front of me, knowing I'd never want to fight in a war and come home a physically and emotionally broken man, like he had." Jerry hung his head.

I swallowed my shock. I'd been an either/or option? "So I was used as leverage?" How humiliating. "I thought the deal was they'd pay off your college loans...which they did, right?"

"They did that too. Dad was set on spending time with his grandbaby, and as you know, barely did at all. I think he was already too sick by then. I should have stood up to him, but he was an overbearing SOB. He probably knew he wouldn't be with us much longer. I wanted to do the right thing and make him proud, for once." Jerry's dad died before Karley turned three.

He looked up at me. "Anyway, do you remember Hal?" His fingers shredded the beer label.

"Yes. Joe mentioned it happened at one of Hal's parties."

"Yep, it was right after Bob and Dana had moved here, and I didn't know her. They were barely talking to each other, fighting over the business I think. Joe had a bee up his ass, insisting Dana wanted me. I was super drunk and, like a dumbass, believed him."

He looked at me. "You gotta understand, I was young, drunk, unhappily married, and it didn't take much to convince me. Dana had about as much interest in me as a bug, but Joe had been sneaking Everclear into our drinks all night and telling her I had the hots for her. Joe got us to follow him to the pole barn for something, and then he snuck out."

Jerry swallowed. "I struggled to even walk. I don't remember a lot of it, but the next morning, I recalled enough. So did Dana." His voice cracked. "She confessed the next morning to Bob, and I give him credit, he didn't come over and castrate me. I hoped like hell I'd imagined the whole thing, but I hadn't. Bob called me the next night, and asked to meet me."

My stomach clenched. Where in the hell had my head been that I didn't notice any of this? The tension should have been palpable. But I knew. My total focus was on my kids and providing what I interpreted as the best environment for them. I couldn't provide happy parents for them, but I could play let's pretend with the best.

Out of beer, and his label shredded to pieces, Jerry rose and grabbed another one. Instead of sitting back down, he paced his narrow kitchen. "So, I met with Bob and I'm thankful he didn't kill me. Our friendship was never the same. A year or so later, he said he forgave me and we kind of put it in the past, but it was never like before. I didn't blame him. Dana took her share of the responsibility and also said she thought somebody slipped something in her drink.

"When Bob mentioned that, I told him the same thing. I had been drinking whiskey, but usually could hold my own. It wasn't until I talked to Joe the next day that I found out what he'd done. He thought it was funny. You know Joe, he doesn't think of the consequences." Jerry stopped pacing and studied his beer again. "I'm sorry about it all. The alcohol, everything, they weren't an excuse."

His voice faded away. "Dana and I talked about it, and she pretty much hated my guts for a few years. They were busy getting their business going and starting a family; we didn't see each other much. When you two became friends, I was afraid it would all come out. Of course, why would Dana bring it up? We both wanted to forget about it."

My nerves were chilled like icicles as I shrugged back into my jacket. As painful as this was for both of us, what was coming next was worse. But if I'd learned anything from the women in the Hell Club, it was that taking responsibility for our mistakes was the best way to move forward. Jerry was being painfully honest. It was time for me to do the same.

"Don't go yet. I need to talk to you about something else." Jerry said as I put on my jacket.

"I'm not going, I'm cold." *And scared to death to match you secret for secret.*

He sat back down. "Things weren't good with us then, you gotta admit. Hell, they've never been good with us, have they?" Jerry winced as if in pain, and I wondered what was coming next. I wanted to unload my burden, but I had a feeling I'd have to wait my turn.

Jerry cleared his throat. "Which brings me to Angela. When I went back to college the fall after we met, before I found out you were pregnant, I met someone at a party. Things were going good between us, and although you and I talked a few times, I got the feeling you weren't expecting anything from me. Anyway, it was a real shock when you called to tell me you were pregnant. Of course it changed everything between me and my girlfriend."

I fiddled with my wine glass. This was news to me. It had never occurred to me he might have been dating someone back then. Even though I was thinking about Greg at the time.

Jerry's elbows rested on the table. "That was Angela, the woman I'm dating now. And Dana looked a hell of a lot like Angela when I first met her; long blonde hair and petite. I think it didn't help me walk away from the barn that night."

A million thoughts raced through my mind. Had Jerry been seeing Angela all these years? Is she why Jerry moved out when he did? And did it matter?

Jerry continued. "Angela and I broke up before you moved to Minnesota. She wasn't too keen on dating a guy who was going to be a dad. She moved to Colorado after she graduated and got married. She moved back here last fall. When she bought a house that needed remodeling, she looked me up to do the work."

"What happened to her husband?"

"He died in a snowmobiling accident a few years ago in Colorado. She moved to be close to her parents again since their health has been poor."

"So, she knew you had your own construction company?" It was a good indication they'd been in contact at some point. An even better one was Jerry avoiding my eyes. He had no cause for worry. My secret was going to wipe out anything he'd done with Angela over the years.

I took the lull in our conversation as an indicator it was time for me to jump in. I finished off my wine, and opened my mouth off and on, like a fish fighting to breathe out of water. The words that would break his heart struggled to stay inside me. I could no longer allow it.

"It doesn't matter. And you're right; we should've never gotten married. It's my fault. Oh, God, I made mistakes." I wasn't even sure he heard me; my hands were cupped over my mouth.

"I think we both did, Perfect. I mean, Peyton." Jerry flashed a half-smile. He was trying to be nice, and no doubt thought our conversation was on the upswing…problems solved, secrets aired, and I must be forgiving him. Oh, how I wished it was that easy.

I held up my hand. "Please, let me talk. I need to tell you something else, and I ask you to give me time to explain." His eyes widened as he sat back in his chair. I struggled to breathe.

Did I dare ask for another glass of wine? *No, Peyton, you can do this without liquid encouragement.* "This is the hardest thing I've ever had to say, so please just listen, okay?" I licked my lips. "You knew when we met that summer, I told you I'd only ever had one serious boyfriend before you—Greg. Well, he looked me up that summer when he was home for a weeks' vacation. We got together a couple nights, and then he left. I knew he was joining the seminary after college. I put him out of my mind, went back to college, and then two months later, found out I was pregnant." I pinched my hand just to remind myself this was real and not just another nightmare.

"When Karley was born, I struggled to get through the days, probably a little post-partum depression mixed in with extreme grief over my mom's sudden death. You're right; I was planning on turning tail and going back to live with my parents." I raised my eyes to meet his. "After mom's death, I thought of what a great upbringing I had, and felt Karley deserved the same. I hinted to your parents that I thought we should get married."

"That's why my dad pushed so hard. He said he wanted to be able to see his grandkids." Jerry nodded, as if it all made sense now. His fingers drummed over his mouth. I pushed on.

"After we married, you know things never got better. When Josh was born, and we heard comments about how much he looked like you and Karley looked like me, I didn't think much of it." My heart galloped like a race horse. I was going to die in Jerry's apartment.

"Remember how Karley's eye teeth were crooked before she got braces? And how she has that tiny piece of extra skin on her right earlobe?" Unshed tears burned my eyes, pain bubbled like an overflowing caldron in my throat. My agony must have been obvious since Jerry's face was now etched in pain, staring at me as if I were going to tell him he had cancer. That piece of news would've been easier to handle than what I was going to say.

When the dam exploded, my words burst out in between sobs. "Karley got those features from her biological father, my old boyfriend." The room was dead quiet. The world had stopped. And I wanted to get off. Anything to avoid the agony in the room.

After a handful of shocked seconds of silence, Jerry pushed himself away from the table as if he could escape my message. My words were strangling me and I stood up, gasping for air. As I stumbled into his small kitchen, I sobbed over and over "I'm so sorry!" I couldn't look back at him, couldn't witness his horror. I searched for tissues and settled for paper towels, mopping the mess from my eyes and nose. Finally, I snuck a peek at Jerry. His head was buried in his hands, his back heaving in sobs. I should have run to comfort him. Cement planted my legs.

"Jesus Christ, Peyton!" His hands muffled his words. "What the hell did we get married for?" Each word sliced the air between us. Words I had no answer for.

The best I could do was hand him some paper towels while I apologized for the hundredth time. His red eyes bore into mine as I sat back down across from him. I now understood the term "if looks could kill." At the moment, I was certainly dying.

"I didn't know! I didn't know she was Greg's until I saw him again last year! And what you said earlier is right; you have curly hair, and you're tall—two things that I assumed Karley got from you. Unfortunately, Greg also has curly hair and is tall. And yes, we were together twice that summer, but you and I had way more unprotected sex than that." I wiped my tears with the back of my hand. "Greg's hair is almost black. Karley was always fair, like you and me. And she has my blood type. What was I supposed to think?"

I was close to hyperventilating; I knew the damage my secret had caused. No bandage could fix it. No words could smooth it over. Yet I tried. "What if we'd have adopted Karley? It would be no different. She's still your child as much as if we adopted her." My words tumbled over each other, like an auctioneer, hoping to make a quick sale.

"You are the one who taught Karley how to ride a bike. *You* are the one who cared for her when she was one, and I was laid up because I'd had appendix surgery. *You* are the one who helped support her and love her unconditionally—the same way she loves you.

"None of that has changed, Jerry. Please realize that." My vision blurred through tears. Someone had squeezed my heart through a ringer. It would never beat the same again.

I couldn't bear to watch Jerry dismembered by pain, his legs shaking like jackhammers. I averted my eyes to his kitchen window, overlooking a parking lot. "Why are you telling me now?" His words moaned through his clenched jaw.

My back was rigid as I turned around. I owed him at least enough to face him. "Because Karley found my high school yearbook this morning and saw Greg's photos with me. And letters from him."

I didn't have to spell the gut-wrenching scene out for Jerry.

A lifetime passed between us before he dropped his head into his fists. "You need to leave. Now." His hollow voice reached into my soul, haunting it.

I wasn't going to argue. I quietly let myself out of his apartment. Jerry hadn't moved a muscle in his chair since he told me to leave.

It was the first time in my life I wanted to stay by him.

I thought of the land mines we both had trudged through. What a hot-mess. From the beginning, our relationship reeked of deceit.

It was four o'clock when I drove away—emotionally drained, as if someone had performed a lobotomy on me. It would have been a welcome relief, forgetting all the pain between us over twenty-two years. I let myself into my home twenty minutes later and decided a long soak in a bubble bath would help ease the fifty stress knots in my body.

A bone-deep remorse set in as I closed my eyes and soaked up to my neck in the hot bubbles. Ever since my talk with Grace at Christmas, I'd reflected on how my brain had managed to suppress the remote idea Karley could possibly have been Greg's child. It had been easy to do.

Was that how child abuse victims felt years later when they allowed the horrors of their past to trickle into their present? Was it because the only option had been to assume the baby was Jerry's? Was I protecting Greg so he could pursue becoming a priest? Percentage-wise, my time with Greg was minimal compared to being with Jerry. I'd gambled—betting on the odds. And we'd all lost. Big time.

* * *

There had been no word from Karley—or Jerry—in over a week. Not that I expected either to call. It was a time bomb they'd had to swallow whole. It would take a while to digest.

Bob and I had talked about me helping him to get their garden going again before I moved. I biked over there one night to visit him and check out his garden.

We visited about my upcoming move as we walked out to his garden. His children were going to a hotel for the weekend with Dana's parents. This would be the first time he and Liz had a weekend to themselves. We talked about that—the whole sex thing—after being with your spouse for years.

Somehow, our sex conversation narrowed in on being faithful all those years, and the thought popped into my head so unexpectedly, I clammed up mid-sentence.

"What is it, Peyton?"

"Nothing."

"You sure?" Bob stopped walking and studied me. I looked the other way, unsure what to say. I caved. "Um, you know, that night?" It was vague enough where if Bob didn't want to talk about it, I could make something else up, divert the conversation.

He opened the garden gate. "Yes." Bob's one word held a lot of emotional history. We stared at each other, feeling each other's pain by telepathy.

"Dana told you. Wasn't it hard to hear?"

He didn't answer right away. "Listen, it was a long time ago, it's in the past." He folded his arms over his chest and looked at me. "How did you find out?"

"Dana wrote about it in our last time capsules. It was her one big regret."

"I can only tell you how Dana felt. Jerry and I haven't talked about it since that first year." He shook his head. "I guess I forgave a long time ago, but for you, it's still fresh."

"I talked to Jerry about it last week. In the case of our marriage, it doesn't matter at this point. I just wanted to try to understand."

"And did it help?"

"A little." *Actually, it was a walk in the park compared to our conversation that followed.*

"The thing is, Peyton, after a bit, I couldn't just blame Dana for the rift in our marriage. In reality, what happened between them helped our marriage somewhat. I know it sounds crazy, but their actions forced Dana and me to bring things out in the open." He crouched down and sifted the soil through his hands. "The pain over miscarriages, the stress of starting a business—we were spiraling out of control—too much stress and not enough communication."

I crouched down next to him as we played with the rich soil. "I'd like to have pointed a finger at Dana, at Jerry, but after it was all said and done, I had played a part in it all too. And for us, it was worth putting in the past." Bob continued. "You never know how you'll react to things until they happen. Every marriage has a pivotal point in their relationship where you look at it and both know, 'this thing could go either way. It could break us apart or make us stronger.' For me, it was easy. My heart was always with Dana."

As I rode my bike home an hour later, I thought about what Bob said. When was Jerry's and my pivotal point in our marriage? The point where we looked and said, "Our marriage could go either way?" Whenever it was, we'd chosen the wrong way.

Chapter 32

I had until the end of June to be out of the house. Not the home. Not our house, just a building which held memories, both good and bad. I squared my shoulders, taking in a deep breath of old items too long stored. The prayers of "Oh, how I wish it was six months from now," or a year…those prayers were gone. I was no longer wishing my life away.

I'd hit the reset button on my life.

The other day I ran into Britin, the soon-to-be owner of our house, at the grocery store. Mallory told me her husband had been killed in Afghanistan. As I watched her corral her three young ones with a shopping cart, I was tempted to walk over and invite her to the next Hell Club event.

Many times I thought the club should have business cards made up saying, *"Have you had some bad shit happen in your life? Do you need others to help lift your chin off the ground? The awesome been-there-survived-that women from the To-Hell-And-Back Club can help!"*

It was a project I'd work on in my spare time.

Reaching out to others made me stronger. The way swimming had strengthened my body, needing others in my life had made my soul stronger.

And there was Daniel. He was meant to be in my life; I was certain of it. I'd hoped for that kind of bond with Jerry for years. It hadn't been there for us, yet it seemed not only had I found someone I wanted in my future, but Jerry had found the woman he lost all those years ago. Talk about a long breakup period for them. It made it easier for me to be happy when Jerry was too. We just couldn't make it work to be happy together.

Josh was plugging along in his own way, working more, playing less, and doing his best to stay clean. I was proud he'd taken the step himself to attend meetings, and knew nobody could change things but Josh. He rolled with the punches; worry was not in his genetic makeup. Karley did enough for both of them, so it was a blessing Ben was sent into her life to bring balance and fun.

* * *

I became a college graduate a few days later, like I should have been at twenty-two, yet I was more appreciative of my accomplishment now at forty-three. I also had a few job interviews under my belt, one of them a strong possibility with the hospital in Brainerd. Funny, it was because of their impending outsourcing I'd taken the leap to complete my degree. How ironic I might work for them again in a higher paying job.

I also knew I'd have to give up some things in my current life. Most likely no more swimming lessons to teach, no more working at The Pines, and I'd have to cut into my volunteering... It all couldn't continue. But, I refused to go back to all work and no life. Work was eight hours, there was so much life left after that.

Mallory and Maren were moving into an apartment with her husband who'd be home from Afghanistan in May. Daniel and I reminded each other our empty nests were not a death sentence.

May twenty-second had started like any other day...until I checked my mail and there was the golden envelope containing my final divorce papers. What a week—college degree, divorce final, and finalizing my house-hunting. Papers or not, it would take a long time before I no longer thought of Jerry as my husband, which was odd considering I had no problem thinking of Daniel as my boyfriend. But nobody ever said life would make sense.

I'd been looking at homes for rent for more than a month, and sometimes Jane or Mary Beth joined me. Location-wise I was trying to stay within a twenty-mile radius of Brainerd, assuming whatever job I got would be located somewhere nearby.

Especially if it was the hospital. When they called to schedule a third interview, I'd wondered out loud to Eunice about how many interviews there could be in the process. "The higher the job, the more interviews," Eunice stated as I helped her with some spring cleaning at her home.

"Good point." I was anxious to get a job. In the end, it was Eunice who found me the duplex to rent. Eight miles from Pine Lakes, the town I'd called home for the past twenty-five years, and closer to Brainerd, where most of the jobs were located. And still close to my new circle of friends. That was important to me.

It was a three bedroom, two baths, pet-friendly, well-kept place nestled in a circle of four duplexes in a quiet, wooded section near the river, and was within my budget.

I could move in the end of June.

When I took Michelle, Charlee, Molly, and Lily to my soon-to-be home to give them a pre-moving-in tour the Sunday before Memorial Day Weekend, Michelle brought along a packed picnic basket filled with champagne, cheese and crackers, grapes, chocolate, and a book for me. "Now that your divorce is final, you're going to need some help, girl. This should do it, and I want a full report when you're done reading it since I could use a few tips myself." Michelle winked as she handed me a crisp copy of GETTING NAKED AGAIN, by Judith Sills. I looked at the white cover with a photo of a negligee on it. I sure as heck didn't own one of them, yet.

We'd talked about the next event we'd organized—Molly, Lily, and me telling our stories. "Mary Beth has the pontoon rented for Memorial Day," I said. It would be the six of us—Mary Beth, Charlee, and Michelle too since they'd been the angels who steered us to the Hell Club.

"The weather looks nice for the weekend. We'll have to figure out who's bringing what for food," said Molly.

"Speaking of food, let's eat," Michelle said. We had ourselves a picnic smack-dab in the middle of my cream-colored living room, sitting on a cushy grass-green blanket Lily had brought along. "It's like being outside, and this way if we spill our champagne, it won't wreck your pretty carpet." We clicked our plastic champagne glasses together, and as we all shouted "Cheers!" I surprised myself by erupting into tears. It hadn't been the only time recently. With all the changes, there were a lot of emotions close to the surface for me, and I let them spill over.

"Aw, don't cry now. This is such a great place for you to start over." Charlee hugged me.

"I don't know what's up with me. I *am* happy. I think it's the finality of so many things." Molly handed me a wad of napkins to mop up my tears and blow my nose.

"You've gone through a lot. There's no need to pretend it doesn't affect you. The reality of change takes a while to sink in, the reality of loss. It's like a person with a terminal disease. Everyone knows they're going to die. Yet when it happens, they still mourn the loss." Charlee held my hand.

Michelle wiped a tear from my cheek and smiled. "Hey, if you waltzed through it all without a care, we'd start to wonder if you were made of stone."

We lightened the mood a little with another toast, and I felt the weight of my tears drain away. *What would I do without girlfriends?* I, of all people, knew.

* * *

I'd walked by my time capsules on my dresser for months. It was time to open them before I moved. It was the Friday of Memorial Weekend, and I planned to spend the day packing more household items. Saturday night I was going with some friends to a concert in the town park—featuring Daniel's band. On Monday, the six of us from Hell Club were renting a pontoon for the day.

I took the capsules out to my patio table, the sun already intense. I chose my old capsule.

"*June 2, 2001—Myrtle*" I'd written across the top of the paper. It was Lauren's birthday, and we had sat passing a bottle of wine around. In with my list was a tampon, sealed in its pink plastic wrap. Karley had gotten her first period around then. The other item was one of those cards you get with flowers that say things like "Happy Birthday." In my case, it said "I'm sorry. Jerry." I sat with it in my hand, feeling the painful memories of a night I'd managed to forget.

Karley's twelfth birthday had been a couple of weeks before then, and she didn't want a birthday party with friends. Instead, she wanted her family there and for me to make her favorite meal: spaghetti and chocolate cake with cream cheese frosting. Jerry had gone golfing during the day somewhere with his friends. After golf, they headed to the clubhouse where they drank the night away. He didn't come home until after midnight. We didn't own a cell phone and I had no way to contact him to remind him he was missing his daughter's birthday party.

To his credit, Jerry was as upset with himself the next morning as I was. Poor Karley. In my heart, I knew the reason she wanted our family dinner. She could already see the family threads being pulled apart, and it was her small way of trying to sew us back together.

When I got the flowers and card from Jerry, I told him it was Karley he needed to apologize to. For him, as he had learned from his parents, demonstrating love was a tough job.

Remembering he took Karley out for dinner the next night, just the two of them, reminded me he did try. In Jerry's own way, he did try. I tossed the card back in the jar along with the tampon, and proceeded to read my first list.

MY NOT-SO-SECRET WISH—to finish college
MY FANTASY DREAM—to move back to Texas with my children
MY LEAST FAVORITE FOOD IS—mushrooms
I WANT TO BUY—a dog
FANTASY JOB—have a cooking show on TV

I was proud to cross "finish college" off my list. I had a wonderful dog, and although I would most likely never have my own cooking show, I was cooking for people who appreciated it at the soup kitchen. And I could now visit Texas whenever I wanted to.

My second jar was a little bare. I remembered that night too. It was a cool autumn night, and we hovered inside the car writing our private thoughts. I'd had a little too much to drink.

Besides my short list dated, *"October 8, 2004—Myrtle,"* one of the two items in the Mason jar was an extra car key. Karley was taking her Driver's Ed classes. The other item was a junior high football program of Josh's. He'd been Captain that year. Both were good memories and I was thankful. Then I read what I'd written.

I WANT TO—get back into swimming again
MY WISH-IT-COULD-A-BEEN-DIFFERENT—I'd had more kids
MY DEEP DARK SECRET—I blame myself for mom's death, she took up running because of the stress I caused in her life
MY HOPE FOR THE FUTURE—to be the best mom I can be
MY BIG REGRET IS—marrying a man I don't love

I fingered the paper; rereading my secrets. Now I'd answer them different. The decisions I'd made while pregnant with Karley were my wish-it-could've-been-different, my deep dark secret, and my big regret. It was something I couldn't fix and couldn't change. I'd buried it deep inside me.

I'd achieved my hope; I didn't have more children, but I had tried to be the best mom I could be. Yes, there was a rift between Karley and me that only time and understanding would fix, and I'd had to let Josh take responsibility for his mistakes… Yet I hoped in the long run, my relationship with my children would come back around. They were the true loves of my life.

As far as the rest of my list, I was swimming most every day, an achievement I was proud of. And I was no longer carrying the guilt that somehow my mom had died because of me. Bad things happened in life, and her brain aneurysm would have happened anyway. Me getting pregnant in college and her taking up running to help handle the stress in her life did not cause her death. As for my big regret, Jerry and I had taken care of it. Yet our lives would forever be entwined, thanks to our kids.

I walked around the yard which would be mine for a few more weeks. The garden I'd never plant here again, the beds of perennial flowers. But I'd plant somewhere new, start over, just as I'd done with so many other things in my life. As I made my way back in my house and tucked my dreams and secrets from years ago inside my sock drawer, I accepted that I'd managed to push ahead and start over, thanks to the Hell Club.

* * *

The sun was setting when Molly, Michelle, Lily, and I headed to the bandstand in the park. Daniel's band would start at nine. He'd gone right from a long, busy day at his sport shop to practicing with the band before their performance. I was excited to hear the band play again, and now I could focus on Daniel playing instead of being stuck with Todd, like that dreaded date long ago. For a music lover, how had I never dated a musician in high school or college?

When they stepped on the bandstand stage and broke into their first song, "Born in the U.S.A.," the crowd erupted in cheers and whistles. Their lead singer had the raspy voice of The Boss, and their energy lit the crowd up. The night was perfect: calm, warmer than usual for the end of May, and the stars sparkling across the sky gave the weekend dedicated to military men and women the right decoration, like part of a big flag over our heads.

The park was packed. They had outdoor concerts a half dozen times during the summer months, usually on the long, busy weekends. Many sat on blankets strewn all over the grass; some brought chairs; many of us stood on the sides. It was easier to dance that way.

Seeing Daniel play guitar stirred me, gave me a warm feeling deep inside my stomach. I couldn't deny the fact. Put a guitar in a guy's hands and their sexiness level was raised considerably. Homer Simpson could look cool playing the guitar. Daniel's sexiness was revved up so high that I wanted to run up on stage and throw myself at him, much like a groupie would. I willed my feet to stay planted, or I'd be sorry.

How old was I? I couldn't remember, because I felt eighteen. In a sense, I was. I'd given up over twenty years of my life to a man I'd never managed to love. I was finally living my life again.

* * *

I dragged myself out of bed at seven on Monday. I still needed to pack for the pontoon picnic I'd be going on in the afternoon with Molly, Lily, Mary Beth, Charlee, and Michelle.

Molly, Lily, and I were telling our stories today. There were details of what brought me to the club that I'd share, but Karley's biological father wouldn't be one of them.

As I slid into the driver's seat to head out to the cemetery, I received a text from Daniel, and a smile crept across my face. He was a great reminder of taking chances in life. I still had a lot of living to do. I reminded myself of it every day…something I hoped would make my old friends proud.

The Memorial Day service at the cemetery started at nine and I wanted to have a good heart-to-heart with my old friends before the crowd arrived. They'd had the guts years ago to write down their painful secrets—it was time to come clean with them and divulge my own.

I was alone in the peaceful cemetery, damp grass tickling my feet as I stood in my sandals at the foot of their graves. So lost in my thoughts and silent confession to my friends, I didn't hear a car door slam on the gravel road, didn't sense someone quietly walking toward me from behind.

"Mom?" A voice I treasured cautiously spoke, ten feet behind me. I spun around, my silent conversation with my friends cut short.

"Karley!" I was as surprised to see her as I'd have been if one of my friends rose from the grave. Her pale pink mouth quivered, and her arms opened wide as I rushed toward her.

"I figured I'd find you here," she mumbled into my neck as we embraced in the most cleansing hug I'd ever experienced.

"Just talking to my friends." I leaned back and smiled as I dabbed at my eyes.

We walked back to their graves, arms around each other, and stood reverently in silence. So many things had changed in my life: my marriage status, my job, even my relationship with my children. And although the pain of losing Maggie, Lauren, and Dana had lessened, my memories with them would never change.

They were my "Remember When" friends, the only three women who held twenty years of shared memories with me; memories I'd forever treasure by myself. They were irreplaceable, and I missed all three of them something fierce. Some things never change.

THE END

ACKNOWLEDGEMENTS

Every writer should have a writing community. I found mine in WFWA (Women's Fiction Writers Association), thanks to author, Amy Sue Nathan. I was lucky enough to join before they even formed their association.

WFWA changed my writing life. Through the association, I was paired with two poor souls who became my Critique Partners: Kerry Morgan and Lynne Marino. These women read enough drafts of my book to test their sanity, and their feedback has been priceless.

When I received "the call" from Zara Kramer, publisher of Pandamoon Publishing, I was thrilled to hear how she "got" my book, my characters, and their emotions. I sincerely thank Zara and all the Pandamoon crew for their hard work in helping birth this baby!

There are so many pay-it-forward authors who have helped me along the way, it would take a whole page to list them all. These authors guided me in everything from query input and marketing, to talking me off the "I'm-giving-up ledge." A special thanks to author Sandra Kring for helping me in the early stages, and her brilliant idea of finding a way to link my first and second books together (which is how the "Hell Club" was formed!) The writing community is truly amazing.

To my beta readers: Heidi Thomsen, Jamie Anderson, Liz Deshayes, Sharon Beaman, Cindy Schufman, Arlene O'Connor, Carissa O'Connor, Sue Cebelinski, Ginny McDonald, Mary Havenor, Karen Koupal, and Michelle Klecker, for their very helpful "reader view" on my story.

To magazine editor, Meg Douglas, for giving me my start in writing, and to Five Wings Art Council, who awarded me a grant provided with funds from the McKnight Foundation. A special thanks to author Jessica Topper for her eagle-eye input. I'd like to thank the valuable ARC (advance review copy) readers for taking time to read and review my book, along with the people who connected me to them. Also, thanks to the book bloggers and book reviewers out there who support authors every day, and especially to *you*, the reader, for choosing my book to read.

And most importantly, I want to thank my husband, Don. He has witnessed the crazy amount of time and effort I've put into my writing…and loves me anyway.

If you read a book you enjoy, the best favor you can do for the author is: read, recommend, & review. The power is in *your* hands!

ABOUT THE AUTHOR

Voted "Most Imaginative" in high school, Jill Hannah Anderson assumed everyone else looked at life with "what-if" questions. She's often told that she asks too many questions, but finds it a great way to learn about people.

Jill lives on a lake in a small town in Minnesota with her husband and their empty nest. It is rarely a quiet nest though, as they enjoy their six adult children and ever-increasing number of grandchildren when they come to visit.

For nearly two decades, Jill has worked at a communications company. She also has written part-time for a Minnesota women's magazine for over ten years. Her debut women's fiction novel is *The To-Hell-And-Back Club*, from Pandamoon Publishing.

She is a member of Women's Fiction Writer's Association (WFWA), and is currently at work on her second women's fiction novel, *Crazy Little Town Called Love*, Book Two in the To-Hell-And-Back Club Series. When she isn't working, writing, or reading, you'll find her running, curling, biking, and enjoying the great outdoors.

Connect with her at: www.JillHannahAnderson.com, and on her Facebook page at: www.facebook.com/jillhannah.anderson/.

Thank you for purchasing this copy of *The To-Hell-And-Back Club*. If you enjoyed this book, please let the author know by posting a review.

Growing good ideas into great reads…one book at a time.

Visit www.pandamoonpublishing.com to learn more about other works by our talented authors.

Mystery/Thriller/Suspense

- *122 Series Book 1: 122 Rules* by Deek Rhew
- *A Flash of Red* by Sarah K. Stephens
- *A Tree Born Crooked* by Steph Post
- *Fate's Past* by Jason Huebinger
- *Juggling Kittens* by Matt Coleman
- *Knights of the Shield* by Jeff Messick
- *Looking into the Sun* by Todd Tavolazzi
- *The Moses Winter Mysteries Book 1: Made Safe* by Francis Sparks
- *On the Bricks Series Book 1: On the Bricks* by Penni Jones
- *Southbound* by Jason Beem
- *The Juliet* by Laura Ellen Scott
- *Rogue Alliance* by Michelle Bellon
- *The Last Detective* by Brian Cohn
- *The New Royal Mysteries Book 1: The Mean Bone in Her Body* by Laura Ellen Scott

Science Fiction/Fantasy

- *Becoming Thuperman* by Elgon Williams
- *Dybbuk Scrolls Trilogy Book 1: The Song of Hadariah* by Alisse Lee Goldenberg
- *Everly Series Book 1: Everly* by Meg Bonney

- *.EXE Chronicles Book 1: Hello World* by Alexandra Tauber and Tiffany Rose
- *Fried Windows in a Light White Sauce* by Elgon Williams
- *Revengers Series Book 1: Revengers* by David Valdes Greenwood
- *The Bath Salts Journals Volume One* by Alisse Lee Goldenberg and An Tran
- *The Crimson Chronicles Book 1: Crimson Forest* by Christine Gabriel
- *The Crimson Chronicles Book 2: Crimson Moon* by Christine Gabriel
- *The Phaethon Series Book 1: Phaethon* by Rachel Sharp
- *The Sitnalta Series Book 1: Sitnalta* by Alisse Lee Goldenberg
- *The Sitnalta Series Book 2: The Kingdom Thief* by Alisse Lee Goldenberg
- *The Sitnalta Series Book 3: The City of Arches* by Alisse Lee Goldenberg
- *The Sitnalta Series Book 4: The Hedgewitch's Charm* by Alisse Lee Goldenberg

Women's Fiction
- *Beautiful Secret* by Dana Faletti
- *The Long Way Home* by Regina West
- *The Mason Siblings Series Book 1: Love's Misadventure* by Cheri Champagne
- *The Mason Siblings Series Book 2: The Trouble with Love* by Cheri Champagne
- *The Mason Siblings Series Book 3: Love and Deceit* by Cheri Champagne
- *The Shape of the Atmosphere* by Jessica Dainty
- *The To-Hell-And-Back Club Book 1* by Jill Hannah Anderson

BOOK CLUB QUESTIONS

1. Like Peyton, do you ever look back at things in your life and think of the domino effect of things in your life, based on a split decision you made?

2. What types of decisions were they and were you happy or sad with the results?

3. Can you relate to the Hell Club, and the need for it?

4. Can you relate to a specific club member mentioned?

5. As much as Peyton feels she knows her best friends, they all had a big secret she uncovers in the time capsules. Have you experienced that with a friend?

6. Do you think Peyton and Jerry should have stayed together? What do you think may have worked to keep their marriage going?

7. What do you think Peyton's greatest strengths are? Her greatest weakness?

8. What do you think the most important theme of this story is? Forgiveness? Friendship? Being responsible for your happiness? Allowing others to help you?

9. Do you have a favorite character? If so, why?

10. Would you have handled things different than Peyton if you realized years later that your husband wasn't the father of one of your children?

11. How did you feel about Peyton's relationship with Greg? With Daniel?

12. Were you satisfied with the ending?

13. Which Hell Club members would you most like to learn more about in future Hell Club books?

CRAZY LITTLE TOWN CALLED LOVE
BOOK TWO IN THE TO-HELL-AND-BACK SERIES

COMING IN 2018
FROM JILL HANNAH ANDERSON AND PANDAMOON PUBLISHING

Crazy Little Town Called Love features fellow Hell Club member, Molly O'Brien, and her story. Molly's cushy life tanks when her long-time boyfriend loses his job and bails on her, along with their underwater-mortgaged home.

Selling her designer shoes and purses on eBay can only float her for so long. It's time to shed the acrylic nails and roll up her sleeves. She needs a place to live and a new job—and the answer to both may be in a little town called Love. A town where her deceased mother grew up, a town where a woman Molly never met has willed an old General Store and home to Molly's family...a town with secrets.

Molly is embraced by the townspeople, including Jackson, a bossy thorn-in-her-side-turned-fun boyfriend. They introduce her to Love's uniqueness: bar stool races down snowy hills, fish-house parades, harvest field dances...and it is at one of these get-togethers where Molly is first attacked. Apparently not everyone is happy to have Molly in town.

SEP 1 9 2017

CPSIA information can be obtained
at www.ICGtesting.com
Printed in the USA
LVOW05s1755280817
546679LV00012B/1328/P